GIRL WITH SECRETS

CAROL RIVERS

CR

Don't miss Carol's free stories and monthly Newsletter! Details at the back of this book.

DEDICATION

Hello my dear readers! Many of you know me via social media and we have become close chums, but I rarely meet you personally, especially now Covid 19 has changed our lives (much like Daisy's life was changed in 1940). But that's not to say I don't think of every one of you as you read my book, whether paper or electronic or listening with Audio. You see, I write directly to you because I know what interests you and touches your hearts, just as it does mine. I know you've loved and lost. I know you've grieved. I know that you helped someone, somewhere at a point in your lives when you needed help yourself. That's what happened in both the World Wars; people put others before themselves and even gave their lives to enrich and sustain others. I want to tell of these people - of you - of us and our families, and add to the social history archives for the next generation to read and realise that we really did the best we could in troubled times. The wars didn't defeat our spirits, nor will Covid. We are resilient and we have the capacity and compassion to love beyond measure.

So, with all my love, I dedicate this book to you - to us - and to our future.

Fond hugs as always, Carol XX

EPIGRAPH

Remembering with love and eternal gratitude Patsie Duggan, his thirteen-year-old sister Maureen and the team of brave children and teenagers who saved many from the flames and carnage of the blitz over 76 terrifying nights of bombardment on London's East End 1940. They were better known as the "Dead End Kids" and saved many lives while losing some of their own. Forever in our hearts and stories and never forgotten.

ABOUT GIRL WITH SECRETS

Nine-year-old Daisy Purbright is a country girl at heart. Together with beloved brother Bobby, they've enjoyed the endless freedoms of rural England. But when her entrepreneur father gambles the family's fortunes on a speculative investment in London's docklands, little does he realise the catastrophic mistake he is making.

The Purbrights attempt to settle to a new life in the East End but the whisperings of war grow louder. Then, one late afternoon in September 1940, Adolf Hitler conducts a paralysing bombardment on London.

Life changes dramatically and closely guarded secrets begin to threaten the Purbrights' happiness. As war tightens its grip on the country, can Daisy stay loyal to her friends and family during one of the most fateful events of the 20th century?

CHAPTER 1

London, Isle of Dogs, 1938

ONE FROST-WHITE MORNING at the beginning of November, when the first scent of Christmas clung sweetly to the high ceilings of the spacious mid-Victorian villa, nine-year-old Daisy Purbright woke, as usual, long before the rest of the household.

For a few moments she listened to the sound of her brother, ten-year-old Bobby, snoring softly under the covers of the camp bed. Only a tussle of white-blond hair, the same shade as her own, showed on the pillow. Whereas Bobby had short, determined curls, Daisy's hair was straight and silky without a bend or swerve in any direction. Pops had informed her that although there were only two surviving senior male Purbrights, himself and his brother Uncle Ed, a noteworthy characteristic of many previous Purbrights was snowy hair, arctic blue eyes and robust complexion.

Curious to discover what the new day held she crept

from her bed and tiptoed to the landing. Here, a little shivery in her nightgown, she pressed her ear against the door of their older brother's bedroom. All was silent. Daisy suspected that seventeen-year-old Matt would be lost in dreamland wooing his drippy sweetheart, Amelia Collins.

She adored her teenage brother, but was also a tiny jot jealous of Amelia who lived in Poplar, a bicycle ride away. Somehow Amelia had spun her web and Matt had fallen into it, mesmerised, just like the moths that flew too close to the Tilley lamp flame.

Daisy loved her two brothers and father Nicholas with a passion. Pops was tall and handsome though he walked with a slight limp, a Great War injury. Matt was just as handsome, a younger mirror image of their father. Consequently, Daisy was thoroughly spoiled as the only daughter of the Purbright family. Her mother, Florence Purbright, posed more of a challenge, for Daisy had not yet decided where her true loyalties lay. Mother was beautiful and elegant. However, she dished out the discipline which was a definite minus. On the plus side, she was an exceptional cook and had long ago figured out Daisy's weak spot. Basically, her stomach.

'To poach or steam an egg might seem simple,' Mother had once explained. 'But your masterpiece might turn as hard as nails with overcooking.'

And oh, how Daisy enjoyed Mother's eggs! Her mouth would water at the soft succulence and sprinkling of pepper on the sunny crown. Mother would smile knowingly, as if sharing a secret, somewhat in line with the secrets she shared with Daisy's father, but, Daisy suspected, of quite a different nature.

Daisy was not only blessed with exceptional inquisitiveness but a keen ear too. She was eager to be in on all the gossip and intrigues of the Purbrights. Florence Purbright often remarked that her daughter had the look of an angel but the tactical mind of a politician. Daisy did not really understand what a politician was, but had accepted the title with good grace. And that was Daisy all over. A one off, so her Pops insisted.

'They broke the mould when they made you, my treasure,' Pops declared only yesterday. 'We'll see you in the House one day, arguing for women's rights just like Mrs Pankhurst.'

'Nicky, please don't give the girl high ideas,' scolded Mother. 'She has enough of her own right now.'

'My high ideas won you over, dearest,' Nicholas Purbright teased. 'Without them I would surely have been rejected.'

'Nonsense,' argued Mother, but blushing all the same.

Daisy's father had winked behind the newspaper only to be interrupted by Matt who contributed a particularly dull comment of his own.

'After Germany's occupation of Czechoslovakia, Chamberlain's chaps have unveiled plans for a National Register,' Daisy's brother spouted. 'Telling everyone what they should do when war starts.'

'Just rumours, Matt,' Mother dismissed. 'Europe has had its fair share of conflict. Our leaders have more sense now than to rise to Hitler's baiting.'

'Not rumours, Mother,' Matt objected heartily. 'Haven't you heard, the dockyards are riveting the ships for action already? Why, some lads I know are joining up.'

'Well, you are not,' Mother returned.

'Pops was seventeen when he enlisted!' Matt protested.

'The matter is settled,' Mother decided. 'As soon as you leave school, you'll follow your father into the family business.'

Daisy's complaint however, was not with this supposed "war" in Europe with which her brother was so enamoured, but something much closer to home. Why must it be Matt who was to follow Pops into business? Why not her or

Bobby? Matt might be the oldest Purbright offspring but he hadn't the least bit interest in electrical engineering. Whereas Bobby actually knew who Isambard Kingdom Brunel was - the most famous engineer in the land. As for Matt, likely he wouldn't have a clue!

Daisy emerged from her thoughts and returned to the bright, crisp morning. Bobby's proper bed was next door in Matt's room, or it had been until the appearance of Amelia Collins. After which, Matt had begun to insist on privacy and Bobby transferred to the put-u-up in Daisy's room, with a promise of the box room next week.

Not that Daisy minded sharing, for there were definite advantages. Tidiness, cleanliness and Godliness - Mother's mantra - had all gone to pot the minute Bobby had decamped, bringing all his clutter with him.

So Daisy had escaped housework, which suited her fine. And besides, she quite enjoyed their nightly discussions concerning the day's observations. Bobby was one year up at school, but for a boy he was quite a card.

She was closer to Bobby in looks and nature than anyone else in the family. Bobby was her ally. She could always count on him for support. Whereas Matt teased her unmercifully, unaware how silly he himself sounded when he drooled over Amelia!

Quietly, Daisy left the figure of her slumbering brother and went to the window. Here, a shaft of light spilled in through the curtain just as it had in their old house in Wattcombe village, south of London. Until two years ago, the Purbrights had existed serenely, though in Daisy's mind, rather boringly, amongst the fields and fauna of the countryside.

Sweet smells had meandered off the fields. Bats skittered against the lattice windows. Every floorboard creaked. Mice enjoyed a carefree existence in the barn. The thick walls of their home had kept out winter's bite. But when Pops accepted a partnership with his brother in the dockland's electrical engineering factory, everything had changed.

Yes, everything! Even now Daisy was disappointed to realise that she was forgetting the look of those fields and the delicate little mice and the fragile black wings that stroked the lattice at night.

She was forgetting - and somehow it felt wrong. For hadn't she lived such a happy - if undisturbed life - in Wattcombe? Where there had been no talk of war or of fighting or of terrible things that happened in other countries and might soon happen in Britain.

Drawing the curtains wide, Daisy undid the catch softly and sniffed the sweet air of the new day. Craning her neck, she could glimpse the city where there was not one thatched roof in sight. Instead, there were energetic hordes of people, unlike Wattcombe with its drab, mumbling farmers and stuffy village shopkeepers.

London was energetic and vibrant. Foreign visitors of every shape and size wandered the streets. Bowler hatted gents walked briskly to their offices. Ladies in furs hailed taxis. Theatres abounded, huge glass-fronted shops like Hamleys displayed their delights. Then of course there was the river, Daisy's most breathtaking discovery. For here in the house in which they now lived, a home tucked neatly away from the busy thoroughfares of the East End, she could view the unbroken line of the snaking grey waters.

Should she peer westward, over the roof tops of Poplar Park Row, the river sparkled in the dawn's light, bright as a diamond. A rowboat's ride directly across the swirling pools, lay Greenwich Observatory. This view was breathtaking to Daisy. Sir Christopher Wren - like Isambard Brunel - was another of her heroes. His magnificent old Royal Naval College was a stone's throw from the famous Queen's House.

She had learned at school that this historic building had been designed by Inigo Jones, a famous architect of the 1600's. But never would she have imagined when living in Wattcombe that one day she might view this spectacle from her window.

Dawn broke as Daisy made her way downstairs; above the front door a milky hue stole through the skylight. Here she paused; at this hour of the morning talk of "*the war*" was thankfully absent. So too were the whispers of bombing and deadly weapons dropped from the sky to destroy London below. Daisy thought this event quite impossible and sided with Mother on the topic. Yet even as she and Bobby walked home from school, there were groups of raucous men rallied on street corners cursing this enemy called Hitler. Worse still were the awful, ugly gas masks and drills for emergency action should a warning siren sound. Some children at school had helped their parents to dig holes for the proposed air raid shelters that were arriving in the New Year.

Mother had once asked Pops if he would have to go away again to fight this war.

'Ye gods,' he'd replied in a startled manner. 'No chance of that! Service in seventeen was my lifetime's contribution.'

'War is easier to make than peace, Nicky,' Mother returned on a sigh. 'People still clamour for it. To our own son war appears heroic and dashing. But we know the truth of it, don't we?'

Daisy, observing carefully, had watched Mother smile. Yet underneath the wing of her light brown hair swept back from her pensive face, the frown had deepened.

As it often seemed to these days.

CHAPTER 2

DAISY BLINKED, putting aside these distracting thoughts as the peaceful moment resumed. If she was to be asked, which wasn't often, since it was usually Daisy who was doing the questioning, what she thought of her new home she would have said that gradually, she and her new home had become friends. At first they had both been unwilling to grasp a new future. An elderly headmistress, Miss Ayling, its previous occupant, had left an air of order and obedience about the place. Quite the opposite, Daisy reflected, to the dusty, creaky rooms of the old Wattcombe house, where everyone came and went without bothering to wipe their boots. But here - well, this was another kettle of fish altogether!

'Living in London is the chance of a lifetime,' her father had encouraged on the day they'd moved in. 'We have a new home to enjoy. The city to explore and the river, the greatest in the world, bringing trade from all nations, right to our doorstep!'

'But all our savings have gone, Nicky. We have nothing behind us.' This from Mother who was not at all enthusiastic about the expense of leaving Wattcombe.

'I'm an engineer, Flo. I put things together. Make them work. The factory is where I should be.'

'You did very well as Wattcombe's estate manager. We enjoyed a comfortable living.'

'Is that how you saw us existing for the rest of our lives?' her father had argued. 'Tenants of the landed gentry, under the thumb until we grew old?'

'What is so wrong with that?'

'Come on Flo,' he'd urged, 'you know I was hopeless in the country. This damn gammy leg had me stuck behind a desk all day - '

'I know this,' her mother had interrupted sharply, 'that you are supremely talented and just aching to make the world's next unrivalled discovery with your electrical valves. But we have a growing family. Expenses to be met. Bills to be paid.'

Daisy had overheard this heated discussion through the open window as she'd played in the garden, attempting - and failing - to find as many nooks and crannies to hide in as there had been in the country. The convenient wind had blown the quarrel her way and once she'd got into the gist of things, she knew that life for her parents was not all the good things they pretended it to be.

'Ed's my best pal as well as my brother,' Pops reasoned. 'I trust him. He wouldn't invite me into the business if it wasn't financially feasible.'

'He wouldn't ask you unless he needed our savings.'

Daisy had cramped inside at the bitter tone of her mother's voice.

'That's not fair, Flo.'

'Not fair, perhaps, but true.'

After a short pause, 'I'm sorry you still miss Wattcombe, my darling. I know your family is there, well, at least, Pat and your mother. But we go back to visit, don't we? Just as I promised before we moved to London.'

'I'm not complaining, Nicky.'

'Just consider the benefits our current situation has to offer,' Pops suggested. 'Poplar Park Row is quiet and untroubled. We are not isolated as we were in Wattcombe. And we even have a plumbed in bathroom upstairs!' He laughed, but when Mother remained silent he added coaxingly, 'Bobby and Daisy are happy at their new school. London's West End is only twenty minutes drive away and the factory a few minutes walk. Once Ed and I have patented our new valves we'll be in profit. All our money problems will be solved.'

'I hope so, Nicky,' Mother had conceded. 'I really do hope so.'

Her parents had gazed at each other, like eager swimmers diving into a pool. Often their affection was so intimate, that Daisy could not bear to look.

Instead, she had hurried back to her bedroom and gazed out of the window across the river to the needle tops of the goose-necked cranes. Here, she was restored by the sight of her new world and the silhouette of Uncle Ed's factory puffing grey smoke from its chimneys like a slumbering dragon.

Her dream was that one day she would board a fine ship sailing down the river. Sail off to a country like Neverland. Oh, she knew quite well that Neverland was made-up. Wendy and Peter were not real. But what counted was how you felt when you set your imagination free. Without a doubt, there must be somewhere in the world where there was no talk of war or threat. A world of discovery and excitement where she would never get bored again.

Daisy found herself in the kitchen, where a black-leaded stove stood opposite the sink positioned directly below the window. An oblong table covered by a cream cloth stood in front of an oak sideboard. On its wooden shelves stood a variety of the headmistress's fine china. On the far wall was the pantry where the faint perfumes of cinnamon and spices still clung to the walls. Beyond this, a laundry room complete with stout wash-boiler and a creaky old door that led outside to the garden privy. The room Daisy disliked most was the cellar, accessed only by a flight of stone steps. This gloomy underground space harboured not only a giant species of spider but all Miss Ayling's unwanted clutter that Pops had not had the heart to throw out.

The living room, in contrast, was bright and cheerful with wide bay windows. Daisy stood there now, imagining the parties that Mother and Pops might host. Just like the exciting parties Aunt Minnie and Uncle Leo held in their Soho studio.

She twirled energetically, holding up the hem of her dressing gown and pirouetted around the couch. Taking a flying leap to the open fireplace, she righted a wobbly landing and missed the brass fender. Impressed by her ballet, she vaulted the wooden rack in which Pops kept his newspapers. Misjudging the distance, she landed heavily on all fours, momentarily winded. Fortunately, no part of her was injured.

As she jumped to her feet, she heard a noise.

Daisy cocked her head, listening carefully. Was there movement in the house? A footfall? Or perhaps someone breathing? Closer now. But where exactly?

'Who's there?' she whispered. Had she imagined the breathing? But the household was sleeping. Could it have come from the garden? It was said that Hitler would arrive in the dead of night. He'd steal into people's houses and take them prisoner. A girl at school claimed her father kept a vicious dog and hadn't fed it for at least three months. Another boy insisted his mother had baked poisoned cakes to be offered to an invading army.

'Wh … who's there?' she mumbled, dreading an answer.

A soft breathing sound came; an evil gurgle.

Daisy froze.

Was someone lurking at the front door? Could this be the invasion all of England feared?

Before she could take a breath, a hand planted itself between her shoulder blades. 'Help!' she cried, falling heavily on the couch.

Her brother giggled as he pinned her down. 'Don't yell or we're for it!'

Daisy gasped for breath. She was so relieved that the war hadn't arrived and Hitler hadn't sailed down the estuary overnight that she forgot to be really angry. 'Bobby, you daft ha'p'orth!' she scolded. 'You frightened me!'

'Got you back for yesterday.'

Daisy pushed him away. 'I didn't do anything,' she declared, knowing very well she had.

'You split on me.'

'Didn't.'

'You told Mother I socked Peter Brady in the eye.'

Daisy defiantly stuffed her hands in her pockets. 'I told Mother the truth.'

'You don't understand what it was all about.'

She felt as though somehow she'd let Bobby down. 'What do you mean?'

Bobby took his time answering. 'If you must know,' he said eventually, 'Peter Brady calls Sammy Berger, "Fritz".'

'Is "Fritz" bad?'

Bobby rolled his blue eyes. ' 'Course it is.'

'Why?'

'Sammy's parents are German. They came to England to escape the Nazis. But Sammy's mother died and now, because of the war, the government is suspicious of any German who lives here.'

Daisy considered her brother carefully. 'Poor Sammy.'

'He's frightened they'll take his father away.'

'What will happen to Sammy?'

Bobby shrugged. 'Those men we saw trying to kick down Mr Berger's door the other day? Some of them were Blackshirts. Peter Brady said he'd join the Blackshirts if he was old enough. That's what started the fight.'

Daisy shivered, recalling the afternoon when she and Bobby had passed Sammy's house on the way home from school. The crowd outside Sammy's house had been very angry. It had been very upsetting to watch and Bobby had hurried her on.

'It was brave of you to stand up for Sammy,' she said.

Once again Bobby shrugged. 'He doesn't have many friends.' Bobby stood up and stretched. Daisy realised how much he'd grown since leaving Wattcombe. He stood a head and shoulders taller than her now; arms and legs too long for his old blue and white striped pyjamas. Mother had called Bobby a "slow grower". Yet now he was close to Matt's height after a sudden spurt this year.

'So tell me little sister, why were you snooping around so early?'

She pulled a face. 'I wasn't snooping. I was thirsty.'

This time he gave a whistle. 'What a whopper, Daisy Purbright! You were on the prowl, sniffing out other people's business. Eavesdroppers never hear any good of themselves, you know.'

Daisy gave him a hearty shove. 'Oh, buzz off you silly bee!' she exclaimed to hide her embarrassment.

But Bobby only laughed all the more.

CHAPTER 3

'Your hair's messy, Mother,' Daisy announced later that day as they sat at the breakfast table. 'It sticks up in funny places.'

'To be expected,' Florence Purbright answered calmly as she poured the tea. 'Unlike some, I've not had time to spend on myself lately.'

'Why's that?'

'It's what mothers do - care for their families. Put themselves last, even down to combing their hair. One day you'll be a mother yourself and then you'll understand.'

Daisy sincerely hoped she would not become a mother! At least, not until she was very old. Mothers, it seemed to her, led a very boring life indeed. Unlike fathers and brothers who were always out and about, allowed to do just as they pleased.

Aware of Matt and Bobby sitting opposite her, shovelling the Saturday treat of crispy rashers into their mouths, Daisy persisted. 'You should have it cut into a modern style, Mother. You'd look much younger.'

'Daisy!' Her father looked up from his newspaper. 'That's enough now.'

'Well, I think - '

'We all know what you think,' he interrupted. 'Now eat your porridge before it goes cold.'

'Yes, do eat up,' Matt mimicked. 'The lumps are the best. Quite more-ish!'

'Then why are you eating bacon?' Daisy retaliated. 'Porridge is much better for you. In Scotland they eat it every day.'

Her brother roared in amusement. 'Just as the French eat snails! Morning, noon and night, it's snails, snails, snails.'

Ignoring his taunt, Daisy continued. 'Anyway, porridge tastes even better in Miss Ayling's little china bowls. Not like it did in those ugly old dishes we used in Wattcombe.'

'If Miss Ayling had lived in Wattcombe,' Mother declared, 'no doubt she would have used the same serviceable bowls as we did. But Miss Ayling lived in the city and led a very different life to us.'

Daisy tossed her flaxen plaits over her shoulders. 'Miss Ayling's china plates with the blue pattern make roasted potatoes even more crunchy.'

'Then Miss Ayling was a magician,' chuckled Matt. 'Borrowed a few of Houdini's tricks, no doubt.'

'That's silly!' Daisy exclaimed. 'As silly as you look when you try to kiss Amelia.'

'Daisy!' Mother gasped. 'That's enough now!'

Annoyingly unseen, Matt poked out his tongue.

'When you've finished your breakfast,' Mother continued, 'you can help me in the kitchen. Your father and Matt must go to the factory. Bobby's at football. So you and I have all morning to bake.'

Daisy's heart plummeted. The very thought of being cooped up in a hot and stuffy kitchen gave her an instant headache. 'Its been ages since we've visited Aunt Minnie,' she suggested inventively, recalling the glamorous event at her aunt and uncle's Soho apartment celebrating Aunt Minnie's thirtieth birthday. 'And that must be months ago.'

'Two weeks in fact,' mocked Matt.

'Fourteen days, five hours and seventeen minutes,' Bobby exaggerated.

'Whether it was two weeks or two months is neither here nor there,' Mother decided, 'since Aunt Minnie is taking Will to the cinema today.'

'What's on?' Matt enquired disinterestedly.

' "Discovering England," ' enlightened Mother. 'A very interesting educational documentary.'

'Does it have dancing or singing?' Daisy enquired.

'I shouldn't think so.'

'Or Charlie Chaplin?'

'Definitely not.'

Aunt Minnie was her mother's younger sister and married to Uncle Leo Drake, a photographer. He took pictures of very special people, like the Prime Minister Mr Chamberlain and Amy Johnson, the brave lady pilot who had flown all the way from England to Australia. William their son, was seven and had more freckles on his nose than even she did. Will told the most awful fibs and frightening stories. Daisy thought Aunt Minnie very pretty. She had enormous deep grey eyes and blonde wavy hair that originated, so Mother inferred, from a bottle in Boots. She wore unusual flowing dresses which Mother called "arty". As for Uncle Leo, he had long, untidy, but rather nice, dark hair. He smoked French cigarettes and kissed Aunt Minnie in public. Daisy loved visiting the Drakes. There were always celebrations going on like the wonderful birthday party Uncle Leo had thrown for Aunt Minnie, overflowing with delicious food and music and people who dressed "arty" too.

'And before you suggest a visit to Aunt Pat and Grandma,' continued Mother, raising her eyebrows, 'you know Aunt Pat suffers from her nerves and likes time to prepare. Besides which, Wattcombe is in the country and the best part of an afternoon's journey. As Pops will tell you, petrol is not easy to come by.'

Daisy had no idea of what bad nerves meant, nor had an explanation ever been offered. When being crushed by Aunt Pat's merciless skills in Mahjong, Daisy had seen no evidence of this mysterious affliction.

'There is Aunt Betty,' Daisy blustered. 'She might need letters delivering. Or a message delivered.' Aunt Betty lived with Uncle Ed in Poplar just a bicycle ride away but on Saturday she was sure to be working at the factory.

'Since you are in such a helpful mood, Daisy,' answered Mother, 'I shall enlist your services. There are floors to be swept. Surfaces to dust. Bed linen changed. Houses don't clean themselves. '

Daisy groaned inwardly. All hope of escaping was gone. How dreary it was to be a girl! She thought longingly of the outside world where Bobby would go to football and Matt and Pops to the factory while she must stay at home.

'Perhaps you could visit the hairdresser, Mother?' Daisy suggested sweetly. 'I could go with Pops to help Mrs Hayes with the tea trolley. She said I did very well last time. Pouring and all that.'

A burst of laughter erupted from her brothers.

Daisy blushed angrily. 'Shut up, you two! I'm very good at tea-making.'

'Daisy the tea-maker,' Matt teased. 'Whatever next? You'll be Prime Minister soon!'

Nicholas Purbright held up his hands for silence. 'Now, now, boys and girls. Let's not argue.' After a short but meaningful pause he addressed his wife. 'Might not be such a bad idea, Flo. Take the Austin today. I won't need it. Daisy's right, you deserve a treat. And she can come to the factory with us. She'll make herself useful, I'm sure.'

Was she to be rescued from the brink, Daisy wondered joyfully? So she composed her features in such a way that she knew if she gazed at her father for long enough and her mother for not too long, and shut out the sight of her brothers' beastly smirking faces, she might - just *might* - be granted a reprieve.

CHAPTER 4

'DOES SHE LOVE HIM, do you think Mrs Hayes? I mean she should, shouldn't she, if they're going to be married?' Following Mrs Hayes's instructions, Daisy idly spooned sugar into the white china bowl. Having escaped to the factory with Pops and Matt, Daisy was now in her element, discussing factory politics. In this instance, Daisy's attention had been riveted on a young woman operating a small lathe and the much older man who hovered over her.

'Who's to tell, ducks?' Mrs Hayes raised her voice above the thunder of every cog, wheel and oiled machine racing towards the tea break in fifteen minutes time. As round as a barrel and only a few inches above Daisy's own height, the tea-lady's well-worked fingers adjusted the flowered turban squashed over her frizzy grey hair.

Above them, the cavernous factory roof rebounded the roars, grunts and groans of the great mechanical arms and legs - as Daisy often thought of them - that built electrical apparatus. Fifty men and thirty-seven women worked in this storm of dust, perpetual noise and invisible energy. But it was Mrs Hayes's commentary that fascinated her the most; a cocktail of courtings, engagements, marriages, tiffs, trials and domestic tribulations.

Mrs Hayes was the one person in all the world who answered her questions fully. They were answers that Daisy could understand; not wrapped up in long words. Things like who on the factory floor was walking out. Who was suffering heartbreak. Or who had recently had a brother or sister or someone in the family locked away in prison. Or banished to the country for nine months.

'Forty years I've been here, man and girl,' Mrs Hayes continued. 'I worked under old Mr Charles before your Uncle Ed took over five years ago. I know every face on the floor, my ducks, and each of those faces has a story to tell. The latest event of note is Elsie Shiner and Joe Rawlings' engagement party. They threw a right old shindig at Joe's house. I stopped by for half an hour and enjoyed a stout.'

'But Elsie's young and pretty and Joe's old,' Daisy protested. 'They don't seem to match.'

'Takes all sorts, my ducks. But yes, you're right. Joe must be twenty years her senior.'

'Elsie likes that other man.' Daisy had been watching from the small recess where the tea trolley was stored. Pretty Elsie was certainly not looking at Joe, her intended, but at a handsome young man who worked on the assembly line nearby.

'Oh, *him*,' replied Mrs Hayes with a disapproving frown. 'Micky Wolf.'

'Micky Wolf looks at Elsie like Matt looks at Amelia.'

'You mean your brother and his girly friend?'

'Amelia is young and pretty too.'

The older lady smiled knowingly. 'Don't all depend on looks, no, not at all. Trouble is, when you're young you don't see that.'

'I'm never getting married,' Daisy declared firmly. 'Instead, I'm going to catch a ship. How would I get a ship to stop, do you think, Mrs Hayes?'

Mrs Hayes licked a drip from the tip of her finger. 'First, you'd need a big cabin trunk for all your clothes. Then something called a passport. And most important of all, your sea legs.'

'My sea legs?' Daisy looked down at her feet. 'Why not the ones I've got?'

'Sea legs are different to land ones. No sense in me explaining; you'll know what sea legs are the minute you find you haven't got them.'

This complicated mystery remained unsolved as Mrs Hayes lumped a firm hand on Daisy's shoulder. 'Now, my ducks, make scarce of yourself while I'm on me rounds.'

'I'll go and visit Aunt Betty.'

'Remember to knock on her office door first.'

'Why's that?'

'Gives the person time to put a smile on their face.'

Mrs Hayes disappeared with the clanking trolley and Daisy ran up the stairs towards the covered walkway. It was cold and draughty compared to the stuffy workplace she had just left, so she skipped along the dirty floorboards to keep warm. At the end of the corridor she squeezed through the flimsy partition leading to the offices.

At the door marked 'Secretary' she paused and remembering Mrs Hayes's warning, was about to knock when she saw it was slightly ajar. Quietly she positioned herself for the best view inside the room. Aunt Betty's tall, slender figure stood at the window. Beside her - very close beside her - stood Mr Calder, whom Daisy knew to be the accounts manager.

'Betty, you must think of an excuse to get away from him,' he said urgently.

'It's not that simple, Neville,' replied Aunt Betty. 'I rarely go out in the evenings without Ed.'

'Not even to a friend's?'

Aunt Betty stroked back a curl of her short dark hair as Mr Calder stepped closer. 'Neville, please don't - not here.'

Daisy held her breath as Mr Calder did - *almost* - what Matt had done to Amelia. That thing with their lips nearly meeting.

Daisy gave a little choke of surprise. Aunt Betty quickly stepped back and Mr Calder bent down to the desk.

'I'll take these papers with me,' he said in a formal voice. 'Thank you Mrs Purbright.'

'Of course, Mr Calder,' replied Aunt Betty. 'Good morning.'

Daisy scurried away as fast as her feet would take her. Retracing her steps along the walkway she was sure she hadn't been seen.

When eventually she rejoined Mrs Hayes, she had come to the conclusion that it was very odd to find her aunt and a strange man standing so close to one another. If Mr Calder was not deaf - and surely he was too young to be hard of hearing - then what excuse was there for his behaviour?

After turning this over in her mind, it became clear to Daisy that she did not care for Mr Calder at all and didn't see how Aunt Betty could like him either!

'Cheer up, ducks, you look as though you've lost a pound and found a penny.' Mrs Hayes steered the rattling trolley towards the canteen at a rate of knots.

'No, I haven't found anything. Well, not really.' Daisy trotted beside the tea lady trying to keep up, listening to the tea-stained mugs clink violently against each other. A quick manoeuvre to the left swerved them down another walkway in the opposite direction to the offices.

'Either you have - or you haven't,' the tea lady objected. 'Speak now or forever hold your peace.'

Daisy was not certain how - or even if - she should reveal what she had seen. If she was to tell anyone at all, it would be Mrs Hayes or even Bobby, but was there really something to tell?

Perhaps she had imagined Aunt Betty standing close to Mr Calder? Had peering through one eye with the other closed distorted their figures? The more she thought, the more she was uncertain. Yet still the imprint of what she had witnessed remained in her mind. Just like Matt and Amelia's almost-kiss.

Mrs Hayes launched the trolley into the doors of the canteen, where the scarred and dented flaps flew open. Once safely into the deserted room filled with stout wooden tables and chairs, smelling strongly of the cleaning agent that was used to kill the roaches and mice, the trolley was abandoned.

'There now, all done,' sighed Mrs Hayes, planting her hands on her hips as she studied Daisy. 'Did you find your aunt?'

Daisy hesitated. 'Yes, but I didn't actually speak to her.'

'Why not?'

'She was with - she had - a visitor.'

Mrs Hayes screwed up her eyes. 'Who was that?'

'Mr Calder.'

'They was doing the accounts, no doubt,' Mrs Hayes said in a tone that brooked no argument as she waved a wooden spoon in Daisy's direction. 'A very important job is accounts. They've got to be kept up to date. Takes some doing; two heads is better than one.'

'Is it?'

'Just like cooking or tea-making.'

'I suppose,' Daisy agreed, not at all convinced.

'Your aunt is busy. Don't go pestering her again.' Mrs Hayes's fierce, unmoving gaze held Daisy's. 'Why don't you go up to the Lab? Bound to see your dad there. Odds on he'll be inventing something that goes bang and ends up in a puff of smoke.'

Daisy nodded though she feared Mrs Hayes was employing diversionary tactics, just as her mother and father did. Mrs Hayes had never done this before and Daisy found it rather disappointing.

'Look here, ducks,' said Mrs Hayes, resuming her cheerful old self. 'I've got a nice fat banger for you. I'll wrap it in baking paper. It's cold from yesterday, but still tasty. Eat it on the QT. Don't let anyone see or they'll want one too.'

Daisy swiftly stuffed the disguised sausage into her pocket.

'Run along now. The cleaners are coming.'

With a final twirl of the spoon, Mrs Hayes returned her attention to the big double ovens. Daisy made her way to the laboratory. The Lab as it was known, was where her father conducted his investigations into how, why and where a thing might work. It was a room full of test tubes and bottles and strong smelling chemicals and little flames that danced out of the Bunsen Burners.

It was here that she felt as though she was witnessing one of Houdini's magic tricks, as stuffy Matt might say. A trick coming true right in front of her eyes.

Daisy smelled the room on the upper floor long before she arrived for the Lab had a particular odour; gassy and smoky and altogether exciting.

She slipped out her parcel, nibbled at the treat and leaped the stairs. Mrs Hayes had never given her a sausage before. It was as if - well, if Daisy didn't know better - the sausage had been offered in conjunction with the tea-lady's spoon-warning about Aunt Betty and Mr Calder.

CHAPTER 5

DAISY THOUGHT LONG and hard about that Saturday morning and her observations at the door of Aunt Betty's office. Nor had she forgotten the warning expression in Mrs Hayes's eyes. Sharing with Bobby would be no help at all; he might claim it was her punishment for spying on people.

So Daisy kept her thoughts to herself, hoping she had been mistaken about Aunt Betty and Mr Calder. It wasn't until a few weeks later when the whole sorry episode was brought to light in the least expected manner.

After school one day, she and Bobby returned home to find Aunt Minnie seated in the living room with Mother. Though there was nothing unusual in Aunt Minnie visiting, both her mother and aunt sat with slightly flushed cheeks and talking in a hushed manner.

'Shoes by the front door!' Mother ordered as Daisy and Bobby burst in.

'But - '

'Do as you're told.' Mother shooed them away.

'They don't want us to hear,' Daisy whispered to Bobby as they returned to the hall.

Bobby kicked his shoes to the doormat. 'Trust you! Always dreaming up a drama.'

She stared at her uncooperative brother. 'They stopped talking when we came in.'

'It was just grown-up stuff.'

Daisy took off her shoes. Why was Bobby not listening? He had lost interest in what she had to say or regarded them as trivial. Did this happen to every boy once they had turned ten?

'Hello you two,' Aunt Minnie welcomed when they reappeared. Stroking her long corn-coloured hair behind her ears she held out her arms. 'Hugs twice over please.'

Daisy watched with interest as Bobby allowed himself to be pulled close. But not for long. How like Matt he was becoming! Hugs and cuddles had slipped into the category of girl's stuff. His recent move to the box room had set the seal on their nightly discussions.

Daisy fell eagerly into her favourite aunt's arms. She relished being overcome by Gardenia and the feel of a smooth, rouged cheek against hers. Aunt Minnie's playful tug on her plaits made her giggle. Bobby, she noted, awkwardly kicked his heels.

'Where's Will?' he asked as Aunt Minnie released her.

'Manners, Bobby,' their mother interrupted. 'Aunt Minnie would like to be asked how she is.'

'Oh, nonsense, Flo!' Aunt Minnie protested. 'Bobby can see I am in the peak of good health. Sadly though, Will has a howling cough. Leo is taking care of him. Though it could very well be the other way round.' Aunt Minnie tinkled a laugh. 'Your uncle is rubbish at medicines and things.'

'Oh,' mumbled Bobby vaguely.

'My goodness, you both look smart. Flo, how do you manage the uniforms?'

'It's difficult,' Florence answered her sister. 'I've made do and mend with some of Daisy's and Bobby's Wattcombe clothes.'

Daisy had learned about shortages first-hand. She still wore her mackintosh from Wattcombe Primary jumble sale. She and Bobby now wore the uniform of Poplar Park School, but Bobby's shorts were too small and her gym slip a faded navy.

'Is tea ready yet?' asked Bobby.

'I've brought rock cakes,' offered Aunt Minnie. 'Sadly, they were all I could find. Like uniforms, good pastries are in short supply. Goodness knows what we'll do for Christmas.'

'Minnie, you spoil us,' worried Mother. 'But thank you all the same.' Turning to Daisy she nodded briefly. 'Why don't you and Bobby have your tea? Aunt Minnie's rock cakes are in the larder.'

'Thanks, Aunt Minnie!' Daisy threw her arms around her aunt. 'I love it when you visit. You always bring nice treats.'

Soft laughter echoed as Daisy chased Bobby to the kitchen.

'I'm taking my cake upstairs to eat in my room,' Bobby threatened as he opened the pantry door.

'Mother won't like it if we don't sit at the table.'

'She won't know if you don't tell.'

Daisy watched her brother shovel another into his pocket.

'Why don't you ever stop to talk to me?' she pestered.

'Talking's for girls.'

'Bobby I need to tell you something,' Daisy called as Bobby left the kitchen. 'There's something I saw at the factory - '

But her brother had already gone. So Daisy sat alone at the kitchen table. Unusually, her appetite had disappeared. Instead there was an uncomfortable weight on her chest. If she couldn't share this dilemma, she was going to burst.

Daisy had finally eaten her cake and was about to follow Bobby upstairs when she heard Aunt Minnie's voice drift out from the living room.

'I know something's wrong, yet I can't put my finger on the trouble.'

'What sort of trouble?' replied Mother.

'Betty said she wanted to go to the pictures to see - what is that film called with Ronald Colman? *The Prisoner of Zenda?*'

'Wasn't it playing up West last year?'

'Apparently, it's showing again. And Betty seemed eager - '

'Why did she ask you?' Mother interrupted. 'Why not Ed?'

'He was working late - apparently,' Aunt Minnie suggested. 'Betty seems to think I'm somewhat of a picture-goer. Not that she really wanted my company. In fact I got the distinct impression she didn't.'

'How so?' Mother questioned.

'I was about to explain that we were expecting a visit from one of Leo's stuffy old clients when Betty told me the cab she'd ordered was was arriving as we spoke. As if she hadn't bargained on me going with her in the first place.'

'How curious,' replied Mother.

'Yes, I thought so too.'

Daisy was puzzling this conversation when the next sentence dropped like a bombshell.

'Anyway, the thing is - and this took the wind right out of my sails - Betty then asked me to tell Ed, if he should ever enquire, that I had gone to the cinema with her. She said something about Ed not liking her to go out on her own what with the threat of war on our doorstep but she was eager not to miss the film and didn't want to upset Ed.'

Another strained silence, but the information about Aunt Betty wanting to go out on her own gave Daisy the shivers.

'So I agreed,' Aunt Minnie continued helplessly. 'I actually agreed to fib on Betty's behalf!'

Mother gasped. 'Heavens, Minnie, you didn't!'

'What was I supposed to do?'

'I … I'm not certain.' Daisy heard her mother hesitate - which was unusual in itself. 'But lying on behalf of anyone is wrong, whoever it might be.'

'I know,' agreed Aunt Minnie sheepishly. 'I just didn't have time to think. Please keep this to yourself, Flo.'

'Of course. Did Betty *actually* go to see this film?'

'I suppose she must have or else I'd have heard from her.'

'Did you tell Leo?' asked Mother.

'No, only you.'

Mother gave a sniff of disapproval, a sound that Daisy knew well. 'I should try to put it from your mind, Minnie. It's probably all quite innocent.'

'I hope so, but - '

'Minnie, don't say it. Don't even think it,' warned Mother, but Aunt Minnie refused to give up.

'I always thought Ed and Betty were well suited. But now I'm having doubts. Ed seems besotted with his wretched valves and Betty might feel ignored.'

'Why should she?' Mother countered icily. 'Like Ed, Nicky is quite passionate about his discoveries. Our men are only trying to make a decent living.'

'Yes,' agreed Aunt Minnie hurriedly. 'But you and Nicky have a family to balance your lives. Leo and I have Will. Ed and Betty are childless. It doesn't seem fair somehow.'

The voices then dipped to an inaudible whisper, forcing Daisy to return to her bedroom where she sat fretfully at her desk. Her times-table exercise book remained unopened. Her pencil lay idly in its groove. What could Aunt Betty be thinking of when asking Aunt Minnie to lie? What if Uncle Ed should learn the truth?

A few minutes later, Aunt Minnie put her head round the door. 'Darling, I'm off now.'

Daisy jumped to her feet. 'Aren't you staying for supper, Aunt Minnie?'

'Heavens, I'd love to. Another time perhaps. Give your father a hug from me.'

Daisy was bathed in Gardenia as she embraced her aunt. A short while after Aunt Minnie had left, she was still sitting, trying to gather her thoughts, when Mother appeared.

'What are you doing, Daisy?'

'I've been learning my times tables.'

'How very industrious.'

'When will Pops and Matt be home?'

'Not long now.'

Daisy left her desk and wound her arms around her mother's slender waist.

'What's all this for?' Mother asked, kissing the top of her daughter's head as they hugged.

'Nothing. I just ... well, it's nice being all together, isn't it?'

'You are a funny girl.'

Daisy melted in the warm embrace of motherhood. She felt reassured after the uncomfortable thoughts stirred inside her. She wasn't able to say why - exactly - she had felt so peculiar. After all, tiny white fibs didn't matter much, did they? White fibs weren't like huge black, unpardonable lies.

All the same, Aunt Minnie regretted her fib and Mother had offered no answer in their place. The fact that Aunt Betty had done something to cause Aunt Minnie to confide her secret to Mother was bad enough. But worse by far - much, much worse, was that Aunt Betty it seemed, had done exactly what Mr Calder had told her to.

CHAPTER 6

DAISY STOOD in the headmistress's office with three other pupils of Poplar Park School.

'Girls, I have chosen you to decorate the assembly room where the school play will take place. We haven't any holly, but we'll make do with a few twigs from the playground. There is a box of decorations in the caretaker's cupboard. Since we've no real tree this year, we must improvise and use a coat stand.'

Daisy loved Christmas and all its trimmings. For the past two years she had helped to decorate the school. Delivered on the first week of December from Cox Street market, the arrival of the tree caused a stir of excitement. But this year her heart sank for the hall stood empty and lacklustre. The scarred red brick walls and scrubbed wooden floors indented by scores of Blakeys hammered into the cheap soles of the children's shoes, were barren. All down to the shortages and hardships posed by the rumoured conflict.

'What will we do with a coat stand, Miss Bailey?' one girl wanted to know.

'Ask Mr Potter for a sheet to drape over it. Use your imagination.'

Daisy didn't think for a moment that Mr Potter would oblige. As old as the hills and clearly suspicious of any child in the vicinity, the caretaker stoically guarded the school's property cupboard. 'Please Miss, what if the cover's not green?' Nora Fudge, the class know-it-all, enquired.

'Any colour will suffice, Nora. We have very few choices.'

Daisy and her friends left to scour the girls' cloakrooms where a suitable coat stand was eventually found. Mr Potter unexpectedly provided a torn grey tarpaulin together with a battered box labelled, "Christmas Decs".

In the cold assembly room, the box revealed ancient pupil-made decorations which helped to disguise the sheet. At home, Daisy cut out a star from a large brown envelope that Pops brought from the factory.

'From Aunt Betty,' he explained. 'And look here, some coloured chalks. You're bound to do wonders with these.'

'Are Aunt Betty and Uncle Ed coming to watch the play?' Daisy enquired, a strange little shiver creeping down her spine as she thought of Aunt Betty's secret.

'Indeed,' he assured her. 'Just as they always do.'

Daisy recalled with pride the many Nativity plays produced at Wattcombe Primary. She had never been chosen to play Mary or Joseph or even a wise man, but she had excelled at helping to dress the cast. Over the years she had secured belts and braces, stretched towels and turbans over tiny heads and made shepherd staffs from the many donated walking sticks. One year, a farmer's donkey had been led into the school yard. Mary and Joseph, head-height to its belly had been terrified at the sound of its braying. Daisy remembered with fondness her village school even though she had never won a great role in the play. So she had been more than surprised last year at her new school, when Miss Bailey had given her a solo to perform.

'You've wonderful lungs, Daisy,' she encouraged. 'Let's hear you make use of them.'

Daisy had done her very best and the applause after her solo of *It Came Upon the Midnight Clear* had been unexpectedly rewarding. Mother and Pops had watched from the second row and Aunt Betty and Uncle Ed sat to their left. Aunt Pat and Grandma who always stayed over at Christmas had joined Aunt Minnie, Uncle Leo, Matt and Will, in the row behind. The whole family had applauded so loudly, that Daisy's moment of triumph had seemed a little embarrassing. But Miss Bailey had congratulated her afterwards and Daisy's reward was in being chosen again this year.

'As the finale, you will sing a solo verse to *Land of Hope and Glory*,' Miss Bailey decided. 'Please learn the words carefully. I shall ask Mrs Jones to take you for practice. Nora, you will be Daisy's understudy.'

Daisy glanced enviously at Nora Fudge. As school monitor, a day didn't pass without her shiny brown hair being tied studiously away from her face. A waft of Sunlight soap followed her wherever she went and the perfection continued in her sweet singing voice.

Daisy reminded herself that it was she, Daisy, who had been chosen to sing the solo, even though Nora was cleverer and prettier than her.

As she wrestled with her doubts, a soft ray of sunshine fell on the silver threads of the old tarpaulin. It lit up the five pointed star balanced on the top of the coat stand and a breeze twirled the paper decorations hanging from its stick branches. Mr Potter's dustbin had been secured for the ballast and a curl of excitement tickled in her stomach. She couldn't wait for practice with Mrs Jones the music teacher. Even if Nora was present as understudy. Even if Nora looked down her freckled nose at Daisy as if she was smelling something unpleasant. None of that mattered. It was she, Daisy, who was to sing a solo verse of *Land of Hope and Glory*.

Miss Bailey gave a smile of approval. 'Keep up the good work, girls. I fear this will be a Christmas to remember, so please make the very most of our celebrations.'

Later, at break, Daisy hurried to the cloakroom with her friend Sally Watson to put on their coats. Nora and her friends made a great show of excitement, but Daisy ignored them.

'Me dad wouldn't half give them cows a piece of his mind,' Sally muttered as they dressed. 'They need pulling down a peg or two if you ask me.'

Sally was a tall, thin girl who had attached herself to Daisy in her first term at Poplar Park School. Her uniform was faded and patched and once Daisy had noted the little white eggs nestling in the parting of her untidy ginger hair. Miss Bailey had sent her home to have it washed and cleansed of nits.

'I don't care about them,' Daisy shrugged.

'Me neither,' agreed Sally with a grin.

'What did you think of our tree?' Daisy asked as she slipped on her shoes.

'For a coat stand it don't look too bad.'

Daisy hurried with Sally along the corridor. 'At least it won't die.'

'No, but we might,' replied Sally.

Daisy came to a sudden halt. 'Die?'

'Yeah, when Hitler arrives.' Sally was always eager to pass on the news gleaned from her docker father. 'Dad said London will be the first to fall.'

'Fall where?' Daisy asked innocently.

Sally tucked her hair firmly behind her prominent ears. 'Me dad says *they* - meaning the Germans - will sail up the estuary to cut off the capital. It's like snapping the head from a live chicken, Dad says. The rest of its body will still run about but its brains are quite dead.'

'Sally, that's not true,' protested Daisy with a shudder. 'Once a chicken is dead, it's dead.'

Daisy had no intention of falling into the trap of discussing the war; she heard too much of it at home. But Sally was insistent.

'What would you do if a German parachutist landed in your back yard?' she demanded. 'Me dad's got a gun hidden under the bed. And he's gonna shoot the first German he sees right between the eyes.'

Daisy turned on her friend with a gasp. 'A gun?'

'Would you rather be killed?'

'No, of course not. But the German might not have a gun or anything. Not if he's just jumped out of an aeroplane. He might even be friendly.'

'Why would he be friendly?' Sally asked as they left the cloakroom. 'The Germans are our enemies, right? Me dad says everyone should have a gun in the house to defend their family with. They should be government issue really. Dad lost two fingers and four of his toes in the trenches. His hand and foot nearly dropped off from gangrene. He says he's not going to give the bloody enemy any more body parts. Not likely.'

Daisy wondered if Mr Watson ever overbalanced with an almost toeless foot? Not that it would be less or more painful than being shot in the calf, as Pops had been. However, Pops rarely talked about his "gammy leg". Everyone in the family knew he was reluctant to discuss his service in the Great War. Quite the opposite it seemed, to Mr Watson who frequently revealed the details to Sally who word for word, repeated the gruesome details.

Once outside in the playground, Daisy and Sally made

their way to the corner set aside for playing marbles. But long before they got there, Daisy stopped still, unable to believe her eyes. Bobby was crouching on the ground, shielding his head with his arm. Above him towered Peter Brady. The first kick found Bobby's ribs and he cried out in pain. The second blow went into Bobby's exposed shin.

Daisy watched in horror as the assault continued. Where was the duty teacher? The playground seemed unattended. Only the children were present, gathering in groups around the spectacle of a smaller boy being bullied by a much larger one.

Bobby tried his best to crawl away, like a beaten dog, attempting to dodge the wicked boot that tormented it. Daisy felt a stab of revulsion. How could this possibly happen in broad daylight with everyone watching and doing nothing? It seemed to her that some of the children were even enjoying it.

Suddenly there was a high-pitched, searing scream. Daisy gulped. The sound appeared to be coming from her. She knew it was a frightful noise, yet she couldn't stop making it.

All the faces turned towards her as she flew like the wind across the playground. It was as if her feet weren't touching the ground. She didn't care how she looked. The louder and uglier the better. She only cared about Bobby. Nor did she know what she was about to do. Her fingers tingled. Her hands stretched out, waving and clawing.

Before Peter Brady could move, she launched herself on him. Her nails met the unguarded skin of his face and and they fell to the ground.

CHAPTER 7

'DAISY, what have you to say for yourself?'

Miss Bailey's office stood in the corridor three doors before the First Aid Room. Daisy could hear the faint echo of Peter Brady's cries as Mrs Potter, the caretaker's wife, applied tincture of iodine to the raw scratches on his face. Daisy knew of course that Peter's protests were exaggerated. His act was for the benefit of the headmistress.

'Peter claims that you assaulted him without reason. Your brother, whilst being attended by Mrs Potter, asserts you were not involved. Now which of these stories am I to believe?'

Daisy kept her eyes down. She knew that her offence carried with it some kind of punishment. On the other hand, if she didn't protest Bobby's innocence and explain why she had flown at Peter Brady in a rage, how would the truth come to light?

The last thing she remembered was clinging to Peter Brady with some sort of miracle strength. Her nails had done their work without any thought on her part at all. When he'd bashed her on the mouth, she'd spat at him and made him blink so fiercely she'd managed to get in another blow, knocking him off balance. He'd soon recovered and was about to deliver a clenched fist when Bobby appeared. Dirt streaked her brother's face and muddied his hair. But with arms around Peter's neck, Bobby had strangled and jostled until Peter's face had reddened, deepening the scratches on his cheeks to crimson.

At that moment the duty teacher had returned and the boys pulled apart. Daisy was left flattened, the inelegant subject of the entire school's gaze.

Miss Bailey sat ramrod-straight under her woollen twin set. 'Have you nothing to say for yourself?' she demanded.

Daisy ached to say so much but how could she? Both hers and Bobby's punishments, detentions or the cane, or inconceivably both, simply could not be avoided.

Sighing deeply, the headmistress took a thin sheet of paper from her drawer. 'In that case, I shall write to your parents,' she decided. 'They will be extremely disappointed in you and your brother. A disagreement is one thing, but physical violence on another pupil will not be tolerated. I hope for your sake that Peter's injuries are not serious enough to warrant a doctor. Mrs Potter is doing her best to repair the damage.'

Daisy was afraid to look up in case Miss Bailey read her angry thoughts. The bump on her nose throbbed so violently she was sure it was vibrating. Her lip tasted salty-sweet with blood. If Peter Brady's injuries were only half as painful as hers, then she wished she had scratched him all the more.

'Daisy, you will forfeit your opportunity to sing solo at the Christmas play. Nora will take your place.'

Daisy's head jerked up. The world felt as though it was collapsing around her ears. Had she heard right? She was to be robbed of her solo! Yet what punishment had Peter received? Not even a reprimand? She choked back her sob.

But she would not cry. Not even let the furious tears close. Well, not now anyway.

'Tomorrow you will apologise to Peter. You have broken school rules. I hope this punishment will teach you to think carefully before acting on impulse.'

Oh, it certainly will, Daisy longed to say. If being deprived of her starring role in the choir was earth-shattering, apologising to Peter Brady was about the most awful, unjust thing she had ever heard of.

She hadn't understood the words that Peter Brady had been yelling, but she knew they were bad. She recognised a bully when she saw one. Peter would grow up to be like the men outside Sammy Berger's house; the same awful men who had daubed the words, "Filthy Yid," on Mr Berger's front door.

'What kind of trouble have you landed us in now?' Bobby demanded as they walked home from school. They were the last two pupils to leave, except for Peter Brady who was still being treated by Mrs Potter.

'I'm not a telltale,' Daisy protested, hurt that Bobby could even think such a thing. Once again, the tears of injustice pricked. Why was Bobby so angry with *her*? She had only tried to help him.

They marched on in silence past the shabby two-up, two-down terraces of the Isle of Dogs until Daisy swiped her runny nose with the back of her hand.

Bobby stopped abruptly. 'What's up with you now?'

'Nothing.'

'You're crying.'

'It's all so unfair,' she burst out. 'Peter Brady isn't punished, but we are.'

'You're too young to understand,' Bobby said impatiently.

Her tears turned to anger again. 'You're my brother,' she spluttered. 'I couldn't stand by and watch you get beaten up.'

Bobby reached out and grasped her shoulders. 'You shouldn't interfere in a boys' fight.'

'Peter Brady is beastly. He deserved what he got.'

'It's not your concern,' Bobby persisted. 'Peter's parents are against Jews, so Peter bullies Sammy.'

'Is that why you stuck up for Sammy?'

'He's got no other mates,' Bobby dismissed casually.

Daisy felt a swell of pride. Bobby was fearless. Even though Peter Brady had a gang, Bobby had defended Sammy.

'I quite like Sammy too,' she said, her eyes stretched wide. 'Even though he's a bit smelly and dirty.'

Bobby withdrew his hands from her shoulders. 'Sammy and his dad are poor. Sometimes they don't have anything to eat. Can you imagine starving?'

Daisy tried to imagine being hungry and not having a meal to look forward to. This, she discovered, was almost impossible. For Mother and Pops saw to it that their family was fed and clothed and given a happy, harmonious home to live in. Unlike the slum where Sammy lived.

'You've got a great big bruise on your shin.' Daisy pointed to Bobby's injured leg. 'It's where Peter kicked you.'

Bobby pulled up his sock. 'Doesn't show now.'

'You can't see my cut either.' She tried to keep the tremble out of her voice. 'Lucky, it's on the inside of my lip.'

They were half way home when Daisy realised the biggest challenge of all was still looming ahead. 'What shall we tell Mother?'

Bobby replied in a tone that sent fresh shivers over her skin. 'We don't say a word!'

'Why not?'

'Grown-ups want to know why you've been in trouble,

but really they don't. Sorting it all out is a big problem for them.'

Daisy stared into her brother's brave, bright blue gaze. This time she thought she understood. Aunt Betty, for instance, had a problem. So she had shared it with Aunt Minnie who, also unable to solve it, had passed it on to Mother.

This process, Daisy decided, was like giving someone a cold. It gathered pace, and infected lots more people. If Aunt Betty had never stood close to Mr Calder, then she wouldn't have passed the cold to Aunt Minnie and Aunt Minnie to Mother.

It was quite clear to Daisy now, from what she had learned from Bobby, that the more people who got involved, the worse it became.

'Did you get detention from Miss Bailey?' Bobby asked.

'No,' she replied resentfully. 'Nora Fudge has been given my solo.'

Bobby whistled through his teeth. 'Poor old you.'

'I don't care,' she insisted, though of course, she did. 'What should I say to Mother when she reads the letter?'

'Don't say a word. Leave the talking to me.'

Daisy's heart filled with admiration. Bobby was her brother, but more than that, he was her hero.

She would never, *ever* let him down. Showing him she was loyal had been worth losing her solo.

CHAPTER 8

'IT WAS JUST A SCRAP,' Bobby explained after Mother had read the letter.

'What caused it?' Mother enquired from her chair beside the fire.

'I can't even remember what it was.'

'So it wasn't serious?' Mother questioned. 'Not something I should know about?'

Bobby shook his head. 'We don't get on. I think he's an idiot. He thinks I'm one.'

Daisy watched her brother shrug and automatically, she shrugged herself. This gesture caused Mother to glance her way. 'And you, Daisy. How did you get involved?'

'She was meddling as usual,' Bobby answered before Daisy could speak. 'Got in the way like she always does.'

Daisy wanted to protest but Bobby kept talking.

'Not that she meant to scratch his cheek,' he elaborated. 'Girls are useless when they fight. Like cats.'

'Is this true, Daisy?' Mother asked.

Daisy chewed on her sore lip. 'I s'pose.'

'Miss Bailey writes she is most upset,' Mother said sadly.

'And I am too. You fought over something so trivial that neither of you can remember what it was. Yet this boy has been physically injured.'

Daisy felt as if she had been dealt a stomach blow. More, she felt ashamed. Guilty, even. But it simply wasn't fair! The fight had not been over something small, but very big indeed. A grown-up problem passed like a cold from Peter's parents to their horrid son and eventually to school and Bobby and then Miss Bailey. No one knew the real cause.

'Have I your word this won't happen again?'

Bobby nodded. Daisy forced herself to follow.

Mother folded the letter back into its envelope. 'Of course, Mr and Mrs Brady will have something to say about their son's injuries. Scratches on the face can be most painful.' With a quick glance at Daisy she added, 'They are also tremendously obvious.'

Daisy raised her eyes carefully and met Mother's gaze. She quickly looked down again.

'You'll both apologise to Peter tomorrow.'

'Yes,' agreed Bobby.

'Yes,' said Daisy, 'but I don't see why - '

'We're sorry,' Bobby interrupted, pressing his arm hard against hers.

'Such a pity,' sighed Mother. 'We all look forward to the Nativity play. Really, Daisy, has your involvement in something that was never your business in the first place been worth losing your solo?'

Despite the insistent pressure of Bobby's arm on hers, Daisy had the most enormous urge to defend herself. To reveal that Peter Brady was the architect of their misfortune. It was Peter Brady who was the nastiest, cruellest, slyest bully in all of London.

'And it won't happen again?' asked Mother.

Bobby shook his head firmly. Daisy, asserting a good deal of will power, followed suit.

Their mother's face was full of suppressed feelings; love and sadness, pride and regret, trust and suspicion. Tears threatened Daisy again at the wrongness of it all.

'I love you both,' said Mother. 'But you must learn that life doesn't always work in the way we want it to.'

But why should they apologise to Peter when there was nothing to apologise for? Grown-ups, Daisy decided, just as Bobby predicted, inhabited another world altogether.

The following day Daisy apologised to Peter. He grinned smugly and put out his hand for her to shake. As Miss Bailey was present, she had to take it. He squeezed her fingers so hard she almost cried out in pain. He'd done the same to Bobby too. Oh, how she loathed Peter Brady!

After that, whenever he saw her in school, he drew his finger across his throat. She knew what this meant. She was for it.

'Take no notice,' Bobby instructed. 'Don't walk home without me. Wait in the girls' cloakroom until my detention is over. Never let him catch you alone.'

'You and Bobby can come to my house after school if you like,' Sally Watson suggested. 'We live just round the corner. My dad will tear Peter off a strip. There's more than one way to skin a cat, he says.'

Daisy was horrified at the thought. 'Sally, please don't tell your parents about this.'

'Don't see why not. I'll bet Peter never gave Miss Bailey's letter to his dad,' Sally guessed. 'Probably said he fell in some bushes. Didn't want his dad to know he'd lost a fight to a girl.'

Daisy felt an unexpected twinge of guilt. What must it be like to go in fear of your parents, rather than loving and respecting them?

That afternoon, as Daisy took her seat in class, she heard a rumpus outside. The screaming was so loud everyone stood up to look through the window. By the school gates, Peter Brady had managed to get his big head stuck through the railings. Mr Potter was trying to free him.

'Sit down,' ordered Mr Gulliver, the English teacher. 'Don't leave your seats again. Get on with your work while I go and investigate.'

Freed of supervision, Daisy, and the whole class scrambled back to the window. A tall woman pushing a battered pram arrived on the scene. Two tiny infants accompanied her. Both children had filthy faces and tousled hair. Their clothes looked like rags.

'That's Peter's Mum,' someone said.

Daisy had a dreadful, sinking feeling. Had Mrs Brady come to lodge a complaint? She imagined being hauled into the headmistress's room where she would be put through an interrogation.

'She keeps on thumping him,' said someone else.

Mr Potter began to protest at the assault on Peter. Miss Bailey and Mr Gulliver joined in. But it was Mrs Brady who made everyone gasp when she pushed Mr Potter to the ground.

'Peter's in for it,' said another boy. 'His dad will knock seven bells out of him. My mum once saw Mr Brady break a man's arm. It took six rozzers to arrest him an' all.'

When Mr Gulliver returned to the classroom his thin fair hair was dishevelled and he looked very pale. 'Pack up your books,' he said in a shaky voice as the bell-ringing fire engine arrived to set Peter free. 'We'll finish our lesson in the assembly hall where we shan't be disturbed.'

That evening Daisy told Bobby all that had happened. 'I thought Mrs Brady had come because of me,' said Daisy with a shudder. 'But it was because Peter got his head stuck.'

'Peter won't tell on you,' said Bobby cryptically. 'But he will get his own back, so watch out.'

As she lay in bed that night, Daisy tried not to think of Peter Brady. Instead, she listened to Mother preparing the spare room at the top of the house for Grandma and Aunt Pat while Pops drove to Wattcombe to collect them. If only Grandpa was coming too!

Daisy tried to recall the big, strong man who she barely remembered before his death when she was young. But instead she fell asleep, only to dream of Peter Brady and Mr Calder, and a man called Hitler and she woke with a cry on her lips.

Climbing out of bed, she stood at the window. The silhouettes of the factories were illuminated by the moon's silver rays. The world at night looked spectacular. A million stars glittered brightly in a vast, deep blue sky that was almost black. On the water, trembled a delicate ribbon of silver light.

On Christmas Eve she and Bobby would hang their pillow cases on the hearth. By Christmas morning they were filled. A delicious dinner appeared as if by magic on the dining table. Games were played until exhaustion set in.

Then she remembered tomorrow and the Nativity play. If she hadn't interfered in the boys' fight, she would still be singing the solo verse of *Land of Hope and Glory.*

And Christmas would be just like it should be.

CHAPTER 9

'YOU'RE DEAD!' Peter hissed as Daisy left the playground lavatories. Miss Bailey had sent her to check they were clean and tidy before the parents arrived. Peter must have seen her and lay in wait.

She stopped, frozen by Peter's threat. Even on an important day like this, the day of the Nativity play, he smelled like he hadn't washed in months. His menacing eyes peered out from under a large forehead that was emphasized by his closely shaved skull.

He prodded her violently in the shoulder. 'You hear me, you little bitch?'

'Stay away,' Daisy squeaked and stumbled back.

'I'm going to make you pay, now I've got you alone.'

Daisy felt faint. The smell of his breath was worse than horse dung. He moved closer, a grin on his lips.

'I've got a knife in me pocket. Guess what I'm gonna do with it?'

Would he really hurt her in broad daylight, Daisy wondered in terror? She didn't know if he really had a knife, but could she take that chance? Should she try to escape? Or call his bluff?

'I … I'll scream if you come any closer,' Daisy threatened.

'Who's gonna hear you?' Peter smirked. 'Your gormless brother? Well, hard luck. I made sure he was inside before I followed you.'

'Everyone will know what you did,' Daisy croaked. 'You'll get put in prison for ever.'

The sloppy smile slowly left his face. He grabbed her arm. 'Prison? No bugger's putting Peter Brady in prison.'

Daisy shrank back as far as she could against the cold brick of the lavatory wall. She couldn't imagine a worse death than bleeding very slowly until all your blood was gone. What part of the body emptied first? Would they find her lying here on the cold earth, without even her coat on. She wished she'd taken the trouble to dress warmly before rushing out on her errand. Now look at her. Shivering like a jelly in her gym-slip and white blouse which before long would be stained crimson red.

Peter reached into his pocket. Daisy gulped. So he really did have a knife! Her head swam in circles. Her breath stopped in her throat.

'Daisy!' A familiar voice echoed across the playground. 'Daisy, we're here!'

Peter let go of her arm. He turned to see who had called and Daisy sprang forward. She ran like the wind across the playground.

'Grandma!' Daisy called, her heart feeling as though it would jump out of her chest.

'What a welcome,' said Grandma as Daisy fell into her arms.

'Where's Pops and Mother?' Daisy asked.

'They'll be here soon. Aunt Pat and I came early.'

'I'm glad you did.'

'Is there anything wrong?' Grandma enquired.

'Not really.'

'I'm sure the play will go splendidly. When I was a girl, I was just the same - stage fright I think they call it. I loved the school plays and belonged to the drama club but before an event I was all at twos and threes. I remember one year especially … '

Grandma continued to reminisce but right now, Daisy couldn't concentrate on anything but keeping out of Peter Brady's way. How she wished the Fire Brigade had failed to release such a hateful boy. From the corner of her eye, she watched Peter slink past. Had he really been going to stab her?

Aunt Pat arrived then, a little out of breath. 'We're very excited to hear you sing Daisy.'

'I'm not singing,' Daisy moped, 'at least, not by myself.'

'Yes, so Mother told us,' said Grandma with a dismissive wave. 'But being part of a choir is just as important. Now, dear, show us to our seats, will you?'

By the time Aunt Pat and Grandma were settled, Daisy had recovered a little. She saw Bobby and another boy on the stage trying to hang a handmade star to the stable roof. She wanted to warn him about Peter Brady and waved to catch his attention.

'Daisy Purbright, what are you doing?' The music teacher tapped her shoulder.

'Nothing, Mrs Jones.'

'You are supposed to be practicing.'

'I was just - '

'Doing very little,' Mrs Jones scolded. 'Now follow me.'

Daisy reluctantly obeyed. But would Peter catch Bobby alone, as he had her?

The rehearsal room was filled with members of the choir. Mrs Jones sat at the upright piano and played the first chords of *We Wish You a Merry Christmas*. Daisy saw Nora Fudge, enjoying celebrity status. Her glossy brown hair was scooped back into a band and she wore a gleaming white blouse under a faultlessly knotted school tie.

Daisy joined in with the chorus but suddenly felt a sharp pain on her elbow. Peter Brady stood next to her. He was carrying a chair and had deliberately knocked her.

Mrs Jones stopped playing. 'Heavens, Daisy, you are singing flat!'

Daisy blushed red. Everyone turned to stare.

'Concentrate now. Once again from the start,' Mrs Jones commanded.

Peter Brady skulked away, but Daisy was left shaken. He always turned up at the least expected of times.

Once on stage, she tried to sing her best. It wasn't easy remembering the words and following the tune at the same time as thinking of Peter. She looked down at the smiling faces of the audience. Mother and Pops had joined Grandma and Aunt Pat in the front row. Aunt Minnie, Uncle Leo and Will were seated just behind. Her whole family were there, except Matt who had remained at the factory in Uncle Ed's place. But all the joy had gone from Daisy's special day.

Nora's voice was pure and sweet and drifted tunefully into the air as she sung her solo. The audience rose to their feet and applauded.

Daisy saw her family cheering. That was, everyone except for the one person who was missing. Aunt Betty.

CHAPTER 10

After the performance was over, Daisy was careful to keep with Sally.

'Can't see Peter anywhere,' said Sally as they walked down the corridor.

'He might have given up,' Daisy replied hopefully, gently rubbing her sore elbow. 'What with so many people here.'

'Look, there's my mum and dad,' said Sally and pointed through the window. 'I can't hang about as Dad's got to get back to the docks to clock out.' Sally's mother wore a faded headscarf and Mr Watson wore his rough working clothes. 'See you after Christmas. At least you won't have to worry about Peter Brady now.' Sally grinned and waved goodbye.

Daisy made her way to the playground where Mother stood in her new camel-haired coat with its dainty black fur collar and Pops in his best business suit. Uncle Ed wore a dark winter's coat and was in conversation with Aunt Pat and Grandma. Aunt Minnie, as usual, looked like a film star, in a flawless cream suit. Uncle Leo on the other hand, looked a bit scruffy in a kind of crumpled linen jacket. Will wore his best shorts and striped woollen jumper, though he had already loosened his tie and shirt collar in an unsuccessful attempt to sit still.

'Seen Peter?' Bobby asked as Daisy joined the family group.

'I was outside,' Daisy confessed. 'Peter crept up. He said he had a knife in his pocket.'

'A knife!' Bobby went pale.

'I got away, thanks to Grandma.'

'From now on, we stick together. Right?'

She nodded solemnly. Thank goodness the long Christmas holiday stretched ahead! But what would happen in the new term? Bobby couldn't be with her every single moment.

Uncle Ed clapped Bobby on the shoulder. 'Well done, old sport. We saw you working on the scenery. And Daisy, what a magnificent effort from the choir!'

'Where's Aunt Betty?' she asked, remembering the vacant chair.

Uncle Ed looked uncertain. 'Your aunt had to visit the doctor.'

'Is Aunt Betty ill?'

'No, it's just a cold,' Uncle Ed assured her. 'Wouldn't want to spread it, would we?'

'Such a nuisance for Betty,' Mother agreed.

'Absolutely,' confirmed Pops.

'Hateful things,' said Aunt Minnie with a shiver.

'Yes, yes,' mused Uncle Leo, who had nothing else to add.

It was Grandma who spoke next, recalling all "the good old days". How Wattcombe had served teas and home made cakes at the Easter fair. How Grandpa had driven his cart, filled with children, through the streets of the village.

This evoked conflicting comments.

'I remember the cart. A two-seater, wasn't it?'

'No, an open trap, I believe.'

'Those two Shires were the apple of his eye.'

'Black as night, most impressive.'

'They were chestnuts,' Grandma corrected. 'His horses were cobs, not Shires. And he drove a wagon. Covered in winter. Open in summer.'

'Yes, yes, that was it!'

'I remember now.'

Another silence which Daisy deemed to be even more awkward than the first.

'You must all come to tea,' Mother eventually declared. 'I'm sure everyone is famished.'

'I'd like to,' said Uncle Ed. 'But I'd better see how Betty is.'

'Yes, of course,' replied Mother.

'We'd love to,' sighed Aunt Minnie. 'But Will has piano practice.'

'Not until much later,' protested Will. 'Anyway it's boring. I'd much rather go to Bobby and Daisy's.' Whereupon Uncle Leo took hold of Will's shoulders and marched him away.

Then, quite without warning, she saw Peter Brady. He stood by the gate with a man whom Daisy had never seen before, but was a head and shoulders taller than anyone else in the vicinity. Was this the terrifying, arm-breaking Mr Brady? Another boy joined them. A menacing older double of Peter!

Daisy glanced at Bobby and he at her.

'Can we go now?' Bobby asked urgently.

Daisy made the same request, adding that she and Bobby hadn't eaten for practically the whole afternoon. But it was not hunger that scraped at her stomach like a claw. It was the sight of Peter Brady and his frightful family.

CHAPTER 11

AUNT PAT'S knitted stocking had grown as long as Pinocchio's nose. An unmissable pillar box red, the toe and heel were in stark contrast, an emerald green. Daisy had been enlisted to wind the heavy skeins of wool whilst taking her turn at Monopoly and Mahjong. All games had now been done to death though currently, Bobby was failing to survive a particularly fierce round of cards with Matt.

'What do you think?' asked Aunt Pat as she looped off the last stitch. 'Ready in time for our visitor tomorrow.'

'Aunt Pat, there is no such thing as Father Christmas,' laughed Bobby.

'How do you know?' Aunt Pat asked calmly.

Daisy watched Matt throw down his cards. 'I love you dearly Aunt Pat, but only a fool would believe that a fully-grown man with a long white beard could wriggle his way down a million chimneys.'

'Then I must be a fool,' replied Aunt Pat with a sigh.

'Rubbish,' objected Matt and got up to pop a kiss on her cheek. 'You are a very wise aunt and we adore you. But now, since Amelia is spending Christmas Day with her family, I must say goodbye.'

'Ah, young love,' said Aunt Pat wistfully. 'Another kind of magic.'

After Matt had gone, Aunt Pat slipped off her spectacles. 'What if your presents didn't arrive, Bobby? Would you stop believing in Christmas?'

'No, but I would be disappointed,' replied Bobby.

'Would you care if the milkman delivered them?'

'A bit,' Daisy admitted.

'What if the baker brought them?'

'Christmas wouldn't seem so special,' admitted Bobby, collapsing beside Daisy in front of the fire.

'Precisely,' said Aunt Pat. 'Christmas is a very special season. A family season. And we would all do well to remember that.'

Just then, Mother and Pops arrived back from Poplar. Daisy jumped to her feet. 'Did you see Aunt Betty and Uncle Ed?'

'Yes,' said Mother unwinding her long scarf and taking off her coat. 'We wished them a very merry Christmas.'

'Are they visiting tomorrow?'

'I'm sure we shall see them soon.'

'But they always come on Christmas Day,' Daisy insisted. 'Has Aunt Betty's cold gone?'

'Cold?' repeated Mother with a frown.

'Did the doctor give her some medicine to cure it?'

'Oh, *that* cold,' said Mother with an unconvincing nod. 'Yes, yes, I'm sure he did.'

'My word, Pat, what a grand stocking,' said Pops as Mother hurried out of the room. 'I'll fix it to the chimney tonight. In time for the arrival of our special guest.'

Daisy gave her father a hug, reassured by the gassy smells of the laboratory on his coat. 'I love Christmas, Pops.'

'Of course you do,' he agreed in his deep, steady voice. 'So let's try to make the very, very most of this one.'

Daisy glanced up, in time to witness the expression on his face. Though she couldn't decipher its meaning, Miss Bailey's remark came to mind. *"I fear this will be a Christmas to remember."*

Was it the word "fear" that alarmed her so? And why should it be this year that had to be made the *very, very* most of? Weren't there dozens more wonderful Christmases to come?

Daisy woke early. At last Christmas Day was here. All the ups and downs of the previous weeks, were behind her.

After slipping on her dressing gown, she hurried to her brother's room. 'Bobby are you awake?' She gently pushed open his door.

'What do you want?' he grumbled from under the bed clothes.

'It's Christmas. Time to open our presents.'

Her brother crawled out from under the covers and dragged on his plaid dressing gown. Together they made their way downstairs in the dawn's light.

'It's full!' Daisy exclaimed when she saw the fat red stocking hanging over the hearth

'Pops must have got up very early,' yawned Bobby.

'Perhaps it wasn't Pops after all,' suggested Daisy, trying to rekindle the feeling of wonder that Aunt Pat had described. The room seemed to take on a special light. All the decorations that she and Bobby had made, were strung around the walls. There was even a Christmas smell in the air, like snow and icicles might smell in the North Pole.

'There's no Father Christmas. There never was,' muttered Bobby irritably. He kicked the pouffe as if it was a football. 'So don't go harping on about it.'

'I'm not harping on,' argued Daisy. 'Why are you so grumpy?'

Bobby attacked the pouffe again. This time with a vengeance. It spun over and collided with the fireside tongs. The clattering noise echoed through the house.

'Now see what you've done,' he accused.

'Didn't do anything,' defended Daisy. 'You lost your temper. It's Christmas as well.'

Bobby carefully righted the tongs. He gave a half-hearted smile. 'Truce?' he mumbled.

'Truce,' Daisy agreed, even though she felt it wasn't her who had started the quarrel.

'Let's see what we've got.' Bobby unhooked the stocking and set it on the floor.

Daisy thought about what Aunt Pat had said about the special magic. Perhaps there really was a very kind man who visited children on Christmas Eve? He would have to own a car, because sleighs couldn't fly. And he'd have to start off from the North Pole very early, in order to make all his deliveries. If some people believed you could dig all the way to Australia, why shouldn't Father Christmas be true?

'I'll always believe in magic,' Daisy said as they sat cross-legged on the floor.

Bobby took out the first parcel. 'My name's on this one. It's my favourite too. Rowntree's York Chocolate.'

'I've got Duncan's Hazelnut,' said Daisy excitedly.

'Look, what's this? Oh gosh!' He held out a pair of new football boots. 'Just what I want. My old ones don't fit any more. They've given me dreadful blisters.'

Daisy's next present was a writing pad with lines running across each page. A pair of plimsolls followed.

'Look, we've got oranges, apples and toffees.'

Daisy recognised them at once. 'The sweets are from Aunt Pat's Saturday Assortment.'

'Let's divide them up.'

Daisy devoured hers immediately while Bobby stowed his in his pocket. 'I wonder if Pops will play football with me today?'

'I don't care what I do as long as it's not cooking or cleaning.' Daisy licked her lips. 'I hope uncle Ed and Aunt Betty come today. They give us such nice presents.'

Bobby flopped on his back lifting a foot to examine his new boot.

Daisy saw her chance. 'Bobby, I've got something to tell you.'

'What?' her brother asked vaguely.

'Do you remember how odd everyone sounded after the play? No one wanted to come home to tea.'

'Perhaps they weren't hungry.' He jumped up and stamped his booted feet. 'The boots are a bit big. It won't take long to grow into them.'

'Bobby, are you listening?'

'Yes, but don't make a drama out of everything.'

'I'm not. Aunt Betty has a problem. She asked Aunt Minnie to solve it, but Aunt Minnie couldn't. So Aunt Minnie gave it to Mother, who couldn't solve it either. And didn't you tell me never to give a problem to a grown-up that they couldn't solve?'

'So?' Bobby dismissed.

'You see, I was helping Mrs Hayes one day. While she served the teas I went to find Aunt Betty. I was about to knock on her office door when I heard voices coming from inside. The door was open a bit. I saw Aunt Betty and Mr Calder, the accounts manager, standing ... well, very close.'

'They were just talking I expect.'

'Mr Calder said Aunt Betty must find an excuse to get away. Aunt Betty said she didn't go out in the evenings without Uncle Ed. And then - well then, they nearly ... you know...'

The chocolate she had eaten was beginning to make her feel sick. 'That day Aunt Minnie called to see Mother,' she struggled on, 'it was to tell her that Aunt Betty was going to the cinema to see a film about a man in prison. Aunt Minnie couldn't go with her, but Aunt Betty asked her to say she had.'

Bobby rolled his eyes. 'Didn't I warn you about spying on people? That one day you would hear something bad about yourself? Now you have heard something bad about someone else. And that's even worse.'

Daisy was mortified. 'I didn't listen deliberately.'

'It's none of your business what Aunt Betty does,' Bobby said coldly, hobbling to the door in his boots. 'You must stop spying. If you don't, your ears will fall off and then your nose.'

After her brother had left the room, Daisy felt miserable and sick. How had she managed to eat so many sweets all at once? Would Bobby's remark about her ears and nose come true? She vowed there and then, never to listen to other people's conversations again. Even if she had to block up her ears.

Her tummy rumbled.

She didn't feel like Christmas dinner at all.

CHAPTER 12

DAISY GLANCED down at her dinner plate. Under normal circumstances, she would have helped herself to at least four roast potatoes. Now she could barely manage one. At three o'clock in the afternoon, she was feeling very poorly.

'Perhaps our little sister is love-sick?' teased Matt as he helped himself to a generous portion of cabbage.

Daisy felt too weak to argue. She lifted her fork and toyed with the slices of roast chicken that Pops had served.

'It must be all the excitement,' decided Mother as she spooned out the greasy baked trimmings.

'What a sumptuous meal!' Pops exclaimed. 'We're so fortunate to be spoiled by Grandma and Aunt Pat. If it weren't for their supplies, our dinner wouldn't be half so impressive.'

'All down to Mr White from the Wattcombe parish council,' replied Aunt Pat. 'He insisted we bring some of his allotment vegetables.'

'Then many thanks go to Mr White,' Pops agreed. 'Top man.'

Daisy wished Mr White hadn't been quite so generous. She was struggling to eat more than a mouthful.

'Christmases were very different in nineteen sixteen,' said Grandma on a reflective sigh. 'Our boys were fighting in the trenches. They had nothing to eat but bully beef. There was not much variety to speak of in England either, though we did better in the country than the towns and cities.'

Matt and Bobby were served generous seconds but Daisy couldn't raise even a smile, let alone more food to her lips.

'Daisy are you unwell?' Mother asked.

'Not like you at all, treasure,' said Pops.

'Save a space for Christmas pudding,' advised Grandma cheerfully. 'I baked it with ale from the Cat and Fiddle. Flo, if you've custard, I think the pudding will go down a treat.'

At the mention of this concoction, Daisy could bear it no longer. She jumped to her feet and rushed from the room. When she reached the lavatory, the volcano inside her erupted.

Slowly, Mother's face came into view. 'Oh dear, it's a day in bed for you, I'm afraid.'

Daisy couldn't have climbed out of bed if she'd tried. Well, she had tried. In the early hours. But she'd felt so ill, she'd fallen back down and immediately gone to sleep.

'I feel a bit sick,' she groaned. 'I'll never eat another sweet again.'

Mother smiled. 'I'm afraid you've a temperature.'

Daisy groaned. 'My throat's sore too.'

'I'll fetch some water and then you must rest. Not what you want to hear at Christmas, I know.'

But Daisy hadn't the least desire to move from under the

covers. She hoped the fever would go away if she lay still for long enough.

She dreamed of school and wearing Bobby's new boots. So heavy and clumsy was the footwear, that she could not escape from Peter Brady who rode on Grandpa's cart, cruelly whipping the backs of the four black horses. This dream was followed by the lonely figure of Uncle Ed standing in Pops's laboratory. The litmus paper in his hand was white. Mr Calder appeared in a puff of smoke and set fire to the Bunsen Burners while Uncle Ed wasn't looking.

Daisy woke up. She had been calling out Uncle Ed's name. She was trying to warn him about Mr Calder. Through the window the bright light of day had faded to a dusky evening hue. She reached for the glass of water that Mother had left on the bedside table and gulped down its entire contents.

As she sank back again, she could hear voices. Bobby was outside in the garden with Pops. They must be playing football. But Bobby's new boots were at school, she fretted. That's where she had left them in her escape from Peter Brady and the horses.

'Bobby,' she croaked in delirium. Staring up at the ceiling, she lay, on fire just like the Bunsen Burners. How would she put out the blaze? The litmus paper was white.

It should have turned red.

CHAPTER 13

THERE WAS the smell of bread baking when Daisy woke. 'Welcome back,' said Pops, from his chair beside her bed. 'Awake at last!'

Daisy smiled the best smile she could. There was a little twitch to her lips that had never been there before.

'Here, drink this.' Pops held the glass to her lips. 'Better?'

She lay back, refreshed.

'You know, we've been worried about you.'

'Have you? What day is it?'

'Wednesday.'

'How many days is that after Christmas?'

'Three. And you've slept them all away.'

Daisy guiltily recalled eating the sweets from Aunt Pat's stocking. 'I ate too much toffee.'

Pops chuckled. 'No, you've had the flu.'

'Did you play football in the garden with Bobby?'

'Not yet. We'd rather you get better first to cheer us on.'

'But I heard - ' Daisy stopped. Was it all in a dream?

'Are you hungry?' Pops asked.

'A bit, I s'pose.'

'Mother is making bread and chicken soup with Grandma.'

Daisy didn't know if she could eat anything, but it was nice having Pops beside her. 'Did Aunt Betty and Uncle Ed call round?'

Pops gave a little cough and shook his head. 'Not yet.'

'They always visit at Christmas.'

'Rest a little more, then come down for tea.' He tucked her hands inside the cover, refilled her glass and went softly out of the room.

Daisy listened to his footsteps on the stairs.

Daisy's jumbled thoughts spun in and out of her mind. Why hadn't Aunt Betty and Uncle Ed called? They always visited at Christmas. It was tradition. Just like on New Year's Eve, when everyone gathered at Aunt Minnie and Uncle Leo's in Soho for a party. More worryingly, Pops hadn't given her a proper answer when she'd asked after them.

Daisy's eyelids were so heavy she couldn't keep them open. This time she dreamed of Sammy Berger's father hiding in his house from a gang of men. Someone had nailed two strong lengths of wood across the front door. But if no one could get in, how would Mr Berger and Sammy get out?

It was Friday and the day before New Year's Eve. By this time, Daisy had passed on her infection to Bobby. Mother told her that Matt had gone along to Amelia's house in the hope of seeing her.

Grandma and Aunt Pat spoiled her, propping up her cushions in Pops's big fireside chair and brushing out her hair. Mother ferried rations of water and a small jar of chest rub up to Bobby who was confined to bed. All prospect of attending Aunt Minnie's party the very next evening had vanished with the uncooperative flu germs.

'Never mind,' consoled Aunt Pat who mysteriously found a new tin of Saturday Assortment in her luggage. 'We can enjoy ourselves and play games.' She opened the tin and placed it in front of Daisy. 'There are plenty of toffees left.'

Daisy felt her stomach protest. She shook her head vigorously. 'No, thank you, Aunt Pat.'

'Still feel a bit dicky?'

'Quite dicky, Aunt Pat.'

'Sensible not to then.' The lid went back on and Grandma nodded.

'Sweets on a poorly stomach can be fatal,' she agreed, settling back in her chair.

'Not that sort of fatal, Mother,' corrected Aunt Pat mildly as, from her pocket, she drew the fortune cards in their mother-of-pearl case.

'I only want good news,' instructed Grandma, eyeing Aunt Pat warningly.

Soon the air was fragrant with woodsmoke drifting from the crimson logs in the grate and Aunt Pat's soft voice was soothing as she announced a return to good health for Daisy. 'And what's more,' she continued, 'I see a new friend, yet strangely, an old one.' Her eyes sparkled as she met Daisy's expectant gaze. 'A friendship to last a lifetime.'

'What's their name?' she asked curiously.

Aunt Pat wagged a finger. 'The cards are telling me you know it already.'

'Is it Sally? Because I've known her ages. She's not new.'

Suddenly there was movement on the stairs.

'Put the cards away, Pat,' Grandma commanded. 'Not everyone appreciates your gift.'

The cards were instantly scooped up and slipped back into their mother-of-pearl case as Mother appeared. But Daisy looked at Aunt Pat and shared a secret smile.

CHAPTER 14

THE LETTER ARRIVED on the first Saturday of 1939, shortly after Grandma and Aunt Pat had returned to Wattcombe. Daisy sat with her two brothers as Pops read from the official looking document the postman had just delivered.

' "This is to confirm the delivery of your air raid shelter. It will measure six feet six inches by four feet six inches. Your shelter must be sunk into the ground and can be extended for larger families if requested. Priority has been given to householders in London's twenty-eight metropolitan boroughs and other potential target cities around the country." '

'*Our* shelter?' questioned Mother. 'But why should we want one? They must have written to the wrong address.'

Pops read it over again. 'No error, not at all. The address is correct.'

'The docks have been given priority,' gushed Matt. 'We are the enemy's first target.'

'Surely not,' cried Mother in alarm. 'This can't be true.'

Daisy watched her brother shrug gently. 'I'm sorry, Mother, but I did warn you.'

'Don't let's panic,' advised Pops. 'This may be just a precautionary measure.'

'What's it made of, this shelter?' asked Bobby, now recovered from his flu.

'Says here they are steel,' replied Pops with a frown.

'Can we sleep in it?' Daisy enquired. 'Is it like a tent?'

'Daisy, you are not sleeping in anything but your own bed,' scolded Mother. 'Now Nicky, you must do something about this contraption. Get them to cancel it. Or give it to someone else.'

'Mother,' said Matt seriously, 'don't you read the newspapers? Our Territorial Army's anti-aircraft and coastal units have been mobilised for war. There are appeals everywhere for emergency workers, plans for evacuation from the city and even patients from hospitals. Food rationing will come at any moment. We are on the brink.'

Daisy sat up. 'Does rationing mean we won't get anything to eat?'

'Of course it doesn't,' said Mother impatiently. 'If rationing were to happen - and only if - I'm sure the government would provide for us all equally.' She looked at Pops and waved her fingers. 'Enough of that letter, Nicky. Put it away and let's try to enjoy the rest of our weekend.'

Daisy watched her father fold the letter into his pocket. Breakfast was subdued and she wondered why Pops did not even pick up his newspaper.

'Can I go to football?' Bobby asked.

'I really think you shouldn't,' said Mother doubtfully. 'It's cold and you're only just well.'

'I'm bored,' Bobby insisted. 'I want to try out my new boots.'

'A boy needs his exercise, Flo,' Pops agreed.

After Bobby had gone out, Aunt Betty arrived. 'I'm sorry

we didn't call at Christmas,' she apologised. 'Are you better now, Daisy?'

'Yes, thank you.' Daisy was relieved to see her aunt at last. 'Where's Uncle Ed?'

Aunt Betty frowned.

'Is he coming to see us?'

'Daisy!' interrupted Mother sharply. 'Enough now!'

'Your uncle is at work,' replied Aunt Betty very quietly with a downcast expression.

'I'll be off to join him,' said Pops formally. 'A happy New Year, Betty.'

'Thank you, Nicky. You too.'

'Matt, are you coming?' Pops called.

Daisy watched her older brother thunder down the staircase, peck their aunt on her cheek and follow Pops from the house.

'Make yourself comfortable, Betty. I'll brew a fresh pot of tea,' said Mother.

Daisy was eager to open the presents that Aunt Betty had brought but there was something quite odd about this visit. Why was everyone talking so politely, as if they were strangers? Why had Pops left for work so abruptly?

'I hope you like your presents,' said Aunt Betty, taking a seat by the fire.

'A skipping rope!' exclaimed Daisy as she tore open the parcels. 'And a brush and comb set with lovely bluebirds and blossoms painted on the handles. Oh, thank you, Aunt Betty.'

However, there was something definitely amiss, Daisy decided, as Aunt Betty stared, preoccupied, into the fire and when Mother returned with the tea, she suggested that Daisy might want to try out the skipping rope.

So Daisy dressed warmly and went out into the chill winter's air to skip on the lawn. But there was only so much skipping a person could do with frozen fingers and eventually she sat on the swing hanging from the apple tree's strong branch, where she considered returning to the house. However, a glance through the window as she swung herself to and fro told her that would not be a good idea quite yet. For two figures were huddled together in the light of the fire; Aunt Betty was weeping and Mother was trying to comfort her.

Daisy played in the garden until her fingers and toes went blue. Going back indoors would be a mistake at this point for it was evident that Mother and Aunt Betty were not to be disturbed.

Instead, she paced out six feet six inches, the area described in this morning's letter. What would a tiny steel house look like? Would it be warm? Could you cook in it? More importantly, could you play in it?

Eventually she opened the front door and gave a slight cough. The whispering continued. Had Aunt Betty and Uncle Ed received a letter from the government too? Were they to be a given a shelter for their garden? Was this the reason for tears?

Daisy was about to set foot on the first stair, when she heard Aunt Betty's pleading, tear-filled voice. 'Flo, what am I to do? I feel torn apart.'

'You're a married woman, Betty. You love Ed, surely?'

'I - I did, I do! But I was very young when we married. Things change.'

'Ed is a wonderful husband,' insisted Mother. 'He worships the ground you walk on.'

'Perhaps that's it,' said Aunt Betty on a sigh. 'Living up to an ideal is no fun at all.'

'Is that what you want - fun?' Mother questioned.

'Why not?' asked Aunt Betty sadly. 'Five years of working hard at the factory. Of trying to conceive and hoping that any day I'd find myself pregnant. Pretending that we didn't care and putting all our energies into the business. Making sure we were solvent. Balancing the figures. Every day consumed with ambition to succeed, making the business our child. Protecting it, feeding it, giving it our all. And forgetting ourselves. Ed and I, we've lost touch. And when - when Neville came along, I just knew that I couldn't go on pretending. At least, not to myself. And I suppose, not to Ed.'

Daisy had vowed never to eavesdrop again. And she wasn't - intentionally. She was trying to get up to her bedroom. Forcing herself to the next stair, she refused to listen.

Stair three, four, five, six ...

Each stair echoed with a sob or sigh from Aunt Betty. In the safety of her room, she flung herself on the bed. Covering her head with the pillow she tried to forget. But nothing could shut out the words of Aunt Betty. Or her mother's shocked response. And worse, so much worse, was that this hateful secret, the one that she had been hoping would disappear like the genii did in the lamp, just like you saw on the films.

Yet this was real life and not make believe.

CHAPTER 15

IT WAS NOT Aunt Betty but Peter Brady who occupied Daisy's thoughts on the first day of term. It was likely their arch-enemy was laying in wait somewhere as she walked to school with Bobby. Peter would be with his gang; he was too much of a coward to confront them on his own. He was the kind of bully who needed an audience.

'Stay with Sally,' Bobby instructed as they walked hurriedly towards the school gates. 'We've been lucky so far but he could be anywhere. Don't go wandering off on your own.'

Daisy had no intention of being caught unchaperoned. As soon as she saw Sally in the playground, she joined her. 'Did you have a good Christmas?'

'Me dad's rolling drunk again,' said Sally with a grin. 'We had more knees-ups than a birthday in a brothel. What did you do?'

'I got the flu.'

'What, you silly cow!'

'I thought I'd eaten too many sweets from Aunt Pat's Saturday Assortment.'

'So you missed all the excitement?'

Daisy nodded dismally.

'I've got something to tell you,' Sally said as they lined up for class.

'What?'

'I'll tell you in assembly.'

Daisy couldn't see Peter as they filed into the hall, but his horrible mates had caused a fuss, refusing to stop swearing and cussing at the younger children. The teachers, Daisy suspected, were turning a blind eye after the attack on Mr Potter.

'So?' Daisy urged, as they sat on their seats and waited for Miss Bailey to appear.

'Peter's not coming back to school - ever.'

'What!' Daisy couldn't believe this was true.

'The word is, he got in trouble with the rozzers at Christmas.'

'Trouble?'

'Nicking at the market and clobbering a copper who tried to nab him.'

'Are you sure?' Daisy asked doubtfully.

'Dad heard it from the blokes at work,' Sally insisted. 'Like I told you, the Bradys have a reputation second to none. Peter is following in his old man's footsteps they say. Odds on they'll stick him in one of them bad boys' homes.'

'What's a bad boys' home?'

'Dad says it's like a prison, but for kids. The boys are thrashed until their bums bleed. They take the birch to 'em.'

'What's the birch?'

'Blimey, Daisy, you don't know much for a posh kid.' Sally sighed impatiently. 'It's like lots of sharp wood used as a whip. The poor sods almost bleed to death.'

Daisy shuddered. 'That's dreadful.'

'It's the only way to knock any sense in their heads.'

Daisy digested this frightful snippet as they sung the school hymn, *All People That On Earth do Dwell.* Could it really be true that Peter would be tortured in such a way? He might be the school bully and hated by just about everyone, but such a fate was far worse even than the flu or painful boils and red spots.

Miss Bailey welcomed the school back but Daisy couldn't concentrate. She wanted to ask Bobby if he'd heard about Peter. Or could it be that Mr Watson had been falsely informed?

At break time, she met Bobby in the playground. 'Do you know Peter has been sent to a bad boys' home?'

Bobby nodded. 'All the school knows. But I've a feeling he'll show up.'

'Oh, no he won't,' Daisy blurted, 'because Aunt Pat said - ' She stopped, remembering just in time that Bobby disapproved of the fortune cards, so she'd have to make do with confiding in Sally whose mother read the tea leaves.

Bobby frowned suspiciously. 'What's Aunt Pat got to do with Peter? And it's not called a bad boys' home,' he corrected. 'It's a reformatory.' Since Daisy couldn't think of anything as exciting to say she was not surprised when her brother soon left to find his friends.

'Bet you and Bobby are pleased to hear the news about Peter,' said Sally as she joined Daisy. 'I reckon he got what was coming to him, don't you?'

Daisy glanced round to confirm they were alone. 'My Aunt Pat reads the cards,' she whispered. 'They predicted a big thing was about to happen. And it has.'

Sally gasped. 'Never!'

Daisy had a stab of conscience. 'But I didn't wish the birch on Peter. Just the flu or boils. You don't think I made it come true, do you?'

'Don't be daft.'

'Perhaps it's not right to know the future.'

'Why not? The leaves are never wrong for my mum.' Sally narrowed her eyes. 'Did the cards say anything about me?'

Daisy considered tweaking the message to include Sally, just to please her friend, but decided against it. A tweaking might add something even more terrible to the already alarming events the cards had so rightly predicted.

For the entire month of February Daisy bathed in the luxury of her newly freedom. The boys at school who had lost their leader were kept in line by the teachers and she and Sally played skipping or hop scotch without interruption. Even Bobby returned to his good-humoured self.

Though Daisy felt one of Aunt Pat's predictions had come true, the second was still missing. A new old friend had not appeared. Daisy wasn't disappointed. She felt she had tempted fate and still had guilty pangs. Was Peter's bloody birching her doing? After all, she had wished him ill - and with vengeance.

It was on a soft spring day, not long after the Peter Brady episode, when Matt decided to deliver his own shocking news.

'The RAF take delivery of more than four hundred aircraft each month,' he informed the family at breakfast.

'Rightly so,' agreed Pops, 'since Germany already has almost five thousand up its sleeve.'

'Our airforce is the best in the world,' agreed Matt glancing warily at Mother as he pressed home his point. 'They are asking for reserve and volunteer flyers. Chaps like me who are the right age and intend to sign up.'

'The airforce can ask all they like,' replied Mother harshly and Daisy watched her face tighten. 'Your responsibilities are here at the factory, Matt.'

'Mother, my heart is set on flying,' Matt insisted. 'There's no two ways about it.'

Daisy stared at her older brother and saw the determination in his eyes.

'Son, with the best will in the world, I applaud your decision,' coaxed Pops, 'but there will be a right time to enlist. No hurry just yet.'

'Pops, there is no getting out of this war,' said Matt firmly. 'Hitler has entered Prague. Who is next to fall?'

Daisy jumped as Mother quickly left the table.

'Will there really be a war?' Bobby asked quietly.

'There is every chance of it, brother,' Matt affirmed.

Daisy studied her father. His gaze was downcast. Tiny lines ran out from his eyes and disappeared into his whiskers. Was there now a scattering of grey in those delicate little hairs?

'I'd better go to your mother,' he said and left the table too. Daisy saw his breakfast was untouched. The question of war hung in the air, as real and immovable as if the war had already started.

CHAPTER 16

'Good morning.' Miss Bailey stood at the podium in the assembly hall. 'I have an announcement to make. It concerns each and every one of us, for after today, our lives might never be quite the same again. Your teachers and I want you to know how proud we are of you. We know that you will support your family and friends through whatever might befall our country in the days ahead.'

To Daisy it seemed impossible that even the news of Peter Brady leaving school had been overshadowed by unimaginable worldwide events. Pops had read from his newspaper each morning. Britain, France and Poland, so Pops explained, were planning to sign a pact together to form an alliance.

At school, Miss Bailey had glued a map of the world to the wall in the assembly hall. Mr Gulliver had pinned little flags on the countries concerned; green for the pact allies, red for the enemy. Each week the red flags seemed to be getting closer to the British Isles.

Daisy felt Sally wriggle beside her. 'Me dad reckons we won't be at school much longer,' she whispered. 'All the kids are being evacuated.'

Daisy glanced at her friend doubtfully.

'It's Hitler, ain't it?' persisted Sally. 'He's joining up with this Italian bloke to conquer the world. They'll be over here soon. It's the docks they're after.'

Before Daisy could respond, Miss Bailey spoke again. 'You are all aware that Spain's civil war has ended. Those with relatives involved in that dreadful conflict will be relieved to hear of this development.' Miss Bailey folded her notes and braced her shoulders under her woollen grey twin set. 'However, since then our Prime Minister has offered Poland and France our assistance.' Miss Bailey cleared her throat. 'Today we are informed that preparations for a war with Germany are in motion. The army, airforce and navy are being doubled in strength. I am quite certain that members of your families will volunteer. Some have already done so and are waiting for their orders. This will affect many of your families, which in turn, will affect you. Many of you will be evacuated to safer regions.'

Sally whispered, 'Told you so!'

Daisy frowned. 'But Pops wouldn't send me away.'

Sally shrugged. 'Me dad says he's sending me to the country. Wish we could go together.'

Daisy stared at her friend. What did this mean? Did Pops and Mother know about evacuation?

'The board of school governors,' Miss Bailey explained, 'are putting into place certain safety measures. Sadly, our school will close as from today.'

'Crikey,' muttered Sally. 'That's quick!'

'But where will we go to learn our lessons?'

'That's just it,' said Sally. 'There ain't nowhere on the island.'

'We have written to your parents to explain,' broke in Miss Bailey above the sudden chattering. 'I should like all those pupils who know either one or both of your parents are at home, to leave the assembly hall quietly, gather your things and say good bye to your friends. Those who have no one at home to care for them will go to the exercise room, where Mr Gulliver and Mrs Jones are waiting and will be with you until four o'clock. Please stay calm and join the queue in an orderly line.'

Daisy watched her friends as they began hurrying to the doors, jostling and pushing. Could school really be shutting down?

Sally grabbed her arm. 'Don't just sit there, we've got to go.'

'But - '

'There ain't no buts, Daisy. This is it. Dunno when we'll see each other again.'

Daisy looked at her friend. Sally had been right all along. Or, at least, Mr Watson had been right.

Sally threw her arms around Daisy's neck. 'I'll miss you.'

'Me too.'

'Remember the school anthem. Britain never will be slaves, right?'

Daisy held back the tears as she watched her friend leave. It seemed the whole school was disappearing before her eyes. Even Miss Bailey had vanished.

Suddenly Bobby was at her side.

'Sally's being evacuated,' she complained. 'I don't know when I'll see her again.'

'Get your coat,' said Bobby unsympathetically. 'We have to meet Sammy at the gates.'

'Why?'

'He's in trouble.'

'But shouldn't we tell Miss Bailey?'

Bobby rolled his eyes. 'You really don't get it do you? No one cares about Sammy, only us. Now hurry up, or else I'll go on my own.'

CHAPTER 17

'UNCLE LEO'S Riley is parked outside our house,' said Bobby as they arrived in Poplar Park Row. 'And Aunty Betty's bicycle is by the wall.'

'I'm going,' said Sammy, taking a backward step.

'No,' insisted Bobby, catching hold of his arm. 'I told you, Pops will sort something out. He always does. But first we need to get you cleaned up.'

'Perhaps it's a party,' said Daisy hopefully, averting her eyes from the sad picture of a bedraggled and wounded Sammy. She didn't have a strong stomach for bruises and bloody noses.

Bobby rolled his eyes. 'Trust you to think of a party!'

'Well, why shouldn't there be?'

'You'll soon find out,' Bobby warned. 'Now listen. We'll go down the hall to the kitchen first so Sammy can wash.'

Daisy didn't like Bobby's idea at all. Why shouldn't there be an occasion to celebrate? Perhaps Uncle Leo had sold one of his photographs for lots of money? Or even more wonderful, perhaps Pops and Uncle Ed had discovered their new valve? Whatever it was, she was eager to find out, yet Bobby only seemed concerned with Sammy.

'Come on,' said Bobby tugging Sammy's arm. 'You can sit in the kitchen. No one will see you.'

Still Sammy didn't move. Daisy was even more convinced this wasn't a good idea. He'd followed them home with hunched shoulders, every now and then stopping and gasping for breath. There was even blood in his thin black hair - which was very thin indeed.

Bobby smiled at his friend. 'Daisy stay with Sammy. I'll go in and make sure the living room door's closed.'

'Mother will give you something to eat, I'm sure,' she said cheerfully when Bobby had gone. 'You must be hungry.'

Sammy continued to stare, as if the mention of food meant nothing at all. Which was surprising to Daisy as he was so thin.

'Perhaps my aunt has brought pastries,' Daisy tried again. 'Do you like rock cakes?'

There was no reply as Sammy edged away from her.

Did he even know what rock cakes were, Daisy wondered? So she stood in silence until Bobby returned.

'The coast's clear,' he announced breathlessly. 'You go first, Daisy.'

'Why me?'

'Because I said so. Now hurry up.'

Reluctantly Daisy made her way into the house. She heard familiar voices coming from the living room and considered an immediate detour. But fearing Bobby's wrath, she continued to the kitchen.

All was quiet here, though there was definitely evidence of a meeting. Miss Ayling's teacups, saucers and side plates were piled haphazardly on the draining board. The teapot was missing its cosy, suggesting there was no tea left to keep warm. Had the party ended she wondered?

Bobby soon followed, pulling Sammy with him. 'I need a cloth,' he told her. 'Do you know where the medicines are kept?'

Daisy recoiled. Was she expected to remove the congealed blood from Sammy's nose?

'Oh, don't look like that,' Bobby snapped. 'I'll find them myself.'

Her brother gently drew the dirty raincoat from his friend's shoulders. Carefully, he lifted Sammy's shirt.

Daisy had never fainted before. She didn't even know what a faint was. Once she had fallen from the barn roof in Wattcombe and hit her head as she'd landed on the grass. But even then, she hadn't fainted. The closest she'd got to a faint, she supposed, was when she'd had flu. But the sight of Sammy's horribly marked thin chest, with stripes of still sticky blood oozing from the vicious cuts, caused her to reach out to the table and steady herself.

Daisy didn't hear the movement behind her; her cousin Will looked like Uncle Leo, she decided, with a shock of fair hair that fell untidily over his freckled face. His legs, which were always on the move under his short school trousers, were even thinner than Sammy's. Today he was wearing a striped knitted jumper that looked as though it might be the handiwork of Aunt Pat.

'Hello,' he greeted, frowning at Sammy.

'Why are you here?' Bobby demanded. 'You should be at school.'

'Got a day off,' said Will. 'What's wrong with his nose?'

'Nothing to do with you,' replied Bobby gloomily.

'A bomb might drop on your factory,' announced Will in a sing-song voice. 'They might have to close it down.'

'Do shut up, Will,' Daisy snapped. 'You haven't a clue what you're talking about.'

Daisy watched her brother gently clean Sammy's wounds, relieved she wasn't expected to help.

'My dad might have to go in the army to take photographs of dead bodies,' continued Will as he tried to balance on one leg. 'Though they might not be quite dead. You could bleed and bleed and still stay alive. That's why soldiers tie knives to the end of their guns, to finish 'em off.'

'Oh do stop, Will,' Daisy protested again. 'Go and play outside.'

'There's nothing to do on my own.' Will stood his ground as Bobby dabbed at Sammy's eye and nose. Daisy thought it was as if her brother knew what to do without anyone telling him. She couldn't possibly have got that close to Sammy who smelled at the best of times.

'If my dad gets shot,' prattled Will, spreading himself over the big wooden table like a spider, 'there'll be no money for food or toys. We'll have to leave Soho and move to Iceland or Australia. Or Eastbourne.'

'Will, Uncle Leo isn't going to get shot,' Daisy said, almost out of patience. 'You mustn't say such things. You mustn't even think them.'

Bobby drew Sammy's shirt back into place. 'That's as much as I can do,' he said as he washed the cloth out under the tap. 'Will, make yourself useful and stay here with Sammy. Me and Daisy will go in and speak to the family.'

'What are we going to say about Sammy?' enquired Daisy.

'I've told you before, leave the talking to me.'

Daisy followed Bobby from the room. She wondered how much of what Will had said was true. Although she wanted it to be make-believe, as it usually was, she had a suspicion that Will hadn't lied about evacuation.

CHAPTER 18

THERE WAS a drift of Aunt Minnie's perfume hidden in the fog of cigarette smoke. Every seat was taken. Beside Aunt Minnie sprawled Uncle Leo, his arm resting lightly on the back of the couch. His dark hair had grown wild, like Will's. Daisy noticed that his open-necked shirt was unbuttoned accompanied by a silk paisley scarf her mother would call "arty".

Aunt Betty and Uncle Ed sat smoking by the window. A vase of cut flowers from the garden and an overflowing ash tray stood on the gate-leg table between them.

Pops reclined by the hearth, one elbow balanced on the mantel. Beside him was Matt, dressed in his sports jacket and white flannels. But there was no Amelia. Daisy felt a selfish pang of pleasure. The family did not yet include an outsider, however pretty.

'We've been expecting you,' Mother said as she rose from her chair. 'This morning we received a letter from the board of governors. I'm afraid the schools nearest the docks must close as from today. It's rather short notice, but I'm sure we'll manage.'

'How much have they told you at school?' Pops said quietly.

'Not much,' replied Bobby. 'Are we going to war?'

'There's a chance, a small one,' said Pops, 'that we might not, if the PM successfully appeases Hitler.'

'What's a-peas?' Daisy ventured.

'It's giving a bully what he wants, little sister, in the vain hope he'll back off and leave you alone,' said Matt grimly.

'Matt,' cried Mother in alarm, 'we shouldn't make light of the Prime Minister's efforts to avoid war.'

'Why not, Flo?' Uncle Leo countered. 'Let's face it, we let Herr Hitler make a mockery of the Treaty of Versailles. He took what he wanted and now he wants us.'

Daisy thought how her uncle might have been talking about Peter Brady. Had it not been for Peter's arrest and banishment to the reformatory he would still be demanding more. It was only the police who had stopped him.

'London and the docks in particular are Hitler's next goal,' continued Matt angrily. 'He'll achieve it if Chamberlain ducks out.'

'Sally's dad, Mr Watson,' Daisy broke in, 'said it will be like snapping the head off a chicken, while its body still runs about. Mr Watson's going to shoot the first German he sees right between the eyes. And Will told us that Uncle Leo might have to join the army and Aunt Minnie will have to leave Soho.'

'Heavens, what rubbish has our son been talking?' cried Aunt Minnie in a fluster. 'Leo, for goodness sake, we must do something about Will! He'll put the fear of God into everyone. Where is that boy?'

'He's in the kitchen,' said Bobby. 'With Sammy.'

All heads turned toward Bobby.

'Who is Sammy?' asked Pops.

'Our friend,' replied Bobby.

'Our best friend,' confirmed Daisy.

Mother narrowed her eyes. 'Why isn't he with his parents?'

'Because,' said Bobby slowly, 'Sammy's house was burned down by the Blackshirts and his dad was taken away.'

Daisy looked round the room. By all the startled expressions, it was as if Bobby, like Will, was telling tall stories. But what Bobby had told them was true. Daisy had seen the evidence for herself.

'I didn't know what to do,' protested Bobby. 'School was closing and Sammy had nowhere to go. So we brought him home.'

'Why is Sammy in such trouble?' said Mother hesitantly. 'Burning down someone's house is a crime.'

'Sammy's frightened of the Blackshirts,' Bobby insisted. 'Because Mr Berger is German.'

Once again the room fell silent.

'How long has Mr Berger lived in England?' asked Pops after a while.

'Don't know,' Bobby answered with a shrug. 'But Sammy was born here.'

'You say he was attacked?' Uncle Leo enquired doubtfully.

'His nose was bleeding,' Daisy volunteered before her brother could reply. 'And he's got a black eye that's gone purple and blue.'

'That's quite enough, Daisy,' interrupted Mother sharply. 'Stay here while Bobby and I speak to Sammy.'

Aunt Minnie rose and extended her hand. 'Come along, Daisy. I've smoked far too many cigarettes today. A breath of fresh air will do us good.'

For once, Daisy went unwillingly with her favourite aunt. She wanted to know what Mother would say to Sammy. After all, she had claimed that Sammy was her best friend too.

But as usual, boys could do everything girls couldn't.

'Your father has driven Sammy to the doctor,' said Mother later after everyone had left.

'Is Sammy ill?' Daisy asked.

'We shall have to wait and see,' replied Mother as she washed Miss Ayling's cups and saucers, placing them on the draining board for Daisy to dry. 'Miss Bailey should have helped him.'

'She didn't know he was in trouble,' Daisy defended. 'He was outside the school gates.'

'Oh dear,' sighed Mother. 'I can't imagine how frightened the poor child must have been.' She sat down on a chair and sighed. 'From the little Sammy told me, his parents came to England from Germany to escape persecution. His mother died from tuberculosis when he was just a baby.'

'Why did the Blackshirts hurt him?'

'Some Blackshirts hold very radical views and have been the cause of untold misery here in London.'

'Why don't the police stop them?'

Mother considered this for some moments. 'The British believe in democracy, Daisy - freedom of speech for everyone. Only when caught in the act of violence can these people be stopped.' Mother slipped an arm around her shoulders. 'I'm sorry, but you are learning that the world can be very unfair sometimes.'

That night Daisy lay under the warm covers, waiting for Pops and Bobby and Sammy to return. How terrible it must be for Sammy and his father to live in fear and not be able to be proud of who they were or what they believed in.

The bedside clock said ten minutes past ten when Daisy woke next morning. Pulling on her dressing gown she hurried downstairs. The house was strangely quiet. Usually Mother would be working in the kitchen and Bobby getting ready for school, but of course, there wasn't any!

Instead she found Pops sitting at the big dining room table surrounded by his ledgers. He wore no tie and the two top buttons of his shirt were undone. Not like Pops at all who dressed smartly for the factory. His curly blond hair had fallen over his eyes which looked rather red and tired. She could smell cigarette smoke on his clothes, and by the evidence in the spilling ash tray, he had been working for many hours.

'Good morning, treasure.'

Daisy sat beside him. 'Where's Mother and Bobby?'

'Mother is shopping and Bobby's at football.'

'What's happened to Sammy?'

Her father shuffled aside his papers and leaned his elbows on the table. 'Sammy's cuts and bruises can be treated,' he explained. 'But his breathing is quite another matter. The doctor thinks it could be tuberculosis. Do you know what that is?'

Daisy nodded. 'Mother said it's when you have bad lungs.'

'After seeing the doctor I took him to the hospital who will send him to a sanitarium.'

'What's that?'

'It's a place where very sick people go to recover.'

Daisy felt sad. 'I wish I'd been nicer to Sammy.'

'You and Bobby brought him home to us and we were able to help him. This was possibly the kindest thing you have ever done for anyone. Please God, it won't be too late to save him.'

And there it was, Daisy thought - the hammer blow. The

real truth hidden in careful words so as not to be too shocking. Like Miss Bailey's "I fear this will be a Christmas to remember," and Pops's "Let's try to make the very, very most of this year."

Her father nodded understandingly. 'I know it's hard for you, Daisy. Your friend has been taken away. School has closed. And the world is in turmoil. Changes in life are unsettling. But we are a family and will see this through together, war or no war.'

'Will you get a gun like Sally's dad?'

'I rather think not. '

'Did you shoot someone in the first war?' Daisy saw the little muscles in his jaw begin to move.

'Taking away even one life has far-reaching consequences,' he explained. 'I was fortunate. My injury was nothing in comparison to others.' He straightened his shoulders and smiled. 'We must hope and pray for peace. That Mr Chamberlain will somehow pull us through.'

'Are we still having a little house in the garden?' she asked.

Pops looked into her eyes and nodded. 'Oh yes.'

'Can we play in it?'

Pops smiled. 'Why not? Now, how about something to eat? Happy eggs and soldiers perhaps? Like our breakfasts in Wattcombe where we ate eggs fresh from the barn.'

Daisy smiled at the memory. Just for one second everything returned to normal. Nothing had changed and the war was just a bad dream.

CHAPTER 19

September 2nd 1939

"SHORTLY BEFORE 6AM YESTERDAY, Friday September 1st, German forces crossed the Polish frontier in the wake of heavy aerial bombardment. The Wehrmacht force of 1.25 million swept into Poland including six armoured divisions and eight motorised divisions with armoured units," said the cut-glass voice from the wireless set in the living room.

Daisy sat quietly next to Bobby on the couch as Matt paced the floor. Pops smoked a seemingly never-ending cigarette. Mother occupied the fireside chair. Daisy saw how tight with apprehension her face had become over the past few months.

She knew this was an important day. More important even, than her tenth and Bobby's eleventh birthday back in the summer. Practically every household in Britain, Pops had said, were tuning in to hear Mr Chamberlain speak.

'The invasion's begun,' said Matt heavily as he paused by

the fire which had been lit early that morning to ward off the first chill of autumn. 'The government have no choice but to announce this soon.'

'Is there any chance we'll be kept out of it, Nicky?' asked Mother.

'I had been hoping so,' replied Pops. 'This disaster has been condemned by almost every sovereign state. The Poles are in a terrible fix. Russia is aiding and abetting Germany, damn it. Tearing apart the spoils like wild dogs.'

'The Poles are helpless,' agreed Matt fiercely. 'The French guns are pounding the German lines on the Western Front, but they haven't an earthly without back-up.'

Daisy listened to her family discussing international events, fearing that sooner or later and probably sooner, that horrid word 'evacuation' would crop up. Though their parents had done the very best they could in trying to prevent the talk of war, a day had rarely gone by without a mention.

'We've no time to waste,' said Mother with a studied look at Daisy. A meaningful, 'you do understand look'. A silent message that Daisy didn't want to understand at all. So she averted her eyes swiftly and settled them on Pops.

'We must make provision for you and Bobby, very soon,' he explained. 'To keep you safe. Out of harm's reach.'

'You mean we're to be evacuated?' said Bobby, giving voice to Daisy's own fear.

'Just until things have settled,' confirmed Mother. 'Aunt Pat and Grandma have your room ready. Won't it be good to be in Wattcombe again?'

Daisy would have once welcomed the idea. But evacuation was different. Evacuation wasn't holiday. It felt more like punishment.

'Cheer up, you two,' said Pops with a forced smile. 'Think of the fun you'll have when you meet up with old friends.'

'All the games of Mahjong and Snap you'll play,' added Mother. 'And there's the Webber's farm and all their animals.'

'How long do we have to stay?' Daisy asked.

Pops slapped his hands jovially on his knees. 'Just a few months, I guess. You'll manage that, won't you?'

A few months, thought Daisy despairingly. A few months! How was she possibly going to bear it?

'What's up?' Bobby whispered in the darkness. 'You should be asleep. Everyone else is.'

Daisy had curled herself into a ball in the fireside chair. She was watching the last little bursts of crimson die under the ash in the grate. She had lost count of time. It must be the dead of night. Today had been like another bad dream, only this time she couldn't wake up.

'I can't sleep either,' said Bobby as he sat on the floor and hugged his knees. 'At least we'll be together in Wattcombe.'

'I shan't see Sally for ages.' Daisy sniffed. 'I don't even know where she's gone.' She was feeling very sorry for herself. 'I don't want to leave home,' she whined.

'It's for our own good,' replied Bobby, gazing into the fire.

'You sound like Pops.'

'Pops told me even the factory might have to close.'

'Why? Because of the bombs?'

'Not really. The machinery's old and needs replacing. It'll cost a lot of money to buy new.'

Daisy had been so preoccupied with her resentful feelings that she had hardly given a thought to the factory.

'Pops is meeting up with some important men soon, hoping to save the factory.'

'So he won't be driving us to Wattcombe?'

'I doubt it,' replied Bobby and jumped to his feet. 'He has more important things to consider than us.'

'I wouldn't mind going on a train.'

'We'll have to see.' Bobby nodded towards the stairs. 'We'd better get some sleep. It's Mr Chamberlain's announcement tomorrow.'

Daisy felt sure she wouldn't sleep. Why hadn't Pops talked to her about the factory that day he was working at home? Once again she felt left out, just because she was a girl.

CHAPTER 20

THE NEXT MORNING breakfast was eaten hurriedly in order to be ready for the Prime Minister's announcement at eleven o'clock. But as the time drew close, there was a knock at the door.

'I'll get it,' said Matt and dashed to the hall. He returned with Amelia by his side. 'We'd like you to know that a week ago I asked Amelia to marry me and she has accepted. Amelia, show everyone your ring.'

Amelia, blushing to the roots of her hair, stretched out her left hand. A simple ring with a single pale jewel glimmered on her finger.

'Oh, Amelia - that's beautiful,' began Mother and was about to stand when Matt continued. 'The other thing is, I've joined the airforce and am now a member of the Air Defence Cadet Corps.' He coughed lightly. 'At least, I signed on the dotted line and await my orders.'

There was a united gasp. Daisy stared at her brother and his wife-to-be. Not that she didn't want Matt to marry Amelia. She was reconciled to this as lately they had been inseparable, not wanting to be in anyone else's company but their own. But if Matt had joined the airforce then he was sure to have to go away.

'I hope you'll all support us,' said Matt hurriedly, holding Amelia's waist tight. 'We love each other and want to be together for the rest of our lives after this bash is over. Amelia is one hundred percent behind my decision to fly.'

Daisy saw Mother put a handkerchief to her eyes. Her shoulders were shaking and Pops got up from his chair. He paused by Matt and Amelia. 'Well done, you two,' he said quietly. 'Grand news.' He took Mother's hand and helped her to her feet. 'Be brave, my darling,' Daisy heard him whisper. 'Come and congratulate this lovely couple.'

Soon there were hugs and handshakes and plenty of tears all round. The ring was examined and shown off in the light and scrutinized until Amelia looked about to faint with joy.

Daisy surreptitiously noted that Amelia never took her eyes from Matt; little wet beads glittering on her eyelashes and sparkled against the sheen of her coppery brown hair. Trailed wisps, dampened by tears, tumbled over her forehead.

A few minutes later the wireless was turned up. "I am speaking to you from the Cabinet Room at 10 Downing Street," said Prime Minster Chamberlain. "The British ambassador in Berlin handed the German government a final note stating that unless we heard from them by eleven o'clock that they were prepared at once to withdraw their troops from Poland, a state of war would exist between us. I have to tell you now that no such undertaking has been received and that consequently, this country is at war with Germany."

Daisy felt a lump swell inside her chest. There was something extraordinary about this moment. An engagement to be married, the overwhelming pride she felt for her brother and the terrifying and momentous declaration of war.

Miss Ayling's teapot was refilled twice after the Prime Minister's speech. Daisy was given the job of emptying the dregs in the pig bin outside, where the momentary waft of decaying food returned her with some force to hers and Bobby's predicament. Not only had Mr Chamberlain joined Miss Bailey and the board of school governors in the certainty of war, but it was clear there would be no escape from evacuation. She and Bobby were to be carted off to Wattcombe, hidden in the depths of a countryside that didn't have goose-necked cranes and busy docks and factories and people like Mrs Hayes to whom you could turn for every bit of vital information.

On Daisy's last visit to the factory in summer, Mrs Hayes had remembered it was her birthday and given her a pretty card. When Daisy had related the saga of Sammy and the Blackshirts, Mrs Hayes had looked ferocious. 'They're rotters through and through,' she'd cried. 'Your poor little friend. Him and his dad must've been frightened out of their wits for no reason at all.'

'Bobby said the reason was because Mr Berger was German,' confided Daisy as she helped with the trolley. 'Mother said it was because Sammy's mother was a Jew. What does that mean, Mrs Hayes?'

'It means it don't matter what a person's religion is, or what colour they are, or if they've got two left feet or none at all, a decent person don't go behaving like them Blackshirts did.' Mrs Hayes had puffed out her chest and adjusted her turban with some force. 'Gawd love that poor little Sammy. And to end up with TB, well, it don't sit right with me, it don't.'

'He'll get well, won't he? Like cousin Irene?' Mrs Hayes

had once told Daisy of the saga of her distant cousin Irene who'd beaten the dreaded TB.

'Please God he will,' Mrs Hayes had nodded. 'Them doctors will see him right. They know their onions.'

'Is it nice in a sanitarium?'

'Not bad,' Mrs Hayes had replied. 'Not good either. In between I'd say. But they get you better like they did our Irene.'

'Was Irene pretty?'

'Told you once, it don't all depend on looks. Our Irene looked forty when she was four and forty when she was sixty.' The trolley had come to a shuddering halt. 'Go up to see your dad, now, but give them offices a miss.'

Softened words that meant a great deal, Daisy had decided. For if she was to avoid the offices, then there could only be one reason for doing so. Mrs Hayes must know as much - possibly even more - than she did about Aunt Betty and Mr Calder.

Just as Mother and Aunt Minnie came into the kitchen there was a terrible shriek. 'The siren,' cried Mother. 'We must be under attack!'

'Already?' gasped Aunt Minnie. 'Goodness, where's Will?'

Daisy barely recalled what happened next. Everyone began to charge here and there, with Uncle Leo bearing down on Will and Pops, Matt and Amelia, together with Uncle Ed and Aunt Betty rushing like the wind through the hall and into the kitchen.

'To the shelter!' Pops yelled at the top of his voice. 'Everyone to the shelter!'

It was first time Daisy had been inside the little metal house, but it would not be the last by a long shot.

CHAPTER 21

'THERE'S NO LIGHT!'

'There's hardly any room!'

'Just squeeze up. The benches aren't finished yet.'

'Where are the candles, Nicky?'

'Here! Has anyone a match?'

Suddenly there were little halos of light flickering in the darkness.

'Stay still, people. Let's count heads. Make sure we're all here.'

'One, two, three ... '

Daisy found herself kneeling on the cold, scratchy tarpaulin Pops had laid over the earth. It was not at all cosy as she had imagined the little house might be. And yet it was also thrilling. She could barely breathe for the excitement of it all.

'The siren's stopped, thank God!'

'What a dreadful noise!'

'Good thing we weren't driving home,' said Uncle Ed. 'Anyone hurt in that mad scramble?'

Daisy saw all heads shake. To Daisy's delight Aunt Betty

was squeezed close to Uncle Ed with his arm firmly around her shoulders.

The candles were passed around. One went to Aunt Minnie, the other to Aunt Betty and one to Mother. Startled faces came slowly into view.

'Do we have any gloves?' asked Uncle Leo, from behind Will's bobbing head. 'Some bod in Whitehall said to put gloves in our kit, should poisonous gas be dropped.'

'Hardly likely,' said Pops at once. 'We all have our gas-masks with us, don't we? Everybody's been issued with one along with our identity cards.'

'Absolutely. We're supposed to take them everywhere we go.'

'Didn't think we need them so soon,' confessed Aunt Minnie. 'Ours are somewhere in the car boot I think. Or perhaps I didn't bring them at all.'

'Ours are in the stair cupboard,' said Mother. 'What a nuisance!'

'Can anyone hear planes?'

'Not a thing.'

'Or the emergency services?'

'Quite the opposite. Just a rather odd silence.'

'I hope my family are safe,' said Amelia in a timid voice. Daisy saw she was clinging to Matt. Her big brown eyes looked even bigger in the candle glow with their thick, dewy lashes. Deep red glints trailed in her long brown hair against the creamy smoothness of her skin. Daisy thought yet again that she hadn't seen many girls any prettier; Amelia's tiny nose hadn't a freckle to spoil it. Her high cheekbones set in her heart-shaped face was like an image cut out from one of Mother's magazines.

'Like us, they'll be in their shelter,' Matt assured her.

'Mother dreaded this day,' Amelia whispered. 'And now it's come.'

'There's no sound of bombers,' Pops said hopefully. 'They may have gone in another direction.'

Daisy looked at Bobby who sat beside her on the lumpy tarpaulin. He was staring at the shiny surface of the corrugated roof. Already the condensation had formed droplets from so many people breathing in a confined space. The wood to make the bunk beds provided temporary seating together with a cupboard that was to be used for food and drink. The air was stuffy and Bobby drew his hands across his eyes, blinking at his surroundings.

'I should have been more prepared,' said Mother anxiously. 'We'll need cloths to wash these wet walls and disinfectant to prevent mould.' She turned to Aunt Minnie. 'When the men were digging the hole I thought, this can't be happening. Not in our lovely garden under the fruit trees. But today it seems very real.'

'We'll soon get ourselves sorted out,' consoled Pops. 'Matt and I will soon have the place ship-shape.'

'We haven't even got a shelter,' said Will, wriggling to free himself from his father's firm grasp. 'Only the tube.'

'At least we're close to the underground,' replied Aunt Minnie. 'But I won't care for the awful dash there's bound to be.'

'We'll share our Anderson with the couple next door, won't we darling?' said Uncle Ed, squeezing Aunt Betty's shoulder.

'Yes,' agreed Aunt Betty, stiffly. 'I suppose so.'

'It's a small size, but enough for the four of us. Nice to get to know our neighbours better.'

Daisy studied Uncle Ed in the glow of the candlelight. He wore a troubled frown but was prevented from replying by the sudden wail of the all-clear siren.

It was as though no one knew quite what to do.

'What do you make of that?' said Pops bewilderedly.

'Most peculiar,' agreed Uncle Leo. 'Must have been a practice run.'

'Let's take a look.' Pops took down the blanket from the door and heaved it open.

'Daylight!' gasped Aunt Betty, quickly unravelling herself from Uncle Ed.

'That settles it,' Mother decided, looking shaken as she climbed out. 'You two are going to Grandma's tomorrow.'

'We don't want to go,' wailed Daisy. 'It's not fair!'

'Daisy, don't cause a fuss now.'

'But the planes could easily fly over Wattcombe instead of London!'

'No dramas Daisy,' scolded Pops and planted a firm hand on her shoulder. 'Your mother and I have decided.'

CHAPTER 22

THE FOLLOWING morning Daisy stood with Bobby in the hall, dressed in their winter clothes.

Mother drew the tip of her pencil over the list she had made. 'Have I forgotten to pack anything?'

'I don't need half as much,' protested Daisy. Her arms ached from carrying her case downstairs. 'We're only staying for a short while.'

'Better to have more than less,' replied Mother. 'The bus arrives in half an hour, so let's hurry.'

'Will the driver know the way?' Daisy asked as they set off.

'I'm sure he has a map.'

'I wish Pops could see us off too.'

Mother only shrugged. 'He has another of his important meetings. In any event, we shall be up to see you next weekend.'

Daisy knew she would miss the new friends she had made whilst playing in the streets close to home. Like Iris Brown and her brother Sidney, whose parents owned a confectionary shop in Poplar and were very generous when sharing their sweets. Her other two friends, the twins Gary and Grace Mellish, were twelve. Like Sally's dad, their father was a dock labourer. They lived in a house near the allotments and knew all the good hiding places.

Grace and Gary and Iris and Sidney were going to a new school in Poplar away from the docks. When Daisy had asked Pops why she and Bobby couldn't go to this school too, he had said the arrangement was not long term. To leave one school and start another only to repeat the process over again, he insisted, was not good for their education.

The bus arrived, rattling its way to the appointed stop.

'I love you,' said Mother, kissing them both. 'We'll see you very soon.'

Daisy watched Bobby climb aboard. She could see the many faces at the windows. Children of all ages, peering out, their noses squashed up to the glass. She wondered if this was the bus that Sally had caught and if so, where it might have taken her friend?

Mother urged Daisy up the step. 'Pops sent a letter ahead. Look out for Aunt Pat.'

Daisy joined Bobby in the aisle. There was no room to sit down. Every seat was occupied. The din the evacuees were making was deafening. Daisy's courage failed her. She made a desperate attempt to return to the door before it was closed.

'Stand back!' the driver ordered.

The bus began to move. It chugged and vibrated so fiercely that Daisy dropped her case and grabbed the nearest rail. She saw Mother waving and felt a lump in her chest. Mother held a handkerchief in her hand.

A sure sign that things were not as they were supposed to be.

'How far is it to Wattcombe?' Daisy asked her brother. She felt hot and cramped as they stood in the aisle. It didn't take her long to realise that she didn't want to stand for the whole of the journey. 'I'd like to sit down.'

'The bus is full up. We'll have to wait until a seat is free.'

Daisy peered at the names of the streets as the bus travelled onwards. Westferry Road, Millwall Dock Road and East India Road. The endless rows of terraced houses and smoke-stained roofs gave way to larger properties of three and four floors. At Blackwall the bus stopped again for yet another intake. 'How many more can this bus squeeze in?'

Bobby shrugged as he stood with his case between his ankles, holding on to the back of the nearest seat. Daisy did the same, though it was difficult to keep her balance as the bus jerked unsteadily along. It seemed hours before the bus eventually pulled up at a garage.

The driver shouted, 'First stop. Anyone for Fernley village?'

Bobby grabbed his case and threw himself at the first vacant seat. Daisy landed beside him, though not without injury. She had fought off competition and scraped her heel in the process.

Another girl had snatched her hair ribbons as she passed. But this time Daisy didn't complain. She was seated beside Bobby with her case at her feet and that was all that mattered!

CHAPTER 23

'GOOD JOURNEY?' asked Aunt Pat as they left the bus after what seemed an eternity to Daisy.

'Yes thank you, Aunt Pat.' Bobby pushed Daisy forward, whispering, 'Don't moan, whatever you do.'

Daisy frowned at her brother. She was exhausted and her heel was sore.

'Whatever's happened to your hair, Daisy?' Aunt Pat enquired. 'And you're limping.'

Daisy looked down at her scuffed and wrinkled ankle sock. Bobby pushed his arm against her. She knew he would be angry if she complained.

'Never mind, we've not far to go,' said Aunt Pat brightly. 'We'll walk up an appetite. Grandma has baked an apple pie for tea.'

Daisy brightened. Grandma's apple pie was always a favourite at Christmas. She even preferred it to Christmas pudding, though last Christmas of course she'd had neither, being under the weather with that dreadful flu.

They made their way into Wattcombe village, past the quaint old shops. "Jane's Wool Patterns" and "John Carson,

Butcher" and "Peggy Altwhistle's Tea Rooms." She remembered that if they turned down the lane by the village hall, they would come to the school.

A large hand-painted sign with wobbly writing announced the lane was blocked off. A few men, rather old and doddery walked in and out of the village hall.

'The council are very busy,' said Aunt Pat proudly, 'making plans to defend our village should it be attacked. The Germans will have a surprise when they try to invade Wattcombe.'

Daisy didn't think the Germans would ever find Wattcombe in the depths of the countryside, not if they took the long and winding bus route.

She looked up and down the street and wondered what these secret plans could be. Elderly ladies led spaniels on leads, or rather, the spaniels led them. Aged old men rode bicycles that wobbled from side to side.

'Are we nearly there?' Daisy asked as Aunt Pat marched ahead. Although Daisy knew Aunt Pat suffered from bad nerves, they obviously didn't affect her long stride.

'Not far. Don't you remember?'

Daisy shook her head. Her memories of Wattcombe were vague.

She glanced at Bobby. He was very quiet, changing his case over from his left hand to his right. Daisy was convinced they had taken the wrong turning. One country lane after another unwound in front of them. Trees arched thickly overhead and the hedgerows grew thickly each side.

A tractor approached and chugged to a stop in the middle of the lane. The driver pushed back his cap and hailed Aunt Pat. They began to gossip and Daisy pulled down her sock to examine her injury. The blister was bright red and extremely sore.

Bobby sat on his case, resting his elbows on his knees. 'It

seems we've been walking for miles. Though I expect we shall do a lot more.'

'What do you mean?'

'Aunt Pat and Grandma haven't got a car. As far as I could see in the village, there weren't any. So where ever we go it will be on foot.'

'I hadn't thought of that.'

'There's just one bus stop too.'

'I'm hungry,' Daisy complained. 'More hungry than I've ever been before. And I'm tired. And I don't know if the blister on my heel will burst.'

Bobby rose to his feet and lifted his case. 'Well, you're about to find out.'

'Come along you two,' beckoned Aunt Pat, stepping aside to let the tractor pass. The driver looked down and smiled at them.

'Mr Webber said you can go to his farm to muck out the yard in the mornings. Just like you used to do,' said Aunt Pat with a cheery smile.

'What's muck out?' Daisy whispered to Bobby as they tried to keep up with Aunt Pat's lightening pace.

'It's shovelling away the animals' poo.'

Daisy tried to recollect the poo clearing, but the agony of her heel was distracting her. There seemed no chance of pausing as Aunt Pat's bad nerves drove her healthily on at a record pace as she hurdled a style that led into a green field stretching as far as Daisy could see.

'Give me a hug,' said Grandma as Daisy hobbled into the house. Whilst in the smothering arms of her grandmother, she was relieved to spot a huge crusty brown pie in its baking tin perched on the top of the black-leaded stove.

'Come here, my boy,' said Grandma, pulling Bobby close. 'You are growing into a fine young man.'

'Now, off you go, up to your room,' shooed Aunt Pat. 'While I make your supper.'

Daisy followed Bobby from the kitchen, making her way through the dark, musty-smelling hall to the stairs remembering that no matter where you stepped, each stair creaked. Daisy thought of the three floors above which were never used, not since Grandpa had died. Grandma had refused to move into a smaller property and nothing would change her mind.

When they were younger, Daisy recalled how she and Bobby had decided the creaking old building was haunted. One expedition had led them up to the top floors that were not connected to electricity and remained in permanent gloom. But they hadn't stayed long to investigate; the darkened, dusty rooms with their worm-eaten furniture and shuttered windows proved far too frightening for imaginative young children.

The door of their room screeched as it always did when Bobby opened it. A deluge of lavender and mothball hit them full force.

'I'd forgotten how funny this place smells,' said Daisy, lumping her case on one of the two single beds. Each bed had a fancy pink pillowcase and frilly floral cover.

'I don't like sharing,' said Bobby disdainfully.

'We used to share, remember?'

'We were just kids then,' said Bobby in his grown-up voice.

'My heel is really sore.' Daisy rolled down her sock. 'The blister's going to pop.'

Bobby threw himself on the nearest bed while Daisy

lowered her case to the other. She snapped open the two brass locks and took out Aunt Betty's brush and comb set. The pretty birds and blossoms painted on the handles reminded Daisy of home. She arranged them on the doily of the old-fashioned dressing table. 'There's room here for your things too.'

Bobby yawned. 'No thanks.'

Daisy sat down with her back to the wall. She could smell the damp plaster of the ceiling reminding her of the times they had come to visit in the past. There was a broken pane in the window just as there always had been. On the other side of the room a hole had appeared in the wainscoting. A small pile of sawdust had accumulated.

'Come on, let's hang our coats in the wardrobe and go downstairs for tea,' Bobby said, jumping up.

Daisy pulled off her coat and joined Bobby at the wardrobe, a huge dark brown polished monstrosity. Bobby tugged at the door. It suddenly flew open.

Daisy screamed as a small brown animal shot out. 'A rat!' she cried running to the bed and jumping on top.

Bobby watched it scoot away. 'It was just a tiny mouse, that's all.' He looked at Daisy cowering on the bed and began to laugh. Soon he was laughing so much, the tears streamed out of his eyes.

Daisy began to laugh too. Fancy her being scared of such a tiny creature!

CHAPTER 24

DAISY WAS WOKEN at the crack of dawn, or so it seemed, as Aunt Pat shouted up the stairs, 'Rise and shine, lazybones!'

They scrambled into their clothes and hurried to the outside closet in the pouring rain, for the weather was on the turn. A dank, poo-smelling mist was swirling around the house.

Breakfast consisted of two thickly carved slices of bread laden with dripping. The strongly brewed tea was poured into mugs and more toast offered with sticky homemade jam.

'Grandma is a fiend for thrift,' Aunt Pat confided as she sawed off a slice of cooked rabbit for the casserole. 'We were raised to be careful. Waste not, want not. Second nature to the Taylor girls.'

'I wouldn't mind porridge,' Daisy ventured.

'Winter's not on us yet,' Grandma decided. 'We'll make the most of summer's crop first.'

After breakfast Daisy showed Grandma her heel.

'Looks nasty, I'll put some iodine on it.'

'Will it hurt?'

'Not at all,' said Grandma, but the pain of the disinfectant made Daisy's eyes water. 'Once the air gets to your heel, you'll soon mend. Don't put your shoes on or the wound will get worse.'

Daisy spent the day with one sock on and one off. She wandered around, trying not to feel like a prisoner. At least Bobby could go outside and amuse himself.

Grandma gave her a few jobs to do and Aunt Pat brought out the Mahjong. But time passed so slowly that it was quite a relief when the next day came.

'Another letter,' called Aunt Pat as she came rushing in to the kitchen. 'It's from your father.'

Daisy and Bobby jumped up. 'What does he say?'

'I'm afraid they have to postpone their visit as they're driving Matt to cadet training, in Lincolnshire.'

'Where's Lincolnshire?' Daisy asked.

'Up north.' Grandma bustled in with a tray. 'A heck of a long way.'

'Is Amelia going too?'

'Doesn't say.' Aunt Pat handed round the mugs of cocoa. 'But seeing as they're engaged I wouldn't be surprised.'

Daisy sat down with her hot drink. Their parents weren't coming after all. The long days of autumn in Wattcombe stretched ahead.

'Cheer up, you two. You'll be starting school soon,' said Aunt Pat.

Daisy's head shot up. 'Will we?'

'I earmarked a place for you. Spoke to the Head, myself.'

'But we're going home in November!' exclaimed Daisy.

Grandma said nothing and Aunt Pat made scarce of herself.

Daisy glanced at Bobby. He looked as miserable. Not only had they not said goodbye to Matt, but Pops and Mother weren't coming. Not even a hint of when they might visit.

We've been abandoned, Daisy decided.

Forever.

It was a cold and bitter day in October when Daisy and Bobby made their way to Wattcombe Primary. Daisy shivered under her winter coat and woolly hat which Aunt Pat had produced from a drawer of mothballs. Her blister had all but disappeared, but had been revived by the galoshes she'd worn to muck out at Mr Webber's farm.

Daisy giggled. 'Now the cows will have to clean up.'

Bobby laughed. 'I'd like to see that.'

'I quite liked the farm,' Daisy added as an afterthought. 'Mrs Webber made us hot scones. And the cow's milk is the best I've ever tasted. Not like powdered milk that we get at home.'

'Cows are quite friendly,' Bobby said with a grin. 'Though they never do as they're told.'

They were still discussing the farm when they arrived at school, only to find the playground filled with bedraggled children of all shapes and sizes.

'Welcome to our school for evacuees,' shouted a tall, elderly man. 'I am Mr Keen, your headmaster.' Daisy wondered if Miss Bailey would approve of his crumpled grey handkerchief and drip on the end of his nose.

Waving a sheaf of papers, he began to call out names. 'The two Purbright children? Where are you?'

Daisy and Bobby put up their hands.

'Daisy, you will be in Class Two, Bobby in Class Four. Please school, make sure you bring your outside shoes with you, as well as plimsoles. Packed lunches too, since the school no longer has catering facilities.'

'I hope we've still got Mr Pine and Mr Fraser as our teachers,' Daisy said as she and Bobby made their way inside.

'Sit where you can find a space,' said the teacher of Class Two who bore no resemblance at all to Mr Pine, a young man who loved to take the children on nature rambles. Mrs Gardiner was white-haired and stood with the aid of a walking stick. 'Daisy Purbright?'

Daisy stood up.

'You are the oldest pupil. It's up to you to monitor the class.'

Daisy looked around at the very young children, some of them clutching battered teddy bears, or dolls. 'Please Mrs Gardiner, what do I have to do?'

Mrs Gardiner sank with a heavy sigh on the chair behind the desk. 'You look like an intelligent child. Start with reading to the children and then go on to numbers. The books are on the shelf there.'

Daisy could not believe her instructions. Was she to teach the children?

'I want to wee,' said a timid voice behind her.

Daisy looked round at the little girl.

'Too late,' muttered Mrs Gardiner. 'There's a mop in the cupboard. Clean up the mess immediately.'

CHAPTER 25

'I HAVE TO LOOK AFTER BABIES,' Daisy complained to Aunt Pat and Grandma that evening as they ate supper. 'Some of them can't even count to five.'

'Poor souls,' said Grandma sadly.

'None of our old friends are there. The children are all evacuees from different places.'

'Like you, my dear,' said Grandma, dolling out the mash potatoes.

'Mrs Gardiner is very old. Older than you, Grandma.'

'Well, that's a comfort. There's hope for me yet,' smiled Grandma.

Daisy found her complaints, unlike at home, fell on deaf ears. Bobby, she discovered, had his own problems. He was almost the youngest in a group of older, rougher boys. His teacher was not Mr Fraser but a Mr Musgrave who relied heavily on a faulty hearing aid and spectacles with very thick lenses, one clear and one opaque.

'It's not a proper school,' Daisy decided that night as they lay in their beds. 'I wish we had Mr Pine back.'

'War changes everything,' Bobby agreed. 'As we've found

out.'

'I wonder what Matt's up to?'

'He's having a much more exciting time, flying planes and shooting down enemy aircraft.'

Daisy shook her head fiercely. 'Matt wouldn't kill anyone.'

'Don't you know anything?' Bobby demanded. 'In war, people get killed. It's not like you've seen at the pictures where everyone gets saved.'

Daisy felt very upset. She had got used to the idea of Matt being in the airforce, and wearing a smart uniform, but not to actually shoot bullets into something or someone. Or worse, the enemy shooting at Matt. 'Do you think we'll all be together for Christmas?' she moped.

'Aunt Pat and Grandma have never missed coming to London for the holiday,' Bobby replied. 'Pops can't leave us behind.'

Daisy felt better. Perhaps Bobby was right.

'Can we go out?' Daisy asked after lunch on Saturday. 'We've cleaned our room and made our beds.'

'Be careful of the traffic,'warned Aunt Pat. 'The village can get very busy at weekends.'

'There's never any traffic in Wattcombe,' Daisy giggled. 'And I don't want to go to the village.'

'Neither do I,' agreed Bobby. 'Let's walk to our old house instead.'

Daisy nodded eagerly. 'I wonder if it's just the same?'

After half an hour's trudge down a narrow lane, a large notice came into view.

'What's that long word?' Daisy pointed to the board in the hedgerow with bright red lettering.

'Demolition,' said Bobby. 'It means something's being torn down.'

As they rounded the corner, Daisy gasped. 'Oh, Bobby, what have they done to our old home?'

The pretty garden that Mother had created, full of roses and flower beds was now overgrown. The old front door and windows were boarded. A blackish shadow crept over the red bricks as though they had been dusted with soot. The smell of burning hung in the air.

They walked slowly round to the kitchen garden and stood with their mouths open. Daisy had planted some of the herbs and vegetables herself; she remembered Mother showing her how to sow the fragile little seeds in tidy rows. Beyond, the chicken coop netting had fallen away and the hens' house was just a pile of old wood. Now everything had been eaten up by slugs, weeds and waist-high grass. The pretty stone path where Daisy loved to play hop-scotch was covered by slippery green moss. The most shocking thing of all was the vast black hole in the roof which wasn't an ordinary hole either, but a charred, gaping void into which the thatch had collapsed.

'There's been a fire,' said Bobby.

Daisy felt sad too. 'Can't it be mended?'

Bobby shook his head. 'No. That's why they're demolishing it.'

Daisy looked up at her bedroom window, now covered by pieces of board. A torn, burned piece of curtain squeezed out as if trying to escape. 'I used to see the bats fly against the glass,' she mumbled. 'And the swifts used to nest in the eaves.'

'That's why Grandma and Aunt Pat didn't tell us,' Bobby said firmly. 'They knew how upset we'd be.'

They stood for a while, staring at the pitiful sight, inhaling the bitter smell of charred wood. Daisy saw that even the pigeons were reluctant to land on the remains of the chimney stack. It was Bobby who turned away, as if unable to bear the scene any longer.

'Come on, let's go. Perhaps we'll watch the parade after all.'

Daisy followed, her heart heavy as they made their way towards the lane. She was deep in thought when she heard a faint rumbling noise. She stopped. 'What's that?'

Bobby stood still, listening. He turned and peered up at the sky. 'Look!'

Daisy followed his gaze. 'Planes!' she gasped.

'Planes,' Bobby confirmed.

'There's so many of them.' Daisy felt a wave of fear. The throbbing of their engines shook the trees and made the ground tremble beneath her feet. 'Are they going to drop bombs on us?'

'Don't know.' Bobby grabbed Daisy's hand and dragged her into the wood. He pulled her through thickets of scratchy bushes until they came to a toppled tree. Together they scrambled underneath its bare, brittle branches. Daisy clapped her hands over her ears and buried her face against the damp ground. Would a bomb fall and kill them?

'Keep still,' Bobby shouted as he thew himself on top of her.

Daisy was too terrified to move. Even her skin was shaking. She could feel Bobby's body protecting her.

Gradually the ear-shattering noise began to subside. 'Have they gone?' she whispered as Bobby climbed off her, staring up at the sky.

'Don't worry. They were ours after all.'

'How do you know?'

'I spotted the round circles on their wings. Spitfires, I think. They were amazing.'

Daisy scrambled beside him. 'Where are they going?'

'London, perhaps.'

Daisy felt a great miss of home. 'Pops read from the newspaper every day. We always knew what was going on. Here we don't know anything.'

Bobby looked at her and grinned. 'Now I understand why Matt wants to enlist in the airforce. Did you hear them? Did you feel their power? I want to fly too. I'm going to enlist when I'm old enough.'

'Bobby, don't say that.'

'Why not?'

'I don't want you to go away.' Daisy tried not to cry. It seemed she had been on the brink of tears all day. She forced back her sob. 'Anyway, you're only eleven.'

Bobby smiled. 'Remember that ship you wanted to catch?'

'I've changed my mind.' Daisy blushed as they walked to the lane. She wished she hadn't told Bobby about her silly, childish dreams. 'I just want us all to stay together. And war to go away. And Matt to come home and marry Amelia. And I could look after their babies.'

Bobby burst into laughter.

Daisy sulked a little. She didn't care for being laughed at. But then again, Bobby had protected her in the wood. He must think a great deal of her even though he sometimes pretended not to. 'Shall we tell Aunt Pat and Grandma that we saw our old house?'

Bobby shook his head. 'Don't think so. Don't want to upset them.'

Daisy smiled at her brother. Even though he was a boy he was really quite nice.

CHAPTER 26

'DID you see our planes fly over?' said Aunt Pat that evening as they ate their pie and mash.

Daisy nodded but Bobby looked down at his plate.

'Britain is gearing up for war,' continued Aunt Pat. 'Especially after the terrible news of the Royal Oak.'

Bobby dropped his fork with a clatter. 'What happened?'

'It was on the wireless,' said Grandma, helping Daisy to a second serving of mash. It was mash with every dinner yet Daisy didn't like to refuse.

'Our greatest battleship was sunk by a torpedo at Scarpa Flow,' explained Aunt Pat.

'Where's Scarpa Flow?' asked Daisy.

'Scotland, where that foreign plane was shot down.'

'What plane?' demanded Bobby, his jaw falling open even more.

'A Nazi warplane landed in a Scottish moor.'

'Did the pilot parachute out?' Bobby's eyes were wide with sudden interest.

'Couldn't say,' Aunt Pat shrugged. 'What about a game of Ludo before bed?'

'I'm a bit tired.' fibbed Bobby.

'That's not like you.'

'I was just thinking,' said Daisy quickly, 'about Christmas.'

'Don't speak with your mouth full, dear.' Grandma waved her hand.

Daisy swallowed quickly. 'Christmas is soon, isn't it?'

'Not long,' agreed Aunt Pat. 'Perhaps we could read the fortune cards tonight. I know you like them, Daisy.'

Daisy wasn't at all certain she did like the fortune cards. They reminded her of Peter Brady and the birch and how she might have brought the awful punishment down on his head. Predicting the future wasn't such a good thing after all. If she'd been told when they moved to London that her old home would become a burned out wreck and had to be torn down, she would have been very unhappy indeed.

'I'm tired, Aunt Pat,' she said. 'I did too much walking.'

Aunt Pat and Grandma glanced at each other. 'Yes, enough excitement for one day,' decided Grandma and began to clear the dishes.

Alone in their room, Daisy voiced her suspicions. 'I think Aunt Pat and Grandma guessed where we went today.'

Bobby nodded slowly.

'Why don't they want to talk about it?'

'People have other things to think about.' Bobby climbed under his floral cover.

Daisy shivered under the cold sheet. She knew Bobby wanted to forget about what they saw today. 'I miss Mother and Pops and Matt,' she yawned. 'Wattcombe's not the same as it was.'

Bobby drew the cover over his head. 'Go to sleep, Daisy.'

She closed her eyes and listened to his soft breathing. Her thoughts drifted to London and the family and Sally whom she missed dreadfully. Pops only ever sent telegrams. Mother had written, but short letters that were rather boring. It wasn't as if Daisy hadn't written herself. She had composed all of three long letters and described almost everything that had happened in detail.

All except going to the old house.

That was too big a disaster to write in a letter.

'Merry Christmas, you two!' Mother and Pops stood at the open door on Christmas Eve.

Daisy couldn't believe her eyes. She had been down in the dumps. Every dreary day since coming to Wattcombe was like a heavy winter's coat that she could never take off. It just got heavier and heavier, weighing down on her shoulders. They had been evacuated and as Grandma would say, "that was that!" Was she dreaming as she gazed into the faces of the two people she missed most in all the world?

'Aren't you going to ask us in?' grinned Pops. 'This isn't the welcome we expected.'

Daisy was overcome with joy as Bobby flung himself into their arms. The next moment she joined him. Tears spilled as they hugged and kissed.

'Gracious me,' said Aunt Pat as she appeared from the kitchen.

'Well, I never did!' cried Grandma, 'This is a surprise!'

'We would have come sooner,' said Mother. 'But petrol is scarce.'

'So many shortages,' grumbled Pops as he slipped off his trilby hat. 'And so much red tape.'

Daisy felt excited. 'How long will you stay?'

'Until Thursday, treasure.'

'I only hope I've enough food,' worried Grandma as they all hurried in to the warmth of the fire.

'Don't worry,' said Mother. 'We've brought provisions with us.'

'You can sleep in our beds,' volunteered Bobby eagerly.

Grandma smiled. 'The children will be comfortable enough down here.'

'I'll put the kettle on,' said Aunt Pat in a fluster.

'I'll help,' said Mother.

Daisy followed her mother into the hall. 'We want to come home,' she whispered. 'We miss you.'

'I'm sorry Daisy, but you'll have to wait until it's safe.'

'But - '

'Daisy?' called Grandma. 'Where are you? Your father is asking about school.'

'Run along,' said Mother giving Daisy a tap on her bottom signalling the end of the matter.

CHAPTER 27

'Mr Musgrave is nearly blind, well, not quite, but almost,' regaled Daisy. 'Mrs Gardiner nods off quite a bit. She often forgets our names. I read stories to the children each day, but they aren't very interested. They can't read themselves so I've taught them small words like "but" and "and". When I get to a "but" or "and" I tell them to shout out as if it was a game. Some of them I've taught to say their ABC and some of them their numbers, like two plus two, and four plus four. But no one knows their times tables. Not even the older ones.'

'But surely there is some kind of school management?' Pops protested, looking baffled after enjoying his cup of tea that took at least half an hour to arrive from the kitchen.

'A child of ten shouldn't be teaching but learning,' he decided.

'It's different here,' Bobby explained carefully. 'The kids are all evacuees.'

'They think the war is a holiday,' chimed in Daisy. 'They don't want to learn, but take it all as a bit of a joke. Tell Pops about Mr Musgrave, Bobby.'

Bobby looked embarrassed. 'Mr Musgrave can't see very well so the class just mucks around.'

Pops looked shocked. 'What happened to Mr Fraser?'

'He's in the army now, like Mr Pine. Mr Keen, the new headmaster said all the younger teachers have been called up. The retired ones have taken their place.'

'Some of the infants have dreadful accidents,' exaggerated Daisy. 'They cry for their mothers nearly all day. Others make disgusting smells and just giggle.'

Pops shook his head wearily. 'We thought Wattcombe was the best chance of an education for you.'

'It was,' agreed Bobby politely. 'It was nice when we were younger.'

'I forgot my numbers,' added Daisy with a rush of feeling. 'I've nearly forgotten everything I learned at school.'

'My goodness,' said Pops. 'What a poor show.'

'Do you want another cup of tea?' Daisy was pleased with her performance.

'Not now.' Pops frowned. 'Perhaps I'd better bring in the luggage. You two can help me.'

'You needn't have worried Pops,' hissed Bobby as they put on their outdoor clothes.

'Well, it's the truth.'

Daisy understood the importance of exaggeration when it was needed and it was needed more now than ever before. But she also knew her brother was a stickler for facts, just like Pops. So she endured a painful silence with gritted teeth comforted by the memory of Pops's horrified expression when he learned of the pitfalls of Wattcombe's wartime education.

As they joined Pops outside, she told herself that for the first time ever, she knew better than Bobby.

'Happy Christmas one and all,' said Mother the next day after enjoying Grandma's roast chicken dinner. 'The meal was delicious.'

'Mouthwatering,' agreed Pops.

'Thank you, Grandma and Aunt Pat,' said Bobby, forking the last potato on his plate.

'Thank you,' said Daisy. She wished now she had made more of an effort to make decorations. If she had known Mother and Pops were coming she would have brought some chalks and paper from school. Mrs Gardiner wouldn't have noticed. These days, she spent more time dozing than teaching

The smell of cooking wafted pleasantly in the air as Daisy helped her mother and aunt. When all was clean and tidy they joined the others in the living room.

'It's impossible to find wrapping paper,' complained Mother. 'We had to use newspaper.'

'Doesn't matter,' said Bobby, tearing open his present.

To Daisy's dismay, there were very few treats; a dog-eared girl's annual and exercise book minus its first page. Bobby received a board game with its dice missing and an elderly railway encyclopaedia.

'Thank you,' said Bobby, looking forlorn.

'We can play games tonight,' suggested Aunt Pat cheerfully. 'I'll borrow the dice from Snakes and Ladders. Why, it'll be just like old times.'

But Daisy thought how unlike old times this Christmas was. There were no new football boots for Bobby or plimsolls for her or Rowntree's York Chocolate or Duncan's Hazelnut.

'I tried for fruit,' Mother apologised. 'But there was none left.'

'All a bit depressing,' said Pops from the fireside chairs.

'How are the family?' Aunt Pat asked.

Daisy was shocked when Mother replied. 'Betty has taken leave from the factory.'

Aunt Pat looked surprised. 'Why's that?'

'She's joined the Women's Voluntary Service.'

'But who will be secretary?'

'We've employed a young woman,' said Pops with a shrug. 'She'll manage the accounts now Neville Calder has been called up to the navy.'

Daisy could hardly believe her ears. Aunt Betty had left the factory and Mr Calder had joined the navy! She wanted to clap her hands.

'However, the factory has been requisitioned,' Pops said gloomily. 'We're making armaments for the war effort.'

'But that's good,' said Grandma doubtfully. 'Isn't it?'

'Yes,' agreed Pops half-heartedly. 'But we've had to ditch our new valves. Just when we'd found something special.'

'You and your valves, Nicky!' Aunt Pat dismissed.

Pops thrust back his wave of thick hair and sat forward. 'That's just it, Pat. Valves are the heart and soul of electronics. You could compare a basic radio valve to your good old King Edward spud. But you know a real potato when it's new and freshly dug from the ground. Ordinary valves for instance, can be generated in such a way as to completely outshine their counterparts. Just think of the power they could produce for the whole of mankind.'

'Darling, I'm sure everyone's heard quite enough of your pet project,' interrupted Mother patiently.

'Poor, Nicky,' said Aunt Pat, 'your valves mean so much to you.'

Daisy wanted to say that no one understood Pop's inventions, not even Mother. He sat back in his chair, quiet again.

'And Matt?' asked Grandma. 'Has he flown yet?'

'No,' said Mother with a frown. 'He's with Amelia and her parents. The poor boy only managed a few days leave.'

'How grand for them to be together,' said Grandma.

Daisy didn't think it grand at all. Matt had chosen to be with Amelia and her stuffy parents rather than Mother and Pops. But even so, she was not downcast for Aunt Betty had escaped the evil clutches of Mr Calder. Her secret would be safe forever.

CHAPTER 28

'WE'RE GOING to walk to the village today,' Bobby told Daisy the next morning as they woke up.

'I'd rather ride in the car.'

Bobby chuckled. 'Cheer up, little sister.' He ruffled her hair and made her giggle. Bobby could always make her smile when he wanted to.

After breakfast they set off. Pops carried lemonade and homemade cake in a basket and they sat on the bench usually occupied by the breathless members of the village council.

'This feels much more like Christmas,' Daisy said, enjoying her slice of cake.

'It's a very different Christmas,' said Pops, grinning.

'Has Matt gone up in an aeroplane yet?'

Daisy knew Bobby was keen to know everything about the airforce.

'He's learning his theory,' said Mother as she packed away the picnic things. 'It's very hard work. Every cadet has to pass his exams before he can fly.'

Daisy glanced at Bobby. She hoped the mention of hard work might put him off joining the airforce.

'We saw Spitfires flying over Wattcombe,' he said, disappointing her. 'They were in formation. They were amazing.'

'Were they now?' Pops said. 'They must be stationed at the aerodrome west of here.'

'An aerodrome?' cried Bobby. 'How far is it?'

Pops threw back his head and laughed. 'Too far, I'm afraid.'

Mother waved her gloved hand. 'And anyway, these places are secret. No one is allowed in.'

Daisy knew that Mother didn't want to encourage talk of the airforce as one son preparing for active duty was enough.

The next day it began to drizzle and so Aunt Pat brought out the entertainment. Daisy didn't mind playing the games they had played at least a hundred times whilst staying in Wattcombe. It wasn't boring with Mother and Pops here. There was laughter and fun and jokes and teasing. Grandma made a wonderful supper which Daisy helped to prepare. There were slender slices of left-over chicken, together with cheese and pickles and some of Mr Webber's delicious cow's milk, followed by hot, baked scones. Mother had brought a little butter which melted into the soft, scented dough.

'We didn't tell them about the fire in our old house,' said Daisy that night from her makeshift bed on the couch.

'It would only spoil Christmas,' yawned Bobby. 'They might know anyway.'

'I suppose it's just another secret that we aren't supposed to know.'

Bobby yawned loudly. 'Go to sleep, Daisy.'

She drifted off, trying to think of a reason to prevent Mother and Pops from leaving. Was she sick? Unfortunately she felt very well indeed and couldn't muster up a hint of flu or a tummy ache or even a toothache.

So that, as Grandma would say, was that.

On Thursday morning the wind howled, the gutters dripped and the rain lashed against the windows.

'Nicky, are you sure you'll be safe driving back in this awful weather?' asked Grandma at breakfast.

'Wait another day,' Daisy begged. Perhaps God had sent a storm to stop her parents from leaving?

'I wish we could,' replied Pops, finishing his cup of tea with a final gulp. 'But my meeting is at six sharp.'

'The car might get washed into a river,' Daisy protested. 'Or the engine might stop.'

'A chance we'll have to take, treasure,' said Pops, regretfully.

'Come along, Pat,' said Grandma, 'you can help me in the kitchen.'

'I've made a list of things I need to send to you,' said Mother as they stood in the hall. 'I promise to tell Aunt Betty to reply to your letter. Is there anything else you want?'

'I'd like to write to Sally, but I don't know where she is.'

Mother smiled. 'I'll do what I can to find out.'

Bobby looked up at Pops. 'And I'd like to write to Sammy.'

'The doctor may know,' Pops replied as he piled one suitcase on top of the other. 'But don't get your hopes up. London is in chaos.'

He gave Bobby a hug then swept Daisy into his arms. She could smell the slightly damp gabardine of his mac and the familiar waft of cigarettes. She hugged him and the tears fell.

'Now, now, treasure. It won't be long before you're home.'

Daisy felt a stir of hope. 'We could catch the bus to London. There's a stop in the village.'

Pops looked amused. 'You've got it all worked out, Daisy Purbright.'

'Be good,' said Mother as she hugged Daisy tightly. 'Look after each other.'

Daisy watched through the rain-soaked window as Mother and Pops hurried to the car. When would she see them again?

CHAPTER 29

'Welcome to the new children,' said Mrs Gardiner on the first day of school in January. 'Daisy will tell you all about school and help you with your lessons. Now get out your pencils and paper.'

'I ain't got none,' shouted a mischievous looking little boy.

'Nor 'ave I.'

'Daisy will get you some from the cupboard.' Mrs Gardiner sank down into her chair, which was now bolstered by cushions so that she could rest more comfortably. Before Daisy had time to hand out the necessary supplies, Mrs Gardiner's chin had dropped to her chest. Little snores echoed round the classroom.

There were giggles and shouts from the class and Daisy clapped her hands. 'Be quiet, everyone.'

But very few listened. The new children were unruly and urged the others to disobey everything Daisy said.

'I want me mum,' wailed a little girl of about five.

'I do too,' cried another.

'I wanna go 'ome.'

'I've wet meself.'

By twelve o'clock, Daisy had spent more time taking the children to the cloakroom and making sure they left the toilets clean and tidy, than in class. When the bell rang, the children all ran out, refusing to form an orderly line.

'Is it four o'clock?' Mrs Gardiner asked when she woke up.

'Not yet, Mrs Gardiner.' Daisy wished it was.

'Where are they?'

'In the playground, Mrs Gardiner.'

'Then you'd better go after them.'

Before Daisy had reached the door, the elderly lady was snoozing again. Daisy wished with all her heart that Pops could be here to witness this depressing state of affairs.

The next day there were light showers of snow and though the countryside looked very pretty, the complaints came in thick and fast from the evacuees. Many had no heavy coats or warm scarves. They came from homes where clothes were handed down from an older brother or sister and were very thin and patched. As for walking to school, they were frightened of this new world that surrounded them. Some had never seen cows or bulls before. Others liked to make a show of throwing stones or chasing any animal that appeared. As the snow melted to wet footprints, muddy patches streaked the corridor. Daisy was never without a broom or mop close to hand. Since there were icy patches on which the younger children fell over, there were always scratches and bruises to wash clean.

'Wrap up well,' Grandma warned one morning before they left for school. 'I've never felt so cold.' Shivering, she huddled under her shawl.

'The children will freeze in the classroom,' said Daisy as she put on her coat.

'So will we, if the coal merchant doesn't deliver.' Aunt Pat shook the empty scuttle.

'Don't worry about that,' dismissed Grandma. 'We'll manage.'

But when Daisy and Bobby got home from school that day, the house was freezing.

'Where's Grandma?' they asked.

'She went to bed.' Aunt Pat was in a fluster.

'Did the coal merchant come?'

'He called to tell us there's none available. Even worse, the stove broke down.'

'What's wrong with it?' Daisy asked.

Aunt Pat shrugged. 'It just stopped working.'

They all shivered their way through supper. 'What are we to do if it's just as cold tomorrow?' Aunt Pat asked. 'Oh, dear, I fear we'll all freeze.'

'Don't worry,' said Bobby at once. 'At first light, Daisy and me will take the barrow and search for wood.'

Daisy watched Aunt Pat as she went to the kitchen. Without Grandma, she seemed lost.

'I'm going to bed,' Bobby said, yawning. 'Tomorrow we'll get up early.'

When Daisy went to say goodnight to Aunt Pat, she found her in the kitchen, struggling to light the paraffin stove. 'I want to make Grandma a hot cocoa, but the match keeps going out.'

'Let me help.' Daisy's fingers were more agile and seconds later the wick was alight.

'This is all very vexing,' complained Aunt Pat. 'I can't seem to think straight. Mother doesn't look well - and nothing works! ' She flopped into a chair. 'Oh, Daisy, I'm all at twos and threes.'

Daisy turned off the whistling kettle and sat beside her aunt.

'I'm sure Grandma is asleep by now.'

'I don't know what I would do without her.'

'Grandma is strong, Aunt Pat. She'll soon be well.'

Aunt Pat took out her hanky. 'I remember the last time we had a storm - it was when ...when I was just seventeen.'

'Was it as icy as this?'

'Oh yes, very. The winter of 1916 was dreadfully cold.' She took a deep breath and burst out, 'I shall never forget that winter. My sweetheart was fighting in the trenches of the Somme.'

Daisy gasped. 'You had a sweetheart?'

'His name was Lloyd and he was a year older than me.'

Daisy thought she knew all the family stories off by heart; she had listened to so many. But she had never heard of Lloyd before.

Aunt Pat bowed her head. 'We did something - something very wrong.' She wiped a tear from her eye. 'In those days it was a terrible disgrace to love a man before marriage. We didn't mean it to happen, you see. B ... but we were young and we only had a few days together before Lloyd joined his unit.'

Daisy realised Aunt Pat was confiding something very intimate to her. She sat quietly waiting, as a deep sadness filled her aunt's eyes.

'Your grandfather was alive then. He was very angry. I was sent away to a special home for girls in trouble. It was there my baby was born.'

Daisy frowned. 'You had a baby, Aunt Pat?'

'I caused my parents a dreadful shame. Grandma I believe, has never recovered.' A tear ran down her aunt's cheek. 'Little Lloyd died in my arms soon after he was born. Oh, Daisy, he was so beautiful.'

Daisy could not imagine that her spinster aunt whose entire life revolved around Grandma, had once given birth to a beautiful baby boy. Tears sprang to her own eyes. It seemed that here in this freezing kitchen where she had only ever known warmth and companionship, lingered a deep unhappiness that remained with Aunt Pat all these years.

'My sweetheart perished in the trenches,' continued her aunt. 'He never knew of our boy. When I came home to Wattcombe Father had let it be known that I had worked for a short time in service for a wealthy family.'

'That's very sad, Aunt Pat.'

'I don't know what's come over me to burden you with my secret.'

If only she could tell Aunt Pat, that nearly everyone she knew had secrets. Like Aunt Betty and Mr Calder and Elsie Shiner and Micky Wolf, and even Bobby who had vowed to join up to the airforce, which if Mother knew, might break her heart. It seemed that life was full of secrets found in the most unexpected of places.

'I think I'll go to bed now. Goodnight Daisy.' She kissed Daisy's cheek and whispered, 'Thank you.'

Daisy sat alone in the cold kitchen thinking of her aunt's sad story. She knew that Aunt Pat feared losing Grandma, which had caused her to open her heart and reveal the love she still had for her lost beau and baby son.

The next morning was even colder and Daisy dressed in her thickest jumper and winter coat. 'I'll boil some water on the Primus and take tea to Aunt Pat and Grandma,' she told Bobby who was reluctantly climbing out of bed.

'Do you know how to use the Primus?'

'I helped Aunt Pat last night.' She wanted to share with Bobby the story that had unfolded, but Aunt Pat had confided in her. Anyway, it wasn't something, Daisy guessed, that a boy would understand.

When Daisy turned on the tap in the kitchen, no water came out. There were icicles hanging from the window. Bobby joined her and tried again, but it was no use.

'The pipes must be frozen,' he said.

Aunt Pat came in to the kitchen. 'Grandma is very sick,' she mumbled, shivering in her dressing gown.

'I'll go for the doctor,' said Bobby at once.

'I'll come too,' said Daisy.

Aunt Pat nodded. 'Dr Norton lives in the lane near Mr Webber. Hurry please.'

Though they took care to wrap up warmly, when Bobby opened the front door a gust of icy wind almost blew them over.

This was a very unexpected turn of events.

Despite her shorter strides Daisy kept up with her brother. The landscape could have been a scene from one of the school's geography books; Iceland, or Greenland, or Finland, the countries marked with a deep blue star to indicate their low temperatures.

'We'll take a short cut I know,' said Bobby, heading off at a pace. The narrow lane soon became a wind tunnel, twirling around them as they ran, forcing her to stop and bend sideways to remove the stitch in her side. The hedgerows had spidery frozen icicles woven into their branches and the trees made violent creaks.

'Where are we?' Daisy puffed unable to feel her nose and lips any more. She looked around, not recognising any landmarks.

'Mr Webber's farm is close by, I think,' panted Bobby, stopping to gasp a breath. His cheeks were bright red under his woollen hat. 'Dr Norton's house must be down that lane.'

'Do you know for sure?'

'Not really.'

Daisy pointed to a gravel path leading off into a clump of woods. 'Could it be down there?'

Bobby looked uncertain. 'I don't know.'

Daisy hugged herself, trying to stop her teeth from chattering. If they took the wrong road, they could be lost for hours.

A howling gust of wind made her stumble once more.

'You should have stayed with Aunt Pat,' Bobby cried above the wind. 'This is no job for a girl.'

'Don't call me a girl.'

Bobby blew air through his cold lips. 'Daisy, you can be so - ' A loud, chugging noise drowned out their quarrel. From a rough track to their left came the familiar sight of a blue tractor.

'Hello you two!' Mr Webber drove alongside them. The black, smelly smoke from the tractor engine blew in their faces. 'What are you doing out in this weather?'

'Grandma's not well,' Bobby shouted. 'We're looking for the doctor's house.'

'The stove's broken,' yelled Daisy. 'And the pipes are frozen.'

'I'll see what I can do,' Mr Webber yelled back. 'Follow the track there and get yourselves up to the farmhouse. I'll fetch the doctor first.' The farmer revved up his engine. It gave an enormous pop.

'I told you so,' said Daisy as the tractor trundled away. 'We almost got lost.'

Bobby turned his back on her.

She suddenly felt guilty. He had looked after her in the best way he could, even if he'd nearly led them on a wild goose chase.

CHAPTER 30

MRS WEBBER GAVE them cocoa to drink as they sat in the farmhouse kitchen. Their wet clothes aired above them on the wooden dolly and something delicious simmered in a pan on the stove.

The farmer's wife dried her hands on her apron and sat down on a wooden stool. 'Now, tell me what happened?'

'Grandma's ill and we ran out of coal,' explained Bobby. 'Aunt Pat sent us to find the doctor. I took a short cut but nearly got us lost. Then Mr Webber came up on the tractor.'

'And the stove doesn't work either,' said Daisy. 'It made a loud noise and puffed out soot.'

'Don't you worry my dears,' said Mrs Webber. 'Bill will sort it all out. Now, sit at the table and I'll dish up. Those empty stomachs of yours need filling.'

'Do you think Mr Webber found the doctor?' Bobby asked as he ate.

'No doubt about that.'

All Daisy could think of was Grandma and Aunt Pat; they were alone and hungry in the freezing house. She put down her spoon.

'Now, now,' scolded Mrs Webber, 'what's this? Lost your appetite?'

Daisy nodded as tears filled her eyes.

Mrs Webber sat beside her. 'You've got to keep your spirits up. Your gran don't want to see you looking poorly.'

Daisy sniffed. 'Grandma said she'd never felt so cold.'

'There'll be lots like her this winter. It's bitter out there.'

'Will she get better?'

Mrs Webber smiled. 'Dr Norton will see her right. Now come along and get that hot broth down you.'

Daisy did as she was told. Mrs Webber's cooking was delicious. She only wished that Grandma and Aunt Pat could enjoy it too.

~

That afternoon, there was the sound of an engine outside. A gust of cold wind sprayed icy raindrops over the kitchen as Mr Webber and the doctor helped in two bedraggled figures.

'Grandma, Aunt Pat!' Daisy ran to hug them. She could only see her grandmother's bleary eyes moving under her woolly hat. Aunt Pat was wearing a scarf tucked into her coat collar.

'Oh, you poor souls!' exclaimed Mrs Webber. 'Take them down to the parlour, Dr Norton. I've got a good blaze going in there.'

Daisy and Bobby followed. When the doctor helped Grandma into a fireside chair, her eyes closed. Aunt Pat sat beside her. 'Th...thank you everyone for helping us,' she stammered, her lips blue with cold. 'I didn't know what to do. I thought we would turn into blocks of ice.'

'And so you might if these two children hadn't raised the alarm,' said Mr Webber.

'It doesn't bear thinking about.' Mrs Webber began to unravel a pile of blankets.

Mr Webber gently took Daisy's shoulder. 'Come along, you can see your folks later.'

In the kitchen, the farmer warmed his big red hands by the oven. 'That house was colder than an iceberg. The pipes are frozen and the stove is dead as a doornail. If you hadn't found me when you did, there's no saying what might have happened.'

Daisy sniffed back her tears and looked at Bobby. His cheeks were very pale. She knew he too had been shocked at the sight of Grandma.

It seemed a long wait before the doctor appeared. 'I'm afraid the cold went to your grandmother's chest,' he explained. 'She'll need nursing, which Edith has offered to undertake.'

'As for you two,' said the farmer, 'you can stay until your parents come.'

Daisy forced back the tears.

'Don't be upset, my dear,' consoled the doctor. 'Your grandmother is strong and will be in the best of care.'

But this was no consolation for Daisy. She loved Grandma dearly and didn't want her to be ill.

That night, Mr and Mrs Webber made up beds on the parlour floor. 'I hope you'll be comfortable, my dears. Your Grandma and aunt are sleeping in the spare room. A good night's rest is what everyone needs.'

'I'm up early to tend the cows,' said Mr Webber. 'To sing 'em their favourite tunes.'

'Do cows like songs?' Daisy asked incredulously.

'No doubt that,' said the farmer. 'They give the best milk with a dash of Harry Lauder's *Roamin' in the Gloamin'* or Georgie Leybourne's *Champagne Charlie*.'

'Take no notice,' Mrs Webber dismissed. 'Mr Webber

enjoyed a mis-spent youth in the music halls see? That's why all the cows have got names. Like Vesta 'cos she's so sassy just like her namesake Vesta Tilley.'

'Nothing wrong with music halls, love,' argued Mr Webber good-naturedly. 'Not if you've got a voice like mine.'

Daisy and Bobby were nearly deafened as Mr Webber bellowed out a chorus from a song called, *The Daring Young Man on the Flying Trapeze.*

'Out of the way, Caruso,' commanded Mrs Webber, pushing her husband aside. 'Now these should fit you,' said the farmer's wife and handed them sets of striped pyjamas. 'They belonged to our children, Mark and Susan.'

'Where are they now?' asked Daisy, growing more and more curious about this very nice couple who had so many hidden talents and colourful family history.

'All grown up, dear, with kiddies of their own.'

'I've left a pail in the passage for you to wee in,' said Mr Webber. 'Make sure you don't kick it over.'

'Goodnight and sleep well,' said Mrs Webber, closing the door.

'It's getting cold now the fire's going out,' said Bobby as he quickly stripped down to his vest and pants, put on his pyjamas and crawled under the covers.

But Daisy was thinking about other things. Grandma's house would be dark and empty without them. How many icicles would grow over the windows? Like Sleeping Beauty's castle, everything was frozen in a wintry spell.

'Hurry up, Daisy,' called Bobby, 'and get into bed.'

Daisy undressed and put on her pyjamas. 'These are much too big for me.'

'Who cares? You're not going anywhere.'

She pulled back the blanket. 'When the sun shines will it un-freeze Grandma's?'

'Not much chance of that,' said Bobby, his teeth chattering. 'Mr Webber says there's worse to come.'

'How does he know that?'

'The cows all lay down in the field.'

'Do cows know when it's bad weather, too?'

'Mr Webber says so.'

Daisy shivered and pulled the covers up to her chin. 'I hope the cows are just tired. And Mr Webber sings them the songs they like.'

Bobby laughed. 'Your turn to switch off the light.'

'Why?'

'Because you were last in bed.'

Daisy didn't want to get out. It was so cold that even in the warmth of the parlour she could see her breath.

~

'Where's Bobby?' Daisy asked Mrs Webber the next morning when she came down to breakfast.

'He's helping Bill with the cows.'

'He must have got up early.'

'On a farm everyone gets up early,' said Mrs Webber. 'Eat up now before your breakfast goes cold. That's real oats with proper dairy milk. You won't have tasted anything better.'

'It's delicious,' Daisy said enthusiastically.

'Cows have got their uses.'

'I wish we didn't have to go to school today and could stay home and help you.'

Mrs Webber turned from the sink and smiled. 'Careful what you wish for, dear. Postie said the school is closed because of bad weather.'

'That's good!' Daisy exclaimed but corrected herself

quickly. 'It's not that I don't like school, but I have to look after the babies.'

Mrs Webber tutted. 'Oh, dearie me. You're supposed to be learning an' all.'

'Pops was disappointed when I told him I hadn't learnt a thing.'

Mrs Webber chuckled. 'I remember your dad. Worked as the manager for Wattcombe estate.'

'He's got a factory now and invents things. '

'My word!' Mrs Webber bustled about the kitchen. 'Good job we've got brainy people like him to see us through the war.'

Daisy had almost forgotten about the war. It was spoken of so infrequently in Wattcombe that it seemed unreal. That was, until they'd seen the planes fly over.

Daisy took her empty bowl to the sink. 'Do you think Mother and Pops will come to collect us?'

'Doctor wrote a letter to 'em dear,' Mrs Webber replied. 'Meanwhile, there's plenty to do on the farm. You can help me gather the eggs first.'

'I'd like that. I used to help Mother collect eggs when we lived here. We only had a few chicken in the back garden and they all had names. One was called Queenie, because she laid the best brown eggs. The other was Princess because she didn't. And the others - '

'In that case,' Mrs Webber interrupted gently, 'You've got yourself a job.'

Daisy beamed, pleased her day wasn't to be spent looking after babies, but the hens instead.

CHAPTER 31

'It's snowing heavily,' the doctor said the next day. 'If it gets any worse we might be cut off from the rest of the county.'

'Does that mean that Pops won't come?' Daisy asked, disappointed.

'The government has advised people against long journeys.' He patted her shoulder. 'Now I must go and see your aunt and grandmother. They have a nasty bout of flu.'

Daisy had not forgotten her own battle with the flu. She had slept away three whole days and nights. She felt very sorry for Grandma and Aunt Pat.

'At least we don't have to go to school,' Bobby said that night as they made up their beds. 'Not if it keeps snowing.'

Daisy looked out of the window. Although it was dark, a bright moon lit up the landscape. 'It's all white out there and very pretty.'

Bobby giggled. 'Even the cows have icicles on their udders.'

'Do they really?'

'Of course not.'

Daisy ignored the tease and pushed her cold feet into the warm blankets. 'Can cows catch the flu?'

'No, silly. Mr Webber says their milk keeps people healthy.'

'I hope so.' She fell to sleep and dreamed of the evacuees screaming and running around school, pushing over the desks and chairs. In the dream she tried to stop them, but they locked her in the cloakroom with a huge key and all the while Mrs Gardiner sat in her chair, undisturbed by the chaos. An icicle grew from her nose.

The following day the announcer on the wireless warned of the violent storms battering the country. Dressed in waterproofs and heads down against the icy wind, they fought their way to the barn to collect the eggs.

Once back in the farmhouse, they took off their wet clothes and hung them to drip in the porch. 'Put the kettle on, luv,' said Mrs Webber as she weighed out the eggs. 'Your brother and Bill will be in from milking soon. Meanwhile, I'd better go up to see how your gran and aunt are faring.'

'Shall I make some tea?' Daisy lifted the big kettle expectantly.

'Not just yet, dear.' The farmer's wife took several bottles and two small glasses from the cupboard. 'This is a little pick-me-up, for your gran and aunt.'

'It doesn't smell very nice.'

Mrs Webber gave Daisy a wink as she took a sip from one of the glasses. 'Port wine and brandy is an acquired taste, but better than any medicine.' Smacking her lips she lifted the tray. 'I'll be down soon and we'll do some baking, like I used to do with my Susan.'

Daisy wrinkled her nose at the strong smell left in the

kitchen reminding her unpleasantly of the cough syrup Mother administered.

~

The next day, Grandma and Aunt Pat came slowly down the stairs. Mrs Webber waited at the bottom, arms outstretched. 'Go careful, my dears. Are you feeling better?'

Grandma nodded. 'Yes, thanks to your nursing.'

'Into the warm you go,' ordered Mrs Webber.

They all sat in the parlour in front of the blazing fire. Daisy tucked blankets across Grandma and Aunt Pat's knees.

'Is it time for your Liquafruta?' Daisy asked.

Mrs Webber chuckled and Grandma and Aunt Pat smiled.

'All in good time,' said Mrs Webber, trying to hide her amusement. 'I'll go and make us a nice hot cup of tea first.'

Daisy knelt at her grandmother's feet. 'Bobby's helping Mr Webber with the cows. Did you know, Grandma, that cows can tell when the weather is going to be bad?'

Grandma smiled and gave a little yawn.

Aunt Pat blew her nose.

'Cows are very clever,' Daisy continued and went on to tell the story of the mischievous evacuees and how Mrs Gardiner dozed most of the day and how, when the freeze had set in, she and Bobby had battled a great storm in order to reach the doctor.

'We're very proud of you,' said Grandma sleepily. 'Aren't we, Pat?'

'Very,' sniffed Aunt Pat, blowing her nose once more.

Suddenly a great shudder went through the farmhouse. Daisy jumped to her feet and ran to the window.

'What is it?' Grandma asked, waking up.

Daisy narrowed her eyes through the snow. 'A tree has fallen down. Mr Webber and Bobby are going towards it.'

'Oh dear,' said Grandma.

'Oh dear,' said Aunt Pat.

Daisy held her breath. Under the tangle of branches she could see a dark shape.

The parlour door flew open and Mrs Webber rushed in. 'Is everyone all right? I was in the kitchen and everything shook.'

Daisy pointed outside. 'A big tree's fallen down.'

Mrs Webber gasped. 'Heavens' above, it's the old chestnut. Look, there's something under it!'

'What's happening?' said Grandma, sitting up in her chair. 'Is someone hurt? Oh dear. Oh dear.'

'I'll go and see if I can help.' Mrs Webber took off her apron. 'Stay with your gran, Daisy. We don't want her fretting not with that bad chest of hers.' She rushed from the room.

Aunt Pat waved her hand anxiously. 'What's going on?'

Daisy returned to her observation post. 'Mr Webber and Bobby are clearing away the branches that fell on top of a car.'

'Oh dear,' said Grandma again. 'Is it Dr Norton?'

'There's someone getting out … '

'And?' urged Grandma curiously.

Daisy blinked hard. It couldn't be, could it?

But it was.

CHAPTER 32

THE KITCHEN DOOR flew open and in stumbled four snow-covered figures.

Daisy hugged her parents. 'Did you get hurt when the tree fell down?'

'Hush,' said Mother in a wobbly voice. 'We're both a little shaken, but no damage done. Except perhaps to the car.'

'There, there,' said Pops as he pulled Daisy to him. 'We had a lucky escape.'

'I should say so,' said Mr Webber, pulling off his wet cap. 'That tree could have killed someone.'

Daisy gave a muffled gasp at the thought.

'Bill, you're frightening the child,' Mrs Webber scolded. 'Now let's take those wet coats and hang them over the dolly.'

Daisy looked at Bobby who was very quiet. He had snow in his hair and on the tip of his nose. All their coats were covered in layers of white ice.

'Now, go along all of you into the warm,' Mrs Webber instructed. 'Bill, take some of these kitchen chairs into the parlour. There will be a lot of us to sit down to supper this evening.'

'I asked the doctor every day if you'd come,' said Daisy as Mother dusted the snow from her cheeks.

'We wrote,' Mother said, 'but you can't have received our letter.'

'Said we were driving down before it snowed,' Pops explained rubbing his cold hands together. 'But half way here we were caught in a blizzard. Apologies if we've arrived unannounced.'

'I'm glad I didn't know,' said Mrs Webber cheerfully. 'I would have worried meself sick that you were on the road.'

'That tree couldn't have fallen at a worse time,' said Mr Webber, shaking his head.

'Or perhaps it was the best time,' said Bobby. 'You might have been driving your tractor under it.'

'Well now, there's a thought,' said Mr Webber, smiling.

When supper was over Daisy helped in the kitchen.

'It was a delicious meal,' said Mother as she cleared the table. 'But I didn't expect you to feed us, Mrs Webber.'

'It's Edith, my dear. And we've got plenty of milk, butter and cheese to go round. None of us will go short. '

'I do hope Nicky can move the car tomorrow,' Mother worried as she laid out cold slices of ham, pickles and home-made bread. 'And it won't be frozen up.'

Mrs Webber chuckled. 'Don't you worry none about that. Bill will bring out the tractor. The old brute might not look up to much but it could shift a lorry if it had to.'

'You've been so kind,' Mother said on a deep sigh. 'My mother and sister are so lucky to have neighbours like you.'

'Think nothing of it, my dear. Us country folk pull together when the chips are down. Bobby has helped Bill in the dairy and your Daisy there has been a blessing, helping out with the chickens. Fact is, I'll miss 'em both something awful.'

Daisy was rewarded with a glowing smile of pride from Mother.

Later, in the parlour, the talk turned to practical matters.

'What do you think is wrong with the stove?' Pops asked the farmer who scratched his head and looked perplexed.

'Wasn't a flicker of life in it when I looked. P'raps in all this cold, it just gave up the ghost.'

'Never say never,' said Pops with a grin. 'I still have a few tricks up my sleeve.'

'If the stove is mended,' said Grandma eagerly, 'we can go back to the cottage.'

'And we can go home too!' Daisy exclaimed, before she could think what she was saying.

'Tired of your poor Grandma already?' said Grandma and pulled a sad face.

'No, Grandma, of course not, but - '

Grandma laughed and everyone laughed too.

The household woke early the next morning from a restless night's sleep. Daisy and Bobby had slept on the parlour floor which was cold and draughty and Mother and Pops had tried to sleep on the couch. All their faces were pinched and tired but a cooked breakfast soon put them right.

'Can we help to clear the branches?' Daisy asked after she'd eaten her fill.

'Wrap up well,' warned Mother. 'And don't get in the way.'

Daisy couldn't wait to play in the snow. But her boots soon got sucked into the deep drifts and her fingers went numb inside her gloves as she helped Bobby pile up the wood.

'Just a small dent in the roof,' Pops decided, as he examined the car. 'Let's see if it will start.'

After a great deal of cranking with the starting handle, the engine burst into life.

'Jump in you two,' yelled Pops and Daisy and Bobby scrambled inside. There were fierce groans and grunts from the engine, but the car began moving.

Daisy smiled. This was an adventure she had never had before.

CHAPTER 33

THE COTTAGE LOOKED AS PRETTY as a postcard, Daisy decided. Dappled with snow and tiny glints of sunshine spinning off the windows, the old house looked welcoming. But it was another matter when they stepped inside.

Daisy shuddered. 'It's freezing in here!'

Pops rubbed his hands together and blew a white cloud from his lips. 'My goodness, given an hour or two without heating we might turn to blocks of ice. Bobby, fetch my tools from the boot.'

'Can you mend the stove?' Daisy said through chattering teeth as Pops peered up in the chimney breast.

'Hmm. This might not be so straightforward as I'd hoped.'

Daisy's spirits sank as Pops prodded about. Showers of dust and dirt fell down onto Grandma's clean floor.

When Bobby reappeared, Pops opened his tool box and surveyed his tools. 'Now let me see ... '

'Do you need our help, Pops?' Bobby asked, stamping his feet to keep warm.

'What?' Pops unwrapped a small leather pouch and drew out a pair of spectacles. He balanced them on his nose and glanced up. 'What? Oh, no. You two go off and amuse yourselves.'

Daisy and Bobby couldn't wait to get outside. 'Let's build a snowman,' Bobby said. 'I'll use the garden shovel. You find twigs for his arms, and stones for his eyes.'

'What a shame we've got no hat,' Daisy said when the snowman was finished.

'There's an old one in the shed.' Bobby ran off and returned with a frayed straw boater. He squashed it on the snowman's head.

'What shall we do now?'

'Let's have a snowball fight.'

By the time they had finished pelting each other with snow, Daisy was beginning to get cold. 'I can't feel my fingers,' she giggled. 'Or my toes.'

Bobby brushed the snow from his face. 'Let's see if Pops has mended the stove.'

When they walked in the kitchen, Pops was completely covered, from head to toe, in soot. Two round white patches covered his eyes where his spectacles had been. He drew his fingers over his face and mopped the soot from his hair with a rag. His white teeth appeared as he beamed a smile. 'Success!'

'Is it working?'

'Of course!' The white smile grew even wider.

They giggled all the more at the unrecognisable man who slightly resembled their father.

That evening, Daisy told everyone the story. There was laughter and pats on the back. Pops had mended the stove and was congratulated many times over.

'Now we can go home,' said Grandma with relief, but Mrs Webber looked doubtful.

'No harm in waiting a few days, my dear.'

'No time like the present,' replied Grandma, obstinately folding her arms across her chest.

Daisy knew Grandma wouldn't change her mind. Her stubborn expression told everyone she was going home come what may - and in her very own words, that was that!

'Goodbye!' Mother waved from the car window as they left the farmhouse the next day. 'And thank you!'

Daisy knew that as much as she loved London, Wattcombe would always hold a special place in her heart. Living with the Webbers had reminded her of what it had been like to grow up in the country. The war had not been talked about much and true neighbourliness had been shown to those in trouble. She would always remember the farmer and his wife's kindness.

Now, as they all crammed into the back of the car, with Grandma and Aunt Pat wrapped in blankets, it was an unexpectedly sad moment.

Mrs Webber stood tearfully on the doorstep. Mr Webber saluted goodbye as Daisy looked out of the window.

The Webbers soon disappeared and, as was the plan, Pops drove carefully towards Grandma's house. The car was stuffy and the windows soon wet with condensation. Grandma sat quietly looking tired but still as resolved to reach home, while Aunt Pat's teeth were chattering.

'Nearly there,' said Pops, turning on the windscreen wiper as rain began to fall. When the house came into view Daisy felt Grandma shudder.

'At last,' she sighed. 'Edith and Bill were kind enough, but oh, how I've missed my cottage!'

Pops brought the car to a halt. 'I'll check on the stove.'

Everyone leaned anxiously forward to watch as he entered the house. When he reappeared, he looked very sombre.

Grandma gasped. 'Oh dear. Oh dear.'

Aunt Pat sniffed.

Mother put her hand to her mouth.

Then a big smile appeared on his face. 'You'll be pleased to know the stove is working!'

Grandma and Aunt Pat hugged each other. 'There's no place like home,' sighed Grandma, giving a tearful smile.

Daisy thought of London, her own real home; of her perch at the window where on misty, sunny mornings she would narrow her eyes to the skyline of the greatest capital in the world and breathe in the salty, sweet tang of the never-ending River Thames.

CHAPTER 34

February 1940

SNOW HAD TURNED to rain overnight and Daisy sat at her makeshift desk in Cawdor Road School. Just a few inches away from her seat, the drips from the roof leaked directly into a bucket, making loud plopping noises. This would have distracted the pupils but now everyone was used to the array of buckets often filled to the brim and waiting to be emptied. Close by were rows of gas masks in their little square boxes hanging from hooks.

Daisy loved the disused warehouse with its high roof and central location adjacent to Poplar High Street. It smelled, she imagined, like a house would smell in a foreign land; rice and spices and tea and coffee and even timber had been stored here at one time or another.

There was also another attraction; their friends Iris and Sidney Brown and Gary and Grace Mellish, all attended Cawdor. So when she and Bobby had been allocated places after their return from Wattcombe, she hadn't minded returning to school even though their benches and desks were just rough planks propped by bricks. Books, pencils and papers were in short supply, but the laughter was not.

Best of all at break times, they were allowed to run free in the waste ground backing on to the warehouse. Bobby and his friends could kick footballs as high and as far as they liked. Surrounded by old Victorian commercial buildings, there was no chance of the ball going astray or breaking a window.

As for the girls, they played on rough patches of scrub fenced in by worm-eaten posts from a bygone era, unobserved by the teaching staff.

The call-up had widened to men as old as forty, and many of the young male teachers had vanished. So Daisy was not surprised to find volunteers like Mrs Gardiner and Mr Keen, retired folk who turned a blind eye or deaf ear - literally - to their pupils misdemeanours.

She liked Cawdor the best of all the schools she had attended and when lessons started, Daisy and her classmates took their lessons seriously. They all knew they were fortunate to have their elderly widowed teacher, Mrs Howard to teach them. With her soft, refined voice and small, calm presence she had a way of engaging them. She always gave a daily update on the war effort. Even the youngest children of seven and eight sat quietly to absorb the news.

'In January of this year,' said Mrs Howard on one such morning, 'two million of our young people were called up to serve our country. An immense number of souls. Here on the home front, rationing began. Your parents will have registered with a local grocer and butcher and received ration books. Now who can tell me what some of these rationed foods are?'

Since these lessons always turned out to be more like

quizzes Daisy shouted out with the rest of the class. Over twenty-five voices replied. 'Bacon, butter, sugar!'

'Very good. Now who can name some of the countries who have remained neutral in the conflict?'

'Sweden!'

'Norway!'

'Denmark!'

Daisy had paid close attention to Mrs Howard over the past few months, so too had everyone else. All the children had family or friends who were involved in some way with preparations for war.

'In February, our Allied shipping was under a very dangerous threat. Very sadly, the valiant HMS Daring was lost. Can you tell me how?'

'Torpedoed, Miss!'

'A German U-boat got 'er!'

'Very good,' said Mrs Howard.

'Me brover's in the navy,' shouted Jimmy Burns, a little boy who sat at the front of the class. 'He's gonna sink all 'itler's submarines.'

Most of the class giggled and Daisy watched Mrs Howard smile sadly. 'I'm sure he'll do his best, Jimmy.'

Though this was a lighter moment, Mrs Howard was as usual, quite practical. 'Who can tell me what countries were invaded in April despite valiant defence by the French and our Royal Navy?'

'Denmark and Norway,' everyone shouted.

'And bugger to the Nazis!' yelled a tall boy with a thin, hungry face.

Mrs Howard wagged a finger. 'Richard, less of the bad language please. Now, we come to last month and the most harrowing turn of events so far. Our Dutch and Belgian friends fell to Hitler's Blitzkreig. After which, German troops reached Amiens on the Somme, only sixty miles from Paris.'

Daisy thought of Aunt Pat and her beau, Lloyd, who died such a gruesome death in the flooded trenches of the Somme. How could it be that only twenty years later the world had allowed the same tragedy to happen again?

Above all, she thought of Matt who had secured leave to come home in just a few days.

'They'll be 'ere next,' an older boy said who sat next to Daisy. 'Our blokes are gonna get wiped out over the Channel. They'll be like rats caught in a trap.'

Mrs Howard straightened her back and looked her pupil sternly in the eye. 'It's true our British Expeditionary Forces are outnumbered on the beaches of Dunkirk. But we were driven back by an unbelievably huge German army, after the surrender of Belgium.'

'Me cousin Reggie's on a warship,' piped up Gary, one of the Mellish twins. 'Reckon our navy'll give Jerry hell!'

Mrs Howard nodded, but her placid face was worried. 'We'll say prayers for your cousin, Gary, just as we will for every soul in combat.' She clasped her fingers and bowed her head.

Daisy did the same. No one was giggling or making fun. They all understood how desperate the situation was. Only last night on the wireless, it was said that a miracle was needed to save the lives of the Allied troops stranded on the coast of France.

CHAPTER 35

DAISY AND BOBBY were allowed to stay home from school on the day Matt started his twenty-four hour leave. Mother baked cakes and Amelia arrived early in order to help with preparations. Daisy thought how young she looked with her coppery brown waves flowing loose across her shoulders, framing her pale face and deep green eyes. She wore a simple white blouse and navy skirt, which Daisy thought made her look very pretty.

'We'll have lunch,' Mother said as they laid the table with Miss Ayling's best silverware, china and neatly starched napkins. 'But afterwards, you and Matt must see your parents and then enjoy an evening together.'

'We want to walk to Island Gardens,' said Amelia simply. 'And sit and talk.'

'Don't you want to go to the pictures or something?' Daisy couldn't imagine the park would prove the least bit exciting.

Amelia blushed. 'You'll understand when you get older.'

'Daisy,' said Mother sternly, 'you have the knives the wrong way round.'

When the knock at the door came, everyone rushed at once to open it.

Matt stood on the doorstep and everyone pounced on him. Daisy thought how handsome he looked in his blue cadet's uniform with a side cap perched on his blond hair cut very short at the sides. A little badge was pinned to the cap cloth, with the initials ADCC under the wings motif.

Matt abandoned his kit bag, scooped off his cap and one by one hauled them into his arms. But Daisy saw that his eyes searched for Amelia who stood back, her hands folded nervously together.

They were left alone in the hall to embrace and Daisy followed Mother to the kitchen while Pops and Bobby studied the newspaper in the living room.

When everyone was together, Matt told them a little about his life at camp. 'We aren't allowed to give away specific details,' he said apologetically as he sat on the couch hand in hand with Amelia. 'But I can tell you that my duties at first, included everything but flying.' He gave a deep chuckle, his voice low and confident. 'We've endured hours doing paperwork and clerical stuff,' he continued, 'which reminded me just why I want to be airborne.'

'But that's rotten,' protested Bobby, looking disappointed. 'You won't have to write stuff when you're flying a plane!'

'You'd be surprised, little brother. Records have to be kept and an enormous amount of data is sent up to HQ. But it certainly made me realise that life between four walls is certainly not for me.' He glanced quickly at Amelia. 'I mean, darling, the four walls of a home is quite different to an office.'

Daisy saw Amelia nod, though she did look a little put out.

'What else did you do?' Bobby asked eagerly, perched on the edge of his seat.

'We filled hundreds of sandbags and sorted out stores and equipment next.'

Bobby looked disheartened. 'That doesn't sound very exciting.'

Mother held up her hand. 'Bobby, your brother is trying to give us an account of his life at camp and he can't get on with it, if you keep interrupting.'

'It wasn't very glamorous at first,' grinned Matt giving Bobby a wink. 'But then, the discipline you've learned on the ground, is the same as you have to learn in the air. When things go wrong, you can't panic. You just have to get on with it.' Matt chuckled again. 'It was in spring, when we started handling the aircraft and lending a bit of muscle to the squadrons, that things got interesting.'

Daisy watched as her brother's eyes, far from being alert, seemed to look into the distance as though he had returned to the place he loved most. 'Our chaps had to fly against the Luftwaffe's fastest and most experienced pilots. We knew we were at a disadvantage in numbers and probably in experience. But our squadron commander reckons that Spits are the best in the world for manoeuvrability.' Matt paused, his teeth for one second catching his bottom lip. 'There's a golden rule, you see. Never fly straight or level for any length of time. You've got to weave in and out, avoid colliding with your number one or two and the best bit of advice I heard; keep on your leader's tale. Don't lose him.'

The room was silent and Daisy knew that Matt was up in the air, fighting the Luftwaffe already, even though he had yet to be sent on a mission. It seemed that this, even more than his marriage to Amelia, was what he was meant for. As Daisy turned her gaze towards Amelia, she could see at a glance that she had recognised this too. Her pale face was full of love and longing, but also of a new and desperate acceptance that Matt would never be fulfilled until he had tasted battle.

'Son, you make us proud,' said Pops in a gravel voice. 'But take care.'

Suddenly, Matt returned to the present. 'Don't worry, Pops, I'm not in action yet.'

'But you will be,' said Mums softly. 'Do you know how soon?'

Matt shook his head. 'I've already said more than I should, Mother. But let me assure you we have the finest fliers out there. You should know that no matter what happens, the RAF will run rings around Jerry.'

Daisy saw tears fill Mother's eyes as she quickly stood up. 'I think it's time for lunch, don't you? Daisy, I'd like your help in the kitchen.'

As Daisy followed her mother out of the room, the conversation turned again to Matt's training. So she was not surprised when Amelia joined them, eager to find a space where she could hide her emotions knowing the danger that Matt was in.

CHAPTER 36

IT WAS the beginning of June when Daisy stood at her window and saw the first of the Little Ships leave London. Fishing boats, pleasure boats, launches, tugs and yachts, armies of water-borne ants heading towards the open sea.

Pops had explained that Churchill's plan to rescue the troops in France was imminent. Therefore, everyone who was able had been encouraged to stand on the dock wharfs and wave off the rescuers. Children had been given leave from school. Factory workers, labourers, shop assistants, lorry drivers and just about all of London crowded the dock walls.

'Are you ready?' Bobby called from downstairs. 'We're waiting.'

'Coming,' she called back, grabbing her homemade flag.

Together with the family, Daisy made her way to the factory where all the staff had gathered. She spotted Mrs Hayes at once, perched on an upturned crate clutching her battered old handbag. 'Hello, luv,' Mrs Hayes greeted. 'Me legs have swelled up like balloons, so I'm resting on me bum for a bit. '

Daisy sat beside the tea lady as the many hooters, horns, bells and whistles hailed the outgoing craft.

'Poor buggers are risking their boats as well as their lives,' Mrs Hayes said with a tear in her eye. 'But it's what everyone supposed to do in wartime. Look after others first instead of number one.' She heaved a big sigh. 'Me neighbour's out there. Fred Kennedy. Old boy of sixty he is, fisherman all his life. Sailing up to Ramsgate to meet with all the other Little Ships. He refused to bear the cross of others' judgements - that at his age he was of no use to his countrymen. So yesterday he tidied up his house, locked his front door and knocked on mine.' Mrs Hayes shuddered at the memory. "Goodbye, ducks," he told me. "Be away for a day or two, I expect." Just as if he was taking out his boat like he did every morning ten years before.'

Daisy felt sad for her friend who had always seemed so strong, with firm opinions that often set her apart from others. But now she looked a bent and frail old lady, the warrior inside her, gone.

'Mrs Howard, our teacher, said the British are trapped in a pincer movement,' Daisy attempted, trying to recapture the spirit of when Mrs Hayes had an answer for almost anything and was glad to give it. 'What's a pincer?'

'A death grip on our blokes, ducks,' replied Mrs Hayes, without taking her eyes from the river. 'That's what it is. Can't go back 'cos of Jerry. Can't go forward 'cos our warships are too big to get close to shore. The sea's the only place left to retreat. Die drowning or die with a bullet in your brain. Ain't much of a choice, is it?'

Daisy shivered. This too, was terrible to dwell on. Yet all the people around had family or friends or knew of a distant relative who at this very minute were struggling to survive those cold and unforgiving beaches at Dunkirk. She looked about her, at the familiar faces of the people who worked in the factory; the women who stood in their turbans and grey overalls and the few men who were left behind, bearing the cross that Mrs Hayes had talked about.

'Do you think Micky Wolf is in France?'

The tea lady lowered her voice. 'Not him ducks. He did the proverbial vanishing act soon as his call-up came. Here one day, gone the next. You were away at your gran's at the time. It was the talk of all the factory. Micky was a coward at heart. But as for our Joe ...' Mrs Hayes lifted an eyebrow. 'Appearances can be deceiving as I once told you. Joe offered his services to the country immediately. Would have taken on Hitler single handedly if given a chance. But of course, time has caught up with him and he's had to stay at the factory.'

'Joe must be very brave.'

'He's a good man, Daisy. A bit old and weathered but he's loyal to his wife and country. Not like the Micky Wolfs of this world, all mouth and trousers and after the women. Or, like him over there - that bugger hiding in the shadows - I spotted him a while ago!'

Daisy turned to see Uncle Ed and Aunt Betty, Mother, Pops and Bobby, standing with Amelia. Unobserved - and a few yards behind the family group - stood a tall figure.

Daisy took a sharp breath.

'Failed the medical for conscription,' whispered Mrs Hayes scornfully. 'Colour blind, apparently. Didn't know his greens from his blues.'

Just then, a London lifeboat sailed its lonely way midstream, a Union Jack hoisted above the deck. A loud cheer went up and Mrs Hayes reached out.

'Give us your arm, ducks. I want to stand up and add me own salute to the city's lads.'

After helping Mrs Hayes to her feet, they moved closer to the water's edge to get a better view of the breathtaking sight. But no matter how hard she tried, Daisy couldn't stop thinking about the man standing only a few feet away.

When she looked again, Mr Calder was gone.

CHAPTER 37

DAISY WAS BURSTING to ask Bobby if he'd seen Mr Calder at the factory, but there was no opportunity until they went to bed. 'Did you see who was at the wharf today?' Daisy said as they paused on the landing.

'About a thousand people,' Bobby shrugged. 'Why?'

'I saw *him*.'

'Who's him?'

Daisy looked behind her. 'Mr Calder of course.'

Bobby shrugged. 'So what!'

'He was sort of - hidden in the shadows. As if he was spying on Aunt Betty.'

Bobby rolled his eyes. 'Another Daisy drama. I thought you'd grown out of that.'

'Ask Mrs Hayes. She saw him too.'

'I'm not asking anyone, least of all the factory gossip.'

Daisy gasped. 'That's a dreadful thing to say about Mrs Hayes.'

Bobby had changed since coming back from Wattcombe. He didn't have time for her any more. When they were at school it was as if he was ashamed to be with his younger sister. He only wanted to play football with the boys or hang about with the older children like Gary and Grace. In Wattcombe they had shared so many adventures, like the day when the Spitfires had flown over and had discovered their old house was in ruins. Living in the country again had somehow brought them closer. But now they were in London and Bobby was back to being a boy again.

That night, she lay in bed and her thoughts went giddily round and round. Then she thought of something she had seen at school. At the time, she had dismissed it, but now it all came back. Grace Mellish had been sitting on one of the broken walls that skirted the waste ground. She had been swinging her feet and her dark hair had come loose from her plaits. It flowed down almost to her waist, which made Daisy think how untidy it looked. But Grace hadn't seemed to mind as she shook her waves back and laughed, her dark eyes twinkling mischievously.

At the time, Daisy hadn't thought much about it, but now she recalled the moment distinctly.

Bobby had kicked the football deliberately probably, to where Grace was sitting. The other boys were urging him to hurry, but that hadn't bothered her brother.

He only had eyes for Grace.

~

Before taking the register, Mrs Howard stood before the class. Her sombre expression told Daisy that she had something very important to say.

'Our Little Ships are at this moment evacuating the Allied forces from the beaches of Dunkirk,' she announced solemnly. 'We understand that some have been successful. But others are still labouring against phenomenal odds.'

'We'll win, though, won't we, Miss?' called a boy who sat by Bobby.

' 'Course we'll win,' shouted Jimmy Burns. 'Just like Charlie Chaplin did when he captured the Kaiser.'

'That ain't real,' argued his friend. 'It's just a story.'

Mrs Howard held up her hands for silence. 'But stories are relevant, children, to our own lives. Every man who survives the fighting will have a story to tell. But not necessarily with a happy ending as you see on the pictures, Jimmy. Many men have been lost to a barrage of gunfire. Others have been drowned or died in the wreckage of their planes. But there will be survivors - and they will need your help and support on their return. Prepare yourselves, class. Be strong. And pray that never again will the world see such violent waste of life.'

Daisy saw that the impact of Mrs Howard's words had touched everyone. Why had she been thinking so unfairly of Bobby?

For if Bobby was a little older, he might have been a soldier who died in the sea under a hail of bullets. Or, if Matt had his wings, a pilot who never returned.

None of those terrible things had happened to her family. Bobby and Matt were both safe, at least for now.

CHAPTER 38

A BRIGHT AUGUST sunshine stole through the curtains as Daisy woke to the sound of raised voices. Suddenly the door burst open and Bobby appeared. Already dressed in his white shirt and grey shorts, his cheeks were flushed with excitement.

'Tilbury and Purfleet have been attacked,' he said breathlessly. 'I'm going out in the garden to see if I can see our Spits.' With that, he disappeared, leaving Daisy to put on her dress and quickly brush her hair. Halfway down the stairs, she heard Mother's voice again.

'You must telephone, Lincolnshire, Nicky. If Matt is flying I want to know.'

'I'm sure he's still grounded,' replied Pops. 'You mustn't worry.'

'But I am worried,' Mother argued. 'Our son may be - '

The conversation stopped as Daisy entered the living room. 'What's happened? Is it true what Bobby said? Is Hitler here?'

'Calm down,' said Pops. 'We're quite safe.'

Just then there was a knock at the front door. When

Daisy opened it, she was surprised to find Amelia standing there, looking as though she hadn't had a wink of sleep all night.

'Have you heard from Matt?' Amelia gasped and not waiting for an answer, rushed past Daisy to the living room. 'Mrs Purbright, is there any news?'

Daisy watched Mother take Amelia's hands and guide her to the couch. They sat down together and Mother shook her head. 'Nicky is going to phone from the factory. I … I'm sure Matt isn't on flying duties yet.'

'But there's aircraft overhead,' protested Amelia. 'Smoke is coming from the estuary by Tilbury and Purfleet.'

Pops gently patted her back. 'There, there. We mustn't jump to conclusions. I'll go now and phone the airbase.'

A little while after he'd gone, Bobby rushed in. 'Postie gave me this letter for Pops,' he said, handing it to Mother, who propped it on the mantel.

'Did Postie say anything about the bombing?' asked Amelia urgently.

'He reckons he saw a plane go down.'

Amelia started. 'Was it one of ours?'

Mother wiped a tear from her eye. 'That's enough now, Bobby. We must wait until Pops gets back with accurate news.'

So this is what war feels like, Daisy thought as she watched Amelia and Mother hug each other. Hitler had sent his planes to bomb Britain and no one knew quite what to do or say.

When Pops returned with the news that Matt was still not on operational duties, there were sighs of relief. But everyone suspected this wouldn't last for long.

Each day Daisy and Bobby watched from the garden as the Spitfires and Hurricanes flew south towards the coast. Since everyone was living in a state of emergency, the schools had closed. Even Daisy's eleventh birthday passed without a party because of the intense rationing.

One evening in late August, the newly appointed prime minister, Winston Churchill, addressed the country. "Never in the field of human conflict,' he broadcast when speaking of Britain's young airmen, "was so much owed by so many to so few."

This brought a sob from Amelia as the announcer continued.

"The success of our airforce in the battle for Britain in deterring enemy bombers is attributed to a radio device invented by our scientists. Capable of detecting the presence of enemy aircraft at a distance of seventy-five miles, our fighters become airborne long before the Luftwaffe appears."

'We've done it!' Pops exclaimed. 'We've actually done it!'

'Who did what Pops?' Daisy enquired.

'I can't say exactly, but this is wonderful news.' He went to Mother and embraced her. 'I was certain it would happen. And it has.'

'Yes, Nicky, you were right,' Mother agreed quietly. 'I'm very proud of you.' She tucked her handkerchief into her sleeve. Daisy saw her square her shoulders and smile in a sad way. 'You had better tell the children and Amelia. At least, tell us what you can.'

Pops nodded, still clutching Mother's hands.

Daisy's heart beat faster. She sensed that this was to be another moment to remember as they looked expectantly at Pops.

'There's been a remarkable breakthrough in the war effort,' Pops began, his voice thick with emotion. 'I can tell you very little, only that this news is highly classified and Uncle Ed and I have been called up to the Ministry of Defence.'

Daisy frowned. 'What does that mean?'

'We may have to go away for a short while. The factory will be left in the capable hands of a staff committee, who will jointly govern our business in liaison with the government's officials.'

Daisy held back her tears. Pops was leaving home. Now she knew how it really felt to be part of this dreadful, awful war, that Mrs Howard had warned her about.

CHAPTER 39

IT WAS a late Sunday in August, when Pops and Uncle Ed left home. All the family including Amelia had gathered in Poplar Park Row to wish them well and wave goodbye.

'If only my dad was a spy too,' Will said as he idly kicked a stone against the garden fence. Daisy, together with her brother and cousin, stood waiting for the government's cab to arrive to take Pops and Uncle Ed to their unidentified location.

'Pops isn't a spy,' insisted Bobby, who was craning his neck in order to watch for aircraft.

'He must be, if it's top secret.'

'Lots of things are top secret in war,' clarified Daisy. 'Don't go making things up again, Will.'

'My dad only takes photographs and that's not secret. They're in all the newspapers for everyone to see.'

'Photographs are meant to be looked at,' Bobby said impatiently.

'If my dad was a spy and went away,' prattled on Will, 'I could stay up late. He always makes me go to bed early.'

'Oh, do stop it, Will,' Daisy said crossly.

'I know a lot about spies,' continued Will oblivious to Daisy's disapproval. 'I read a book about a spy who took a pigeon with him behind enemy lines. He hid it in his coat and tied messages to its legs. When he got caught they shot him and the bullet went through the pigeon. There were feathers everywhere.'

'That's silly,' said Daisy, screwing up her nose. 'You're telling stories again.'

'Am not. There was blood everywhere.'

'Will, shut up, will you?' Bobby nodded to the front door. 'Everyone will be out in a minute. Come on. Let's stand at the gate.'

Very soon Aunt Minnie, Aunt Betty and Mother appeared. They were all trying to look happy, but their smiles weren't real. Uncle Leo stood with Uncle Ed and Pops, shaking hands and saying farewell as the large black car drew up.

Daisy rushed into her father's arms. 'I don't want you to go,' she mumbled.

Pops placed his hands on her shoulders. 'Chin up, treasure. Help Mother all you can. Promise?'

Daisy nodded. 'I promise.'

He grasped Bobby and hugged him. 'Take care of everyone while I'm away, son.'

There was not a dry eye as the cab drove off to a secret destination. Daisy saw Aunt Betty, who now wore her WVS overcoat and badge, was tearful too. That must mean she still loved Uncle Ed.

A few days after Pops and Uncle Ed had left, there was bad news.

"This morning the Battle of Britain intensifies as Adolf

Hitler threatens to raze British cities in reprisal for the RAF attacks on Berlin,' warned the announcer on the wireless. 'The government warns us to be vigilant and prepared for aerial onslaught."

'What happened to Berlin?' Daisy asked as they sat at breakfast.

Mother was very pale, Daisy thought. Since Pops had gone, she had seemed quiet and preoccupied. 'Many ordinary people like us were killed.'

Bobby put down his spoon. 'Is Matt flying?'

Mother shook her head wearily. 'I don't know, Bobby.'

'Can't we telephone?'

'I tried the call box. That number is now unavailable.'

'What does it mean?'

'It means, Daisy,' Mother said, lifting her eyes, 'that the army and airbases are not available to the general public. Pops warned me to expect the shut down as part and parcel of our defence system.'

'So we can't reach Matt or Pops?' said Bobby angrily and pushed himself up from the table. 'It's not fair. They're our family. It should be different for us.'

'Bobby, remember what Pops said. His project is top secret. And it must be kept that way.'

Bobby turned on his heel and ran out to the garden.

'We must make allowances,' Mother explained, 'for your brother. Becoming the man of the house is a great responsibility. Go and be with him, Daisy. Now, more than ever he needs you.'

A little reluctantly, Daisy followed her brother outside. She didn't know what mood she would find him in. These days, he was very unpredictable.

'Hello,' she said and sat beside him on the broken end of the wall.

He looked up at the sky and said nothing.

'Have you seen any Spits yet?'

Bobby turned on her. 'Do you always have to follow me around like a lost puppy?'

Daisy was about to insist she had only come out here at Mother's request, when she saw he had been weeping. But boys didn't cry, she thought, at a loss for something to say. So she just dangled her feet, studied her sandals and tapped the wall lightly with her heels.

Which seemed to suit Bobby perfectly.

The next day, Mother patted the cushion beside her and said quietly, 'Sit down, I want to talk to you both.'

Daisy sat silently with Bobby. What was about to happen?

'I don't want to leave London,' said Mother. 'I really don't. This is our home and we cherish it. But, the time is drawing close when we must face facts. If there are air raids on the docks, I can't see an alternative, but to evacuate.'

'The attack might not come,' protested Bobby. 'Our Spits might stop them.'

'I think that's rather hopeful, Bobby.'

'Matt said we've got the best airforce in the world,' said Bobby proudly.

Mother smiled. 'We have indeed got a magnificent airforce. A navy and army too. But we have been warned. And it would only be a fool who ignored those warnings.'

'Does Pops know we might leave?' asked Daisy tearfully.

'Before he left I made him a promise that we would go to Wattcombe when the time came.' Mother twisted her handkerchief between her fingers. 'First, I must give Pops's instructions to the factory committee. Fortunately the government assessors will conduct business in our absence.'

'But what about Aunt Betty and Aunt Minnie? They live in London too.' Daisy couldn't imagine Uncle Leo abandoning his studio and all his expensive equipment. Or Aunt Betty leaving her job with the WVS.

'I don't know,' said Mother on a sigh. 'No doubt we shall hear from them soon.'

Daisy saw the dismay in Mother's eyes and desperation in Bobby's.

She guessed his thoughts. If they were to be evacuated, would they ever see their friends again?

CHAPTER 40

IT WAS A BALMY, cloudless Saturday morning early in September, when Daisy woke to the silence of an empty house. Downstairs, she found a note from Mother saying she'd gone shopping and would Daisy please tidy round in her absence. This had become their weekly ritual. Flying a duster over the furniture, seemed to Daisy, the better part of their bargain. The chore was a lot less boring than standing for hours in endless queues, hoping for groceries that would prove to be unavailable. Besides, Mother insisted on walking everywhere. A car ride was out of the question. The Austin stood gathering cobwebs in the road, now too expensive to run.

Daisy helped herself to several slices of bread and a generous portion of jam. It was very unusual to find herself alone at breakfast on Saturday morning. Bobby would bolt his food eager to tune in to the wireless set and catch any mention of aerial activity over the city.

Daisy missed his company, even though he seemed not to care for hers. She longed to see Sally again and rekindle their friendship. Sadly, Mother had failed to find any information on the Watsons and Daisy supposed that Sally must still be evacuated.

By the time Mother returned, Daisy had finished her chores. She helped unpack the two string baskets though the variety of food was limited.

'I found these,' Mother said delightedly as she placed three unbelievably small eggs on a plate in the kitchen. 'And this!' Next came a tin of sardines, a luxury. 'As for meat, I was late for the butcher and only managed corned beef.'

Daisy helped to stow away the contents of the baskets in the larder. She couldn't imagine how Mother had the patience to wait for ages outside the shops at which they were registered. Last week, Mother had stood in the butcher's queue for at least an hour and ended up with very little reward.

Quite different to life in Wattcombe she often reflected, where real cows' milk - not powdered - was enjoyed by one and all. The farm eggs were large and juicy and the succulent cheese homemade in the dairy. In London, these luxuries, if available, went first to ladies expecting babies and others most in need.

This morning though, it was Bobby - or the lack of him - who held Mother's full attention. 'I barely saw your brother before I left,' she complained. 'He ate very little breakfast and was out of the door in a flash. I know how upset he is that we might have to leave London.' She sank down on the kitchen chair with a deep sigh. 'I do miss your father, you know.'

Daisy sat beside her; it wasn't often that she'd seen her mother so low. 'I miss him too.'

'Of course you do.' Mother touched her hair fondly. 'Where are your plaits, this morning?'

'I thought I'd do my hair differently,' said Daisy. 'I'm getting too old for plaits.'

'You're growing up so quickly.'

'Do you think Pops will write soon?'

'We must expect delays,' Mother said patiently. 'No news is good news.'

'What does that mean?'

'Only that nothing has happened. Nothing - too bad - that is.'

This startled Daisy as she hadn't imagined anything bad could ever happen to Matt or Pops. Matt was her hero and Pops was helping the government. How could anything bad happen to either of them?

'Well now,' said Mother, swiftly changing the subject, 'perhaps we could bake scones for tea and cut them into quarters to make them last.'

Daisy thought again of Grandma and Aunt Pat and the bountiful days in Wattcombe when there seemed very little rationing. Nothing ever was divided into quarters or even halves. There was always plenty to go round.

Daisy was helping to gather the fruit that had fallen from the garden trees. 'The fly has got into our apples ,' said Mother sadly, depositing several brown and mouldy cores in her basket. 'But needs must.' Cocking her head to one side, she stopped still. 'What's that noise?'

'It's the sound of aircraft.' Daisy pointed to a vast black shadow on the horizon. 'They aren't our Spitfires,' she gasped, 'like the ones Bobby watches for.' No sooner had she spoken than the wail of the warning siren lifted eerily into the air.

'Quickly,' ordered Mother. 'Into the shelter!' They sped across the lawn and stumbled down the steps that led to the Anderson.

The door protested with a loud screech but once inside,

Mother gave it a hefty tug. 'I shan't draw the lock. There's still time for your brother to come.'

The wail of the siren was soon broken by the loudest roar Daisy had ever heard. The explosion pitched them forward and into the darkness. Mother caught her hand. 'Are you hurt?' she gasped.

'N … no, I don't think so.' Daisy felt sick with fright. 'Are we going to be killed?'

'Of course not.'

Wave after wave of bombers flew over, causing the dust and earth to fall from the corrugated ceiling. Daisy thought it was like being buried alive. All around them was an ear-splitting clattering and shattering of glass.

When a brief lull came, it was brief. Louder and even more determined than before, the German bombers droned overhead, dropping their deadly cargo on London. Daisy thought about Berlin and how terrified the people must have felt as they too sheltered from the bombs.

'We're safe enough,' whispered Mother as they sat on the edge of the bunk but Daisy doubted that the wrinkled iron roof above them would prove any protection at all.

Eventually they lay, exhausted, Mother on the chair and Daisy on the uncomfortable slats of the bunk. All through the night, the attacks continued.

'Oh Bobby,' breathed Mother into the darkness, 'where can you be?'

'He must have found safety or else he'd be home.'

'Yes … yes, he's a sensible boy.'

'I'm awfully thirsty.'

Mother sighed. 'How foolish it was of me not to store some provisions in here. But there's a little lemonade left in the basket, if I can find where I dropped it.'

To Daisy's relief, a torch was found, the basket retrieved

and the lemonade drunk. Above them, the planes criss-crossed the city, droning like angry bees.

'I want to wee,' Daisy confessed in the middle of the night.

'A pail,' Mother said, 'is under your bunk.'

But when Daisy managed to find it, a huge bang sent her flying.

'I've wet myself,' she sobbed. 'I hate those planes. I hate them!'

'Hush now, Daisy,' soothed Mother. 'Knickers can be replaced, but broken bones can't.'

And by the end of the night, Daisy had decided she agreed with Mother. Damp knickers were very unimportant in the scheme of things.

CHAPTER 41

WHEN DAISY WOKE on the hard wooden slats of the bunk, the cold had eaten into every part of her body. She was frozen, from her numb fingertips right down to the tips of her toes.

Daylight broke in from the crack around the door and speckles of dust danced across the shelter.

Mother was asleep in the old armchair that Pops had squeezed in by the bench. The sour smell of dampness was choking; little beads of water ran down the walls and onto the soggy ground, seeping up into the sheet of thin linoleum.

Her first thought was for Bobby. Was he safe?

Slowly she stretched one leg. Then the other. Would her knees give way if she tried to stand up? She waited, testing them as she rose and shuffled forwards. Placing her hands on the door, she tried to open it.

The was no movement. She tried again.

'Daisy?' Mother stumbled to her side. 'Are you all right?'

'Yes, are you?'

'I think so.'

'The door won't open.'

Mother pushed, but soon gave up. In the distance Daisy

could hear the sound of fire engine bells and sirens. Mother cleared her throat. 'We're alive and that's what matters. I only hope your brother is safe.'

When they had eaten the last few crumbs of scone, Mother stood up. 'Let's try the door now.'

They pushed and pushed, but without success.

'We must keep calling,' urged Mother, coughing as she inhaled the stuffy air. 'It's just a matter of time until someone hears us.'

They continued to shout and call, until they were both completely hoarse. It was sometime later, when she had almost given up hope that they'd be found at all, that Daisy heard a noise outside.

'Help!' she screamed. 'Help, someone!'

Mother joined in. 'Help, help!' they shouted together. 'We're in the shelter!'

'Mother? Daisy? It's me, Bobby!'

'Oh, thank goodness!' Mother exclaimed in relief. 'Bobby, where have you been?'

'I was with Grace when the siren went,' he shouted back. 'I stayed in her Anderson and came home as soon as it was safe.'

'We were so worried,' gasped Mother, 'but you're here now and that's all that matters. Can you let us out?'

'I can't. The bricks from the chimney and the window frame are blocking the door.'

Daisy felt her mother stiffen. 'Is there any other damage to the house?'

'I don't think so,' said Bobby doubtfully. 'There's a kind of fog everywhere. I can't really see.'

'Then you must go for the warden. He'll know what to do.'

Daisy forced back the tears. 'Don't be too long!'

When Bobby had gone, they sat on the bench. After so

many hours trapped in the shelter there was no clean air to breathe.

'One broken window and the fallen chimney is not a catastrophe,' decided Mother. 'But after last night, I've decided to send you and Bobby to Wattcombe. The docks are far too dangerous now.'

'We don't want to go without you,' Daisy insisted.

Mother gave a little sob which she tried to disguise as a cough. 'I'm afraid I've made up my mind.'

Daisy was too tired, hungry and thirsty to argue and quite desperate to sit on a proper toilet.

CHAPTER 42

'STAND BACK FROM THE DOOR,' shouted one of the men whose help Bobby had enlisted. 'We're shifting the debris.'

Daisy huddled with her mother at the back of the shelter, listening to the rumbles, bangs and bawled instructions of the men outside. There were many strange voices, though she couldn't hear Bobby's. But perhaps he too, had been made to stand clear.

After what seemed an eternity, but could not have been more than an hour, the door opened with a great crack. Light flooded the shelter along with an oppressive smell of burning. Swirling motes of dust skittered around as a group of men peered in.

'All clear! Come on out now, missus. Take me hand an I'll help yer.'

They were hoisted up the three brick steps and landed in the open air.

'Mother! Daisy!' Bobby hurled himself towards them. 'I couldn't find the warden, but this is a rescue squad helping to get people out of their bombed houses.'

Daisy wanted to tell Bobby that he was the best brother in the world, but decided a hug would do for now.

'You all right, missus?' enquired a man with a peaked cap and very few teeth.

'Yes, yes, I think so. My daughter and I are unharmed, except for being a little shaken.'

'You're lucky,' he replied. 'Yer 'ouse is still in one piece. An upstairs window's gorn and so has the chimney but it don't seem too bad otherwise. I've told one of me men to have a quick scout round and see if it's safe inside.'

'Are there any other houses damaged in Poplar Park Row?'

'Some's taken a bashing,' said the man, pushing back his cap, revealing his heavily sweating face. 'But we ain't had no casualties.' He pointed to the roof. 'Looks like when yer chimney took a tumble it brought down the window beneaf' wiv' it.'

Daisy could hardly bear to look. 'That's my bedroom.'

'Count yourself lucky, ducks,' said the man unsympathetically. 'It was one 'ell of a night. Buggers was after the docks and got what they wanted.'

'Do you know which factories were damaged?' Mother asked.

'No, missus. There's fire crews fighting with the flames and rescue squads digging their way through the rubble on the docks. Gawd knows how many poor sods they'll find underneath.'

Mother nodded silently.

'You won't 'ave no gas or electrics indoors,' he warned. 'All the mains is turned off. But you might get a dribble of water from yer kitchen tap.' He ran his hand over the shelter door. 'I'll get a bloke to fix this lock. Any other damage inside the 'ut?'

'No, the shelter stood up to the bombing. And we had a little refreshment to see us through.'

'In that case, we'll get on. Word of warning 'afore I go. Kit out yer Anderson good and proper with supplies, 'cos they reckon the buggers will be over again ternight. And t'morra. And Gawd knows for how long after. Gov'ment thinks 'itler's gonna drop more incendiaries so's the Luftwaffe can see their way along the river. Then the perishers will follow up with 'igh explosives. Tell you for nothin', we're gonna be lucky to turn the tables this time.'

'Hurry,' said Mother as the rescue party left. 'Bring the basket, Daisy. If the man's right, we shall need more than lemonade and a scone tonight.'

Daisy did as she was told, however she would rather be anywhere else than cooped up again in that small, smelly, dark space.

CHAPTER 43

INSIDE THE HOUSE the walls and floors were covered in a thick, clinging dust that had seeped into the upholstery and curtains. Even the ornaments on the mantel and the family photos in their frames were tarnished.

Daisy watched Mother trail despondently from one room to another, her hands clenched together in dismay. 'However will I clean all this?'

'We'll help,' said Bobby.

'A mess is to be expected after such an attack,' sighed Mother, lifting a cushion and quickly replacing it as a thick cloud of dust rose in the air. She inspected the windows, tracing her finger tips over the ugly brown tape she had stuck across them. 'Thank goodness the windows didn't blow out and the tape held.'

Daisy was about to go up to her room, when Mother shook her head. 'We'll use the privy first and wash our hands and faces.'

After a visit to the privy which Daisy enjoyed immensely, then a quick wash in the kitchen sink, she followed Mother and Bobby into the hall.

'Be careful where you tread,' warned Mother as they ascended the stairs. 'Though we've been told the house is safe, we must be vigilant. Especially in your room Daisy, where we can expect to find the most damage - ' Mother's voice tailed off as they came to a halt on the landing and stared into her bedroom.

The wind was whistling through the gaping hole in the wall where the window had once been, spreading dust and soot everywhere. Daisy thought it looked as though her room had been ransacked and the burglar had thrown grey paint after him, staining her lovely bedspread and clean white pillows.

'Poor Daisy,' said Mother with a sniff and gently patted her shoulder. 'There's nothing we can do at the moment. But tomorrow we'll move your things to the spare room. For now, collect what you need for the shelter.'

Daisy could only stand and stare. The impact of the blown-out window frame had carved a ragged edge to the bricks where one of the blackout curtains had moulded itself into the mortar. Her chest of drawers had toppled on its side spilling all her pretty trinkets across the grimy floor. Aunt Betty's comb and brush set was covered in the same sooty grey dust.

Daisy's blue eyes were tear-filled as Bobby came and stood by her. 'It probably looks worse than it is,' he dismissed.

'You wouldn't say that if it was your room.'

'I'll ask Mr Cook to fix it.'

Daisy frowned. 'Who's Mr Cook?'

'The man who mended the shelter door. He told me where he lives if we need help.'

Daisy bent down and tried to rub away the dirt from the bluebirds and blossoms on the handle of her brush. 'Nothing will clean this. The bristles are full of soot. I'll never be able to use it again.'

'Stop moaning,' said Bobby impatiently. 'Now, come on. You lift one end of the chest and I'll lift the other.'

Surprisingly, she found her clothes inside her drawers were unmarked. At least she had clean knickers to wear.

'That's everything,' said Mother later, brushing her untidy hair from her eyes as they stood in the shelter. 'It doesn't look so bad now, even quite homely.'

Daisy doubtfully studied their handiwork. What worried her most was the small cupboard that she and Bobby had ferried out from the larder. The wire mesh over its front was sufficient to keep out insects, but would it keep out the dust? After all, the food stored inside it was more important than anything else. At that very moment her tummy grumbled.

Mother smiled. 'I think we deserve a good meal. I've prepared a small snack indoors, corned beef and a little cheese, with buttered bread. Not very appetising, but sustaining.'

'But have we enough food in the shelter?' Daisy anxiously considered the cupboard again. She remembered all too well how hungry and thirsty she'd been last night.

'We have sandwiches, a cold pie, biscuits, a few groceries, a flask of tea and water,' listed Mother. 'I've stowed half a dozen candles and a box of matches in a tin along with a few pieces of china and cutlery - and, oh yes, the stone hot water bottle and kettle are on the table beside the armchair.' She nodded to the bunks now resplendent with two mattresses carried down from their beds and a variety of linen. 'I think we'll have enough blankets and pillows but ... ' she hesitated, 'what is it that I've forgotten?'

'A battery for the torch,' said Bobby.

'Well remembered, dear. I'll see to that at once. Daisy, are you wearing your thickest jumper under that coat?'

'Yes, but I'm too hot.'

'You won't be tonight. Remember how cold it was? We need our warmest clothes, underwear, socks and boots. And, oh yes, mustn't forget gas masks.'

'I've hung them on the back wall pegs,' said Bobby efficiently. 'Pops left tin hats too but they look awfully big for us.'

'I didn't even notice them,' said Mother, shaking her head. 'It was all so dark and sudden.' Her voice broke a little. 'Tonight we'll be prepared. As soon as we hear the siren … ' She paused and taking Daisy's hand and Bobby's, drew them close. 'My better judgement tells me you should be in Wattcombe with Grandma and Aunt Pat. It really is the sensible thing to do.'

'Would you come with us?' asked Bobby.

Mother sighed and shook her head. 'Not immediately.'

'When, then?' said Daisy.

'My dears, I really don't know. Someone has to stay here and take care of the house. It's our home and I refuse to be threatened out of it.'

'Then we want to stay too,' said Bobby staunchly. 'Don't we Daisy?'

Daisy nodded, for however unsavoury the ugly old tin house was and however terrifying the nightly ordeal of the Luftwaffe attacks, they didn't want to leave Mother.

CHAPTER 44

THAT NIGHT the Luftwaffe swept over the city with renewed vigour, releasing even more bombs than the night before. All night long the pounding continued until the early hours of the morning, when at last, dawn broke.

With eyes unaccustomed to daylight, Daisy crawled from her bunk and let herself into the garden. She stood, peering up at the hazy red blush in the morning sky.

'London is burning,' Mother said, joining her. 'What a dreadful sight.'

Bobby followed. 'The guttering's come away from the eaves of our house,' he said, squinting through tired eyes. 'And the drainpipe's broken.'

'The least of our troubles,' sighed Mother. 'When you think of what others have suffered.'

'I'm starving,' said Daisy as they trudged over the dusty brown grass. 'And it will be lovely to have a bath.'

'We have to save water,' Bobby reminded her as they approached the kitchen door. 'The sewers and pipes are what the Luftwaffe are after.'

'How do you know?' Daisy suspiciously studied her

brother whose pale face was streaked with dirt and his hair stood on end.

'All the news is on the wireless,' he retorted. 'But you never bother to listen.'

'Why should I?' she huffed. 'I'd only hear it over again from you.'

'Children, please!' Mother put up her hands. 'Our tempers are short but this is no time to bicker.' She wiped the smudges of dirt on her face with her handkerchief and pushed back her hair that had fallen loose from its hair grips. 'Let's start the day with good intentions.' She opened the kitchen door cautiously. 'Seems to be all right … so today, after breakfast, we'll help to carry your things into the spare room, Daisy. Then, afterwards, we can top and tail in the bathroom.'

'What have we got for breakfast?' Daisy looked hopefully at the larder door as they went in.

Mother smiled. 'If one thing in this world never changes, Daisy, it's your appetite.'

Just after they had begun to carry Daisy's belongings to the spare room, there was a knock at the door.

'Flo, are you there? It's me.'

Daisy rushed to the landing and looked over the banister. 'Aunt Betty, oh, Aunt Betty!' She flew down the stairs and fell into her aunt's open arms.

'Daisy, darling,' whispered her aunt, hugging her so tight that Daisy could barely breathe. 'Are you all right? Where's Bobby and your mother?'

'Upstairs. Oh, Aunt Betty, it was awful,' blurted Daisy as she rushed to explain everything that had happened. 'We were collecting the apples when we heard the planes and there was no time to take anything into the shelter, except the basket. Which was lucky because in it we had a bottle of lemonade and a scone, but the lemonade made us even more thirsty. And Bobby hadn't come home and Mother was terribly worried. And in the morning, guess what happened? There was a huge hole in the house and it was my bedroom window and - '

'Betty!' Mother came running down the stairs with Bobby. 'Oh Betty, it's so good to see you.' They all grasped one another, holding back tears, as everyone tried to speak at once, until Daisy caught sight of a vague reflection in the hall mirror.

She untangled herself to clean the glass with the palm of her hand. They were all blanketed like Egyptian mummies in the wretched dust that, it seemed, was now part and parcel of everyday life. Aunt Betty's smart blue overcoat was a shade of gunmetal grey and her brown, glossy hair was a dull, untidy mop. Mother was speckled with dirt and soot and so was Bobby who had managed an assortment of interesting black stripes and squiggles over his shirt and trousers. Her own un-plaited hair hung about her head and shoulders in lifeless, lank strands, while her face, despite the swift wash in the bathroom sink reminded her of one of the monkeys she'd once seen at the zoo. Two white patches for her eyes and under her nose, a small moustache was imprinted on her top lip.

'Is that me?' she gasped into the mirror.

Bobby pulled a face. 'Horrible!'

Daisy giggled. Aunt Betty laughed. Mother shook her head, unable to hide her amusement. 'We might not look our best - but oh, oh - ' Suddenly she put her hands over her eyes. Aunt Betty held her close and smoothed her hair behind her ears.

'Come now, Flo. We'll face this together. Nothing matters more than that.'

'I'm sorry, it's just that so much has happened,' Mother murmured as she tried to regain control. 'Our lovely house - well, it's ruined!'

Aunt Betty smiled. 'No need for apologies, Flo. This continual dirt and dust is very upsetting.'

Daisy nodded in agreement. 'I wanted to be upset too. But I couldn't because I needed to sit on the lavatory first.'

Bobby gave a hoot of laughter and Mother bent close to hug her. 'Thank you, Daisy,' she whispered. 'You make me feel so much better.'

CHAPTER 45

'COME ALONG, we'll clean the kitchen, then have tea,' said Aunt Betty, taking charge. 'Daisy, I've brought a flask in my bicycle basket and some cheese sandwiches and pickles from the WVS canteen. Perhaps you could get them for me? Bobby, be a dear and pump my tyres. They're a bit soft and I have to cycle back to Aldgate for my shift tonight.'

'Aldgate?' said Mother as Bobby left. 'What on earth do you have to do there?'

Daisy returned with the flask and food parcel just as Aunt Betty was explaining. 'I'm in digs at the moment as I'm more central in Aldgate. I decided to close the house with Ed gone.'

'But Betty, what about all your things? Your personal possessions and clothes?'

'I packed a suitcase and took it with me to Aldgate. In fact, since we have uniforms supplied I need very little of anything except underwear and stockings.' Aunt Betty continued to wipe down the surfaces. 'Life is very different for me now. My days are certainly far more interesting than sitting in the office and typing. Talking of which, I cycled by the factory on my way here and saw a girl I knew from the typing pool. She told me the caretaker management have installed new equipment, retaining only a handful of women to work the machines.'

'Is Mrs Hayes still there?' Daisy asked hopefully.

'I'm afraid there's no canteen now, Daisy. It's just too dangerous to operate. If a bomb, God forbid, should drop there, the gas would explode and cause untold harm. These days most of the workers bring packed lunches and a thermos filled with tea.'

Daisy thought of the happy times she had gone with Pops to the factory and helped Mrs Hayes to make tea for all the staff. Were those days never to come again?

'This war is the cause of so many changes,' sighed Mother sadly. 'Oh, Betty, I do admire you. Your work in the voluntary group must be very rewarding - but dangerous.'

'There's no time to think of the danger, Flo. We're given our orders at the beginning of our shifts and the day flies by. Sometimes it's helping the wardens, sometimes the hospitals, sometimes transport, and those who find themselves homeless.' She gave a long sigh. 'This morning I helped to dig out a family of six from a pile of debris and smouldering bricks. The oldest member was a grandfather of eighty, the youngest an infant in arms. They'd lost all their precious photos and personal effects and were left without a stick of furniture to their name, let alone a roof over their heads. Fortunately they escaped serious physical harm.'

Daisy was still thinking of Mrs Hayes and the never-to-be-seen-again tea trolley when Aunt Betty's heartrending description caused her to imagine what it would be like if one of the Luftwaffe bombs fell on their house. What if all their possessions and photographs went up in smoke like the family that her aunt had helped? The prospect was very sobering indeed.

'I suppose you've heard nothing from Ed or Minnie?' Mother asked after a while.

'I telephoned Minnie yesterday,' said Aunt Betty with the first hint of a smile. 'She told me to tell you they're safe. Because of living in their apartment they have no Anderson, but she refuses to use public shelters. She insists she hasn't the right fashions to befit such an occasion! Instead, they've decamped to Leo's studio which is on the ground floor and leads to a cellar.'

'Minnie can be so stubborn,' sighed Mother. 'I hope she knows what she's doing.'

Aunt Betty shrugged. 'You know Minnie when she has a bee in her bonnet. Not even the Luftwaffe will change her mind.' She reached into her pocket. 'Now for the good news. I've heard from Ed - sort of.' She grinned ruefully and passed a postcard to Mother who carefully studied the image of St Paul's Cathedral on one side, before reading aloud from the other.

"Dearest Betty, this is to let you know I am fine, but missing you enormously. I hope Margaret Kelly's fiftieth went off well - too bad I had to miss it. Sorry, no return address just yet, but we are told one will be forthcoming soon. Ever yours, Ed."

'Who is Margaret Kelly?' said Mother with a frown. 'And why is this card postmarked London? Do you think Ed and Nicky are still in town?'

'No, quite the opposite,' declared Aunt Betty. 'That's what we are meant to think.' She took a breath. 'You see, Ed thought up this ingenious idea, and we created our own code before he left. Yesterday I deciphered some of it.'

Daisy clapped her hands. 'Aunt Betty, how exciting!'

Her aunt smiled. 'The credit goes to your uncle. But yes, it does feel rather wonderful to pit our wits against the powers that be.'

'Well indeed, Betty, I would never have thought it of you!' Exclaimed Mother.

Aunt Betty's eyes lit up as she spoke. 'The postmark is a generic one, probably collected from our men's location and sent off en masse by the war office in London.'

'So we shall never be able to trace where they are?' Mother looked disappointed.

'Don't be too sure of that,' replied Aunt Betty. 'I've developed my own theory on Ed and Nicky's whereabouts. Though I shan't be certain until Ed writes again and I can confirm my deductions.'

'Deductions?' said Mother on a gasp. 'Do you mean Ed and Nicky are to be sent abroad?'

'Good gracious, no,' said Aunt Betty. 'The government, I am convinced, have borrowed our men for very specific missions - here, on British soil. And though we are not supposed to talk about such things, I'm sure what I have to say won't go beyond these four walls.'

Daisy stopped eating immediately. She didn't want to miss a word.

'As I told you, Ed and I hatched a plan,' said her aunt in a hushed voice.

Everyone leaned forward to hear her whispered words.

'Ed guessed that any communication between us would be censored and any letters from him would be postmarked according to government instructions. And so we invented our own code.'

'I wish Pops had invented one too,' said Daisy eagerly. 'It would be so exciting if we could - '

'Shh,' said Bobby knocking her elbow. 'You're interrupting again.'

With great restraint Daisy didn't retaliate which was just as well because Aunt Betty took a dog-eared map from her bag and spread it over the table.

'We decided that any number from one to a hundred would represent the amount of miles from London to their secret location. Over one hundred and we would refer to another code, which this time, isn't used on the postcard. Any name, be it male of female that was unfamiliar, would stand for the initials of the town nearest to this location. Does that make sense?'

'No,' they all said at once.

'Good,' said her aunt with a satisfied nod. 'If you haven't guessed, then our plan is pretty watertight.'

'What does Margaret Kelly's fiftieth have to do with your map?' said Mother, puzzled.

'Everything,' said Aunt Betty with a wry smile. 'Our men are fifty or so miles from London, as the crow flies, living in a town with the initials MK.'

Bobby sat bolt upright. 'I get it, Aunt Betty. That's why you've drawn this circle around London.'

'Well done, Bobby,' said their aunt, indicating the lightly pencilled orb. 'For instance, here to the south is Hastings, fifty or so miles from us. And here, as we follow the shape of the circle is Oxford, fifty miles or so away. And here, at the top of the circle - '

'Margaret Kelly!' burst out Daisy, stabbing her finger on the map.

'Milton Keynes!' exclaimed Bobby. 'Pops and Uncle Ed are in Milton Keynes?'

'By my reckoning, yes,' agreed their aunt. 'We're unlikely to be rumbled, you see, even if the card is intercepted. Ed will send his postcards or his letters and hopefully when I receive a forwarding address, I'll respond with mine, also in code.'

'What a whizzer!' exclaimed Bobby, examining the map closely.

Aunt Betty grinned. 'It's quite simple really. Wherever our men were sent within the British Isles, it had to be north, south, east or west of London, right?'

Everyone nodded.

'So we based our code on one set of numerals per letter or postcard. In this case, Ed wrote 'fiftieth' which corresponds with fifty. As for towns, following the circle, the only town with the initials of Margaret Kelly is Milton Keynes. If their destination was Hastings or Oxford then Ed would have written Harry or Olive's fiftieth. '

Once again Daisy clapped her hands. 'That's brilliant, Aunt Betty!'

'But what if they were in, say Wales?' asked Mother. 'Or Scotland even?'

'Our code for Wales is Tommy and Scotland is Susan. Irene stands for Ireland.'

Daisy slipped her arms around her aunt's neck. 'You're so clever, Aunt Betty.'

'Not at all, Daisy. It was your uncle who thought this trick up. Ed is really, well … ' Her aunt's brown eyes filled with pride. 'He's an extraordinary man.'

This was music to Daisy's ears. For if Aunt Betty spoke so highly of Uncle Ed, then she wouldn't be thinking of Mr Calder.

CHAPTER 46

For Daisy, time passed in an almost identical pattern of scraping up debris and repeatedly cleaning surfaces, the result of nightly bombing attacks. She found herself something of a specialist in trying to defeat the muck that seeped through every crack in the roof. The second someone closed a door or walked upstairs, a shower of fine black particles fell to the floor.

Every two weeks the luxury of a bath was poured. The tub water was reused and hair was shampooed with a delouser, since the nights spent in the shelter had proven a haven for tiny insects and fleas.

It was left to Mother to scout for provisions and make the most of their rations. Daisy couldn't abide the long, boring queues and having to wait for the best or worst that their coupons could provide. Instead, she'd opted for the cleaning and her most dislikable duty, the laundering of their clothes. With no gas supplied to the house, the copper was useless and items had to be hand-washed in the kitchen sink and urged through the groaning mangle.

As for Bobby, after helping Mr Cook to fit a stout panel

of weatherboard over Daisy's bedroom window, he became, more or less, Mr Cook's apprentice. A day didn't pass without Bobby attending some kind of catastrophe in the area. 'I carry Mr Cook's tools and help him to mend stuff. Or sometimes I run errands for him and the other men,' he boasted, much to Mother's concern.

'You must come home before the siren alert,' Mother warned him constantly. 'I should worry about you terribly if you were absent again all night.'

'Mr Cook always tells me to knock off at half past three.'

Daisy giggled as she helped fill the basket for their overnight stay in the shelter. 'What's knock off?'

'Time to stop,' said Bobby. 'Like you are my skin and blister. Skin and blister rhymes with sister, see?' Daisy grinned as Bobby continued. 'Mother is making the Rosy Lee and I'm carrying the blankets for Uncle Ned so we don't get taters.'

Daisy burst out laughing. But Mother stopped pouring the tea into the flask. 'Bobby, that's enough now. Whatever would your father think?'

Bobby's cheeks flared red. 'He's not here, so I don't know.'

Mother looked startled. 'Bobby, you know your father had no choice in going away.'

'But why?' cried Bobby furiously. 'I'd rather have him to talk to than Mr Cook. But as I don't, then Mr Cook will have to do.' He sped from the kitchen and into the garden.

Mother sighed and shook her head. 'This war is such a terrible thing for families. And the worst of it is, there's an element of truth in what he says. Your father could have refused the government, but he felt it was his duty to cooperate.'

'Pops might get leave like Matt does,' said Daisy hopefully.

'Perhaps,' Mother agreed vaguely.

Daisy began packing the basket again but the quarrel with

Bobby had left Mother downcast as they prepared for yet another night in the shelter.

It was on a chilly day in October when two letters arrived.

'This is your father's handwriting,' said Mother excitedly as they sat at the kitchen table and she opened the first.

"My dears, all is well here and the days pass rapidly. So quickly in fact, that I am guilty of neglecting to write to you. However, I've very little news, as is to be expected, that I can announce. But I shall be very happy to receive a letter from you. Here is the address." Mother sighed. 'It's just a war office department.'

'Does he say anything about me?' asked Bobby.

'Only that he loves and misses us all.'

'Is there any code?' Daisy asked.

'None that I can see,' replied Mother.

'When is he coming home?'

'He doesn't say.' With a disappointed expression, Mother passed the letter to Bobby as she opened the second envelope.

'It's from Aunt Pat,' Mother said as she studied the single sheet. 'Apparently several bombs fell near the village, close enough to shatter some of the shop windows. No one was hurt but Aunt Pat sounds rather worried.' Mother put down the letter. 'I must find a working telephone box and speak to your aunt. I shall be back soon.'

Daisy watched her mother slip on a headscarf, then hurry out again.

'Pops's letter wasn't very exciting,' said Daisy as she followed Bobby to the larder. 'Do you think there's a code in it, somewhere?'

'Don't know,' Bobby mumbled over his shoulder. 'Didn't sound like it.'

'Are you going to help Mr Cook today?' Daisy watched her brother set out the bread and carving knife and the last of the apple preserve.

'No,' Bobby replied with a shrug. 'I'm going to see Grace.'

Daisy had almost forgotten the pretty girl from Cawdor School. But Bobby said no more and continued to eat ravenously.

Daisy considered the unappetising looking loaf. She was sure she couldn't eat any more of the unpalatable substance that lodged in her throat. As for the mugs of dishwater tea …

'Can I come with you?' she asked.

'You'd only interrupt all the time.'

'I wouldn't. I promise I won't say anything.'

'Some hopes,' munched Bobby, licking the preserve from his lips.

'I don't want to be on my own,' she confessed.

'Mother won't be long.'

'She might go shopping.'

Bobby scowled. 'The answer's still no.'

How could Bobby be so cruel? Salty tears filled her eyes. These days she took great care never to follow him around or say anything that would upset him or do anything he disapproved of. Since his outburst with Mother, she knew Bobby was growing into a young man who was hard, if not impossible to understand.

Quietly sniffing, she left the table and went into the hall. Everywhere she looked was grimy; the wallpaper was yellowed, the carpet so ingrained with dirt there was no visible pattern. For all her efforts, she might as well not have bothered to clean.

She dragged her tired legs into the living room and sank down on the couch, amidst a cloud of dust. She could even taste it on her lips. If she crunched her teeth, it was like chewing grit. A tear of self-pity rolled down her cheek. She wiped the moisture with the ends of her hair and tried to muffle a sob.

'You can't come with me,' said a voice beside her, 'because we meet at Island Gardens as her dad doesn't like her seeing boys.'

Daisy looked up, startled. Had Bobby really spoken to her in such a pleasant tone?

'But I can bring Grace here if you like,' he offered.

Daisy felt a warm glow inside her. Below Bobby's dirt-streaked cheeks and smudged blond hair and the splash of adolescent spots on his cheeks was an exceptionally good-looking youth. He towered over her now, lean and a little awkward yet his blue eyes looked on her fondly.

'Th … that would be nice,' she stammered.

'Just don't say anything that will embarrass me, right?'

'I won't,' she promised excitedly. Somewhere upstairs in the spare room, in a box, or perhaps in a cupboard were her best clothes. It wouldn't take long to find them.

CHAPTER 47

'HELLO DAISY, I haven't seen you since Cawdor.' Followed by Bobby, Grace stepped through the kitchen door and smiled. 'That's a pretty skirt you're wearing.'

Daisy thought Grace looked very pretty with her long dark hair brushed neatly over the collar of her winter's coat. Despite all Daisy's attempts to find a skirt or dress that wasn't creased, everything was either crumpled, dirty or too short. She'd realised then, because she had been living in trousers for goodness knew how long, that it wasn't only Bobby who'd grown. She had found very little to fit her and in desperation, had opted for a dark green skirt that Mother had lengthened though the original hem line still showed.

'Did you ever find your friend Sally?' Grace asked as she sat herself down on a kitchen chair. 'And that other boy - you know the one you told us about? The one who got in trouble with the Blackshirts?'

Daisy was about to answer, impressed that Grace had remembered Sally and Sammy, when Bobby said quickly, 'No, we haven't seen them.'

Undeterred, Grace dug into her pocket and brought out a small brown bag. 'Would you like a sweet?'

Daisy's gaze fell on the shiny black and white confectionary.

'Guess where I got them?' Grace asked.

Daisy shook her head.

'Iris and Sydney! Remember? Their dad had a confectioner's in Poplar?' Grace pushed the bag closer to Daisy. 'Did you know that a bomb fell on their shop? It was terrible. There were sweets and broken jars everywhere. All the cigarettes and cigars went up in smoke.' Grace giggled at her own joke. 'I must admit it's not very funny. But Iris and Sydney and their parents were safe as they had gone to the underground.' Grace shook the bag enticingly. 'These sweets are all chipped where the bomb exploded. See? Go on, try one.'

Daisy looked at Bobby who gave a brief nod.

'Thank you.' Daisy popped one on her tongue.

Grace smiled. 'Would you like to come up to Island Gardens with us?' she said, her tongue curling over her lips. 'There's an ack-ack station there now.'

Daisy was about to say she would like that very much when Bobby, standing behind Grace, shook his head.

So she managed to refuse politely, claiming she had chores to do about the house. It was the only long sentence she had uttered in Grace's company, and Bobby seemed to approve as the look of fright on his face turned to one of relief.

She watched them leave, their hands brushing slightly. When they were out of sight, Daisy curled herself on the couch and gave her full attention to enjoying the sweet.

To think, she actually had something in her mouth that had been blown up by a bomb!

That night there was no rest at all, for the Luftwaffe rained their lethal cargo on the docks without pause. Explosions erupted in such fierce succession that no conversation was possible, words lost in the roar of the aerial attack.

'Fortunately Wattcombe has not seen any more disasters,' Mother said, explaining her earlier telephone call. 'But the village seems to be directly under the path of the Luftwaffe who discharge the odd bomb or two on their way back across the Channel - '

An exceptionally loud explosion shook the kettle from its stand on the Primus. Then almost at once a deafening screech was followed by an earth-quaking roar.

Daisy was catapulted from her bunk to the floor and Bobby toppled beside her. As they lay there, shielding their heads with their hands, Daisy recalled Aunt Betty's story of the bombed-out family and her heart thudded violently.

Could it be that the shelter was next? Who would find their remains and tell Pops and Matt they were dead?

CHAPTER 48

DAISY SAT up and stretched her arms. At some point in the night she must have crawled back on her bunk and fallen asleep. She wriggled her frozen legs over the side and whispered into the darkness, 'Mother, Bobby?'

'I'm here,' Mother croaked. 'Stay where you are while I light a candle.'

Bobby moved on the upper bunk, unravelling himself slowly, his groans blurred with sleep.

'It was the worst night so far,' said Mother, as she lifted the candle and rose awkwardly from the armchair. 'Are you two all right?'

Daisy stood up, shaking out the dirt from the shelter ceiling that had fallen on to her. 'I thought we were going to die,' she whispered and Mother's arms went round her. Bobby joined them and they remained still, holding one another, unable to believe they'd survived.

When at last they emerged, a sulphur-smelling fog swept in.

'Don't breathe too deeply,' Mother instructed.

Daisy stepped over the rubble, until the fog cleared sufficiently to reveal the outline of the house. At first, it looked as though by some miracle, the building might have remained in tact. But as she pushed open the creaking kitchen door, a curling grey funnel of smoke billowed out. A scarlet flame leapt into the air and Mother grabbed her shoulder.

'An incendiary!' she shrieked, pulling Daisy away.

Almost in the same instant, a dozen other smaller flames ignited and the kitchen became a cauldron of heat.

The last thing Daisy remembered was Mother screaming, an instant before an almighty blast sent her flying. A pain seared across her forehead and lifted her off her feet. It was as if she had been swept up into an invisible force, propelling everything and everyone in its path into the foggy, evil-smelling air.

Daisy woke to the sound of a garbled echo which was somehow attached to a head that wobbled and weaved across her line of vision.

' 'Ello there, ducks,' said a vaguely familiar voice. 'You decided to open yer old mince pies, then?'

The blurry face was smiling and she recognised the dirty peaked cap. Mr Cook gave her a cheery wink. ' 'Ow do yer feel, kid?'

Daisy blinked and tried to move. 'My head hurts.'

'Too right it does,' agreed Mr Cook. 'You took a bit of a wallop.'

Daisy looked down at her feet poking up from under a cover. Apparently she was laying in the back of a large vehicle. 'Where am I?'

'In an ambulance on the way to 'orspital, kid.'

'Where's 'orspital?' asked Daisy trying to fathom what Mr Cook meant. 'Where's Bobby and Mother?'

'They're on their way to 'orspital too. Don't worry, you'll catch up with 'em soon.'

'Wh … what happened?' Daisy looked around at the grey blankets piled on the bench where Mr Cook was sitting. At the stretcher bracketed against the wall. And a strange looking gas mask attached to a long tube.

'Lay back, kid. You've got a massive lump on yer loaf.'

Daisy wanted to smile but instead she burst into tears. Mr Cook took a rag from his pocket and pressed it over her cheeks.

'Now, now, it's the shock, see.'

'I want Mother and Bobby,' she sobbed.

'Course you do. But first we've got to get you right. You took the full whack of the blast, see? Gawd knows how you survived. '

Through her tears, she began to recall the burning hole in what was once the kitchen floor, a great hungry mouth spiting flames.

If only Pops was here.

'Hello,' said a man wearing a white coat. 'I believe your name is Daisy Purbright, is that correct?'

Daisy nodded. 'Is this a hospital?'

'It is indeed. And I'm Dr Deacon.'

'Are Mother and Bobby here?'

'They're quite safe and have been taken elsewhere for treatment.'

'Are they all right?'

The doctor nodded. 'Just a few cuts and bruises, luckily.'

Daisy stifled a sob of relief. She knew something awful must have happened, but Mother and Bobby were safe and that was what mattered.

'Now,' said the doctor firmly. 'I'd like you to relax while Sister Thomas takes care of you.'

Before she could ask more, her head fell back on the pillow, seemingly of its own accord. From this position she watched the doctor leave and a nurse replace him.

'Hello, Daisy, I'm Sister Thomas.' The older woman with a rather severe expression raised an eyebrow.

Daisy attempted to speak, but any movement was far too painful.

'You'll be with us for a while,' continued the Sister. 'I've dressed you in a hospital gown. Your clothes will be put in a locker once you're in the children's ward and returned to you when you're discharged.'

Daisy peered at the long cotton robe that seemed to be covering most of her body. 'Can I get up?'

'Not yet. You have suffered a head wound and smaller abrasions caused by an incendiary bomb's blast. I'm afraid it's a case of bed rest for a while.'

'But Mother will be worried,' she protested as the Sister began to bathe her head.

'Just lay still, my dear.'

'Ouch!' Daisy yelped as the nurse seemed to be pulling at parts of her brain.

'You have small pieces of debris in your injury. It's important they're all removed before having stitches. '

Daisy clenched her hands together in an effort not to cry as the tiny splinters were removed from her head. With a great effort, she managed to grit her teeth and bear the pain that seemed to go on endlessly.

'All done,' said Sister Thomas at last as she discarded the instruments of torture and removed her apron. Daisy lay in silence as the Sister eyed her firmly. 'Dr Deacon examined you when you were admitted. Do you remember what he did?'

While resisting the painful sensation of tiny knife points attacking her scalp, Daisy tried to think back. A faint picture came to mind of someone's hands in front of her. 'He asked me how many fingers I could count. Then there was a bright light in my eyes.'

'Very good,' Sister Thomas praised. 'That means you have good recall - so far. Now, I'd like you to rest while I'm gone. I shall arrange a bed for you on the children's ward in time for supper. I expect you're hungry.'

Daisy was about to agree that she was - when she realized she wasn't. Her head hurt when she tried to speak. And she wanted to remember what had happened before she woke up in the ambulance with Mr Cook sitting beside her.

CHAPTER 49

'HOW ARE WE, THIS MORNING?' enquired a pretty young nurse with fair hair tucked under her cap.

'Is it morning?' Daisy asked as she found herself sitting in an unfamiliar bed.

'You were brought up to the children's ward yesterday. Don't you remember?'

Daisy rubbed the corners of her sleep-filled eyes. As everyone kept asking her if she remembered things, she thought it would be better to say that she did.

'Here, drink a little water.' The nurse helped her to sit up.

Daisy drank as if she hadn't tasted water in years.

'Little sips,' advised the nurse.

Daisy took a breath. 'Do you know where my mother and brother are?'

The nurse frowned. 'I've been told they are being well cared for and you are not to worry.' She took away the glass. 'I'd like to give you a top and tail before the doctor's rounds. Do you feel up to that?'

Daisy nodded, though she wanted to go back to sleep.

'My name is Nurse Gwen, by the way.'

Daisy didn't have to wait long before Nurse Gwen had tended to her injuries. 'You have only minor scratches and bruising. It was your head that took the impact.'

'I can't remember much.'

'You've been a very brave girl.' Nurse Gwen wrung out the flannel in the bowl on top of the cabinet. 'I promise to be gentle as I brush your hair.'

Despite trying to be brave Daisy shied away.

'I'm sorry,' apologised Nurse Gwen. 'This nasty head wound must be painful.'

Daisy was determined not to complain, though she missed Mother terribly.

'Well done,' the young nurse encouraged. 'I'll bring the commode.'

'What's a commode?'

Nurse Gwen chuckled. 'A chair with a po, more or less.'

'I'd rather go to a proper toilet.'

'We'll see what the doctor says after he's seen you. But for now, it's bed rest and the commode is easy to use.'

As Daisy lay there, she listened to the noises in the ward. A child was crying somewhere soothed by the consoling murmurs of an adult. Soft footsteps padded close by and the curtains blew very slightly as the nurses passed.

Daisy held back her tears.

When would she see Mother again? There were so many questions she wanted to ask, but there was no one to give her any answers.

Over the next few days, the prodding, poking, changing of dressings and general investigations of her injuries were exhausting. She heard other children around her, but their beds were often shielded by screens as the nurses and doctors came and went. Could she get out of bed and walk, she wondered? But as she moved, what felt like a huge marble rolled around in her head. And then, frustratingly, she would fall asleep.

'Good morning,' said Nurse Gwen one day and peered into her eyes, gently lifting one eyelid and then the other. 'After I've taken your pulse, we'll decide what you would like for lunch.' The nurse took her hand from under the sheet. 'We don't want you wasting away. You're only a wee thing.'

Daisy had been called many things before, but never a wee thing. 'Mother says my puppy fat won't disappear till I'm older.'

'Really? But there's not an inch of fat on you.'

Daisy looked down at the shape of her body under the hospital blanket. 'Where's all my puppy fat gone, then?'

Nurse Gwen chuckled. 'Let's just say, you have plenty of room for a good, solid meal. Today it's a stew. And a very nice one at that.'

Daisy had to agree that the beef broth was delicious. She finished every scrap, followed by a small portion of ice cream. But not long after she had settled down for an afternoon nap, the siren wailed.

'Oh dear, the warning is early today,' Nurse Gwen sighed and hurriedly hung her notes on the end of the bed. The ward Sister appeared through the swing doors, a small, grey-haired woman dressed in her deep blue uniform, who calmly gave all her nurses their orders.

'I'll help you to sit in this,' said Nurse Gwen as she wheeled up an ancient-looking chair to the side of Daisy's bed. 'An orderly will come and take you to the underground wards and I'll join you there.'

Daisy was cosseted in blankets and a pair of hospital slippers put on her feet. With a cushion propped behind her back, she was transported downstairs.

The sloping floor made access easy and along with many other patients in wheelchairs, on crutches and sticks and even in beds, the underground ward was soon filled with patients. The orderly, an older man with a small moustache, parked her at one end of the ward. Casualties of all shapes and sizes joined her until the ward was full to capacity.

Later, meals were served. 'Sit tight and I'll bring yer grub,' said an orderly. 'The nurse will be along soon.'

Daisy felt a churning in her stomach. She was alone and without the reassuring presence of Nurse Gwen. The noises in the underground ward grew louder. Patients called for attention as the orderlies delivered small trays bearing a slice of cold pie and a drink.

Daisy didn't have an appetite. Instead there was a dreadful feeling inside her, as if something terrible was about to happen.

When Nurse Gwen arrived she explained everyone would be safe during the attack. But when Daisy heard the first grumble of aircraft, she tried to get up from her wheelchair. She thought of the hole in the kitchen floor and the flames bursting upwards to lick at the ceiling. Most terrifyingly of all, was that invisible hand catching hold of her, propelling her into the air as though she was made of rags.

'Daisy!' Nurse Gwen was restraining her. 'You must stay seated.'

'No, no!' protested Daisy. 'The bomb will go off.'

'My dear, please calm yourself.' Nurse Gwen prevented her from standing. 'There's no bomb. Really. You are quite safe.'

'It will explode - '

'There are no bombs here,' the nurse assured her.

Daisy was unable to see anything but that great, dark void, with its scarlet flames leaping violently into the air. Her body shook and trembled. She had to escape before the blast that would surely come. Pulling away from the young nurse, she threw herself forward, knowing she had to escape from the fiery monster.

It was as she tried to push her way through the crowded room, that Daisy heard herself scream, just a few seconds before she fell.

CHAPTER 50

AUNT MINNIE'S PRETTY FACE, coiffured blonde hair and red lipstick, was slowly replaced by Aunt Betty's deep brown eyes and gentle smile.

'Daisy, darling … '

'We're here, right beside you,' breathed Aunt Minnie sending over her faint fragrance.

'Gardenia,' babbled Daisy, which drew a weepy sob from her aunt.

'Don't cry, Aunt Minnie.'

'Oh, my dear … ' Aunt Minnie turned away to hide her tears.

'Minnie, pull yourself together,' whispered Aunt Betty from close by.

'I can't help my emotions,' sobbed Aunt Minnie. 'Not everyone is as brave as you, Betty.'

'We mustn't upset her, Minnie. She's still very fragile.'

'Where's Mother?' Daisy attempted to focus on the two people at her bedside.

'Please wait outside,' came a command from Nurse Gwen

who replaced the twin visions of her aunts. 'Now, Daisy, do you feel well enough to sit up and have visitors?'

Daisy nodded, though as she did, her head hurt dreadfully. Holding on to Nurse Gwen, she found herself gently rearranged on the pillows as the cover was tucked firmly across her chest. A cool glass was placed on her parched lips.

'You know the drill by now,' said Nurse Gwen with a smile. 'A few sips at first.'

Daisy drank the reviving water and slipped her tongue around her dry mouth. 'I thought I saw my aunts,' she said.

'They've come to visit you, but you won't go trying to escape again, will you?'

Daisy looked around at the ward she had been returned to. There were no curtains now, but many children sitting or lying in their beds. 'I'm sorry,' she said quietly. 'I remembered the bomb. The one in our kitchen.'

'We call it a trigger,' the nurse explained. 'Your thoughts go back to the time when the bomb exploded. Not unusual after such a shock. Luckily an orderly was there to catch you when you fainted and no harm was done.'

'I can't really remember.'

'Do you feel well enough to speak to your aunts?'

Daisy managed a tiny nod.

'Afterwards your tea will be ready. We must start to build you up.'

Daisy hoped that corned beef and bread wasn't on the menu.

The sight of her aunts was almost more than she could bear. 'Aunt Betty, Aunt Minnie!' she mumbled.

'Oh, darling, what's hidden under that huge bandage on your head?' Aunt Minnie's voice crackled with emotion. 'Are you in pain?'

'No,' Daisy fibbed, trying to smile. She didn't want Aunt Minnie to be upset.

'We've been so worried about you.' Aunt Minnie gave another choked sob.

'Mr Cook told us it was an incendiary,' said Aunt Betty. 'The force of it threw you forward.'

'I had stitches after they got bits out of my head.' Daisy blinked back her tears. 'But I'm all right now.'

Aunt Betty hesitated. 'Your Mother and Bobby are in hospital too. There was no room here, you see.'

'Do they have bits in them too?'

'Nothing for you to worry about,' said Aunt Minnie. 'But like you, they were very shocked. We're going to visit them later. Do you remember what happened?'

'Mother pushed us out of the kitchen.' Daisy frowned, trying to recall. 'I think I felt the bomb go off and it pushed me through the air. Now I keep forgetting things.'

'Quite normal so the doctor says,' reassured Aunt Betty. 'Your memory will come back with time.'

'I hope so.'

'You were all so lucky to escape,' consoled Aunt Minnie. 'But Mr Cook tells us that the house is unstable.'

'Won't we be able to live there again?'

'Well, not for a while.'

'But where will we go?' Daisy asked tearfully.

Aunt Minnie squeezed her hand. 'You'll come to us, of course.'

'I'm afraid time is up,' said Nurse Gwen, firmly pulling the screen around Daisy's bed.

'We'll visit again soon,' promised Aunt Betty.

Daisy watched as Nurse Gwen whisked her aunts away.

When they were gone, rather than reassured, she felt abandoned. All she wanted was to go home. But did she have a home to go to? It wouldn't be a home anyway, without Mother and Bobby.

CHAPTER 51

'London saw its worst night of bombing yet,' Nurse Gwen revealed as she brought Daisy's medicine. 'Our dear St Paul's was hit. An unexploded bomb was removed from its roof, but it still stood up to the attack and people will be able to use it again, just like you'll be able to go home to your house.'

'I hope so,' Daisy said, accepting her pills and dutifully swallowing.

'Cheer up, Daisy dear,' encouraged the nurse. 'Most people feel down in the dumps after a stay in hospital. You'll soon have your happy spirits back.'

Just then, the wail of the siren echoed throughout the hospital and all the nursing staff went into action. Daisy twisted her fingers together anxiously. She didn't want to hear those planes flying over. Or listen to their deadly drone.

She tried to stay calm and think of her bedroom at home and of the many times she had gazed from her window to the towering cranes and workman-like tugs and proud ships sailing by on the river in a kind of regal procession. And of Greenwich and its glistening dome when the sunlight played on its roof like diamond splinters.

Would she ever see these beloved sights again?

~

And so the blitz, as it became known, continued. When the raiders returned at dusk or sometimes even earlier, they caused a mass evacuation from the upper hospital floors to the safety of the underground levels below.

It was five long days after Daisy had been admitted to the East London Hospital, that during one attack, Nurse Gwen failed to appear.

'Gwen's not on duty today,' said a female orderly as she pushed Daisy into the underground ward.

Daisy began to tremble as the thuds of the bombs came closer. 'Please stay with me,' she asked the orderly.

'I have others to attend to, dear,' the woman said hurriedly. 'Try to be brave and sit quietly.'

Daisy knew there were others who were more in need of attention than her, but she was terrified of the muffled drone of the bombers coming closer and the pounding of the ack-ack guns below. She wanted to run away, but where was there to hide?

For the first time since the incendiary had exploded, she found herself quite alone. 'H … help,' she called. 'Please help me, someone.' But no one came and when she tried to stand, she fell over.

~

Daisy woke to the sensation of being lifted into someone's arms. The person was cradling her and she clung tightly to the stranger's shoulders as his rhythmic steps strode purposely forward.

The long walk to wherever it was they were going, was

accompanied by the sounds of the Luftwaffe's attack and the slightly raspy breath of her bearer. Daisy buried her head in his chest and wondered if she was being flown to heaven. Had she died? Could this be a real angel?

When her bearer laid her down on a bed and covered her gently with a blanket, she reached out to grasp his wrist. 'Am I in heaven?'

The face, like Mr Cook's in the ambulance, bobbed and weaved from side to side. 'You won't die, Daisy. I'll make sure of that.'

Daisy smiled. 'I know who you are. You're my guardian angel.'

A quiet, yet husky breath came as her answer. Strangely, amidst the howls and snarls of the planes above and the pounding that shivered its way through the hospital's foundations, she felt safe. Now she was certain she was being watched over by her very own angel who on this day, had taken her into his care.

An angel, she fancied, whose deep, dark eyes and cloud of raven black hair haloed his gentle face.

CHAPTER 52

'WELL, MY GIRL.' Dr Deacon adjusted the stethoscope around his neck, his examination complete. 'I'm relieved to say, you are on the mend.'

Daisy couldn't remember being asleep for that long. 'What happened to me?'

'You ran a high temperature and fell into a delirium.'

'What does delirium mean?'

'It's a condition that may last for a few days, weeks or even months. A person can have vivid thoughts or sometimes see things that aren't there.'

'I did have a dream,' Daisy agreed. 'But it was real.'

Dr Deacon looked amused. 'That's very interesting. What was your dream about?'

'An angel who's going to look after me.'

'Well then, I'm sure you're in good hands.'

Even though the doctor was smiling, she suspected he didn't believe her.

'It's quite understandable that you're a little confused,' he added, confirming Daisy's suspicions. 'You've had a shock and suffered a serious wound. Your dreams are a result of this experience. Now, do you think you're up to having your stitches removed tomorrow?'

Daisy didn't like the idea at all, but thought it wise not to complain.

'That's settled, then,' said Dr Deacon without waiting for her reply. 'I shall see you in the morning.'

When Nurse Gwen appeared at her bedside, Daisy wanted to hug her. 'I missed you,' she croaked.

'And I missed you, Daisy dear. But my shifts were changed.'

'The doctor said I've been asleep for three days.'

'That's true.'

'Are you going to be on duty tonight?'

'Yes, so don't worry.' Nurse Gwen arranged the sheet gently around her. 'I shall be with you. Now, what about something nice to eat? After all, three days without food is a very long time.'

Daisy smiled. She was beginning to feel hungry. 'How long will it be before I'm better?'

'One step at a time, Daisy, dear,' Nurse Gwen advised. 'Once Dr Deacon is satisfied with your progress, we'll have you discharged in no time at all.'

Daisy knew Nurse Gwen was trying not to alarm her. Just as Bobby once explained that it was what all grown-ups did when they wanted to hide the truth.

As the days passed, Nurse Gwen did her best to be with Daisy when the warning siren went. But her shifts often changed or there would be some emergency and Daisy would try to walk a few paces on her own, but then, exhausted and dizzy, she'd flop down in her chair. What was wrong with her? After having her stitches removed she thought she would be back to normal again. But instead she had gained an unsightly scar and lost all her energy.

'Patience,' the doctor had told her.

'You're doing very well,' Aunt Betty had said.

But Daisy was beginning to think she would never get her "sea legs" back.

So when the bombs dropped and the dust rained down from the ceiling, she thought of her angel and prayed he would stay close.

Each day she hoped that Mother and Bobby would visit, but it was Aunt Betty who called by on Wednesdays and Saturdays, keeping Daisy informed of all that had happened in the outside world.

One day, Aunt Betty was late and Daisy felt the old fear return. What if her aunt had been caught in an air raid? Had she been blown off her bike? Was something wrong with Mother and Bobby that no one had told her about?

At visiting hour, in poured the smiling faces and eager footsteps of friends and family, but there was no Aunt Betty. Daisy knew time was limited before the raids began.

Some brought gifts for their children, in particular, small paper bags with twisted corners and mouth-watering shapes inside.

Daisy felt her wound throb. Like a miniature railway track, the scar ran down from her hairline. She touched the tender bumps and her palms grew damp with fear.

A pounding began in her head. Was this another spasm?

'Daisy?' someone said. 'Daisy, it's me.'

A tall figure hovered over her. The man removed his hat and out fell a bunch of untidy curls. Below the unruly blond mop were two very blue eyes.

Strong arms tightened round her, along with a smell she would never forget. Inhaling the damp gabardine and cigarettes of the coat, Daisy shed tears of joy.

CHAPTER 53

'POPS, IS IT REALLY YOU?' she whispered as he hugged her. She hung on so fiercely that he had to prize her away.

'Hey, what's all this, treasure?' His deep, calm voice made her feel as though they had never spent a day apart.

She grasped his fingers with all the strength she had. 'Have you come to take me home?'

'Oh, Daisy, where has my brave girl gone?' He sat on the chair beside the bed and looked into her eyes.

'I'm not brave, Pops,' Daisy insisted, still terrified by the thought he would leave her again. 'I just pretended to be. Instead, I'm frightened all the time.'

'You've come back from a very dark place; it's quite normal to be frightened. If a bomb had exploded close to me, I would be frightened too.'

'I missed you,' she mumbled. 'But I know you had something important to do.'

'Ah, how hearing you say that hurts even more,' he sighed and Daisy saw the pain in his face. A face which was, now she studied him, much thinner and paler than before.

'You are the bravest girl in the world,' he continued,

returning the pressure of her fingers. 'I'm proud of you. You've been in your very own war. If it doesn't upset you, tell me what happened.'

It was as if a dam had burst as the words gushed out; how she and Mother and Bobby had slept every night in the shelter and tried to keep the house and themselves clean and how she hated to return to the dark and cramped space that they had tried to make homely for their nightly vigils. And how on that day in October, they had left the shelter one morning and returned to the house where in the kitchen, a terrible event awaited them.

'If only I'd been with you,' Pops groaned. 'Can you imagine how badly I feel, not being there to protect my family?'

'What you do is important.'

'But not nearly as important as you.'

'I had stitches in my head,' Daisy elaborated, 'and then I went to sleep.'

'So the nurse told me. But like Sleeping Beauty, you woke, thank heavens. Now let me see, what's this?' Pops dug into his pocket and brought out a paper bag.

Daisy gasped 'Saturday Assortment!'

'I know how much you like them.'

Daisy put the bag on her locker. She didn't want sweets. She only wanted to hold tightly to Pops.

'I saw Mother and Bobby this morning at Aunt Minnie's,' he told her. 'They have been discharged from hospital and are missing you dreadfully. Here is a letter from Mother.'

'I'll read it after you've gone.' She placed the envelope by her sweets. 'When can we go home to Poplar Park Row?'

'That, Daisy, is a question I can't answer. I've not been back to see our house, but I understand Mr Cook thinks the damage is extensive.'

'Like our old house in Wattcombe, you mean?'

He frowned. 'Why do you ask that?'

'Bobby and me went there. Oh, Pops, will we never have a home of our own?'

He touched her cheek. 'Of course we will. But this is wartime and we must all do the best we can.' He saw the disappointment in her eyes and said mysteriously, 'Can you keep a secret?'

Daisy wanted to say that she had kept many secrets but decided against it.

'You see ... ' he hesitated and lowered his voice. 'You remember our happy days in the laboratory?'

Daisy nodded, this time smiling at the memory.

'Well, Uncle Ed and I invented something there that will help us to fight and win this war.'

Daisy's eyes flew wide. 'What is it?'

'You won't understand exactly, but the country's secret weapon is to be powered by valves, to be precise, thermionic valves of the type we created in our lab at the factory.' He placed a finger to his lips. 'Uncle Ed and I are using our highly accurate electrical apparatus to aid something - well, something very special.'

'Pops, you're so clever.'

'No, treasure. There are lots of people much cleverer.'

'Are these people in Milton Keynes, too?'

Pops sat upright. 'What makes you ask that?'

'Aunt Betty discovered it,' Daisy whispered. 'There was a code in Uncle Ed's letter.'

Pops looked astonished. 'You must never tell anyone, not a soul. Do you understand now why I have to work away?'

Daisy nodded and would have nodded harder but her head hurt with every move.

'We all have to do our part in keeping our country safe.' He tenderly traced his fingertips over the bumpy scar on her forehead. 'This wound is your badge of honour, Daisy. Be proud to wear it.'

Once again she was in his arms until Nurse Gwen appeared and told them it was time to part.

That evening, Daisy walked unaided to the underground ward. Although she trembled and stumbled several times, she wore her badge of honour proudly. When she was given a place to rest, she opened Mother's letter. Though it was short, her words of love and affection filled Daisy with hope. Bobby had signed with kisses too and Will had scrawled his initials, hidden under a large blob of ink. Although Daisy missed her family dearly, she remembered Pops's words. From now on, she would be brave, and, even when the planes flew over.

CHAPTER 54

SEVERAL DAYS LATER, a letter from Matt arrived. A few lines to tell her how sorry he was to hear of her injuries. He explained he had earned his wings and that he'd visited Amelia who had evacuated with her family to Swansea in Wales. After scrawling numerous kisses, he added a post script.

"I've put in for special leave for early next year, so that Amelia and I can travel to London to be with you. Keep it under your hat, but there's a surprise in store! Now get well and chin up, little sister!"

'You're very lucky,' said Nurse Gwen when Daisy showed her the letter. 'I haven't got a brother, but if I did, I would want one just like yours.'

'I wonder if the surprise is they're getting married?' wondered Daisy. 'I'd like to be a bridesmaid.'

'What a romantic occasion,' sighed Nurse Gwen wistfully.

'I hope the blitz is over by then.'

Nurse Gwen's expression saddened. 'Our boys in the air are brave but it's just as hard for those left at home. Still, Matt has a special reason to stay safe - to visit his little sister.'

'I can hardly wait,' Daisy said from where she sat on her chair beside the bed. 'How long will I be in hospital?'

'Patience is a virtue they say,' smiled the young woman. 'After a serious injury like yours, your recuperation may take time.'

'What does rec - recop - '

'Recuperation means getting better. Even if your body is almost back to being its old self, your mind may be slower in catching up. When patients fall into delirium, we have to monitor them closely for some time afterwards.'

'Will I have a delirium again?'

'There's no reason why you should.' Nurse Gwen squeezed her hand. 'We're going to see to it that you're as fit as a flea when you leave us. Though I'm not certain whether fleas are fit at all. But they certainly jump about.'

Daisy giggled. If there was one person she would miss from hospital, it was her dear friend Nurse Gwen who always brought a smile to her lips.

To while away the long hours, Daisy escaped to the rest room where she joined several others who sat quietly in the comfortable chairs. From this vantage point she could see through the glass door to the window of her ward opposite. Some patients read newspapers or books piled on the table and some discussed the nightly raids and the worry they had for their families. Daisy too worried about Mother and Bobby. Pops was probably the safest of them all, hidden away in a very secret place. She tried to remember the name of his invention which sounded a bit like thermometer. But if she concentrated too hard, her head began to hurt. It was difficult even, to read a book. Her concentration wandered and it was easier just to sit and listen to the hum of conversation.

Just then, in burst a mischievous looking little boy of about six or seven, a newcomer to the children's ward. He had a cheeky smile and a mop of untidy black hair. His legs were extremely bowed and one of them was bandaged up. Daisy recognized him as a recent addition to the children's ward.

The selection of newspapers on the small table caught his eye and very soon, despite the adults' protests, they were strewn over the floor in complete disarray. One by one the patients departed and Daisy was left alone with the troublemaker.

'See how strong I am?' he said to Daisy as he trampled on a newspaper.

Daisy couldn't resist a giggle. 'Yes, you are strong. And what a mess!'

'I ain't gonna pick 'em up either.'

'Nor am I,' replied Daisy with a shrug. 'I think they look better on the floor.'

He came and sat beside her. 'Ain't you gonna bash me?'

'Why should I?'

'Me brover does.'

'How old is your brother?'

'Dunno. But he's bigger than you.'

'I'm not very big.'

The little boy laughed. 'Girls are daft.'

Daisy laughed too. 'They are sometimes.'

'You've got a bash on the 'ead, ain't you?'

Daisy nodded. 'Yes, but the doctors and nurses are making it better. Just like they'll make your leg better too.'

'Me mum says I might die.'

'I'm sure you won't.' Daisy felt very sorry for the child. If what he said was to be believed, he had a very unsympathetic family.

'She says lots of people die in the 'ospital. But you ain't died yet, have you?'

Daisy tried to keep a straight face. 'No, I'm still quite alive.'

'You talk funny too.'

Before Daisy could reply the door flew open. 'Tommy, what are you doing in here?' a nurse demanded. 'You've been told to stay in your bed.'

'We were just talking,' Daisy said and began to pick up the newspapers. 'Tommy was helping me to tidy up.'

The nurse looked doubtfully at Daisy, then marched Tommy off. Daisy restored order to the room, folding the newspapers into a neat pile on the table. Eventually she returned to the ward, where Tommy was sitting in his bed, sulking, as the nurse hovered close by.

The following afternoon, Daisy saw Tommy wriggle from his bed and try to escape once more. Some of the other children called a warning and one of the nurses sped after him. Daisy smiled, expecting Tommy to be captured as he had been the previous day.

Unexpectedly, a loud bellow echoed from the corridor. Very soon Tommy appeared, weeping and scarlet-cheeked. A tall, sturdily-built woman grasped him by his ear and dragged him along.

Daisy gasped when she recognised Tommy's mother. Mrs Brady - Peter Brady's mother - hoisted her young son on his bed and slapped his bottom.

The agonized cry brought Sister hurrying along, but Tommy's mother was in no mood to listen. Daisy recalled a similar scene at school when Mrs Brady had sent Mr Potter flying and how Mr Gulliver had ordered the class into the assembly hall for the rest of the lesson.

'Mrs Brady!' barked Dr Deacon as he strode into the ward. 'Please come to my office.'

Moments later, the screen was drawn around a distraught Tommy and the ward returned to a peaceful calm once more.

When Nurse Gwen came on duty, Daisy asked how her little friend was.

'I shouldn't say but Tommy needs an operation,' Nurse Gwen told her confidentially. 'Malnourishment has caused his bone disease, leaving him with a deformed leg.'

'Will his leg get better?'

'Yes, if he has his operation. But there's very little we can do without the parents' cooperation. They seem to think he's just seeking attention.'

Though Daisy didn't reveal what she knew of the Bradys, her heart went out to poor little Tommy. She knew how difficult life must be for him.

CHAPTER 55

AUNT BETTY breathlessly adjusted her WVS beret and sighed. 'I'm sorry I'm late. There's no buses today because of last night's raid. So I rode my bike but Aldgate was strewn with debris and I've managed to get a puncture ... '

Daisy felt guilty for putting her aunt to so much trouble. 'I have some good news,' Aunt Betty continued. 'Your mother has written to Aunt Pat and arranged for you to stay at Grandma's when you're discharged. Wattcombe will be much safer than here in the East End.'

This came as a shock to Daisy and it was a minute or two before she found her voice. 'But Matt's coming home. He wrote and told me so. I couldn't bear it if we weren't all together.'

'I'm sorry, my dear,' Aunt Betty shrugged. 'But Uncle Leo's studio isn't practical. Your mother is doing her best to arrange things to suit everyone; a particularly difficult job in wartime.'

'Perhaps Grandma and Aunt Pat could come to London instead?'

Aunt Betty shook her head wearily. 'I'm afraid it's just not safe during the blitz - ' Tommy's loud scream interrupted her and Daisy peeked through the gap in the curtained screen. A frightening figure stood at Tommy's bedside. Taller now and broad-shouldered with his head shaven, Peter Brady looked more menacing than ever.

Daisy could barely breathe let alone talk so she climbed into bed hoping fervently that visiting time would soon be over.

'Time for me to leave.' Aunt Betty kissed her cheek. 'I'll see you tomorrow.'

When Daisy eventually had the courage to peer above the covers, she was relieved to see that Peter had gone, but Aunt Betty hadn't. Through the window overlooking the corridor Daisy could see her aunt talking to a man wearing a raincoat. He suddenly caught hold of her shoulder. Aunt Betty's face was white as she tried to step away.

Daisy gasped.

It was Mr Calder.

Dr Deacon jerked an eyebrow. 'How are we this morning?'

'I had a bad dream last night.'

'And what was in this dream?'

'A man. He was very tall and wore a mackintosh. He was chasing Aunt - no, he was chasing me and I tried to get away from him. But there was a bomb. I couldn't see it. And it exploded.' Daisy shuddered at the thought of Mr Calder and the way he had frightened Aunt Betty.

The doctor stroked his chin. 'Vivid dreams and confusion are quite normal under the circumstances. But they can be very frightening. All the same, I'll check you over.'

For once, Daisy didn't mind being examined. Dr Deacon's presence was comforting.

'Now then, my dear, you mustn't fret,' he assured her when the examination was over. 'As far as I can tell, you are suffering from lack of sleep, but no more.'

'Can I go home?'

The doctor chuckled. 'We'll see.'

After the doctor had gone Daisy looked over at Tommy. He was snuggled down under the covers and very quiet. Had Peter upset him as much as Mr Calder had upset her? Had Aunt Betty managed to escape from Mr Calder?

Each day after that, Daisy watched for the tall figure dressed in a mackintosh. When her aunt next came, she arrived just before visiting time.

'Aunt Betty,' Daisy burst out. 'You're early!'

'I can't stay long.' She glanced over her shoulder.

Daisy looked too. She was relieved to see the corridor was empty. 'Are you all right, Aunt Betty?'

Her aunt tried to smile. 'I'm a little tired, that's all. Everyone is at the moment, with these continuous raids.' She put a shaky hand to her cheek. 'I've come with good news, Daisy. Your mother has telephoned the doctor and asked him to discharge you. I think he'll agree as beds in the hospital are scarce.'

'Can I leave today?' Daisy asked eagerly.

'If all goes well, Mr Cook will collect you tomorrow.'

'Do you promise?'

Aunt Betty nodded. 'I won't be with him as there are only two seats in his van. Now, I really must leave.'

Daisy glanced through the window again. 'Aunt Betty, be careful won't you?'

Her aunt smiled gently. 'Don't worry, I'm quite an expert at cycling through the traffic.'

That wasn't what Daisy meant, but her aunt stood up and Daisy stretched out her arms. 'I love you, Aunt Betty.'

'And I love you, darling,' Aunt Betty whispered as they hugged. 'We've all missed you so much.'

Daisy watched as her aunt left the ward. Quickly she put on her slippers and ran to the door. Aunt Betty was hurrying down the passage. To Daisy's relief, there was no sign of Mr Calder.

That evening, as usual, Daisy joined the queues to the lower ward - she hoped - for the last time. Tomorrow she would be going home. Even the dull drone of the bombers over London didn't sound so menacing now that she knew she would be with Mother and Bobby soon.

She thought of Bobby and his dream to join Matt in the airforce. Was Matt at this very minute, flying one of those planes above the city, weaving in and out of the searchlight beams, seeking out the enemy aircraft? She had always thought of her older brother as indestructible. Now she feared he was in jeopardy, fighting for his country up there in the searchlight strafed skies.

She slept very lightly again and was thankful that Mr Calder hadn't appeared in her dreams. When next morning she returned to the ward the sight that met her eyes was shocking. A very subdued Tommy was being wheeled away on a trolley.

'Is Tommy having his operation?' she asked Nurse Gwen.

'Yes,' her friend replied. 'It's his big day.'

'Will they cure his leg?'

'Let's hope so.'

Daisy's eyes filled with tears.

'There, there,' said Nurse Gwen and slid an arm around her shoulders. 'I know you've grown fond of him. But this is wartime, Daisy. Many people will come and go in your life.'

Daisy knew she would miss Nurse Gwen too. 'Will you be here when Mr Cook comes?'

'Perhaps,' Nurse Gwen replied. 'I'll do my best to see you off. Now, breakfast is coming. You'll feel better once you've eaten.'

Daisy sat in her chair where she ate her porridge, but she didn't feel better. She couldn't stop thinking of Tommy. Would he get better? She put on the clothes she had stored in her locker, then sat in her chair.

She must have dozed as she opened her eyes to see Mr Cook beside her.

'Hello youngster,' he said apologetically. 'Sorry, but I can't take you. The roads are in a terrible mess. I'll try again tomorrow.'

'You will come for me, won't you?' Daisy panicked. Would she ever get away from this hospital?

'I'll do me best, don't you worry.'

That night Daisy joined the long queues to the underground level, a place she had hoped never to see again.

~

When she returned to the children's ward the next morning, Tommy's hadn't returned.

'Where's Tommy?' she asked the nurse.

'I'm afraid it's sad news.'

'Didn't he have his operation?'

'No more questions now. I understand you're leaving today. Get dressed and sit in your chair until someone comes for you.'

Once more Daisy put on her coat and studied her knees, peeking out beneath her hem. They looked very white and wrinkly as though they'd been soaked in water. What had happened to Tommy she wondered yet again? She wished Nurse Gwen was here to ask.

Slowly she gathered her letters from Matt and Mother and tucked them in her pocket. Breakfast came and went and so did the midday meal. She sat waiting again, wishing Nurse Gwen was on duty and wondering if Mr Cook would arrive.

'Hello,' said a female orderly at last. 'I've instructions to wheel you downstairs.'

'Has Mr Cook arrived?'

'All I've been told is to take you downstairs. Now sit in, dear, I haven't got all day.'

Daisy reluctantly sat in the wheelchair. She was looking forward to walking and using her legs. The orderly sped off at a rate of knots and finally they arrived at the entrance.

Daisy searched the crowds for Mr Cook. Streams of wounded and sick passed by, but with no sign of the person she was looking for.

'We've waited long enough,' the woman decided. 'I've other patients to see to.'

'Please let's stay a bit longer,' Daisy entreated. 'Mr Cook promised he'd come today.'

'Then you'll have to wait on your own,' snapped the orderly. 'If he arrives, make sure you return this chair to the porter before you leave. If you're still here when I come back, I'll take you back to the ward.'

Daisy found herself waiting alone amidst the milling crowds. She searched all the faces once more, hoping to see Mr Cook and feeling desperate when she didn't. What could have happened? Were the roads impassable again?

'Can't 'ave you 'anging around wiv' all these germs,' said a voice behind her. 'A bit of fresh air'd do you good.'

The wheelchair spun in the opposite direction. Daisy clutched its arms. Where was she being taken and by whom?

She recognised the voice. It certainly wasn't Mr Cook.

No, it was Peter Brady.

CHAPTER 56

'STOP, PLEASE STOP!' Daisy yelped as the wheelchair flew along. She tried to attract the attention of a porter as they passed, but he was too concerned with directing the flow of human traffic.

'No one's gonna hear you,' threatened Peter as he swerved to miss an elderly lady leaning on a cane. 'Everyone's out for 'emselves after last night. Who's gonna bovver about a pasty-looking kid like you?'

'Where are you taking me?' Daisy spluttered, wondering if she could reach down to stop the wheels somehow. But they were going too fast.

'You look like you ain't had a breath of air in ages. I'm gonna put roses in yer cheeks.'

Daisy felt the force of Peter's rough actions as he swerved the chair this way and that until they finally came to a door marked, "Exit Only." He pushed her into the silence of a long, dark passage.

Eventually they stopped at a set of iron gates. Peter stabbed his thumb on a button and they lurched into the empty space beyond. As the doors clanged closed behind them, the creaking lift ascended higher.

'Please take me down, Peter,' she begged, a request which only drew a contemptuous laugh.

He shoved his face into hers. 'I'll take yer down all right. The quick way.'

Daisy had never looked into such cold eyes. He leaned closer and pressed his coarse, unshaven chin against her cheek and whispered, 'Think I didn't see you, Miss Hoity-Toity? Think I didn't know you was hiding in yer bed, a mouse in its hole, all shivery and shaky, while I was over with me brother? Well, he never amounted to much. I'm glad to be rid of him.'

Daisy gasped. 'What do you mean?'

'Runt of the litter he was. Even me mum didn't shed a tear when he copped it.'

'You mean - you mean he died?'

'Good riddance that's what I say.'

Tears filled Daisy's eyes. 'That's a dreadful thing to say. He was a nice little boy,' she whispered fearfully. 'He couldn't help his bad leg.'

'He was a weakling,' Peter shouted, pushing his face into hers. 'An embarrassment to the Brady's. Me dad was gonna kick him out anyway.'

Daisy closed her eyes as they flew along. How could he say such terrible things? Poor little Tommy. He was a mischief but a loveable one. He didn't deserve a family like the Brady's.

A gust of cold air whipped her face as they arrived on to the hospital roof. She gulped at the breathtaking view. A thick, cloying fog accentuated the late afternoon dusk that veiled the blitzed London landscape. Wisps of smoke curled into the heavy clouds above and filled the air with a choking heaviness.

So this was what the city looked like after almost three months of continual bombing! She felt as though she had been asleep and woken up just as Pops had said, like Sleeping Beauty. Only the sight before her was not a scene from a fairy tale, more likely one of hell where people's homes and possessions resembled piles of charred debris and fountains of water erupting randomly from the severed water mains. Electricity cables lay entangled over the rubble like gigantic spiders webs while pavements erupted like treacherous volcanoes. Armies of bulldozers and tractors manoeuvred the broken, steaming earth into jagged hillocks of waste while telegraph poles were strewn like matches that had fallen from their box. A momentary burst of scarlet flame reminded Daisy of the fiery hole in the kitchen and she shrank away from the poisonous view.

'I'm gonna take you right up close for a better view,' Peter tormented, manoeuvring the chair slowly across the uneven, windswept roof.

Daisy screamed. The chair grew closer to the edge of the roof. As the breeze blew her scream away, she could hear Peter laughing. In that terrible moment she understood exactly what he was about to do. Poor Tommy. Had Peter tormented him in the very same way? Now it was her turn. And there was nothing she could do.

'Turn yer nose up at me, would yer?' Peter demanded. 'You think yer better than me with yer posh talk and stuck up airs and graces? Liked lording it over the other kids, did yer? Well, I've never forgotten the day you tried it on with me. I'd 'ave got you back for them scratches you give me if it hadn't been for that old cow making an appearance. Had you bang ter rights at the toilets an' all. I was clever. Made sure no one would've seen me - just like no one will see me now.' He tilted the chair into the wind and Daisy felt her legs go to jelly as the East End spread around them, crushed, battered and bruised. Even from this height she could hear the noises below; ambulances, fire engine bells, the mechanical grunts and groans of recovery vehicles. People in distress and despair as they fought their way out of a crippled world.

'One good push,' Peter growled into her ear, 'that's all it'll take.'

'Peter, please don't,' she begged. 'I didn't mean to scratch you. But Bobby - '

Peter gave a howl of fury. 'Bobby bleedin' Purbright! I should've done 'im in when I had me chance. But it ain't too late, cos I'm starting wiv his sister.'

Daisy was frozen with terror. She stared at the edge of the roof as if hypnotised. One good push and it would all be over. How long would it take for her to reach the ground? How painful would it be when she did? A strangled sob lodged in her throat.

'You ain't starting nothin', chum,' said a voice suddenly. 'Unless it's a stretch at the Scrubs.'

Daisy blinked away the tears that were swimming in her eyes. Who had said that? Was someone else up here too? Was the voice in her imagination? She wanted to look round, but she was too afraid to move.

'Who the 'ell are you?' shouted Peter.

'A friend of the kid, that's who. Now step aside from the chair.'

Daisy knew any movement might send the wheels forward but very slowly she managed to crane her head round.

Peter was backing away across the roof, his mouth open and his eyes wide. Mr Cook was following, fists clenched.

'You're just an old codger,' Peter taunted. 'This ain't none of yer business.'

'You'd be surprised what this old codger can still do,' Mr Cook threatened. 'Besides, meet my chum here. Think you might know him.'

Another figure joined Mr Cook and Daisy gasped as she recognised Sammy Berger. Bobby's friend had grown into a tall and muscular young man, equalling Peter in stature. He wore a brown orderly's coat and Daisy realised he must be one of the hospital staff.

'Remember me?' Sammy said threateningly. 'I've been waiting for a day like this ... '

'So now you know,' muttered Mr Cook, tugging his cap down with force. 'And when the coppers arrive, I'm gonna enjoy watching them nick you.'

'You've got nothin' on me,' blurted Peter and Daisy saw the colour drain from his face. He stumbled two shaky steps backwards, his eyes searching for escape. 'Keep yer distance, Fritz! Or I'll - I'll - '

'You'll what?' challenged Sammy as the breeze caught his dark hair. 'I've learned how to take care of myself. You're just a gutless coward without your pals around you.'

Mr Cook nodded. 'My money's on Sammy, here,' he grinned. 'I reckon he's got a score to settle before the law arrives, which if I'm any judge, should be in the next few minutes.'

'You don't scare me,' croaked Peter. 'Yer bluffin'.'

'Have it your way, son,' shrugged Mr Cook. 'But I warn you, the East End's crawling with rozzers after last night's rumpus. So I decided to give the authorities a bit of a prod and left word at the desk that a fifth columnist was spotted up on the roof.'

'I ain't no fifth columnist,' roared Peter, tripping over his own feet in an effort to run. 'You're bonkers.'

'No, chum,' glowered the older man. 'I've got me head screwed on just where it should be. We all know what happens to traitors like you.'

Peter glared at them, then bolted.

'Let him go, mate,' said Mr Cook as he grabbed Sammy's arm. 'We've done our bit. Let's get this young 'un to safety.'

Daisy held her breath as Sammy took the handles of the wheelchair and guided it to safety. She was shaking so much that when she looked up at her rescuer, intending to thank him, she gave a limp squeak instead.

CHAPTER 57

SHE HELD FAST to Sammy's hand as they made their exit by way of the clanking old lift she had last occupied with Peter Brady. Now however, it was descending and she was in the company of friends who had her complete trust.

Once on the ground floor, they made their way slowly towards the busy entrance, allowing Daisy time to regain her breath before exiting the main doors.

The poisonous air outside was barely breathable, a stark contrast to the cleansed hospital atmosphere and Daisy struggled for a few seconds. The sights and sounds of mass destruction almost overwhelmed her. Sammy urged her forward and she clung to him, grateful for his strength.

They slowly but successfully navigated the broken hospital steps, before stopping by the battered light-coloured Morris van parked at the curb. Mr Cook started the engine and the fierce vibration caused a flurry of scorched paper fragments to fly up from the windscreen.

Sammy opened the door and helped her inside. A tool box rested at her feet, together with a sack of potatoes propped against the wheel-arch. Closing the door firmly, he met her gaze and she wished there'd been time to ask where he lived and what had become of his father. Instead she made do with waving furiously from the window, mouthing her "thank you" as best she could.

His tall figure receded into the grey, swirling smoke and eventually he was gone. Vanished like a shadow in one of her dreams.

'That boy's a good 'un,' said Mr Cook as the van rattled into action. 'Never laid eyes on him before, not till I asked for you at the desk. He was standing close by and must've heard me. When the lady said she'd seen someone pushing a wheelchair out the exit to the roof, we didn't waste no time coming after you.'

Daisy wanted to pinch herself. Could all that had happened today be true? Had Peter Brady really intended to kill her?

'Are the police really going to arrest the five - the fifth - '

'Fifth columnists?' chuckled Mr Cook. 'I told a bit of a porky there. Wanted to see his face when he realised the game was up. Now, I might have to put me foot down sharp, so 'ang on to yer 'olly-ocks.'

Daisy did just that, gripping her seat tightly as she watched the never-ending streams of people coming from every direction. Some were weighed down with bags and suitcases. Others pushed barrows and carts spilling with personal effects. The elderly and lame were assisted by wardens or the Home Guard while the Red Cross manned medical posts or gave out refreshments.

A stomach-turning odour clogged the air as they travelled past fires that were still burning and firemen braved flames to retrieve casualties. Daisy felt sick to her soul as she witnessed the many lines of corpses on stretchers covered by blankets.

When, at last, they could make no headway, Mr Cook

swung the vehicle round, hoping to find a path forward. But instead, they were met by more carnage; city streets dangerously strewn with glass and half-demolished buildings looming perilously above the rescue teams as weary survivors emerged from the ruins, searching for friends and family. The shapes of bodies under blankets, quite motionless. Lined together on stretchers, a dreadful bonding of lives that were alive no more.

The sad sights went on and on.

She thought of the quiet and peaceful countryside of Wattcombe and knew she should be grateful they were leaving London - of course she should! But even though the streets around them were in ruins, disfigured and maimed by war, this was her home and where she wanted to be ... *here* with the people she loved.

Daisy jumped awake to the ear-piercing screech of a siren.

'You alright, youngster?' Mr Cook asked as he frowned intently through the windscreen. 'You've had a bit of a kip, but the bloomin' warning went off and woke you.'

'Are we in Wattcombe yet?' Daisy struggled up from the uncomfortable ball she had been curled in. As always when anxious, her head began to throb. She missed the reassurance of the hospital ward where Nurse Gwen had never been far away.

'Wattcombe?' Mr Cook repeated vaguely. 'No, we ain't going there. For the past hour we've been stuck in the biggest free-for-all I've ever witnessed. Roads are blocked or turn out to be dead-ends. I even lost me way once or twice and I've lived in London all me life. I was hoping to get you to safety before the blackout, but dusk caught up with us.'

Daisy peered out of her window, although it was difficult to see properly as the glass was filthy.

Mr Cook reached over to pat her hand. 'You're still bit confused, gel.'

Daisy felt rather dreamy and a little light-headed. Soothing the scar on her forehead, she mumbled, 'Pops is making thermometers to fight in the war. But it's supposed to be secret.' Giving a yawn, she added, 'You won't tell will you?'

Mr Cook grinned. 'Me lips are sealed.'

Daisy giggled. 'And Aunt Minnie told a fib, just a white one, when Aunt Betty went to the cinema with Micky Wolf. The film was called *Discovering England*.'

'You don't say,' replied Mr Cook bewilderedly.

'And this is the biggest secret, so you mustn't ever repeat it. But Joe Rawlings is colour blind. What do you think of that?'

'Gawd only knows,' replied Mr Cook hesitantly.

Daisy was about to add that, on second thoughts, she might have got some of the information muddled, when an almighty screech and burst of bright light was followed by a huge bang.

Mr Cook swung the wheel to one side and with a yell of 'Duck!' he threw himself across her.

Suddenly she remembered it wasn't Joe Rawlings who was colour blind at all.

It was Mr Calder.

CHAPTER 58

'COR BLIMEY, that was too close for comfort!'

'What happened?' Daisy looked around.

'An incendiary landed behind them houses. Better check the wheels I think, as I felt the van hit something.' He climbed out but soon returned. Opening her door he peered in. 'Bloomin' tyre is flat as a pancake. Your aunt's house is just round the corner so we'll go by Shanks's pony.' He pulled a rag from his tool box. 'I've got a couple of helmets and a gas mask in the back. But that stink of cordite will get down your throat, so tie this bit of cloth over yer mouth. It's a bit oily, but will do the trick.'

Daisy did as she was told and didn't mind the smell of oil at all, but when Mr Cook helped her out, she almost overbalanced.

'Just jelly legs,' he assured her as he pushed a helmet on her head. 'This titfer is too big for you but better than nothing. Hang on to me, gel.'

Daisy could barely see a thing, but they managed to pick their way forward. All the while an ominous drone seemed to be drawing closer.

'Don't worry, we'll get to safety in no time,' Mr Cook assured her.

But no time seemed a very long time to Daisy. It was cold, foggy, noisy and very dark. She couldn't really see where she was going and frequently tripped. At other times she was disoriented since an occasional glance to her right or left told her that she recognised no quaint shops like Mr Carson's butchers or Peggy Altwhistle's tea rooms. Neither was there a lane leading to the primary school and certainly no village hall. Most of the buildings were fatally damaged. Her heart dropped.

Daisy struggled on, but all the while the deep pulse of the planes was growing closer and the searchlights criss-crossed the sky above.

'Nearly there,' Mr Cook said, just as an ear-splitting bang made the ground shiver.

She tried to wipe away the sweat that was running from her forehead into her eyes but her hands were trembling too much. 'Mr Cook,' she pleaded, 'you're going too fast.'

'Sorry gel, I keep forgetting you're only just out of 'orspital. Let's try it this way.' With all the ease of a much younger man, he hoisted her over his shoulder.

When the explosion came, her ears seemed to burst with pain. Mr Cook appeared to be flying gracefully off his feet with her on his back just like Peter Pan who had flown over the silver ribbon of water, winding all the way up to Neverland.

Flowers ... scented flowers ... *Gardenia*!

'Is that you, Aunt Minnie?'

'Daisy!' Aunt Minnie gasped and added in a shrill burst of excitement, 'Flo! Come at once!'

There was a great deal of hustle and bustle around the comfortable chair Daisy found herself sitting in. The last she recalled was the strange sensation of riding on Mr Cook's back as they flew over the river.

But now here was Aunt Minnie who was joined by Will and Mother and Bobby and then came Aunt Betty and finally Uncle Leo.

'Daisy, oh Daisy!' Mother cried. 'I've been so worried.'

'What happened?'

Mother squeezed her hand. 'Mr Cook carried you here to Aunt Betty's house after the fall you both took.'

'I remember now. The van had a puncture.'

'Mr Cook's gone to mend it.'

Daisy studied the faces around her. 'Did you know Tommy died?'

'Who is Tommy?' asked Mother.

'He was Peter Brady's little brother.' She sniffed. 'He had his operation but died. Then Peter tried to push me off the hospital roof and Sammy saved me.'

'Who's Sammy?' Bobby wanted to know.

Daisy giggled. 'Sammy Berger of course. He works at the hospital now.'

Everyone looked puzzled. Mother touched her hot cheek. 'You're a little confused. You must be running a temperature.'

Aunt Minnie, Aunt Betty and Mother all examined her intently.

'What's that on your head?' Will asked. 'It's all red and crusty.'

'Oh, do be quiet, Will,' ordered Aunt Minnie and caught hold of his collar.

Mother gently lifted Daisy's hair. 'What a horrid wound! No wonder you're not yourself.'

'I wish,' said Will admiringly, 'that I had a scar too.'

'Shut up, Will,' Bobby muttered and Will made a face.

At which point everyone looked up at the ceiling. The light pendant shook on its brown cord and a tremor went through the floorboards.

'Jerry's on his way!' warned Uncle Leo.

Mother took Daisy's arm and led her out to the shelter. Behind them, Daisy heard Uncle Leo shouting frantic instructions. The siren grew louder and everyone rushed to perform their tasks as the Luftwaffe approached.

CHAPTER 59

IT WAS dark and damp inside the Anderson shelter, lit only by the weak, flickering flame of a candle. Daisy lay on the top bunk where Uncle Leo had lifted her. Below, Bobby and Will shared a bunk, while the adults huddled together on chairs. Wave upon wave of enemy planes thundered in the sky above and bursts of gunfire from the ack-ack stations were deafening. Every so often there was a lull.

'I wonder what we'll find when we go home,' said Uncle Leo in one such pause. 'When we drove away our street was being sealed off. We were told the Air Ministry had been targeted.'

'Then you must stay here, Leo,' insisted Aunt Betty.

'Thanks Betty, perhaps we will. Although I hope my cameras are safe.' Uncle Leo lit a cigarette. 'I might need them when I'm given my orders.'

'Do you really think they'll call you up?' said Mother.

Daisy listened carefully. Was Uncle Leo going away too, just like Pops and Uncle Ed?

'I rather think they'll need pictorial coverage for the

news,' he answered. 'Though heaven knows, it will be tough to find anything positive.'

Uncle Leo's voice was drowned by a rumble that soon became a roar. Dirt and dust fell in showers from the ceiling. Despite this, Daisy's eyelids grew heavy. The boys had fallen asleep and it was only her whirling thoughts that kept her awake.

So much had happened. Only yesterday she'd discovered poor Tommy had died. Peter Brady had tried to kill her but Sammy Berger had saved her. She'd been driven across the city by Mr Cook. It was impossible not to witness the dreadful outcome of war. Homeless, frightened and injured, the people stumbled through chaos.

Bodies lay unmoving on stretchers …

Uncle Leo was right, the world was in turmoil.

Finally her eyes closed and Daisy fell asleep.

Dazzling daylight streamed through the open door of the shelter.

'Have the planes gone?' she asked Uncle Leo as he helped her down from the bunk.

'All gone,' he confirmed as he thrust back his hair and smiled. 'Do you know a person called Tommy?'

Daisy nodded. 'He was a little boy in hospital.'

'During the night you shouted his name.'

Daisy knew she had dreamed again, but couldn't remember exactly what. 'Tommy needed an operation. But - ' She tried not to feel sad.

'I take it he didn't make it?' Uncle Leo squeezed her shoulder. 'It's hard to lose friends, and there's no real remedy for grief. But you will make new friends, I promise. Now, breakfast is served, m'lady.'

She thought how kind and funny Uncle Leo was. He was very different to most uncles. He liked his hair the way it grew, all tangled and curly and probably didn't ever use a comb. He never wore suits, but preferred baggy sweaters and ancient trousers. He even wore sandals in winter.

When they reached the kitchen door, a delicious smell wafted out. Mother was frying eggs on a Primus. Aunt Betty was making tea. Will and Bobby sat at the table gulping down their porridge. Perched in her high heels at the sink, Aunt Minnie washed the dishes.

Uncle Leo grabbed Aunt Minnie by the waist and tickled her ribs. When he smacked a kiss on her cheek, everyone laughed.

As weary and exhausted as they all were from the gruelling events of the night, the tension was broken. Daisy knew that no matter what happened in the days and weeks ahead, it was wonderful to have a family.

CHAPTER 60

Christmas Eve 1940
Wattcombe

DAISY WAS PERCHED UNCOMFORTABLY on a suitcase next to Will and Bobby in the rear of the car. The windows were all fogged because of the stream of nervous conversation that had not paused since leaving London. But it wouldn't be long now before they reached Grandma's and Aunt Pat's cottage. Perhaps Christmas would not be as bleak as everyone forecast.

'Soon be there,' confirmed Uncle Leo as he steered the car along the narrow country lane. 'And we seemed to have avoided trouble.'

'I'm still not sure that we've done right in making a surprise visit. You know how Mother and Pat like to be prepared,' said Aunt Betty who sat next to Mother on the rear seat.

'We've brought all our allowances with us,' Aunt Minnie assured her. 'We shan't go hungry.'

'I can't believe that Matt is up there flying in those treacherous skies,' said Mother distractedly. 'It only seems like yesterday he was wearing shorts and kicking a ball around the garden with Nicky.'

'Is Amelia still in Wales?'

'I believe so, though we've heard nothing,' replied Mother as Daisy shifted her position in order to hear more of the conversation. 'The problem is, with wholesale evacuation no one knows where anyone is living these days. Half the island has gone away; very few shops remain open and I dread to think how much damage has been done to our house.'

'We'll all muck in to help you,' Aunt Minnie promised.

'Look!' exclaimed Daisy, drawing a circle with her finger in the misted window. 'There's Vesta!'

'Who's Vesta?' demanded Will, wriggling beside her.

'The bossiest cow of all,' Daisy explained patiently. 'All the herd have musical hall names, like Vesta and Marie and Harry Lauder - '

'Harry is a man's name,' objected Will truculently.

'So what!' Daisy protested. 'They all had good voices.'

'Cows don't sing,' Will laughed, deliberately misunderstanding. 'They only moo.'

'No bickering now, children,' interrupted Mother, so ending the debate. 'I know you've been cooped up for ages but we're almost there.'

Everyone shuffled a few inches forward on their seats. Daisy's heart missed a beat. In just a few moments they would catch sight of the elderly thatched building with its glinting lattice windows and smoking chimney. Hidden amongst the trees of the thick wood where she and Bobby had played, its brittle bare branches would be alive with the noisy armies of rooks.

'You were right to bring us all away for Christmas, darling,' whispered Aunt Minnie in Uncle Leo's ear. 'And risk making the journey. Now we're here I'm so glad we came.'

'Me too,' agreed Aunt Betty wistfully. 'Though I do miss Ed. Especially now I've taken a couple of weeks leave from the WVS. I feel a bit of a shirker.'

'You more than deserve a break,' said Mother as she reached for Aunt Betty's hand. 'Ed would be proud of you.'

'Do you think so?' Aunt Betty sighed. 'There's so much I want to talk to him about. Things I have to say ... '

Daisy saw a look pass between her mother and aunt that surely indicated their secret. But Mr Calder seemed like a ghost from the past as Aunt Betty's eyes shone with sentimental tears.

For a moment everyone was very still as Uncle Leo drove slowly down the last few yards of the narrow lane.

Daisy pressed her nose against the window. She couldn't wait to explore the garden and fields again and hide in the wood. Perhaps they could walk to the shops and visit Mr and Mrs Webber's farm again?

After all that had happened to London, the war seemed so very far away ...

But the gasp that left everyone's lips as the cottage came into view was not of joy or expectation. Rather of shock and dismay.

'What!' Exclaimed Uncle Leo, slamming his foot on the brake and stalling the engine.

Daisy stared wordlessly at the once pretty front garden that had been so luscious with wild flowers. Now a blackened and charred skeleton rose above the smouldering mountain of bricks and thatch which was all that was left of the cottage.

'No!' Mother cried, gripping the back of Uncle Leo's seat with white knuckles. 'Oh, no!'

'I can't believe it,' gasped Aunt Betty. 'The cottage has just ... just disappeared.'

Everyone sat as if frozen, until Daisy saw Uncle Leo suddenly shake himself and putting his shoulder to the car door he thrust himself into the wintry air.

They all watched, unable to drag away their eyes. Even Will was silent, which to Daisy was far more disconcerting than Uncle Leo's wild behaviour as he hopped across the path of still warm embers. Kicking pieces of charred wood aside, he finally vanished in the smoke that still wound up from the pyre, yelling out for Grandma and Aunt Pat.

'It's useless Leo,' breathed Aunt Minnie as if he could hear her. 'The cottage is gone.'

'It can't be!' gasped Mother and covered her face with her hands. 'I ... I'm seeing things. This isn't real - '

Daisy felt a kick of panic in her stomach as Mother's tears broke through her trembling fingertips.

Then as if a messenger from the gods arrived to announce the futility of a search, the open car door shuddered. A sudden gust of smoke-filled air covered them all in ash.

Daisy couldn't ever remember quite how they all managed to scramble outside at once, but they did, scraping the thick grey dust from their clothes and coughing, so that the scene was simply chaos.

Daisy choked a breath and covered her mouth with her coat collar. This was - or rather - used to be, Grandma and Aunt Pat's cottage. This ruin was once the family home that had stood for a century at least. It had existed through wind and rain and storms and freezing winters and sultry, scented summers.

The cottage was a place of safety and welcome, a retreat from a city that was slowly burning. Now, Wattcombe was on fire too.

Where were Aunt Pat and Grandma? They couldn't be - she gulped, they couldn't be there, under all that.

CHAPTER 61

Uncle Leo appeared, his hair and beard spattered with tiny particles of grey ash. Shaking his head, he confirmed he had found no one. Muffled sobs came from Mother, Aunt Betty and Aunt Minnie as they hugged each other.

'It's useless,' he gasped. 'There's nothing left at the back, nothing at all. Just - just a jungle of burned shrubbery.' He swiped his smarting, red-veined eyes. 'And the air is like poison.'

'Nothing?' protested Mother. 'Are you sure?'

'Only the stove and that's - well, mangled, I suppose you could say.'

This word made everyone gasp again. The stove was the heart of the cottage and had breathed warmth and life into its character. To think of it as *mangled*?

Daisy looked at Bobby who met her gaze and moved close beside her. She knew the shock was affecting him too. It was only Will who wandered off to the wood, apparently unconcerned.

'Will, come here,' barked Uncle Leo in an unusually stern voice. 'It's too dangerous to go out of sight.'

'There's big tracks,' called Will, pointing to the ground. 'The Germans have captured Grandma and Aunt Pat and put them in a tank.'

'Don't be ridiculous,' said Uncle Leo impatiently. 'I won't tell you again. Come here.'

Daisy heard Aunt Betty inhale a sob. 'Leo, when do you think this ... *this* happened?'

'Going by the warm embers, within the last twenty four hours, I reckon.'

'But why didn't someone alert us?' protested Mother. 'Why weren't we told and why - ' she stopped as grief overcame her.

Daisy blinked back her own salty tears. Grandma and Aunt Pat's cottage was just like the shattered buildings in London, completely unrecognisable. And worst of all was the thought she would never see Grandma and Aunt Pat again.

'Do you think ... do you think Grandma and Aunt Pat are under all that - ' she blurted to Bobby whose eyes were trained fiercely on the devastation. 'Could they be ... '

'How should I know?' he bit back, but added more softly, 'It does look bad, though.'

They watched Uncle Leo make another search, avoiding the glowing embers and leaping obstructions. Once again he disappeared into the haze and his voice echoed desperately as he called out for Grandma and Aunt Pat.

Everyone waited with bated breath, as if hoping for a miracle or at least, some indication that life had not been completely extinguished. Minutes later, he returned, shaking his head again and pushing his dirty hands over his face.

Daisy heard a pitiful whimper come from Mother. Then a choked howl from Aunt Minnie. They were the most heart-breaking sounds she had ever heard.

'There's a chance someone got them out,' soothed Uncle Leo, in a not very convincing tone as he too, stood aimlessly to one side. 'I mean, the cottage might have been empty when it happened - '

'Mother's never out,' shrieked Aunt Minnie as tears glistened on her cheeks. 'She's not been well, Leo, you know that. And as for Pat, who hates even walking to the shops - ' Her cheeks flared scarlet as she fumbled for words.

'But I - ' began Uncle Leo spreading out his arms. 'I didn't mean to - '

'How could anyone survive this inferno?' continued Aunt Minnie, hopelessly. 'How could you possibly think it? We've got eyes, we can see ... there's not a chance - '

Daisy watched her aunt suddenly crumple into Uncle Leo's arms. He held her against him to soften her sobs, but Daisy could bear it no longer. She ran to her aunt and uncle, throwing her arms around them. Very soon, everyone was huddled together, trying to contain their shock and grief. Daisy tried not to imagine the terrible thing that had happened to her grandmother and aunt. Would they have suffered? Did they hear the bomb coming?

'It was definitely the Germans,' called Will. 'They've taken Grandma and Aunt Pat prisoner.'

'Will!' yelled Uncle Leo, turning impatiently to frown at his son. 'Come away from that mess.'

'But Dad, look down there, the Germans have left their tracks.'

Daisy watched Uncle Leo reluctantly peel himself away from the group and with defeated shoulders, amble across to where Will stood. 'Why do you insist on spouting such rubbish, Will - ' he began, only to halt mid-sentence as he followed Will's gaze.

'See?' said Will eagerly. 'It's the tracks of a tank.'

Uncle Leo went down on his haunches and examined the ground. 'Good grief, you're right, Will. Not a tank, but certainly a large vehicle. And what's that over there?' He pointed to a clump of nearby bushes.

No one moved at first, but then there was a mad dash to look at Uncle Leo's discovery.

'It's Mother's!' cried Aunt Minnie, grasping the ancient handbag. 'I'd recognise it anywhere! She's had it for years!'

'You're right,' agreed Mother. 'She never let it out of her sight.'

Will pointed to the half inch of white paper sticking out of the clasp. 'It's a ransom note from the Germans.'

This time no one told Will to shut up. Daisy watched Uncle Leo lift the bag gently. Shaking off the ash, he turned the rusty brass catch. With a click it opened. Inside was a pristine white sheet of Grandma's favourite notepaper.

'What is it?' Aunt Minnie demanded as Uncle Leo drew it out with the tips of his dirty fingers. 'What does it say?'

Slowly he looked up, his face expressionless. 'They're alive,' he whispered. 'Those tracks were left by a tractor - they're with the Webbers.

'Told you,' said Will, looking smug. 'But no one ever listens to me.'

Seconds later, it was another mad scramble to the car. This time, after piling in, Uncle Leo drove furiously back along the lane. As if, Daisy thought, they were being chased by Will's imaginary tank. Mother and Aunt Betty insisted on supposing what might have happened to Grandma and Aunt Pat while Aunt Minnie lit a cigarette for Uncle Leo. Then Mother, who rarely ever smoked shook one from the packet too.

'Did the note say they were both safe?' Aunt Betty said again to Uncle Leo.

'Was there anything about injuries?' demanded Aunt Minnie.

'Where's the handbag? Did we leave it behind?'

Uncle Leo was about to answer but swerved the car to avoid a rabbit. Everyone flew forward, until they careered off again.

'Is this the way to the farm?'

'I think we missed the turning.'

'I'm sure it was the other way … '

'We'd better turn back - '

'It can't be far from here!'

When Daisy saw the field where Vesta and Ida and Harry Lauder were still grazing, she remembered how she and Bobby had almost got lost in this very spot.

'That's the lane to the farm,' she cried, pointing to the sandy track.

There was a united sigh of relief when the Webber's farmhouse came into view.

CHAPTER 62

THERE WERE TEARS, embraces, sighs and tears again as Grandma and Aunt Pat were hugged and kissed to within an inch of their lives.

'It was a stray bomb from an aircraft two nights ago,' Grandma explained as she tottered her way with Aunt Pat and Mrs Webber into the farmhouse parlour. 'No one saw the culprit. We suppose the pilot must have been on his way back to Germany.'

'Sit yourselves down,' interrupted Mrs Webber as she fussed with the fire, piling on more logs. 'You must be frozen. I'll put on the kettle.'

'It was the stove that saved our lives,' explained Aunt Pat. 'It broke down again and we've been living here at the farm ever since. Had we been inside the cottage, well, we shouldn't be alive to tell the tale.'

'But all your personal items, clothes and books?' Aunt Betty asked sadly. 'All gone, I suppose?'

Grandma nodded. 'All gone. But bricks and mortar are replaceable. Lives aren't.'

'Mother kept our ration books and identity cards and a

little money in her handbag,' said Aunt Pat practically. 'Though we emptied it of course before leaving it at the cottage with the note inside. We knew you'd be thinking of us and might even go against the government's advice and risk driving down for Christmas. Bill tried to telephone Minnie just after the raid happened but there was no answer from the studio.'

'We must have been at Betty's,' explained Aunt Minnie. 'Our studio isn't deemed safe to return to after a bomb dropped close by.'

'London is having a frightful time,' said Grandma with a little shudder. 'I worry about you girls living in the city.'

'But look at what's happened to the cottage,' pointed out Mother gently. 'It's not safe down here either.'

'I've no intention of leaving Wattcombe,' Grandma replied in an alarmed voice. 'Pat and I will find a place to rent. Wattcombe is our home and I refuse to be forced out of it.'

'But that won't be easy in wartime,' persevered Mother. 'Nor will it be cheap. Won't you give some thought to coming back to Betty's?'

'Heavens no!' exclaimed Grandma indignantly. 'It's my belief that everyone should save for a rainy day. I have enough put by to see me and Pat all right.'

'Do think again,' pleaded Aunt Betty. 'We'd love to have you with us - '

Grandma shook her head fiercely. 'Very nice of you dear, but I don't care for the city. Bill knows of a place to rent in the village. A small two-bedroom mews at the back of the shops. I've asked him to make enquiries on my behalf.'

Daisy watched keenly as her aunts all looked at one another in dismay.

'Now, I'm sure we could do with another cuppa,' suggested Mrs Webber. 'I'll top up the teapot.'

More tea was drunk and it was finally agreed - not at all to Daisy's surprise - that for better or worse, Grandma should have her own way.

When Mr Webber returned from the dairy, a hearty supper was served in the kitchen. 'Eat up, my dears,' Mrs Webber invited as they sat down to yet another farm feast.

Daisy piled her plate high - almost as much as Will and Bobby piled theirs; thick slices of cold pork and hot boiled potatoes with a knob of butter. Crusty slices of real, home baked bread and Mrs Webber's creamy trifle. Made with thick, buttery cow's cream, probably Vesta's or Marie's or even Harry Lauder's, the spongy, fruity flavoured jelly was lost under the fluffy white topping. Trifles were unheard of in London, but here on the farm, Daisy reflected, life seemed to have changed very little.

'Now, we'll sort out the sleeping arrangements,' said Mrs Webber, getting up from the table and slipping off her pinny, she addressed her husband. 'Bill, fetch the ladder for the attic.'

'But you can't put us all up,' protested Mother. 'You've been very kind, but I'm sure we'll find lodgings in the village.'

'I won't hear of it,' said the farmer's wife sternly. 'We've four beds upstairs and two mattresses in the loft and plenty of bedding. There's put-u-ups for the two men and the children won't mind sleeping in the parlour I'm sure. As for Christmas dinner tomorrow, Bill's bringing in a fresh turkey and we've sacks of spuds and carrots in the store. I'm sure we can make an apple pie or two go round.'

'Are you really certain?' Aunt Betty asked again.

'We're used to entertaining at Christmas but our own Mark and Susan and their children won't be coming this year, what with restrictions and all. Young company will fill the gap they leave.'

'We do have a few groceries in the car,' said Aunt Minnie eagerly. 'Children, help Uncle Leo to carry them in.'

'Before you go, son,' Mr Webber said with a wink, turning to the cupboard and opening its doors. 'Let's see what our friend from the North Pole has delivered.' Two bottles familiar to Daisy were placed on the table and each adult's glass was filled to the brim.

Grandma's medicine, Daisy decided, was very versatile indeed.

Daisy heard Mr Webber tread softly down the stairs in the early hours of Christmas morning and make his way to the kitchen. Soon after the kettle whistled, followed by the seductive smell of frying bacon.

A little later, the thought of breakfast was enough to rouse her from the couch where she had been sleeping. Mrs Webber had draped her coat, trousers and jumper over the fireguard a safe three feet away from the embers in the hearth. Dressing quietly, she tiptoed past the boys on their mattresses.

'Morning, love. Happy Christmas,' Mrs Webber greeted, as Daisy stole into the kitchen.

'Happy Christmas, Mrs Webber. Bobby and Will are still asleep.'

'That's boys for you,' smiled Mrs Webber, rolling her eyes. 'Bill's breakfast is done and dusted and he's gone out to the cowshed. You'll be needing a fry up.'

Daisy sat down to her breakfast; an egg with a juicy yellow middle sitting squarely on a slice of fried bread and topped with a crispy brown rasher.

'We never have breakfast like this in London.' Daisy mopped up her plate with a slice of bread.

'Today's special,' said Mrs Webber, filling the toast rack. 'Thought you and your family could do with a decent meal.'

'Can I help milk the cows?'

'Course you can, love.'

'How do you pull their udders?'

'Easy as eating pie, you'll find.'

'I want to be as good as Bobby.'

'Well, seeing as you're so keen, I'll show you.' Mrs Webber demonstrated with one of Mr Webber's thick socks hanging on the airer. 'You give 'em a bit of a tickle first, like so. Cows like a tickle. Then cup your fingers round the teat gently but firmly, see?' She waggled the sock. 'Now pull. And don't forget to aim in the pail or else you'll get an eyeful.'

Daisy giggled and left the table. Mrs Webber pointed to the many pairs of boots lined up by the door. 'Now put on them galoshes, whatever ones fit best and remember to do a wee in the privy on your way out. Once you get milking you won't want to stop.'

Later that morning, Daisy was perched on a milking stool, her booted feet spread wide. Her warm cheek rested softly against Harry Lauder's round belly. Harry was giving little shudders as if she was enjoying the technique that Daisy had quickly mastered. An occasional moo resonated in the echoey cowshed, followed by another and another, as if the cows were talking. Every now and then, Harry produced an extra generous squirt of rich, white milk into the pail. Daisy's little fingers worked hard to maintain a rhythm as Mr Webber passed the stalls, a bucket in each hand. His floppy galoshes squelched in the smelly, mucky cow pats and he'd whistle a tune or sing.

'We'll make a farmer of you yet, my girl,' he called encouragingly. 'Your Pops will be proud of you.'

'Am I better than Bobby?'

'There's not a jot between you.'

Daisy couldn't wait to tell Pops what she had achieved, in spite of the war. Nurse Gwen had recommended a career in nursing. Mr Webber suggested farming. Mrs Hayes, a tea lady's position. Mrs Jones, the music teacher, had praised her singing and Mrs Gardiner had delegated an entire class of infants to her care! Though Daisy had once dreamed of a world adventure, the dream had somewhat faded. A little ache fluttered near her heart for Poplar Park Row. Was this homesickness, she wondered?

It was a surprise to Daisy that even though she could milk a whole herd of cows if challenged and even though she loved Wattcombe with its peaceful green fields and thick, wild woods - she had grown to love the city more.

CHAPTER 63

CHRISTMAS DINNER WAS, as Mrs Webber had promised, a treat. The turkey and potatoes were browned and basted to perfection, the sprouts and beans drowned in real butter and the fruit cake smothered in homemade cream.

Everyone ate ravenously and not a scrap on their plates remained.

'How can we ever thank you?' said Mother as the table was cleared. 'We must return the favour somehow.'

'You're Wattcombe folk,' replied Mr Webber as he took a small box of cigars from the kitchen mantel, 'and there will always be a welcome for you at the farm. As for you, Leo,' he teased, 'a true city type, you and me have got some smoking to do. Come along, bring your glass, let's listen to the King's speech.'

Daisy inhaled the smell of cigars and the faint aromas of the farm drifting into the partly open window, as they all gathered by the fire in the parlour. The ancient wooden wireless set in the corner was given an encouraging thump to bring it to life. Very soon the crackly strains of the national anthem could be heard.

Daisy felt a lump grow in her throat as she sat cross-legged beside Bobby and Will on the floor. When the King faltered, everyone held their breath as he wrestled with his stutter. But he overcame his difficulty and addressed the nation as the ancient radio set crackled. Daisy felt the overwhelming love and pride that filled the room as he spoke.

Christmas is for children, the King reminded the country and referred to the many British children who had travelled to members of the Commonwealth for safety. When he spoke about the meaning of separation, hankies were tugged from sleeves and mother's hand crept towards Aunt Betty's. She knew that Mother was thinking of Pops and Matt and Aunt Betty's sad smile was for Uncle Ed.

Daisy hoped that Pops was listening at this very moment. Perhaps Matt was too, although it was more likely he would be on standby duty. There had been no letters from either one, though Mother thought this was to be expected since postal services were disrupted.

"Remember this," comforted the King in his gentle voice, "if war brings separation, it brings unity also ... good comrades ... good neighbours."

And everyone looked at Mr and Mrs Webber who had proved to be the very best of friends and neighbours. Uncle Leo raised his glass to their hosts and Mrs Webber's pink cheeks grew even redder with embarrassment. Mr Webber gave a dismissive shrug and returned his concentration to his smoking.

"I have seen a good spirit of fellowship spring up in adversity," the King continued. "We shall need this spirit in our own lives ... and think about others ..."

Daisy glanced at Bobby, trying to disguise her deep feeling of affection for the very best brother a girl could have. Will was - well, he was just Will, and she loved him too. She loved everyone in this room; her family and friends like Mr and Mrs Webber. There were others she thought of like poor Tommy and Sally and Grace and all her friends who lived on the island and Mr Cox and Nurse Gwen whose kindness she would never forget.

There was another name too. That name was Sammy. The boy who had saved her life on the roof of the hospital. Sammy Berger was the person she thought of now, Sammy and his father, wherever they might be.

The King took a long, painful pause and the radio crackled noisily but his last words were clearly audible.

"Our future will be hard but our feet will be planted on the path of victory. With the help of God we can win this war … and make our way … to justice and to peace."

The anthem boomed out, everyone scrambled to their feet and stood to attention. It wasn't as if, Daisy thought, the King had intentionally walked into this room with his mild-mannered voice and aura of deep comfort. But somehow he had, and she knew every other household in the country must think the same.

'Pat, let's have a round of fortune cards,' Mrs Webber suggested later that afternoon as they sat by the parlour fire. 'I want to know if the calving goes well this year.'

Mr Webber coughed politely. 'Time for a walk, Leo,' he mumbled. 'Let's stretch our legs before the next round of milking. Boys, do you want to join us?'

Eager to be away, they all shambled out. Grandma chuckled. 'Men don't approve of this sort of thing.'

Aunt Pat nodded. 'I'm not sure the cards are right for Christmas Day.'

'Oh, go on, Pat,' urged Aunt Minnie with a giggle. 'Let's have a bit of fun. No one takes them seriously, anyway.'

'What do you think, Betty?' asked Aunt Pat hesitantly, though Daisy saw she was already searching her handbag.

Aunt Betty smiled ruefully. 'Just as long as you forecast something nice, Pat.'

Very soon the pretty cards, with their colourful symbols, were dealt. Grandma's were read first, with a predictable interpretation. 'A different address,' said Aunt Pat immediately.

Grandma waved her hand. 'No surprise at all. I don't need the fortune cards to tell me that!'

Mrs Webber showed her hand. 'Oh, what do these mean, Pat? A beautiful sunset over the fields and one with a crescent moon showing?'

Daisy held her breath as Aunt Pat studied them carefully. 'I can tell you there's an opportunity in the offing.'

'Oh good!' Mrs Webber cried. 'I hope it's that holiday we promised ourselves. We haven't taken one in years.'

Daisy watched as Aunt Pat frowned at Aunt Betty's cards. 'You are going to have a visitor, Betty, who I'm afraid, won't be welcome.'

'Oh,' said Aunt Betty disappointedly, her face very pale.

'I can't change it,' sighed Aunt Pat. 'One card is showing a black sheep - an unwelcome caller - it's as plain as the nose on my face. And I don't mind admitting that I've always considered my nose to be my best feature.' Somewhat embarrassed, Aunt Pat turned her attention to Mother. 'Now your card, Flo.'

Aunt Pat considered the hand that Mother had been dealt. 'This lovely card - the Lily, is the symbol of innocence and purity.'

Everyone gathered round. 'But what does it mean?' Aunt Minnie asked curiously.

Aunt Pat smiled. 'New life is is in your aura.'

The room was silent until Mother broke the spell. 'I haven't a clue,' she decided.

'You'll find out,' replied Aunt Pat mysteriously.

Daisy turned her cards over slowly. 'What about mine?'

'This is the symbol of responsibility and protection,' announced Aunt Pat pointing to the card bearing an angel. 'Your celestial being is carrying a seed in her hands. You must take care to grow and nurture it.'

Daisy had no idea what it meant. She wasn't the world's best at gardening. In fact Grandma had once remarked that her granddaughter wasn't blessed with green fingers but sticky ones.

'What a lovely card!' said Aunt Minnie. 'Yet not a bit like Flo's.'

Daisy didn't want to disappoint Aunt Pat so she said quickly, 'I did dream of an angel - once.'

'It was probably delirium,' Mother pronounced doubtfully and began to pack away the cards.

CHAPTER 64

IT WAS past midnight when everyone went to bed. Daisy lay awake as she curled under the blankets on the couch. She still felt the glow of Christmas, as with the blackout curtains drawn, she could see the golden embers of the fire.

A country blackout didn't seem so dark as it did in the city. Bobby and Will's regular breathing from their makeshift beds on the floor, made her feel secure. Without the drone of overhead aircraft and the threat of raids, spirits had been uplifted today. The shock of the demolished cottage had been accepted but what would it be like in London, she wondered?

She thought of Sally again and wondered if Bobby was missing Grace? As for Sammy Berger, was he still working at the hospital? So much had happened in such a short time, yet it seemed an eternity since Pops and Uncle Ed had left for Milton Keynes. Had they too, celebrated Christmas in a different way?

Mother and Aunt Betty had been very brave. Daisy knew that just like her, they were homesick. They wanted to get back to London and hopefully, to Aunt Betty's house where they planned to stay.

Her thoughts wandered for a while until she drifted to sleep. Perhaps she would dream of her card again and learn the meaning of the seed.

~

Daisy enjoyed the rest of the holiday, especially as the weather was good and the family made several visits to the village. Here they inspected Grandma and Aunt Pat's prospective abode where the quaint little mews and its close location to the shops was unanimously approved.

Though Daisy's opinion wasn't sought, privately she was disappointed. There was no pretty garden or wicket gate and tumbledown shed. No woods to hide in, or fields full of cows to visit. Still, Grandma and Aunt Pat were satisfied and invitations given to visit as soon as they'd moved in.

So it wasn't until Sunday that Uncle Leo eventually drove them home under an early morning sky that hung heavy with grey rain clouds.

'Perhaps we should have waited a day or two longer,' said Mother from the rear seat as they approached the edge of the city. 'The Air Ministry wireless reports weren't good, after all. Apart from one night's grace, the raids are continuous.'

'We couldn't have burdened the Webbers any longer,' replied Aunt Betty. 'And anyway, I have to get back to work.'

'Don't worry,' said Uncle Leo resolutely. 'Jerry won't get their act together until the New Year, I'm sure.'

'Let's hope so,' sighed Mother doubtfully. 'Living in the country for a while is wonderful, but you get a false impression of reality.'

Once the island was reached a cutting wind blew the smell of burning into an open window of the car. Daisy gazed out of her window, shocked to see the blitzed and wounded streets. Houses were boarded up or blackened by the smoke of incendiary bombs. People trudged wearily along, collars turned up against the cold.

'Oh, Leo, it's worse than we thought,' whispered Aunt Minnie, leaning forward to study the grim view.

'Much worse,' agreed Aunt Betty just as a warden stepped into the road.

'I hope he doesn't ask where we've travelled,' worried Mother. 'We'll get an awful ticking off.'

'Stop!' the warden bawled, thankfully distracted by a cyclist who almost collided with a pedestrian in the dusk. 'Oi! Watch where you're going. Get orf that bike and go home!'

'Put your foot down, Leo,' insisted Aunt Minnie. 'He can't stop us then.'

Daisy giggled as the car sped on while Bobby and Will made faces from the rear window.

'Boys, no!' reprimanded Mother. 'He's only doing his job. And we're in the wrong anyway to have made an unnecessary trip.'

'Well, as it happened, it was necessary,' reasoned Aunt Betty. 'Mother and Pat might have been in the cottage when it - '

'But they weren't!' interrupted Aunt Minnie sharply. 'I can't bear to think of it.'

'Have we any food at the house?' Mother asked, changing the subject.

'Maybe a tin or two.'

'Let's hope the water's on.'

'It will be nice to sleep in our own beds again.'

'Good grief! There's the warning siren already!' exclaimed Uncle Leo and crashed the gears. 'Thank goodness we're almost there.'

Daisy felt a knot of anxiety tie in her stomach. She knew everyone else was anxious too. They could barely wait until Uncle Leo pulled up outside Aunt Betty's house.

'No damage,' he said, glancing out of the window. 'At least, not outside.'

The car emptied in seconds and Aunt Betty let them in. They stood staring at the dust and soot-streaked interior. 'Well, other than being filthy, the house seems undamaged.'

'There's no time to waste,' said Uncle Leo hurriedly. 'We'll take the same things out to the shelter as before.'

'Daisy, help Bobby and Will to carry the blankets and pails,' said Mother. 'I'll bring Mrs Webber's food parcel.'

Once again, everyone scrambled to perform their tasks and it was not long before they were all safe, but wondering what the night would bring.

CHAPTER 65

Daisy's fond memories of the farm soon faded as the raids deafening assault began. The roar of the aircraft above vibrated the metal casing of the Anderson and shook the earth violently. Blankets were thrown to the ground and Uncle Leo yelled at the top of his voice.

'Get down, hands over your heads!' A command that everyone obeyed. They collapsed in a tangle, their gasps of shock and fear masked by the explosive sounds outside.

Daisy was squashed between Mother and Bobby and Will was somewhere close by. It felt as though the roof of the shelter was about to fall in. Dust and dirt sprayed down relentlessly, causing everyone to cough and splutter. But no one dared move as wave after wave of aircraft deposited their lethal cargo on London.

The minutes turned into hours. Bitter cold and damp crept into bones and muscles as the onslaught felt like the end of the world. Without light, Daisy couldn't see Mother, but she could feel an arm around her. Occasionally soft lips brushed her cheek and consoling words were offered. But hearing anything at all, other than the huge impacts around the shelter, was impossible. A short respite came at some point in the night when the aircraft above retreated - or so it seemed.

'Stay down,' thundered Uncle Leo, 'there's no telling what will happen next. Will, Bobby, Daisy, are you all right?'

Aunt Minnie assured Uncle Leo that Will was beside her and Mother and Bobby both called out they were safe. Daisy managed a shivery acknowledgement but she felt too cold and tired to say more.

Almost immediately, the Luftwaffe returned. With all hope fading of an end to the attacks, or even a break in the intensity, they lay coupled on the ground, adjusting positions when possible.

Exhausted and cold, Daisy fell fitfully into sleep. She woke briefly in the night, trembling at the repeated explosions, wondering if Bobby and Will were just as afraid as she was.

Was Aunt Betty imagining her house a demolished ruin, like Grandma's cottage? Was Mother thinking of Poplar Park Row and expecting it to be completely destroyed? She was in no doubt at all that Aunt Minnie and Uncle Leo feared for the studio. If it had been deemed unsafe to live in before tonight, then what would be its fate tomorrow after such a bombardment? That is, she thought desperately, if there was a tomorrow …

No one heard Mr Cook at first. It was Daisy who recognized his voice and saw the pencil line of dawn light above the door.

'Mr Cook, we're in here!' she shouted, slowly moving her cramped limbs. Her call woke Uncle Leo and with stiff, ungainly movements he heaved himself up.

'Just a second,' he said in a gruff voice and picked his way past the recumbent bodies to release the door.

'Steady as you go,' Mr Cook said as he assisted Uncle Leo and then Daisy from the shelter. A bedraggled group followed, sluggishly dragging themselves into the daylight.

'Thank God. We all came through,' gasped Aunt Betty, brushing back her tousled hair.

'I thought the night would never end,' agreed Mother.

Aunt Minnie shook the dirt from her clothes. 'It's the confinement of the shelter I can't bear. Sometimes I think I'd prefer to be hiding under my kitchen table.'

'You'd be taking your life in your hands if you did,' Mr Cook reminded her as they all stood in the gassy, putrid air. 'Me and my crew have been on the job since dawn. Prepare yourselves for a shock. It was the roughest night so far.'

At this, everyone looked around. The thick, smoke-fuelled air was tinged with the sickening smell of burning.

'What happened?' Uncle Leo asked, clearing his throat and swatting the grey dust from his face and hair. 'Why were we hit so badly?'

' 'itler timed a corker of a raid to coincide with the tide,' Mr Cook explained. 'The high explosive parachute mines and fire bombs broke the water mains. Our firemen tried pumping from elsewhere but their engine's overheated. Buildings were collapsing like nine pins.' He narrowed his eyes craftily. 'But we had an ace up our sleeve - the elements! Just when the Luftwaffe was getting in their stride, the weather deteriorated over German airfields, so our Air Ministry says. Planes couldn't take off. Couldn't land. That's scuppered their plans.'

'We saw storm clouds over London on the way back from Wattcombe,' replied Aunt Betty, wiping the dirt from her face with the back of her sleeve. 'Little did we know what an important part they would play in our defence.'

'You can't beat Mother Nature,' Mr Cook agreed. 'Thank Gawd, last night she was on our side. He inspected them all closely. 'You look as though you've had a rough night.'

'You could say that,' muttered Uncle Leo.

'Get yourselves into the house, then,' said Mr Cook, leading the way. 'Some of your windows are cracked, but the structure is safe enough.'

'Oh no!' gasped Aunt Betty when they reached the kitchen door. 'Just look at this!'

'There's a bit of tidying up to do,' agreed Mr Cook as everyone contemplated the disaster of the kitchen. Bare, dusty shelves and china fragments strewn everywhere, a chair upended, the surface of the table thick with plaster from the ceiling, pots and pans violently shaken from hooks and scattered across the quarry tiles. And over everything lay a thick layer of grime and soot. ' 'Fraid the other rooms ain't much better,' he commiserated. 'And there's more ... '

Everyone spun round to stare at Mr Cook.

'That empty house over yer broken fence? An incendiary landed in a road close by it. Wouldn't have done much harm if the building had been stable. But it collapsed and the disposal blokes have sealed it off.' He turned and wagged a finger at Daisy and Bobby. 'Until the area is given the all-clear, don't play in yer garden.'

'Is it safe to use our Anderson?' asked Aunt Betty anxiously.

'Lucky it's close to the house,' replied Mr Cook.

'But where can we play?' Daisy protested.

'In the street, kid. Like thousands of others.'

This wasn't the reply Daisy had hoped for.

CHAPTER 66

DAISY STOOD IN THE KITCHEN, watching the changing expressions on the faces around her. Mr Cook's latest announcement had unsettled them all.

'There's no imminent danger,' said Uncle Leo. 'Otherwise we'd have been evacuated immediately.'

'It's horrible to think that a bomb dropped so close,' said Mother.

'There's not much room in the street to kick a ball,' complained Bobby.

'Can we just play by the Anderson?' Will asked hopefully.

'No!' shouted Aunt Minnie and Uncle Leo together. 'You heard what Mr Cook said.'

'But - ' began Will truculently.

'No buts, Will,' said Uncle Leo sternly. 'You'll do as you're told.'

'What happens tonight?' asked Mother. 'Is it really safe to use the shelter?'

'I don't see why not,' shrugged Uncle Leo. 'Though I noticed they've erected a public shelter just down the road.

It's much bigger and might be more comfortable. You might try that.'

Aunt Minnie shook her head. 'With the best will in the world, Leo, I can't face it. I want to go home.' Her wan face was bereft of make-up and Daisy thought that she didn't look at all like her bubbly, beautiful aunt with golden hair and scarlet lips. 'If I'm going to die I want to die on my own clean floorboards. Or in our bed with proper pillows and freshly washed linen.'

'But, Minnie,' protested Mother, 'you'll be taking an awful risk.'

'I'm beyond caring, Flo,' replied Aunt Minnie. 'Bruton Mews is our home yet I've begun to feel as though we've no home at all. I've had enough of the way the Germans want to fight this war. If I'm going to fight, then it will be on my own terms from now on.'

A silence filled the kitchen as Uncle Leo shook his head doubtfully. 'But what if the police won't allow us back?'

'Please let's try,' begged Aunt Minnie. 'I need to see our friends again; the couple who live above us and our neighbours next door. And eat pastries from the bakery and buy vegetables from the grocer. Let's try to find some normality in our lives.'

Daisy saw little pearls of moisture shine in her aunt's eyes and Will, scuffing his dirty nose with his cuff, said cheerfully, 'I'm bored too. If we're not allowed to play in Aunt Betty's garden, I want to go home.'

Uncle Leo smiled. 'I must admit, I miss the studio too. But first Betty, we'll help clean up.'

Aunt Betty shook her head. 'Now the decision is made, Leo, you had better set off. We'll cope here.'

'Here, Minnie,' whispered Mother. 'Take some of Mrs Webber's scones with you.'

'And I'll make a flask of tea.' Aunt Betty turned on the tap.

A brown, rusty dribble gurgled out. When a spurt of clear water followed, everyone cheered.

'Thank you for everything,' said Aunt Minnie tearfully. 'But you do understand, don't you?'

Daisy understood perfectly. She knew exactly how Aunt Minnie felt. It didn't matter if there were floods, fire or famine as Mrs Gulliver often quoted from the Bible. The heartstrings always drew you home.

CHAPTER 67

WHEN THE WARNING SOUNDED, it was decided to follow Uncle Leo's suggestion. As they reached the bend in the road that led to the public shelter, the smell reached them in advance; a strong disinfectant mixed with the ingrained stench of urine.

At the entrance, a queue of people pushed and shoved while inside benches were lined up in rows, sufficient for more than fifty people - so the warden informed them.

Daisy hated it on sight. Cramped, noisy, stuffy and smelly, the accommodation was almost unbearable. Much to her alarm, the floors were stained yellow. Worse still, the warden allocated them benches close to the makeshift toilets. Mother was horrified to discover the lavatory consisted of half a dozen pails behind a sagging curtain. There was no privacy and no one got a wink of sleep. Babies screamed and children were fretful. A man had a dreadful cough that he proudly took care to distribute with enormous sneezes. Mother issued hankies to cover mouths, but when an elderly lady collapsed, the air became putrid as puffing and sweating, people tried to assist.

It was a good hour before the patient revived, but by then,

Daisy suspected this nightly arrangement did not bode well for the future. When morning arrived, it came not a moment too soon.

'I prefer our damp shelter,' Mother confessed as they trudged wearily home. 'Besides, tomorrow is New Year's Eve. What will it be like shoulder to shoulder with fifty other people, who I am sure will need to celebrate? In such a confined space I doubt that we'll get a wink of sleep. It's not as if we had any alcohol of our own and could join in.'

Aunt Betty stood still. 'I've just remembered. Ed kept a bottle of apple cider in the old toilet at the side of the house. The ancient plumbing was broken so Ed stripped it out and used the space for storage. He always meant to restore it to its former glory ... ' She smiled fondly at the memory. 'Whether or not there's very much apple cider left in the bottle, or even if it's still there, goodness only knows. '

'All is not lost, then,' replied Mother with a grin. 'As desperate as we are, even a thimbleful each would do.'

By the time they reached home, everyone's mood had lifted. Mother lit the Primus and began to fry eggs while Aunt Betty sliced a loaf.

'After the war is over I'm going to keep chickens,' vowed Daisy as she devoured her breakfast. 'Then we can eat a whole egg every day.'

'Just as long as you remember to feed your chickens,' teased Bobby. 'Eggs don't appear by magic.'

'I know that,' replied Daisy haughtily. 'Mrs Webber thought I was very good at feeding the chickens.'

'I miss the farm's food,' interrupted Aunt Betty. 'But being back in London feels good, despite our frightful experience last night.'

Daisy gulped her tea, wondering if she would like the taste of apple cider and whether or not there might be an alternative - such as a bottle of lemonade hidden somewhere - for children.

~

That night, the Luftwaffe's attack was met with fierce opposition from the British Airforce. The little tin house, as Daisy thought of it, shook and shuddered as the assaults intensified. They were all so sleep-deprived that even the loudest explosions didn't keep them awake.

Yet again, the air was cloaked in a thick, impenetrable fog the next morning. 'We're at the end of yet another year,' Mother said wearily, cautiously stepping into daylight. 'Who would believe it?'

Aunt Betty nodded. 'Thank God, we're all still safe yet thousands of people have lost loved ones. Look, I think the house has survived too.'

All eyes turned to view the dim, but familiar outline. 'What's for breakfast?' Daisy enquired.

'Bacon, eggs and fried bread,' said Mother with a chuckle.

Though the porridge was no where as enjoyable as a fried meal, Daisy ate hers greedily. The hot oats rolled down her throat and quelled her rebelling stomach. The tea, though weak and watery, was hot and comforting.

After breakfast, duties were allotted. Daisy was given the task with Bobby of finding the apple cider. After a thorough search of the storage space, the apple cider was discovered.

'It's three-quarters full,' said Mother delightedly. 'Quite enough to celebrate.'

'Let's hope 1941 is kinder to us,' sighed Aunt Betty, staring through the kitchen window to the end of the garden. 'Mr Cook was right about that empty house. Now the mist has cleared, you can see it's nothing but a ruin. Such a depressing sight. This neighbourhood held such promise before the war.'

'Like so many others,' Mother agreed, joining her at the window, 'and there will be a good deal of rebuilding to do. Who knows if we'll ever go back to Poplar Park Row?'

A short while later, Daisy stood with Bobby on the gravel path that led to the street, outside the kitchen. 'Did you hear what Mother said to Aunt Betty? We might never go home!'

'Pops won't let that happen,' said Bobby confidently as he opened the door of the old toilet.

'But what if our house isn't even there?' Daisy suggested. 'And there's just a pile of bricks instead?'

'Look!' exclaimed Bobby, adroitly changing the subject. 'There's an old crate and some pram wheels under the shelf. They would make a terrific cart.'

Daisy wasn't interested. 'I'll never sit on our swing under the apple tree or go to school again. I'll never see our friends or Sally.'

'Stop moaning and help me.'

She reluctantly obeyed though her heart wasn't in it. When the crate and wheels were successfully dragged out, Bobby examined their finds. 'There's a pot of Uncle Ed's paint on the shelf. It would look better if it was another colour. And with a bit of encouragement the wheels will fit.'

Daisy was unimpressed. She was still thinking about Poplar Park Row and all the things she would miss.

CHAPTER 68

IT WAS midnight and the candle's flame was the only light to illuminate the shelter. 'Should old acquaintance be forgot and never brought to mind,' Daisy sang with Bobby, Mother and Aunt Betty.

She recalled the many new years' celebrations in Wattcombe and none of them had been like this one. She fondly remembered her early years with Grandma and all her aunts and uncles and Matt - who in those early days - had not even dreamed of the brave pilot he would become.

The apple cider was shared into enamel mugs, and Mother made the first toast. 'To Nicky and Ed, Matt and Amelia. God keep you all safe.'

'Come home soon,' said Aunt Betty quietly. 'I've so much I want to tell you.'

Another toast was made for the rest of the family.

'And Mr Cook,' added Bobby, 'and his crew.'

'And Nurse Gwen,' continued Daisy enthusiastically. She was about to include poor departed Tommy when an enormous explosion rattled every inch of the shelter. The mugs were lost and the candle extinguished.

1941 had arrived with ink-black darkness and the sickly smell of a very cold and musty Anderson shelter.

'Happy New Year,' Mother murmured as a familiar wisp of morning light squeezed in above the shelter door.

'Happy New Year,' replied Aunt Betty in a drowsy voice.

Daisy had slept fitfully under the blanket, but now the air tasted sour. It didn't seem like a happy new year at all.

'I'll open the door,' said Mother, unsteadily rising from the armchair. 'Those explosions in the night came very close. I hope we're not trapped.'

To everyone's surprise, the door gave way. 'Our luck's in,' decided Mother, shivering fiercely under her coat. 'But there's that awful fog again.'

Daisy staggered out beside Bobby who stretched his arms and peered around. All Daisy could see were fragments of concrete, dislodged roof tiles and broken bricks. 'Be careful,' warned Mother as they moved towards the house.

'The door is still on its hinges,' called Aunt Betty, first to arrive at the kitchen. 'There seems to be no structural damage.'

They all stood uncertainly until Aunt Betty stepped forward to enter. Once inside they were met with a predictable, but heart-sinking scene. Over every inch of space lay a coat of thick grey dust that would take hours to remove.

'Oh well, it could be worse,' said Aunt Betty cheerfully. 'I'll look upstairs, Flo, if you check downstairs.'

Mother handed Bobby the broom and Daisy the mop. 'The kitchen is yours,' she said with a grin.

'I really hate housework,' Daisy complained to Bobby, who began creating more dust than he was clearing.

'Me too,' he agreed. 'Let's hurry up. Then I can finish the cart and whizz you along the street.'

Encouraged by Bobby's unexpected offer, Daisy took off her coat and rolled up her sleeves.

After breakfast, the letterbox rattled.

'It can't be a delivery, can it?' gasped Aunt Betty, her eyes wide as she pushed back a lock of untidy brown hair and jumped to her feet. Running into the hall, she cried, 'Three letters, Flo!'

'We haven't had a post in weeks!' gasped Mother and quickly followed.

Once seated back in the kitchen a letter from Pops was opened first. 'Nicky's is very short,' said Mother disappointedly. 'He wrote at the beginning of December. Unfortunately this has been heavily censored. Perhaps he mistakenly gave some indication of where they are stationed?' Her voice broke and she took her hanky from her sleeve. 'He writes that he's well and hopes we are too. He wishes us all a happy Christmas.' A tear slid down her cheek. 'But there's no mention of when we shall see him again.'

Aunt Betty hurriedly opened hers. She read it, then sighed. 'Practically the same, Flo. The censorship prevents any real information coming through. And like Nicky, Ed says nothing about leave.'

Daisy watched Mother open Matt's letter. 'The date is December 4th 1940. And remarkably, there seems to be very little deleted.' She paused, catching her breath. *"Dear family, how long is it since we've seen one another? Too long. I hope you received my letters before Christmas. Daisy, I took care to send yours to the hospital and hope you are well and fighting fit by now. Mother, thank you for your letter confirming you're staying with Aunt Betty. Pops, no word as yet from you, but my guess is that your circumstances, whatever they may be, might prevent it. I'll be brief with my own news. Amelia and I enjoyed a special pass just before Christmas. Wales is beautiful in winter, but cold! We spent two days in Pwllheli. Here, we married by special licence. Please, please, be happy for us. Of course we should have waited - but how could we? Mother and Pops, you are to be grandparents. So you see, we are simply ecstatic. It's safe to say I have wings on my feet! Rejoice for us. Celebrate! Stay safe in these dangerous times. Write quickly. I love and treasure you all. Matt. P.S. Sadly my leave has been cancelled. I can't say more about this. Don't be unhappy for there is so much to look forward to."*

Mother looked up, her pink cheeks damp. 'Oh, Matt,' she murmured, 'my darling Matt and Amelia. What welcome news!'

'Goodness!' exclaimed Aunt Betty. 'You're to be a grandmother, Flo.'

'I can hardly believe it.'

'The fortune cards!' exclaimed Aunt Betty. 'Pat was right after all. Your card was a lily, Flo. The symbol of innocence and purity. It meant a grandchild!'

Mother and Aunt Betty hugged one another, but Daisy was disappointed. She wouldn't be a bridesmaid after all.

CHAPTER 69

'I WAS GOING TO BE A BRIDESMAID,' complained Daisy as they stood on the path outside the old toilet door. 'I thought Matt and Amelia would have a big wedding.'

'Mother told you it was highly unlikely. What with the blitz and all.'

'They could have waited until the blitz was over.'

Bobby heaved an exasperated sigh. 'That could be years ahead. And anyway, there's a baby on the way. Now, come on, let's pull the crate out.'

By sheer brute force, the crate and wheels were unearthed from the rest of the junk and Bobby critically studied the proposed cart. 'I'll need to screw the wheels onto the crate, or else it'll come apart. But I haven't got any tools.'

'Uncle Ed keeps his tools indoors. I saw them under the stairs,'

Bobby's face brightened. 'I'll ask Aunt Betty if I can use them.' Her brother made a swift exit.

Daisy gave the cart a little push with her toe. It wobbled forward unevenly. Would she really be able to sit in it? Even if she could, how would Bobby pull it along? Suddenly she recalled a length of rope she had seen at the rear of the storage room. Minutes later, Daisy was skipping on the path.

One skip … two skips … the newly discovered rope turned effortlessly! Round and round it went until the action slowed and she began to trip. On closer inspection she discovered the rope had begun to fray.

Her attention was focused on resolving this when the man appeared. His face was hidden under the brim of a dark hat as he moved slowly from the street towards her.

Then she recognized the mackintosh.

'Hello,' he said in a voice that Daisy remembered from Aunt Betty's office at the factory. 'You're Daisy.' He gave a false smile. 'Do you know who I am?'

Daisy stumbled back, dropping the rope. 'M … Mr Calder.'

The smile vanished. 'So your aunt has told you about me? I'm glad to hear it.' He moved towards her.

Her head told her to run, but her legs were rooted to the spot. She was about to turn when, with lightning movement, he reached out and grabbed her.

'Quiet!' he growled as he cupped his hand over her mouth and pinned her against the wall of the house. 'Listen carefully.'

He was strong and Daisy knew resisting was useless.

'I hoped you would be reasonable, but now you've made things very difficult.'

Daisy's thoughts whirled. How could she raise the alarm?

'Bring your aunt out here. Tell her she has a visitor.'

Wide-eyed, Daisy stared into his gaze. He wasn't at all like the smart, well-dressed man she remembered. His eyes darkened menacingly. There was stubble on his chin and his cheeks were hollowed.

'I'll be waiting,' he threatened. 'If you don't do as I say, I'll come after you. If you scream or make any noise, you won't see your family again.'

Daisy froze. Would he really dare to harm her?

She tried to think calmly. What was she to do? More importantly, what was Mr Calder going to do?

'I've waited for this moment for a long, long time,' he rasped in a husky voice. 'I've been patient, made plans for your aunt and me. I've bought train tickets to take us out of this damned city. We'll be far away from London by this evening. Tomorrow we'll start our new life.' His voice dipped low. 'Tell Betty she must come to me, or it will be the worse for you all.'

Daisy gulped down her fright. Mr Calder was quite mad. She was certain of it. She had to warn Aunt Betty and Mother.

But all her resolve disappeared when he drew the gun from his pocket.

Little lights flickered over her vision. Her ears roared with noise, then dulled to a whisper. She couldn't breathe. Daisy knew she must compose herself, just as Nurse Gwen had taught her.

'Do you understand?' He pressed the muzzle of the gun into her chest.

Daisy fought against the faint. She nodded.

'I have your full cooperation?'

Once again, Daisy nodded.

'Turn very slowly. I am just behind you. I shall pull the trigger without hesitation if I become suspicious.' He slowly let go of her.

Daisy blinked, trying to clear her vision. Her forehead throbbed and her legs felt weak and wobbly.

'Walk!' snapped Mr Calder, prodding her back with the muzzle of the gun.

Daisy walked, but it didn't feel like walking. She felt as if she was floating. It was only a few feet to the kitchen door. But what would she do then? And what if Bobby came rushing out? Would Mr Calder pull the trigger and kill them both?

Daisy stumbled, expecting another instruction. She mustn't faint away. Reaching out for the wall to steady herself, she thought of Mother and Aunt Betty and Bobby and all the things they had been through together. There must be something she could do …

'Daisy! Daisy!'

Someone had called her name. Not Aunt Betty or Mother. But someone so familiar that Daisy could hardly believe her ears. It was Pops's voice.

Daisy opened her mouth and screamed. She screamed and screamed again, waving her hands, trying to warn Pops, to somehow avert the flight of that bullet. She didn't care for herself. But Mr Calder was mad …

'Go away, Pops,' she yelled at the top of her voice. 'Stay away!' Her heart turned over in waves of dread. Was Mr Calder about to shoot her or would he shoot Pops? How long before the bullet entered her body? Or worse, much worse, followed a path towards Pops?

Suddenly a blackness swallowed her.

She had been there before and recognized the landscape. It was fear. She understood now, that fear never left you. The war, the death and destruction, the grey, ruined landscape of the blitz; these were all part of her now. But there was another part too, allowing in the bright and precious light that Daisy recognised as love.

'Daisy, it's me,' said Pops, gathering her in his arms. 'I've got you.'

'Did he shoot us?' she mumbled, clinging to the strong, familiar shoulders. She couldn't feel any pain. Did a bullet go right through you or lodge somewhere inside before it killed you? Pops's face became clearer now; arctic blue eyes and tussle of wavy hair. He was smiling and said reassuringly, 'You're safe, quite safe.'

Mr Calder hadn't pulled the trigger? She was still alive and so was Pops! But where was Mr Calder?

Suddenly there was a flash of lightening and a roar of thunder. She felt Pops shudder and drag her against the wall, until the roar of the explosion subsided. Then all at once Mother and Aunt Betty and Bobby were there, embracing her and Pops.

'There must have been another bomb,' said Mother in a shaken voice, 'under the debris of the demolished house.' The air was thick with the smell of cordite and burning and clouds of dust and vaporous fumes revolved around them.

'Thank God, you're both safe,' Aunt Betty said with tears in her eyes.

'What happened?' asked Bobby in confusion.

'It was Mr C … Calder,' Daisy stammered. 'He wanted me to fetch Aunt Betty. He had a gun and said he would shoot us all if I didn't do what he said. But then Pops came and saved me. And Mr Calder must have run into the garden and - ' Daisy burst into tears.

Mother held her close. 'There's nothing we can do for him now.'

'I didn't want that,' Daisy protested. 'I didn't want him to be killed.'

'You weren't to blame,' Pops said gently. 'No one was.'

'It's me who is to blame,' Aunt Betty assured her. 'I made a terrible mistake, Daisy. Sometimes adults can be reckless. I never guessed at the hurt and sadness such an ill-advised friendship might bring. Your mother and father have been very understanding. Nicky has taken compassionate leave so that we can talk things over before I speak to Uncle Ed.'

Daisy gasped a breath. Her parents knew?

'Uncle Ed and I have to work things out,' Aunt Betty whispered. 'I've never stopped loving him and I hope he'll forgive me.'

Daisy slid her arms around her aunt. 'I'm sure he will,' she murmured, choking back her tears. 'He loves you too.'

Daisy saw the anguish in her aunt's face and in her parents' eyes. She guessed there would be more heartache ahead. The war had threatened everyone's happiness. Yet the conflict had brought this family together. What was more, they loved each other for better or worse, in peace or in wartime, just like a family should.

EPILOGUE

4 months later

It was a mild, sun-swept morning in May, when Daisy sat with Bobby in the rear of the car as Pops drove them through the East End. His long-awaited leave had finally arrived. Uncle Ed had accompanied him and was, at this very moment, with Aunt Betty.

Today's visit to the island had come at last. Daisy found it almost impossible to believe that day had finally arrived. After the terrible event of Mr Calder's accident, the war had become very personal. His death had signalled the end of her's and Bobby's carefree days playing in Aunt Betty's garden. The cart and rope had been abandoned, as if somehow they were attached to that fateful day. The blitz had continued until last week when Germany had turned its attention on Russia. Daisy knew that like every other family in Britain, they were trying to recover and repair their lives.

Before they had left Aunt Betty's, Mother warned them to

expect the worst. Their home might be broken and battered, or like many other buildings, a mountain of smouldering bricks and masonry. Yet returning home was their hopeful dream, a lifeline from their past that they all needed to keep alive.

Daisy glanced at Bobby. Like her, he wore a look of anxious expectation as he stared out from the window. To celebrate the occasion they were dressed in their best clothes; a new skirt for her that Mother had made on Aunt Betty's sewing machine, a pressed white shirt and tie for Bobby. This visit was special. A visit to be remembered. That is, if they were lucky. If they still had a home to return to.

Pops drove slowly through the blitzed streets, flanked by blackened, deserted buildings. The Isle of Dogs bore its untold scars like old soldiers' medals, a maze of boarded windows, fire singed bricks and collapsed roofs. Worst of all, were the gaps that spoke of the missing families, friends and neighbours.

An eerie silence descended as Pops turned the car into Poplar Park Row. Daisy took a breath. Not one house, it seemed, had escaped the cruel ravages of war.

Pops brought the car to a halt. Daisy climbed out and stood with Bobby under the bare, black branches of the plane trees. Every house in the row had been victim to the Luftwaffe's attacks.

'Oh, Nicky,' gasped Mother, as she stepped onto the splintered pavement. 'Look at what this terrible war has done!'

Daisy watched her father's arm slip comfortingly around her mother's waist. 'Chin up, Flo. Look! Our home is still standing, which is more than can be said for many in this area.'

They all paused at the open gate, propped to one side on its creaking hinges.

'Is it safe to go inside?' Mother asked tentatively as they stared at the battle-scarred building.

'Nothing ventured, nothing gained,' Pops replied. 'But let's go carefully.'

Mother nodded. 'But I'm afraid of what we might find.'

'There's nothing we can't achieve together, Flo,' Pops urged. 'We'll repair or re-build after the war is over.'

Daisy listened to her parents' conversation and marvelled at their courage. They were country folk, but had claimed a small piece of the city as their own and refused to abandon it.

'Look,' shouted Bobby, springing into the garden. 'There's my old football!' He leapt towards the side of the house and the apple tree where the swing hung limply from its branches.

It was no time at all before Bobby was kicking the ball and Daisy was swinging as high as she possibly could. How long was it since she had last occupied the little wooden seat? She swung higher and higher, straining to see the crane tops and tall chimneys of the factories. Would she ever see Mrs Hayes again and talk in whispers about Elsie Shiner and Joe Rawlings and the wicked Micky Wolf?

Daisy breathed in the tarry, salty air that was so familiar. The course of her life in wartime had taken her from the island, but her friendships were not forgotten. Fond memories of Cawdor School and playing on the waste ground and Iris and Sidney and Gary and Grace burned as vividly as ever.

Daisy slipped from the swing, planting her feet firmly on the ground. The football flew past her and Bobby ran up, his cheeks flushed. 'You're too big for that swing now.'

'I don't care,' Daisy replied. 'It still works.'

'It's good to be home,' he said, idling around her.

'When we left Wattcombe I thought we'd never get used to Poplar Park Row,' she admitted. 'I missed the village. Then

I slowly forgot. Not forgot exactly, but we made friends here.

'Do you ever think of Grace?' Daisy knew it was the kind of intimate question she wouldn't have asked once. But somehow it was easier now.

'I s'pose I do,' he admitted.

'I miss Sammy too. He was brave,' she faltered. 'He saved my life on the hospital roof.'

Bobby studied her for a while. 'I wonder what happened to Peter Brady?'

'Poor Tommy didn't deserve a cruel brother like that.'

Bobby shuffled his feet, his eyes fixed on the house. 'Do you think we'll ever get our factory back?'

'I hope so. I'd like to see Mrs Hayes again.'

Bobby frowned. 'I suppose it all depends on Bletchley.'

Daisy frowned. 'What's Bletchley?'

Bobby's blue eyes flickered. 'I shouldn't have said that. And it's not a what. It's a where.'

'So,' Daisy persisted, puzzled, 'where's Bletchley?'

'I overheard Pops speaking to Mother,' Bobby replied in a whisper. 'Bletchley is a place near Milton Keynes. I looked it up on the map. And it's all very hush hush. My guess is that the government send boffins like Uncle Ed and Pops to work there. To plan out Britain's defence for the rest of the war.'

'What's a boffin?'

'Someone who knows as much as an encyclopaedia.' He pointed a stern finger towards her. 'You mustn't breathe a word. Bletchley's a secret.'

'I'm good at keeping secrets.'

'You'd better be.'

Daisy smiled. Bobby had taken her into his confidence and that was something she valued. 'I'll play football with you if you like?' She jumped from the swing.

'We'll line up some bricks from the chimney to make a goal.'

Daisy considered the suggestion. 'You can do all the lifting. You're stronger than me. I'm only a girl.'

Bobby's blue eyes danced. 'I'm just surprised you've remembered for once.'

Daisy watched with interest as her brother constructed the goal. This was what girls did; they stood on the sidelines, letting boys take the lead. Or so they thought.

'Daisy? Look what I've found.' Mother waved from the front door. In her hand she held an envelope.

Daisy ran up. 'What is it?'

'This letter's addressed to you.'

Daisy studied the untidy, looped scrawl which covered the best part of the crumpled envelope. 'It's from Sally,' she gasped. 'I recognise her handwriting!'

Mother smiled. 'The letter was trapped under the matt. It must have been here some while. '

Daisy slid her finger along the sealed edge and drew out the single sheet. Sally had written her new address. 'Is Somerset far away?' she asked.

'Too far to walk,' replied Mother.

Daisy returned to the swing, sat down and savoured the brief note. *"Dear Daisy, this is to let you know I got a bilit with an old gel and a dog. I take it for walks. There are 2 other girls here. Not my cup of tea. I want to come home. It's nearly Christmas and all. Please write qwick. Love Sally. ps. Mum wrote to me that all the Bradys got nicked. Good ridance I say. Thought youd be pleased. pps I got my monthlys, have you?"*

Daisy swept a tear from her eye.

'What's that?' Bobby called.

'It's a letter from Sally. She's in Somerset.'

He shrugged and picked up the ball. 'Come on, let's have a kick-about.'

Daisy stuffed the letter in her skirt pocket. It was funny how everything got sorted in the end. She would write to

Sally this evening. Though she wasn't quite as grown up as Sally and hadn't had her dreaded monthlies yet, she did have Bobby's secret; a secret that was better than any secret she had ever kept before.

'You stand there,' her brother ordered. 'I won't kick the ball too hard. But remember, you must stop a goal. That's what being goalie is all about.'

Daisy didn't argue, it was easier to let Bobby have his way. Though she had missed a great deal of schooling, she had learned a good many lessons that she didn't think might be taught as a subject in class. The best, was always to be grateful; to have gratitude for her family and the love that bound them all together. For Amelia and Matt who had just brought a darling baby daughter into the world and for Aunt Betty and Uncle Ed who still loved each other in spite of the distress they had suffered. Gratitude for Grandma and Aunt Pat, now enjoying their new home in Wattcombe village and for Aunt Minnie and Uncle Leo and Will who had returned safely to their beloved studio in Soho.

And lastly, she was grateful for today. For Mother and Pops and Bobby and herself - all being safe and well - if a little anxious about the future, just as everyone was. For it was true the war wasn't over, but the Purbrights were united and strong and there was a glimmer - just a faint glimmer - that their lives might be resumed once again here at Poplar Park Row.

THE END

REVIEWS

If you have enjoyed my book - and I sincerely hope you have - then I would be most grateful if you could leave a quick review on Amazon.

Reviews are the lifeblood of our stories and help the author and reader to evaluate both works of fiction and non-fiction. Again, so many thanks for your support.

Don't miss my free stories and monthly Newsletter! Sign up by going to www.carolrivers.com
I do hope you enjoy your freebies ...

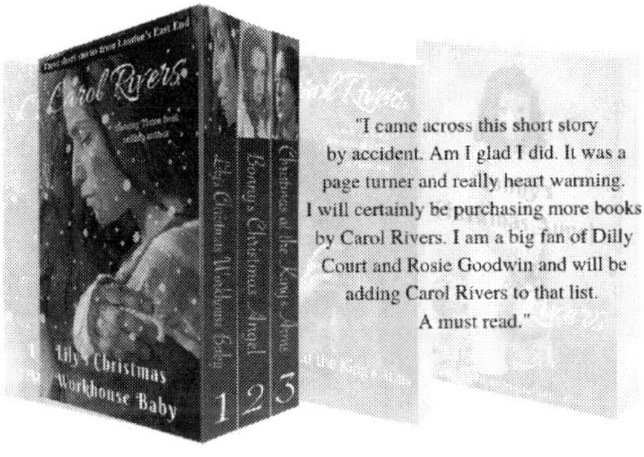

ALSO BY CAROL RIVERS

Also by Carol Rivers

Bestselling Lizzie Flowers series

BOOK ONE LIZZIE OF LANGLEY STREET

BOOK TWO THE FIGHT FOR LIZZIE FLOWERS

BOOK THREE LIZZIE FLOWERS AND THE FAMILY FIRM

Seasonal Christmas themed books

CHRISTMAS CHILD

CHRISTMAS TO COME

TOGETHER FOR CHRISTMAS

A WARTIME CHRISTMAS

IN THE BLEAK MIDWINTER

MOLLY'S CHRISTMAS ORPHANS

LILY'S CHRISTMAS WORKHOUSE BABY (Short story)

Page-turning wartime books

GIRL WITH SECRETS

EAST END ANGEL

TOGETHER FOR CHRISTMAS

A WARTIME CHRISTMAS

Gritty East End family dramas

A PROMISE BETWEEN FRIENDS

A SISTER'S SHAME

EAST END JUBILEE

COCKNEY ORPHAN

LILY OF LOVE LANE

EVE OF THE ISLE

EXCERPT OF CHRISTMAS CHILD

CHAPTER 1

PART ONE

Poplar 1894

THIRTEEN-YEAR-OLD HENRIETTA O'REILLY scuffed aside a lock of curling copper-coloured hair that fell stubbornly over her brown eyes. The icy water in the big china basin where she toiled, was freezing; her fingers were numb to the bone. Yet, after a hard morning's laundering, there was still so much to do.

'A labour of love,' so Sister Patrick regularly assured her. 'You'll be fitting those curling tresses of yours into a halo before long.'

The thought of a halo appealed to Ettie, as she was know by the nuns. All the saints looked radiant in the pictures hanging on the convent walls. Their holy images with auras of gold inspired her. But it was hard to conjure a smile in the ancient orphanage laundry. Draughts as strong as storms rushed in from the broken windows. The mucky steam dampened her clothes. The air smelled strongly of soap and starch, and made her eyes sting.

Not that she minded, for having spent all her life in the care of the Sisters of Clemency, Ettie considered the orphanage her home. Situated in the hamlet of Poplar, East London, it was rare that she ever ventured beyond the high stone walls of the convent.

Sister Patrick was her favourite nun and though she had lived many years in England, she still spoke with her native Irish accent. It was Sister Patrick who, on her way to chapel on Christmas Day fourteen years ago had discovered the dying Colleen O'Reilly.

'Sure, t'was a heartbreaking sight,' Sister Patrick had related many times. 'The ice was hanging sharp as knives from the eaves of the laundry. The snow was banked knee-high. I couldn't believe me eyes when I saw a tiny figure, fallen against the laundry wall. And there you were, safe in the wee girl's arms, a tiny speck of life. With the last of her strength, your mother was keeping you warm against her breast. Wrapped only in filthy rags, she was in no fit state to help herself let alone her baby.'

'Where is she now?' Ettie had asked when she was small.

'The good Lord called her to be his angel.'

'Is she an angel now?'

'She's a Dublin angel for sure,' Sister Patrick assured her. 'Colleen O'Reilly, Jesus rest her soul, was from the land of shamrocks just like me. She was born in a road I know well meself called Henrietta Street and she named you after it. Though saints preserve us, we all got lazy and know you as our darlin' Ettie.'

Ettie never tired of listening to Sister Patrick's explanations of her heritage. It gave her great comfort to know that Sister Patrick and her mother were so closely connected and that Dublin was the city of her mother's birth. 'What did she look like, Sister Patrick? Was she pretty?'

'Ah, as pretty as a picture she was, just like yourself. A replica. Hair and eyes the colour of God's own soil. And her countenance, well, it might have lit up the whole convent if she'd lived.'

'And she really did love me?'

At this, Sister Patrick would look astonished. 'Jesus, Mary and Joseph, child, why wouldn't she? You were her very own miracle.'

'Will I see her again?' Ettie persisted, having studied the bible and her catechism sufficiently to know that angels appeared on earth with great frequency.

'We all have a guardian angel,' Sister Patrick would reply. 'And before she died in my arms, your mother vowed to always watch over you.'

This answer rarely varied. Ettie never felt lonely because she knew her mother was with her. Sometimes she even thought she could see her holy aura lighting up a dark corner. As time went on, this knowledge was sufficient for Ettie to recover from any sadness she might have felt at being orphaned.

Ettie considered the nuns her family. Like a young duckling, wherever the sisters went, so Ettie followed too. At a very early age, she would wait outside the chapel door while they said their office. She understood that praying hard for the orphans was the most important duty of their day.

Later, Ettie's little figure could be seen trotting after the line of black habits into the kitchen where she would be ordered from pillar to post, carrying and fetching. Any help was welcomed by the nuns who somehow managed to run a convent, an orphanage and a schoolroom at the same time.

Every day, at early morning Mass Ettie knelt on the polished pews of the chapel. Here, she thanked God for giving her such a happy life. Best of all she liked helping the waifs, strays and foundlings who turned up at the doors of the convent orphanage. Just as she had.

A wistful smile came to Ettie's sweet face as she thought of the many children who had passed through the ranks. The nuns made sure that their charges learned the alphabet and their numbers. Some rebelled at first. But not for long. It gradually dawned on them that life in the orphanage was much happier than on the streets. Even if they had to learn the catechism, it was worth their efforts.

As Ettie undid the cords of the wooden ceiling rack, she reflected on her hopes for the future. She intended to become a teacher and dedicate her life to orphaned children.

This ambition was like a rosy glow inside her. She woke up with the glow each morning and went to sleep with it at night. Sister Patrick always encouraged her. 'For sure, you are a fine scholar, so you are. Sister Bernadette has taught you a little French, and you've learned your numbers from Sister Catherine. If I didn't know better I'd say meself you were an old soul.'

'What's an old soul, Sister Patrick?'

'Someone who's walked this earth before,' answered the nun mysteriously. 'But no more questions now. Me tired brain can only stretch so far.'

Lowering the clothes pulley, Ettie began to fold the wet wimples and caps over the long wooden struts. With great care she made certain each one was flat. The ironing afterwards, so Ettie had discovered, was easier if the white headdresses were prepared properly. She knew this was another labour of love and would be rewarded by God.

A light voice broke into Ettie's reflections. A raffia basket overflowing with dirty clothes landed on the table. The smiling, unlined face above it belonged to Sister Patrick. 'Ettie, we still have the children's smocks to wash. Mother Superior will inspect us soon, so?' The nun removed her small, round wire pince-nez which were fogged up due to the moist heat of the room and squinted at the newly rinsed articles. 'Ah, so, the wee girl is ahead of me!'

Ettie beamed, for she loved to please. Her training over the years had made her a conscientious worker. After a full day's housekeeping, she went to the schoolroom to help the most needy children. Whenever a pupil struggled in lessons, they were sent to Ettie. She would spend patient hours with them, teaching in her own childlike way, all the lessons the nuns had taught her.

Although Ettie was given Sunday afternoon to herself, she rarely took it. Rather she would help children like seven-year-old Kathy Squires. Kathy was a street beggar who had never attended school until she was sent to the orphanage. And Johnny Dean, who at eleven, had been boxed round the ears so many times by his drunken mother, that he was a bit deaf. At six years old Megan and Amy were twins and had spent most of their young lives thieving. They refused to be parted and even slept head to toe in their bed.

Then there was Michael Wilson, the most unruly and disobedient orphan of them all. A year and a half older than Ettie, he was a rebel. All his young life he had lived off his wits. At first he refused to even look at a book or hold a pencil. And as for a bible or a catechism, he would declare them poisonous.

But Ettie had patiently appealed to his better nature. She found this in his love for adventure stories; Daniel who was thrown into a den of lions. Noah who defied a flood and David who had conquered a giant.

'Can't be true,' Michael had at first argued. 'A lion would eat you in one gulp. You'd never get all those animals on one boat. It would sink. And a giant would crush you under his foot.'

'Believe what you like,' replied Ettie, unoffended. 'God gave these men special strength. There are women too. Like Joan of Arc who fought in battle, as brave as any man. Look, here's a picture of her wearing armour and sitting astride a horse.' She showed him the pages of the old and musty bible. Like all the books that had stood on the convent's library shelves for many years.

Michael had studied the image with interest. Ettie knew that she had gained his approval. From that moment on, she read him stories of heroic action and adventure. One thing led to another. Michael decided to learn to read so that he could investigate for himself.

Ettie came back to the present as Sister Patrick examined the caps and wimples. 'Not a crease among them,' she congratulated. 'What would I do without you?'

Ettie habitually answered, 'You won't ever have to, Sister Patrick. I'll always be here.'

Mostly Sister Patrick's response was the same too. 'I pray to Our Blessed Lady that you will.' But today, the nun's face clouded. She fiddled with her spectacles and played nervously with the wooden rosary looped at her waist. 'Ettie, come away to the dining room. It's time we talked.'

CHAPTER 2

'HAVE I DONE SOMETHING WRONG?' Ettie enquired.

'No, child. But the sooner you learn the truth the better.'

Ettie hurried after the small, squat figure floating over the convent's stone floors. Finally they reached the dining room. All the long wooden tables and benches were permanently set with cutlery, mugs and pitchers of water for the nuns' simple meals.

Ettie kept this room as clean as a new pin. Sweeping the stone flags, polishing the table and lighting the fire on cold winter mornings was another labour of love. Once breakfast was over, Ettie and two young women employed from the local village would clean the children's dormitories and tend to the sick.

Sister Patrick sat down on one of the benches. Ettie had an anxious sensation. The vast room echoed with an eerie silence. The strong smell of wax polish wafted up into the air. A smoky haze from the fire curled around the roof's lofty ceilings.

It was late on a winter's afternoon and Ettie moved restlessly. The boys and girls would be waiting for her. She loved her little friends and they loved her. For they all knew from life's experience what it was like to be unloved.

But Sister Patrick was in no hurry to let her go. 'Ettie, nothing in life is permanent, so?'

A little shiver went down Ettie's spine. 'No, Sister Patrick. Nothing lasts forever. Except heaven.'

'Heaven is our eternal home,' Sister Patrick agreed. 'But in this life we are in the hands of the Good Lord.' The nun's tongue came out and slipped nervously over her dry lips. 'We must accept our fate.'

Ettie did not answer. For she too, had very dry lips.

'The bishop has given us a directive.'

Ettie sat up. This new bishop who had replaced the old one, was very important. When he visited he arrived in a shiny cab pulled by a fine black horse. A special rug was produced for him to stand on; even Mother Superior knelt down and kissed the ring on his finger.

'Rome can no longer support us,' explained Sister Patrick. 'And there are many repairs to be done. The windows are all broken. There are leaks in the roof of the school house.'

Ettie wondered why this was important. 'We catch the drips in pails,' she reminded the nun.

'Those drips are becoming waterfalls,' Sister Patrick objected. 'The chapel too, needs attention. Sure, the big bell is so rickety it's about to fall from its tower.'

'Can't it be tied with rope?' asked Ettie innocently.

The nun smiled sadly. 'Ah, if only the sisters had your youth! We should do a great deal more than we do now.'

Ettie rarely thought about the age of the nuns. They all looked, well, just like nuns. There was perhaps, Sister Francis who walked with the aid of a stick. And Sister Bernadette who sat in a chair most of the day muttering her prayers in

French. But now Ettie realised there were very few younger faces.

'Already Sister Catherine has left for the motherhouse in Belgium,' Sister Patrick added. 'Soon Sister Enuncia will follow.'

Ettie swallowed. 'Then who will teach the children?'

The nun heaved a sigh. 'Sad it is, Ettie, but they too must go.'

Ettie felt a lump grow large in her throat. 'But where?'

A tender smile touched the nun's lips. 'We must pray for guidance.'

'But - '

Sister Patrick put a finger to her lips. 'Quiet, now, Ettie. The problem is that the Sisters of Clemency have lost our patrons over the years. The old bishop took no interest in money. He was a good man but only wanted to save souls. He loved his orphans and thought God would provide. But unfortunately, we are lost without patronage.'

Ettie remembered the wealthy gentry arriving in their fine carriages who once attended Mass in the chapel. But as the East End of London grew poorer, their visits declined. Yet she had been taught that God was loving and merciful. Surely He would save the orphanage?

'God helps those who help themselves, doesn't He?' Ettie boldly protested. 'We could grow vegetables and fruit for Sister Ukunda to sell at the market. Keep hens for eggs and a goat for milk. Perhaps even a cow. Arthur could build a stable to keep them in.'

'Arthur is just our gardener, child. He's not a farmer, just as we are not builders.'

But Ettie would not give up. 'We could learn to be,' she insisted.

Sister Patrick shook her head sadly. 'Shh, darlin' girl. Rome's decision is final.'

Ettie hung her head. She bit her lip to keep her tongue silent.

'Life changes,' Sister Patrick tried to soothe. 'We must accept God's will.'

'But Sister Patrick,' Ettie burst out, 'I can't live without you.'

The nun looked lovingly into her eyes. 'My child, you have all your life to live without me.'

Suddenly Ettie realized that something or someone far greater than either herself or Sister Patrick, was now governing their lives. It was a frightening discovery. Ettie's heart, which usually overflowed with love and gratitude, felt heavy and lost. At last the dam broke. Her sobs echoed in the big room like loud claps of thunder.

'Hush, my dear one,' comforted a loving voice. A voice that she had trusted all her life. A voice as close to a mother's voice as she had ever heard. 'We have spent many happy years together. God only loaned you to me. Now I must give you back.'

Ettie heard someone wailing. The cries were lifting right up to the rafters. They bounced on the sharp glass of the broken windows and against the faded holy pictures on the walls.

These noises couldn't be from her, of course they couldn't! But they weren't from Sister Patrick who was trying to console Ettie.

'I'll never leave you,' Ettie heard herself insist. 'Never!'

'Wherever you go,' Sister Patrick murmured calmly, 'I'll always be in your heart.'

Ettie felt the pain so violently, it felt like an earthquake inside her. But nothing could alter the look of defeat on Sister Patrick's face.

Whether or not the nuns approved of Rome's directive, it had to be obeyed. But it was such a dreadful, unkind and heartless directive! It tore people apart and caused such loss, that Ettie, for the first time, questioned the faith on which she had built her life.

CHAPTER 3

THE CONVENT'S schoolroom was very old, with brown-painted walls and ink stains smudging the desks and floor. A grey and depressing light seeped in from the broken windows. In the very same manner as Ettie had held tightly to Sister Patrick, the little girls held fast to Ettie. 'We don't want to go,' they wailed, cuffing the snot from their noses.

Ettie had just delivered the news. She wanted to tell the children herself. They had to prepare themselves.

'I want to stay here with you,' Kathy insisted.

Ettie lifted the little girl's chin. 'Say your prayers. Jesus will look after you.'

'We're being got rid of!' accused Johnny Dean, scratching nervously at one of his disfigured ears.

'The nuns don't give a farthing about us,' agreed Michael Wilson, who looked very angry as he clenched his fists. Ettie always smiled when he bragged he was older and wiser than her. Though tall and skinny as a rake, he was very strong. 'We'll be turfed out on the street,' he declared. 'Or sent to the workhouse.'

Ettie looked into his rebellious grey eyes. 'Where is your faith Michael?'

'The only faith I've got,' he shouted dramatically, 'is in myself!' His face darkened as he poked a finger at her. 'Can the nuns stop the rozzers from nabbing me the moment I step out of this place?'

Ettie felt her tummy turn over. He could be right, for it was only the nuns intervention with the law that had prevented Michael's arrest.

'God will provide,' she promised. 'He'll answer your prayers.'

'He's never answered them before,' came the reply. 'Why should he answer them now?'

Ettie wanted to remind him that it was only because of the nuns request to the police that he wasn't now incarcerated in the boys' reformatory. But she knew this would upset him even more.

From the smaller children there were sobs and gulps as they listened to this harsh exchange. How could she reassure them?

'Let's say our prayers,' she said and obediently they kneeled on the floor. All, except Michael.

'May God surround us with His light,' she prayed fervently. 'May He enfold us with His love. May He protect us and guide us, so that forever we will remain safe in the palm of His hand.'

'I'm clearing out,' interrupted Michael, kicking his boot against a desk. 'While I've got the chance.' He grabbed his grubby cloth cap from the chair. 'Good luck to all of you. You'll need it.'

The younger ones began to cry and Ettie went to comfort them. 'Michael, don't go,' she pleaded.

'Why should I stay?' demanded the angry boy, his cheeks burning as he stood at the door.

'I don't know exactly, but please think again.'

He pulled up his ill-fitting trousers and tossed back his straggly dark hair. Plonking the cap on his head, he looked outside and shouted, 'I'm off while no one's looking.'

The door banged behind him and the orphans wept even more.

Ettie followed Michael into the cold and draughty passage. 'Michael, you can't leave,' she called.

'Who says I can't?'

'Where will you go?'

He gave a careless shrug. 'I'll manage.'

'But how?'

'Listen Ettie, you don't understand the world. You've lived in the convent too long. You don't know what life's like on the outside.'

Ettie agreed she had led a sheltered life, but how bad could the world be? Hadn't Michael learned to trust the nuns even a little? Tears bulged in the corners of her eyes.

'Crikey, Ettie don't cry.' Michael looked confused. He put his arm around her.

'You're making me sad.'

'I don't mean to,' he said, squeezing her shoulder. 'You and the other kids, well, I like you all.' He added in a gruff tone, 'You, mostly.'

Ettie stared up at him. Suddenly he seemed much taller and older than she was, though only one and a half years separated them.

'I've never said that to a girl before.'

'Really?' Ettie sniffed.

'It means something special when you tell a girl you like her.'

Ettie smiled, forgetting her tears. 'Thank you.'

'But listen!' He pushed her away. 'Don't get no ideas. I'm not staying, not even for you.'

Ettie felt sad. She would miss this boy with the beautiful grey eyes, but who spoke words that could be so hurtful.

'Friends are supposed to look after each other,' Ettie said softly.

'I'd be no good to you if I stayed.'

'Why not?'

Michael stared at her solemnly. 'Do you really think the bishop couldn't help the nuns if he wanted?'

This was a question that took her by surprise.

'Listen, the Roman candles are rich, Ettie,' he continued passionately. They've got more money stacked away than the Queen of England. If the bishop wanted, he could flog that ring on his finger and buy a whole new orphanage! But he won't. 'Cos this is the East End and out of favour with the toffs who fill his coffers. Mark my words, the sisters are done for.'

'Michael,' she gasped, 'please stop.'

'It's the truth. I'm older than you - and wiser.'

Ettie wanted to say that he must be wrong, but the words seemed to stick in her throat. 'Stay for the children,' she begged one last time.

Michael took hold of her shoulders. 'Sorry, kid.'

'You're really set on going?'

He nodded.

She flung her arms around him. 'Oh, Michael, I've grown so fond of you.'

He held her gently as though she was china. 'Tell you what,' he mumbled and made a show of straightening his jacket. 'We'll meet up somewhere like Victoria Park.'

'Victoria Park? Is it close by?'

'Just down Old Ford Road.'

Ettie nodded uncertainly, her brown hair falling across her eyes. 'When?'

'First Sunday in December. Three o'clock sharp at the water fountain.'

'I'll try.'

Michael laughed cruelly. 'You see, you're scared to come, ain't you? You won't even go out on your own.'

Ettie didn't understand Michael when he lost his temper. He'd say things he really didn't mean. She'd always prayed that God would change him. But now she knew that Michael was a lost soul. A tear trickled down her cheek.

'Cheer up,' he said with bravado. 'You're my girl, remember.' He bent and kissed her cheek.

She blushed, trying to ignore the unfamiliar pain in her chest.

'You watch out for yourself Ettie O'Reilly. This world's a rotten place. The sooner you get used to the idea the better.' He waved jauntily. 'See you soon. That is, if you've got the guts.'

Ettie shivered as she watched him hurry down the passage. She felt so cold without him. As if something was dying inside her. She wanted to go with him. But there were the orphans to consider. She had to look after them until they left the orphanage.

Slowly she returned to the schoolroom, trying to forget the awful things that Michael had said. As much as they hurt, there were tender new feelings growing inside her. And she knew Michael was the cause of them.

EXCERPT OF CHRISTMAS TO COME

PROLOGUE

Christmas Day 1940
Isle of Dogs
East London

'TERRY'S COLD, BELLA.' Five-year-old Terry Doyle squatted next to his sister in the dank, rubbish-strewn alley opposite the row of derelict cottages. Bella Doyle, only eight-years-old herself, slid her arm protectively around her brother's bony shoulders, painfully aware his thin white shirt was no protection against the winter's bite.

Terry was starving and today was no exception. They'd been scavenging on the debris all day and found little to satisfy their appetite. If only their mother and that pig of a man she'd picked up at the Rose hadn't decided to come home early! They must have had a skinful, then run out of booze or money or both.

Bella was weighing up this problem carefully; a problem she had been faced with more times than she had eaten hot dinners. In fact, to Mary Doyle's children, a hot dinner was something they could only dream about, and often had.

Bella knew that to enter their home now, a rundown dockside cottage dripping water from its mouldy walls, would be a risky business. After the week-long binge that their mother and her boyfriend Jack Router had enjoyed, even setting eyes on her children would be aggravation to Mary Doyle.

Bella understood the evils of alcohol even at her young age. If asked, she couldn't put it into words. But she knew through bitter experience how it could corrupt a person's nature. Their mother hadn't always been the drunkard she had turned into and Bella somehow understood this. She sensed the sinful nature of Mary's work and the crucifying poverty of their lifestyle, though she suspected that once upon a time her mother had been a child too. Perhaps with a brother or sister or both, and part of a real family. Mary Doyle had been innocent once. Before she had turned into a wild animal and lay with men to earn her living. And the blame for this degradation, Mary had daily informed Bella, lay squarely on her children's heads. They were bastards, appearing unbidden in her life. At the best of times, the sight of them was almost more than she could bear. At the worst, she left them alone with Jack Router.

'What we going to do?' Terry mumbled, trembling with the cold, his hand frozen inside Bella's.

'We'll wait a bit, right? Till they go out again.'

'But the planes might come over.'

Bella shook her tousled and filthy copper curls. 'They won't come over tonight. It's Christmas. Even the Germans know that.'

'Do Germans have kids as well?'

'Course they do.'

'Do they give 'em presents?'

'Dunno. Might do.'

Terry leaned his slight weight against her and Bella sighed heavily. All the buildings in Bow Street were condemned. She knew that because she'd read the notice nailed to their door. "This dwelling is considered unfit to live in and is condemned by the council."

But this had been in the summer before the Blitz started. Since then, the paper had worn away and life had gone on much the same, Blitz or no Blitz. Bella had been thankful that at least, she and Terry still had a roof over their heads. More so, when Mary and Jack were not sleeping or fighting underneath it.

Now snow was drifting across the street and Bella's stomach churned emptily. She had stowed a crust of bread between the floor and the bug-ridden mattress they slept on in a corner of the cottage. Bella had planned to share it with Terry as soon as they'd got home from the debris where they'd been looking for anything of value left over from the raids. But today they had come home empty-handed. And they'd been waiting an eternity in the hopes that the cottage would soon be vacated.

'They must be asleep,' Bella decided, taking off her coat and folding it around Terry's shoulders. It wasn't much protection; threadbare and darned, it was the only comfort she could give him. If only Terry could remember to dress himself properly. He didn't seem to know what kept him warm and what didn't. He had a habit of forgetting and Bella was always looking out for him.

'I don't like it here,' Terry complained, his bare knees knocking under his short, raggedy trousers. 'I'm cold. I wanna go in.'

'So do I,' Bella agreed impatiently. 'But not for a bashing. And we'll get one, as they won't be in no mood to see us.'

'Where we going, then?' Terry asked forlornly, swiping the running snot from his nose. 'To Micky's?'

'Don't reckon Micky would like that, either,' Bella said, shivering in her thin dress that was more tears and holes than fabric. 'It's Christmas Day. His mum will be dishing up the dinner.'

Micky Bryant was their benefactor. The one light in Bella's dark life. He was twice as old as her, but he didn't seem like it. He seemed like her other half. He looked out for them. And all the other street kids. He paid them for what they found. And sometimes gave them grub. He told them to keep shtum, as if his mum knew he was knocking off stuff, she wouldn't be best pleased.

Micky had two brothers too. Sean was all right. But Bella didn't care for the oldest one. She'd seen him at a distance and he looked - well, she didn't know how he looked. But she suspected he wouldn't encourage Micky's friendship with kids from the slums. Micky would laugh at that if she told him. He'd give her a wink and roll his lovely eyes. Micky didn't have airs and graces. Not like his brother, Ronnie.

'I'd like an 'ot dinner,' Terry said hopefully, his thin face and hollowed dark eyes under his thin black hair looking to Bella, like the face of an angel. A dirty, grubby, smelly little angel, but an angel none the less. She loved Terry with all her heart. She'd cared for her baby brother since the day he was born. Mary had brought him into this world with language so foul that even the old girl - who was always in at the deliveries - had turned away in disgust.

Bella remembered the violence of her mother's labour. As though she cursed nature and everything in it for her unwanted condition. But to Bella the miracle of birth had opened her young eyes to the first sensation of love. The blood soaked newspaper on the floor where Terry had suddenly appeared from between Mary's legs had seemed like a royal blanket of welcome. The old girl had slapped his silent body, all mauve and sticky with blood, and Bella had held her breath as she listened for Terry's first cry.

When it came, it was as if her own lonely heart had called back. And because there was no where else to put him, Bella had reached out and there he was! In her arms. This speck of life, staring up at her, with eyes like jewels in an old man's wrinkled face. She'd loved him from the off. And instinct had told her to keep him safe. So she'd kept him away from Mary until his pathetic screams had to be silenced by her huge, milk-swollen breasts. Mostly Mary had fallen asleep and Bella had held him there, snuggled up to the round fullness, his tiny fingers pleated around Bella's as he learned to suck.

Bella looked at her brother now. He didn't have a bad bone in his body. At least, what bones were left after the bashings he got from Jack Router. And that was what hurt her the most. What made her angry. What made her feel so powerless. She could take the man groping her. She made herself take it, so he wouldn't touch Terry. And the one thing in her favour was Mary's jealousy, her need for men as much as their money. She was still young and beautiful in her own eyes. Her daughter's youth was an anathema to her. She resented it. Jack knew that too and he played on it.

Another hour passed and dusk began to fall. The pretty snow flakes stuck to Bella's dark lashes and surrounded her brown eyes like tiny stars. They couldn't stay here much longer. Bella knew they would freeze to death. Terry's lips were blue and his face a ghostly white.

'Come on, we're leaving,' she told him, shaking him awake from the frozen doze he was falling into.

'Where to?' Terry whimpered as she hauled him to his feet.

'Back to the debris.'

Terry's big eyes filled with tears. 'I want to go home, Bells.'

In a grown up fashion far beyond her eight years, Bella took hold of her brother's shoulders. 'Listen Terry, might as well face it. We've got no home. Not when *he's* with her. Not when he thumps you like he does. And certainly not when they're both pissed. We'd be dead meat if we went back now and you know it.'

The tears trickled down Terry's cheeks. He said nothing, just stared at Bella and sniffed back the mucous streaming from his nose. She took his hand and squeezed it. 'I promise I'll find us a place to kip. And something to eat. All right?'

He nodded slowly and Bella took one last glance at the cottage. No sign of them coming out yet. She could only guess they'd drunk themselves daft. There would be hell to pay when they woke; in the absence of alcohol, the fighting and screaming would start. Bella had hoped that her mother would tire of the man, but for better or worse, she kept with him. And as far as her children were concerned, it was mostly the worst.

Shivering uncontrollably herself now, Bella hugged Terry to her. 'About a mile down the road is the pie and mash shop. In the blackout, no one will see us turn over the bins.'

Terry sobbed softly. 'I was sick last time we did that.'

'Listen,' Bella consoled him with her innocent logic, 'if pigs can eat that muck, so can we.'

He hung his head and she pulled him along the alley. It was dusk and the blackout was strictly enforced. There was no light showing, not even a full moon. But she knew every step of the way. When they'd eaten, they'd walk to the debris. She'd seen the remains of a burned-out house today. Some of its blackened rafters hung loosely inside. She'd take Terry there. It was better than sleeping in the open. And if the rest of the roof didn't fall in on them, that would be a bonus.

They could even make-believe they were in a posh house and were having a proper Christmas. They could pretend to open presents from under a Christmas tree. And sit round an imaginary fire opening them. She liked pretending. As they stuffed themselves with plum pudding, she would tell Terry the story about Joseph and Mary riding on the donkey and following a star. Mary and Joseph didn't have no home at Christmas either. In the end, the star led them to a stable where Mary had her baby in the straw. There was cows and sheep and the donkey, too. It was a pity there wasn't no animals on the island, only rats. Thousands of 'em, all over the place. Just as hungry as she and Terry were.

Bella hurried on, dragging Terry beside her. She was eager to investigate the bins at the back of the pie and mash shop and find shelter before it was too dark. And she might be wrong about the Germans. Their planes could be on their way over this minute. P'raps they hadn't even heard of Christmas.

Well, nor had she and Terry, really. Not until last year, when Micky had bunged them both a tanner along with two of his mum's apple pies.

CHAPTER 1

PART ONE

The London Blitz
March 1941

'YOU BUGGER, don't you hit our Terry again!' Eight-year-old Bella Doyle stared defiantly up at the big man whose fist was clenched in readiness to strike.

Jack Router turned his bloodshot gaze slowly from the small boy huddled in the corner to scrutinize the parcel of rags and lice infested hair gazing up at him.

'What did you say, girl?'

Bella moved cautiously backwards, out of reach of the man who had just knocked seven bells out of her little brother. Drunk and swaying Jack Router might be, but when the occasion warranted it, she knew he could turn on a sixpence.

'I said leave him alone. You're a bastard bully for clobbering our Terry. And I'm telling me Mum when she comes home.'

'Oh you will, will you?'

Instantly regretting her quick tongue, Bella knew there was no escape. Above her, the gaping hole in the ceiling where the rafters of the roof hung down and to her right, the closed door and blacked-out window. Not that she'd try running anyway. Not without Terry.

Jack Router curled a thick, grubby finger in her direction. 'Come here now, Bella. We should be friends you and me. Give your Uncle Jack a little cuddle. That's all he wants. And you like it, you know you do, girl.'

With her back pressed hard against the wall of the derelict cottage, Bella inched her way towards Terry. The man watched in amusement, his belly quivering above his belt as he enjoyed the child's terror.

'What's it to be then, eh? You or him?' He reached out his hand and Bella froze as a look of satisfaction crept over his face. Tilting his head, he shrugged lightly. 'You know, it was just a tap I give him, that's all. No more than he deserved for spinning your mother a pack of lies.'

'It wasn't our Terry's fault,' Bella protested in a whisper. 'It was Rita Moult from number nine. I heard her myself. She told everyone.'

'Rita?'

'She's all smiles and winks to you,' Bella burst out, 'but behind your back she told our Mum that you've had more dock dollies than hot dinners.'

'You lying little cow! She wouldn't dare, the bitch!'

Bella began to panic. 'I'm not lying, honest.' She watched furtively as the man thrust hesitant fingers across his sagging jaw his eyes moving slyly in their sockets. After his midday session at the Rose and Crown, he was breathing fumes. Even from where she was standing, Bella could smell him. Her stomach turned as he belched and rubbed his gut.

'Well now, you've got me all confused,' he grunted as his gaze travelled back to the boy. 'Let's see what your brother has to say for himself, shall we?'

Bella knew this was a trap. In a second or two he would swing round and catch her. But she couldn't let him clobber Terry again. Whatever he did to her, was nothing in comparison to what he'd done to Terry.

But this time he surprised her and with a powerful lunge he aimed his boot into the boy's hip. For all the ale in his belly, he delivered a blow that swept the human bag of bones along the filthy floor like a duster.

Without hesitating Bella threw herself forward and sank her teeth into the outstretched hand. Even as he screamed and pulled her up by her hair, she clamped her teeth tight, hanging on like a terrier. He shook her violently but Bella bit deeper, tasting his salty blood on her tongue. She imagined him dying the worst death possible like burning in one of the bombed buildings or boiling in oil. And the wanting of it was so strong it wasn't until all the air was punched from her stomach that her teeth finally parted.

'Look what you've done to me!' the man yelled in pain.

His eyes gleamed as he brought her against him. 'Fight me would you, Bella Doyle? I'll teach you, girl. See this?' He tapped her nose with his knuckles as he held her aloft with one meaty hand. His tongue rolled out to lick the dried beer coating his lips. 'This is for girls like you that need to be taught a lesson.' He pushed hard, sliding his fist over her cheek and finally downwards to her chest.

'Whisper to me, Bella. Say the nice things Uncle Jack likes to hear and it'll soon be over.'

All the struggle was gone from her now. Her legs and arms were suddenly weak as if she'd run up to the top of a hill and down again. It was a familiar pattern and she recognized it, knowing that no power on earth could now save her. Closing her eyes she tried to pretend she was up in the sky above the planes. Her mind began to draw pictures, taking her aloft on the clouds, flying in the blue ocean over the earth where there was release and freedom.

But just as he brought her against him, his fingers peeling away the layers of her clothing, the door flew open. Mary Doyle's faded green eyes flashed as she took in the scene before her. Fully attired in her working clothes, her chipped red nails dug into the worn black skirt that crinkled tightly over her stomach. Above her belted waist, a thin white blouse trembled on her drooping breasts. Slowly, a patch of angry crimson spread over her throat, creeping up into the lifeless red hair that fell on her neck. 'What in the name of Jesus is going on here?'

Jack Router stared innocently at the woman as he dropped Bella to the floor. 'She's an animal, Mary. She bloody bit me. Look! See them marks? All because I was trying to treat her decent.'

Laying still, Bella knew her luck could go either way now. Their mother was as likely to land him a punch as she was to believe him and blame her children instead.

'She was cursing me, Mary, love. I swear on me old mother's life. All I did was walk in that door and they gave me a mouthful before I'd even taken me coat off.'

Mary Doyle's gaze narrowed suspiciously. 'If you've lifted one finger against my kids – '

The man laughed suddenly. 'What'll you do? Chuck me out?'

'As sure as hell I would and you know it.'

'Ah, you drunken slut.' He pushed his face into hers. 'You'd do me a favour if you did. If I found myself a pigsty to kip in, it would be an improvement on this shit hole. I'm sick to death of you and your brats. I must've been mad to take the bastards on.'

'You were willing enough at the time,' she reminded him sourly, returning the crude gesture. 'You had nothing, *were* nothing! And if it wasn't for me you'd be six feet under and still scratching the coffin lid. You're a curse to women, you bag of shite.'

Bella gulped down her fear. Her wary brown eyes looked out from under the tangled curtain of auburn hair; she was waiting for the inevitable, a verbal and physical assault that had begun from the moment Rita, alias *Mouth Almighty,* had set her poisonous tongue free.

The first blow cracked aloud in the air. Jack Router stumbled, the heel of his boot landing heavily on Bella's leg. With a stifled cry she scrambled aside, dragging Terry with her into the only other habitable room of the dwelling. Here they crouched on a filthy mattress covering themselves with a threadbare blanket.

Bella buried her head against Terry's. He stank where he'd peed himself but the room smelled like the bog anyway. She prayed the planes would soon fly over and when the siren went, Mary Doyle and her man would be off, screaming at one another still, but thirst would drive them to search for liquor.

Terry's snuffling grew loud. His mouth fell open as the blood congealed in his nose.

'Tomorrow we'll tell Micky,' she whispered as a plan formed in her mind. Micky would know what to do. He always did.

Bella comforted herself with the picture of Micky's gun, not aimed at the wriggling sewer rats but pointed lightly against the brow of the man's head.

Bella rubbed her bruised cheek as she sat up.

A pale morning light seeped under the blackout. She stretched her stiff limbs as Terry stirred beside her, his long brown lashes laying softly on his swollen face. He'd rubbed the scabs from his nose in the night and was snuggled down in his coat. Both children were frozen, the temperature in the room at an all time low.

'Terry, wake up.'

His almond shaped eyes flickered. He groaned at he sat up. 'Terry hurts.'

'He gave you another bashing, that's why.' Bella took his hand and pushed the blanket away from his tight grasp. 'We're leaving before they come back.'

His eyes filled with tears. He lay down and pulled the blanket back over him. 'Terry don't want to.'

Bella wondered why God couldn't have left just a few brains in his head. Enough to tell him when he was safe and when he wasn't. Enough to make him understand that the man would kill them both after last night. Why had God forgotten Terry?

She ruffled his thin brown hair. 'Be a good boy, now. And do as Bella tells you.'

In the clothes they had worn day and night for more than a month they stole into the street. The cold March wind whipped around them and rain spattered down. Bella gazed up and down the rows of cottages. Only the rats, bugs and fleas that infested them moved in the early light. She looked up at the rotting pile of bricks that comprised number three, at the sunken roof and shattered windows lost in the drifting smoke of last night's raid. She shivered. It was the only home they knew and they were leaving it.

'Terry wants to stay.'

'We've got to find Micky.' She pulled his gas mask tighter

across his shoulder. Jack would be home first, looking for trouble. And resisting the tears herself, she urged him forward.

'Is the bombs coming?'

'Tonight they will.'

'Terry don't wanna run away.'

Bella didn't want to either. But if only God had given him half a mind he'd know they didn't have a choice. The man said one day he would put them in a pot and cook them. And after last night, Bella believed him.

CHAPTER 2

Ronnie Bryant stood in the big kitchen of the rambling three-storey building and frowned out on the cold March morning. He pushed back his hair and stretched his aching arms. From the kitchen window he could see the piles of junk that filled the yards of Piper Street, and spilled around the Anderson like a shark-infested sea. No one would ever guess what was hidden under the floorboards of the air raid shelter. That's good planning, Ronnie my lad, he congratulated himself. The dugout had its uses after all. If the law came sniffing round, they were welcome to sort through all Dad's rubbish piled high on the stones. But it would take a shrewd copper to suspect the neat interior of the Anderson where all the booze and fags him and Micky and Sean had nicked from the docks were stashed safely away.

A gentle dew sparkled on the legs and arms of the ancient furniture and junk going back to the year dot. Their Dad's treasure trove, his legacy to his sons as he was always telling them.

Ronnie smiled, the quirk of his full, sensual mouth giving his young face a touch of maturity beyond his sixteen years.

His cool grey eyes gleamed penetratingly, missing nothing under the heavy shock of raven black hair.

He glanced across the kitchen to his brother dozing in Dad's old armchair by the range. Micky's curly dark hair flopped over his thin face and his size ten boots were filthy from the mud that had congealed on their soles. The lino in the hall needed cleaning before Mum arrived back from Auntie Gwen's. Another bonus that, Auntie Gwen asking her to stay the night. Luckily it was a good bus ride to Poplar from Cubitt Town. The two widowed sisters liked to chinwag and they wouldn't stir once the fire was made up.

Ronnie sighed heavily as thoughts tumbled in his brain. Him and Micky hadn't had a wink all night and hadn't expected to what with dodging the raids and bringing the haul up from the docks in the old van Dad parked under the railway arches. It was a real rust bucket and on its last legs but it had done the job. What a night it had been! They'd worked like stink digging up the Anderson floor and battening down the boards again. When they sold this lot off he was going to give her and Auntie Gwen a good holiday. Send them to the seaside. That's what Dad would have wanted ...

Ronnie felt a moment's deep miss of the father he'd worshipped and the gap in their lives that had never been filled since his death three years ago. His loss hadn't been easy for Mum or indeed for any of them. But Sean had only been eleven when Dad went and taken it the worst. Odd that, as him and Dad had been opposites. Dad was a real man's man, and Sean all curls and a mummy's boy. Still was, in fact. Yet Dad's death had knocked him sideways. Micky on the other hand, had been down the market the very next week, trading junk up the Caledonian or Cox Street. Where there was a gap in the market it was up to a Bryant to fill it, Dad said. Mum didn't know the half of his escapades and never would. And when the Blitz had started last September, well, who wouldn't have made the most of what was on offer? The black market had come into its own and you were an idiot to ignore it.

Ronnie was well aware that 1940 had seen the island at its best and worst. Not a night passing without catastrophe, destruction and death in some poor sod's case. But out of the turmoil came the best living they had ever made. Dad would have been in his element. And whichever way the war went, opportunities like last night were priceless.

There was a loud knock and Ronnie started. But quickly he pulled himself together and went to the front door.

There were two children on the doorstep. The girl, taller than the boy, had hair full of knots and the colour of brass, with eyes as round as pennies. Her coat had more holes in it than his mum's crocheting. The boy's hung down to his ankles. At first he had them down as beggars, but then she asked for Micky by name.

'Who wants to know?'

'Bella Doyle.'

'Well, Bella Doyle, you're out of luck. Micky's not home. Come back some other time, kid.' He was about to close the door, when she stuck her foot inside.

'I'm not a kid. I'm eight.'

Ronnie was impressed. She had a mouth on her all right. 'Yeah, well, the answer's still the same. Micky's out.'

The girl pointed behind him. 'What's he doing there then, if he's not home?'

Ronnie swung round to find his brother propped against the wall. Micky Bryant yawned and narrowed his bright blue gaze. 'What's up then, Bells?'

'Got something to tell you.'

'Yeah? Such as?'

Her eyes darted back to Ronnie. 'Can't say standing 'ere, can I?'

Ronnie looked hard at his brother. 'Not now, bruv. Get rid of them.' He was about to walk away when Micky grabbed his arm.

'Hang on a bit, Ron. These two turn up a few tasty bits now and then. They're as regular as clockwork on the debris come rain or shine. Don't look a gift horse, as they say.'

Ronnie frowned. 'It's not a good time, Micky. And anyway Mum'll be back soon.'

'Well why don't we let 'em stay till she gets back?' His thick, dark eyebrows lifted persuasively. 'She loves kids, probably call them dirty faced angels, feed 'em up and sort 'em out. Take her mind off what we've been up to whilst she's been away.'

Micky had a point, Ronnie decided as he gave the suggestion due consideration. Anything to divert the numerous questions that would come flying at them the minute she walked in. And, with Sean kipping upstairs like Sleeping Beauty, she wouldn't have time to wonder why he was so dead to the world.

He nodded grudgingly. 'Have it your way, but I don't like it.'

'All right, you two can stay for a bit,' Micky said, grinning. 'But no nicking and no pissing on the floor, pal. OK?'

'What's up with the boy?' Ronnie frowned as the children stepped in.

Micky shrugged. 'Got bashed in the head once too often I reckon. You gotta wind him up and push him in the right direction. Their mum's one of them dock dollies that works the Rose. Don't suppose she ever gave it a thought as to why he's a screw loose.'

Ronnie noticed the boy did look a bit vacant under all the

dirt. He went down on his haunches. 'Here kid, what's your name?'

'Terry,' his sister said.

'Can't he speak for himself?'

'Depends what you ask him.'

Ronnie smiled. She was a card all right. 'Where'd he get all them bruises?'

'It's the joker they live with,' Micky offered with a dismissive shrug. 'A big geezer who kips at their mum's gaff over Bow Street. If he's not on a bender he's knocking off any old skirt. Gives the kids a belting every day if they don't make themselves scarce.'

'Thought no one was living over them places any more,' Ronnie said thoughtfully. 'Condemned by the council years ago, weren't they? '

'Yeah, but who takes any notice of a bit of paper slapped on a wall?' Micky yawned once more. 'Funny thing is, Jerry's never landed a bomb on Bow Street. Makes you laugh really, when it'd only take a breath to knock it over.'

Ronnie cursed lightly under his breath. This was the last thing he needed. Two kids and a bastard drunk wasn't his problem today. He had enough of his own to be going on with. But he also knew it was way too late to stop the anger that was already building inside him. If it was one thing he couldn't stand it was a bully. Granted, there were blokes who walloped their women and kids and got away with it. Bullying the weak and infirm was a way of life for some on the island, but not for his own kith and kin. Mum and Dad had brought them up to observe family values. The old ding-dong now and then was only natural. His folks had gone at it hammer and tongs sometimes like all cockneys did. But only a row to clear the air. When an injustice like this got shoved right in your mug, it was hard to ignore it.

'How did they know where you live?' he enquired suspiciously.

'Must've told them, mustn't I?'

Ronnie studied the girl again. Now that he looked she was blue with bruises. The clothes they wore were no more than rags hanging on bones. His Mum would have a fit when she saw them like that.

'You two hungry?' he asked.

The girl's eyes widened. They were troubling eyes, Ronnie noted a little uncomfortably; there was so much hidden in the depths of them.

Micky laughed scathingly. 'Don't mention grub. These two are like bloody gannets. You want to see them demolish the rubbish they find in the bricks. Thick with dust it is and tastes like shit. But it goes down their gobs like dripping.'

Ronnie stared incredulously at his brother. That he could talk so lightly of what in effect was starvation. He was seriously worried about Micky's state of mind. Nothing seemed to bother him these days. It was as if all he cared about was number one. Though if he was really honest, that had always been so, even before Dad died.

'Come on then,' Ronnie said over his shoulder as he led the way to the kitchen. 'But after you've got to clear off.' Now he'd taken a closer look at them he knew he couldn't let them stay. His Mum wouldn't like those bruises any more than he did, a fact that Micky seemed to have overlooked.

In the kitchen he took the loaf from the larder. Carving off four thick slices, he lay them on the oilcloth. There was butter under the china dish, but it was still rationed and if it was one thing his mum loved it was a good helping of her old cough and splutter. The jam though, not that she knew it, was well and truly off the back of a lorry and more where it had come from any day of the week.

The girl wolfed it down and swiped her mouth with the back of her hand.

'See what I mean?' Micky chuckled. 'They'd eat horse dung if you served it up hot.'

'And so would you,' Ronnie answered him shortly, 'if Mum didn't put food in your belly.'

'That's why I help 'em out,' Micky stated quickly. 'If it wasn't for me they'd be brown bread.'

Ronnie sneered. 'Yeah, I can believe that an' all.'

'No kidding, bruv. Nicking from the debris is what keeps 'em alive. If it wasn't for me giving them a good whack for what they find, they wouldn't be standing here today. As half dead as they look it's me what keeps them breathing. Their mum don't give a toss what happens to her kids and sure as hell the ugly bastard that belts 'em don't.'

Ronnie knew the only reason Micky had half of London's back street kids working for him was for his own gain. He worked them like stink, returning the poor sods a pittance. Ronnie had turned a blind eye so far but now he was thinking twice. As for the nutter who used two little kids for a punch bag…

'What is this bloke to them?' Ronnie asked heavily. 'He not family or nothing?'

Micky laughed as he stuffed his mouth with bread. 'He's Mary Doyle's pimp and that's a fact.'

Ronnie cut another slice and halved it. 'Here, put this away, you two.'

They were at it like vultures when someone knocked on the front door. 'Keep quiet,' Ronnie warned them all. 'Not a whisper.' He went to open it. A warden was standing there and his uniform was covered in dust.

'Yeah?' Ronnie asked irritably.

'Is this the home of Winifred Bryant?'

Ronnie nodded. 'She's out.'

'You'd better let me in, son.'

Ronnie put up his hand to stop him from entering. 'Why should I do that?'

He looked into Ronnie's eyes. 'The Luftwaffe hit Poplar bad last night … and your mum …'

Ronnie stared into the warden's face. He must have got it wrong. Somewhere along the line, there was a mix-up.

'We dug this out, well, what was left of it.' He lifted an identity card and his mum's black purse with a metal clasp. Ronnie saw a stain, a dark red one smeared across the felt. Then he knew she was never coming home again.

CHAPTER 3

Nine days later

RONNIE PUSHED his hand under his open shirt collar and squeezed the tense muscles of his neck. Mum would have made him wear a tie, but he hadn't worn one since he was at school and never a suit. Removing his jacket he placed it carefully over the back of his chair as Sean and Micky walked in the room.

Mum would have approved, Ronnie thought as he studied his two brothers who were dressed in identical dark suits. They were wearing what her idea of real class looked like. But now she was gone and her sons being done up like a dog's dinner for the funeral was a sting in the tail if ever there was one. For years she had meticulously ironed their shirts and pressed their trousers, nagging them to smarten themselves up. Now she wasn't here to see the result of her efforts.

'How long is this going to take?' Micky peeled off his jacket. 'I've got things to do.'

'Such as?'

'Dunno, just stuff.'

Ronnie narrowed his eyes, the sense of foreboding that had beset him after Mum's death, growing inside him. 'Whatever it is Micky, forget it. There's family business to be taken care of this afternoon. Now shut up and sit down.' Ronnie nodded to the seat on his right. He had swallowed his irritation all week as Micky's attitude had gone from bad to worse. He accepted his brother was grieving, but he was well out of order today and Ronnie's patience was growing thin.

Micky dragged out a chair and slumped down on it. Sean was already seated; his elbows resting on the big oval dining table polished each day by their Mum for as long as Ronnie could remember. A pang of sadness went through him as he met Sean's red-rimmed eyes. He had wept openly, unafraid to show his sorrow. Of the three of them, Sean had been their mother's favourite and it wasn't surprising to Ronnie that he'd taken her loss as badly as he had Dad's.

When he'd returned home that day after identifying his mother and aunt in the makeshift mortuary, he'd gazed into his brothers' faces, unable to speak. He had felt as if all the life had drained out of him from that moment. Mum and Auntie Gwen had looked as if they were asleep, their faces unmarked by the hand of death.

'You're certain it's them?' the warden had pressed as he'd identified the two corpses lying side by side.

Of course he was certain. The dead women were his family, the only family that he, Micky and Sean had.

'We found her bag straight away,' the man had told him gently. 'I know it's no consolation, but she wouldn't have known a thing.'

No, it's no consolation at all, he had thought bitterly as he stared at the marble white face of his mother that had, twenty four hours ago, been full of life and energy. They loved their father, but all three of them worshipped their mother. Perhaps she had been asleep when it happened? Ronnie hoped to God that it was quick.

He could still hear the rustle of the utility tarpaulins as they were replaced over the two still forms. See in his mind's eye the uniformed man who had taken his arm, intending to lead him away. Felt the frustration in his gut as he'd tried to decide whether it was all some sick joke.

All he could think of then was the fact he wouldn't be looking into Mum's eyes again, their expression alert to whatever catastrophe had befallen her sons in her absence. She wouldn't be conjuring up a fried breakfast. Or chewing them off about they way they refused to get up in the mornings. Life as they had once known it had now come to an end.

Ronnie looked hard at his brothers. 'Sean, I know there's no way we can bring back Mum. But if she was here she would tell us to pull ourselves together and sort ourselves out. So that's what we've got to do, right?'

Sean shrugged helplessly. 'Why did it have to happen to her, Ron? I just don't understand.'

'There's no answer to that question, Seany. I wish I could give you one.'

'She never hurt no one. She'd give the coat off her back to anyone who asked. It was us that's done all the nicking. Why didn't that bomb fall on us?'

'I wish it had,' Ronnie muttered darkly. 'But what's done is done and we're still alive and kicking.'

'But that's just it, Ron, I don't feel right about what we did – you know – just before she went. It's as if it was us who made the bomb fall on her.'

Ronnie jerked his head round. 'That's rubbish Sean, and

you know it. Get it out of your head. We loved her, treasured her. And what we did was all for her, to give her a comfortable life as Dad would have wanted.'

Sean swept the tears from his cheeks with a grubby hand. 'I don't know anything any more, only that Mum turned a blind eye to what we did and we took full advantage. She didn't have a clue as to what was happening half the time. If we'd told her we knocked off a load of stuff and wanted to bury it in the Anderson she would have given us all a slap for even thinking it.'

Ronnie's face tightened. 'Point taken, Sean, but the fact is what the eye don't see, the heart don't grieve over. After Dad died it was too late to change what he'd started and I for one wouldn't have wanted to, anyway. The old man didn't spend his life teaching us the tricks of the trade for nothing. We was Robin Hood and his Merry Men. Give anyone a helping hand if they asked and bugger the sheriff. He kept telling us them stories over and over again. They came out of him like verbal diarrhoea and we believed every word. Still do.'

Sean blinked his long lashes. 'I know Ron. But the country's at war and the punters we deal with are all in this lark for a profit, not to give to the poor and needy.'

Ronnie couldn't argue with that. But his priority was family. If he didn't hold them together now, they'd fall apart. 'Look if it makes you feel any better, I'll agree that expanding the business into black market after Dad died was my decision, and I take full responsibility. I'm not saying I was right to do so, mind. That is a matter of opinion and you are entitled to yours. But I know in my heart it was the road Dad would have gone down. In my book, there was no doubt whatsoever as to continuing the business.' He paused as for a second saw his mother gazing back at him in the form of Sean's honest blue gaze. God only knew how the old man had worked the flankers he'd done and kept the old girl in such blissful ignorance. But he had and Ronnie commended him for it. Now it was history repeating itself and with Mum gone, it was Sean who had taken up her mantle. But Sean was the new generation of Bryants and as such, had either to support the business or get out of it completely.

'Seany, let me put you straight on one thing. Mum never died because of what we did. It was nothing to do with us, so get that through your Uncle Ned. She died because a maniac in another country decided to start a war. And that's a fact you're going to have to accept.'

There was silence in the room. Ronnie glanced at Micky who was sporting a face as long as a fiddle. 'Right, Micky, now it's your turn.' He braced his shoulders back and added firmly, 'I'm not sitting here all day looking at your moody gobs, so speak your mind or forever hold your peace.'

Micky kicked the table leg idly. 'Since you're asking, Ron, what I don't fancy is Old Bill sniffing round. I've been shitting bricks lately, every time the door goes. Stands to reason they know Mum's gone and she won't be here to tell them to sling their hook. So where does that leave us, I ask? And the answer is, we're sitting here like three orphaned ducks.'

'So what is the alternative?'

'I reckon we get shot of this last little bundle. Take a dip on our profits if we have to, but just get clear of it.'

Ronnie nodded slowly. 'Fair point. Any suggestions what we do with it?'

'It's too hot for the markets and it would take too long to flog it round the pubs. What about shoving it Luffman's way? He'll rook us something chronic, but we'll have to swallow on that.'

Ronnie begrudged giving Goldy Luffman the contents of his nose, let alone a generous deal, as he was the meanest sod this side of the river. However, Goldy took anything and everything and asked no questions. 'All right. Suits us this time, but from here on in we'll find somewhere legit to stash our Georgie Woods.' He turned slowly to Sean. 'So, are you up for a clean sweep, Seany?'

'What choice have I got?' Sean replied moodily.

'You've always got a choice in life.' Ronnie stared hard at his kid brother who up until this moment had always been just that, a kid. But with Mum gone he was going to have to step into the real world. 'You don't have to come with us on this one, bruv. Me and Micky will do the business. We'll sort out the Anderson and see Goldy.'

'You *what*?' Micky objected, for the first time sitting up and paying attention.

'I said Seany can sit this one out.'

'But it took all three of us to move it,' Micky protested. 'A whole lorry load it was, buried six-foot down under a bloody shelter. We was at it like navvies and only finished just before the All Clear went.'

'We'll manage.' Ronnie's tone was final. 'Sean's staying put.'

'So what if I decide to sit on me arse all night, too?' Micky sulked.

Ronnie sighed heavily. There was something in both his brothers' attitudes that worried him. Sean was frightened of his own shadow and Micky was in love with himself. They both needed to realize they had to give a lot and take a little between themselves. They were family. And if family couldn't hack it, who could?

Micky continued to stare at him resentfully. There were rings round his blue eyes and a hollow look to his face. With his curly brown hair he was like their Dad, a charmer. Sean had the same intense blue gaze but with his light brown hair and soft, smooth features he was their mother all over. Now Ronnie looked at his two brothers and knew they would never be kids again, at liberty to fight amongst themselves and be stopped by a cuff round the ear. Now there could only be one leader. And as the oldest, he was it.

'Right then,' Ronnie said decisively. 'I'll dig out the van and bring it round as soon as the first raid starts. There'll be no lights on anywhere and plenty of noise to distract any nosy parkers. I'll reverse up to the back wall and Sean, you can help us load the stuff, but then you'll come back in here and lie low. Me and Micky will drive over to Goldy's and be back before first light.'

'It'll be a bloody miracle if we are,' Micky grunted.

'We did it before. We can do it again.'

'That is if Jerry don't drop one on our heads.'

Ronnie smiled. 'He'll have to catch us first.'

Ronnie expected further protest and was prepared for it. But Sean hung his head, trying to disguise his wet cheeks and Micky was busy still kicking the table leg. He had always had a laugh at anything remotely serious. After Mum, he didn't know how to act.

'And just to refresh our memories,' Ronnie continued, his gaze not leaving his brothers' faces. 'We'll keep this gaff ship shape, then. I don't want to find so much as a fag end under your beds – or anything else come to that. In other words, if the law was to shove its nose inside this house, all they'd find is a layer of dust and even that would be sweet smelling. Are you hearing me, you two?'

'Yeah, yeah.' Micky rolled his eyes.

Sean nodded in silence.

'And no outside jobs,' Ronnie added firmly. 'No creeping, no spotting, no fitting. Not even a touch at the market. No nicking wallets, bags or goods. Nothing goes down unless I say so. The Bryants think, act, even shit as one.'

Micky turned to face him and Ronnie was relieved to see a glimmer of humour return to his brother's eyes.

'What about them kids outside?' Sean asked suddenly. 'They've been kipping right on top of the stock.'

Ronnie had almost forgotten he'd allowed them to sleep in the shelter. After Mum's death he hadn't had the heart to send them back to Bow Street.

'They'll have to go,' Ronnie nodded.

'Lambs to the slaughter, I reckon,' Micky murmured, a glint in his eye.

'But they're not our problem,' Sean said anxiously. 'Are they?'

Micky shrugged. 'I reckon sending them back to Bow Street is like feeding mice to a cat. I'd like to see how handy the bastard is with someone his own size.'

It wasn't often Micky made sense, Ronnie thought, but this time he was in full agreement. He felt a grudging admiration towards Micky. More than that, he knew his brother was no coward and had taken his punishment on the streets as well as dolling it out. Inside him there was a vicious streak that was pure hate for authority of any kind. Ronnie knew that if this trait could be harnessed for the good of the family, they would have a valuable asset in Micky.

'You want to sort it out?' Ronnie asked.

Micky's dark eyes lit up. 'Now you're talking, bruv.'

But Sean was shaking his head. 'I don't like it. Those kids are bad news.'

Ronnie was under no illusions as far as Sean went. He was never cut out for the physical. Mum had spoiled him rotten, and him and Micky had understood why. Sean was the total opposite to Micky who, given the chance, would happily take a swing at a bull with a match up its arse.

'We'll start as we mean to go on,' Ronnie said without hesitation. 'Ask yourself this question, Sean. What would Dad have done if we had a sister and some lairy sod lifted a hand against her?' His face was set hard, its handsome proportions chiselled out in the broad daylight. 'This is our patch and we need the respect.' He paused, assessing his brothers' reactions. When no argument was forthcoming he continued. 'Now, are we all done?'

Ronnie looked at them again. Then he stood up and felt the smooth material of his trousers fall over his long legs. He liked that feeling. He liked the fact that he now had his brothers' undivided attention and made a vow to keep it that way.

Before leaving the room he picked up the newspaper. The polish of the table sparkled. He could remember his mum polishing it and the joy she took in doing so. It was a big, solid table, like the family he intended to cultivate. This was the first meeting he had called, but it wouldn't be the last. There would be many more to come.

Now he instructed Sean to change his clothes and put on his working clobber. Ronnie had already convinced himself that the action he was about to take to remedy a bad situation, would achieve a result that his Dad, if not his Mum, would sanction.

Thank you so much, dear Readers, for visiting my world of sagas!

ABOUT THE AUTHOR

"Where there's muck there's money!"
If my family had a royal crest I'm sure those are the words that would have been hewn into the stone above it.
Mum and Dad were both East Enders who were born on the famous or should I say the then infamous Isle of Dogs. They were costermongers selling fruit, veg and anything else that would stand still long enough!
Their family were immigrants who travelled to the UK from Ireland and France, while others emigrated to America.
As a child I would listen to the adults spinning their colourful stories, as my cousins and I drank pop under the table.
I know the seeds of all my stories come from those far off times that feel like only yesterday. So I would like to say a heartfelt thank you to all my family and ancestors wherever you are now ... UK, Ireland, France and America, as you've passed down the magic and love of story telling.

ACKNOWLEDGMENTS

I am extremely grateful to 'library resources' for the many books, papers and scanned documents involving World War 2 events and 20th century historical facts made available to me for this novel.

Grateful thanks and deep appreciation go to the contributors who have afforded me their private diaries, recorded personal experiences, evocative memories, written reflections and intimate personal letters describing this unique time in our history.

Thank you - and I hope my story seen through nine-year-old Daisy's eyes, does justice to your great and invaluable generosity.

COPYRIGHT

Girl with Secrets

First published in Great Britain by Carol Rivers
This edition published 2021

www.carolrivers.com

Manufactured by Amazon.ca
Bolton, ON

21857113R00214